second
chance
summer

Also by Morgan Matson

Amy & Roger's Epic Detour

second chance summer

Morgan Matson

SIMON & SCHUSTER BFYR

NEW YORK   LONDON   TORONTO   SYDNEY   NEW DELHI

An imprint of Simon & Schuster Children's Publishing Division

1230 Avenue of the Americas, New York, New York 10020

SIMON & SCHUSTER BFYR is a trademark of Simon & Schuster, Inc.

For information about special discounts for bulk purchases, please contact Simon & Schuster Special Sales at 1-866-506-1949 or

business@simonandschuster.com.

The Simon & Schuster Speakers Bureau can bring authors to your live event. For more information or to book an event, contact the Simon & Schuster Speakers Bureau at 1-866-248-3049 or

visit our website at www.simonspeakers.com.

Also available in a SIMON & SCHUSTER BFYR hardcover edition.

Book design by Lucy Ruth Cummins

The text for this book is set in Adobe Caslon Pro.

Manufactured in the United States of America

First SIMON & SCHUSTER BFYR paperback edition May 2013

8 10 9 7

The Library of Congress has catalogued the hardcover edition as follows:

Matson, Morgan.

Second chance summer / Morgan Matson.

p. cm.

Summary: Taylor Edwards' family might not be the closest-knit—everyone is a little too busy and overscheduled—but for the most part, they get along just fine. Then Taylor's dad gets devastating news, and her parents decide that the family will spend one last summer all together at their old lake house in the Pocono Mountains. Crammed into a place much smaller and more rustic than they are used to, they begin to get to know each other again. And Taylor discovers that the people she thought she had left behind haven't actually gone anywhere. Her former best friend is still around, as is her first boyfriend . . . and he's much cuter at seventeen than he was at twelve. As the summer progresses and the Edwards become more of a family, they're more aware than ever that they're battling a ticking clock. Sometimes, though, there is just enough time to get a second chance—with family, with friends, and with love.

ISBN 978-1-4169-9067-3 (hc)

[1. Interpersonal relations—Fiction. 2. Family life—Pennsylvania—Fiction. 3. Terminally ill—Fiction. 4. Love—Fiction. 5. Pocono Mountains (Pa.) —Fiction.] I. Title.

PZ7.M43151Sec 2012

[Fic]—dc23

2011052241

ISBN 978-1-4169-9068-0 (pbk)

ISBN 978-1-4391-5752-7 (eBook)

For Mom and Jason

ACKNOWLEDGMENTS

This book wouldn't have been possible without the incomparable Alexandra Cooper. Thank you, thank you, thank you for your patience and faith and brilliant editorial skills.

Thank you to all the wonderful people at S&S: Justin Chanda, Amy Rosenbaum, Anna McKean, Venessa Williams. And a huge thank-you to Lucy Ruth Cummins for such a beautiful cover.

Rosemary Stimola, thank you for your agenting superpowers and your faith in the story from the start.

In the UK, thank you to Jane Griffiths, Kat McKenna, Mary-Anne Hampton, and Franca Bernatavicius.

Thank you to Lauren Strasnick, writing buddy extraordinaire, for your friendship and your invaluable help with this book.

Thank you to my mother, Jane Finn, for more things than I have room to list here . . . but especially for all those magical Pennsylvania summers.

While this book was primarily written in Los Angeles, it was revised all over the place, and I owe a great deal of thanks to those who made that possible:

Thank you to Susan MacTavish-Best, for the use of her beautiful, art-bedecked Mill Valley home. To Eric Berlow, for the use of his cabins in the Sierra Nevada—revising has never had such a gorgeous setting. And thank you to Nancy Quinn and Ginger Boyle, who made the house-renting process in the Poconos so easy.

Finally, and above all, I must gratefully acknowledge Alex MacDonald. Thank you so much for finding us revising cabins, making scrambles, cheering me on, and always knowing when ice cream was needed. I could never have done this without your support and encouragement.

Love is watching someone die

—DEATH CAB FOR CUTIE

The Lake House

chapter one

I EASED OPEN MY BEDROOM DOOR TO CHECK THAT THE HALLWAY was empty. When I was sure that it was, I shouldered my purse and closed the door behind me quietly, then took the stairs down to the kitchen two at a time. It was nine a.m., we were leaving for the lake house in three hours, and I was running away.

The kitchen counter was covered with my mother's plentiful to-do lists, bags packed with groceries and supplies, and a box filled with my father's orange prescription bottles. I tried to ignore these as I headed across the kitchen, aiming for the back door. Though I hadn't snuck out in years, I had a feeling that it would be just like riding a bicycle—which, come to think of it, I also hadn't done in years. But I'd woken up that morning in a cold sweat, my heart hammering, and every impulse I had telling me to leave, that things would be better if I were somewhere— anywhere—else.

"Taylor?" I froze, and turned around to see Gelsey, my twelve-year-old sister, standing at the other end of the kitchen. Even though she was still wearing her pajamas, an ancient set decorated with glittery pointe shoes, her hair was up in a perfect bun.

"What?" I asked, taking a step away from the door, trying to look as nonchalant as possible.

She frowned at me, eyes resting on my purse before traveling back to my face. "What are you doing?"

"Nothing," I said. I leaned against the wall in what I hoped was a casual manner, even though I didn't think I'd ever leaned against a wall in my life. "What do you want?"

"I can't find my iPod. Did you take it?"

"No," I said shortly, resisting the urge to tell her that I wouldn't have touched her iPod, as it was filled solely with ballet music and the terrible band she was obsessed with, The Bentley Boys, three brothers with perfectly windswept bangs and dubious musical gifts. "Go ask Mom."

"Okay," she said slowly, still looking at me suspiciously. Then she pivoted on her toe and stomped out of the kitchen, yelling as she went. *"Mom!"*

I crossed the rest of the kitchen and had just reached for the back door when it swung open, making me jump back. My older brother, Warren, was struggling through it, laden with a bakery box and a tray of to-go coffees. "Morning," he said.

"Hi," I muttered, looking longingly past him to the outside, wishing that I'd tried to make my escape five minutes earlier—or, even better, had just used the front door.

"Mom sent me for coffee and bagels," he said, as he set both on the counter. "You like sesame, right?"

I hated sesame—in fact, Warren was the only one of us who liked them—but I wasn't going to point that out now. "Sure," I said quickly. "Great."

Warren selected one of the coffees and took a sip. Even though at nineteen he was only two years older than me, he was dressed, as usual, in khakis and a polo shirt, as though he might at any moment be called upon to chair a board meeting or play a round of golf. "Where is everyone?" he asked after a moment.

"No idea," I said, hoping that he'd go investigate for himself. He nodded and took another sip, as though he had all the time in the world. "I think I heard Mom upstairs," I said after it became clear that my brother intended to while away the morning sipping coffee and staring into space.

"I'll tell her I'm back," he said, setting his coffee down, just as I'd hoped he would. Warren headed toward the door, then stopped and turned back to me. "Is he up yet?"

I shrugged. "Not sure," I said, trying to keep my voice light, like this was just a routine question. But only few weeks ago, the idea of my father still being asleep at this hour—or for that matter, still home—would have been unthinkable.

Warren nodded again and headed out of the kitchen. As soon as he was gone, I bolted for the door.

I hurried down our driveway and, when I made it to the sidewalk, let out a long breath. Then I started speed-walking down Greenleaf Road as quickly as possible. I probably should have taken a car, but some things were just habit, and the last time I'd snuck out, I'd been years away from getting my license.

I could feel myself start to calm down the farther I walked. The rational part of my brain was telling me that I'd have to go back at some point, but I didn't want to listen to the rational part of my brain right now. I just wanted to pretend that this day—this whole summer—wasn't going to have to happen, something that got easier the more distance I put between myself and the house. I'd been walking for a while and had just started to dig in my bag for my sunglasses when I heard a metal jangling sound and looked up.

My heart sank a little as I saw Connie from the white house across the street, walking her dog and waving at me. She was around my parents' age, and I'd known her last name at some point, but couldn't recall it now. I dropped my sunglass case in my bag next to what I now saw was Gelsey's iPod (whoops), which I must have grabbed thinking it was mine. There was no avoiding Connie without blatantly ignoring her or turning and running into the woods. And I had a feeling either of these options was behavior that might make it back to my mother immediately. I sighed and made myself smile at her as she got closer.

"Taylor, hi!" she called, smiling wide at me. Her dog, a big,

morgan matson

dumb-looking golden retriever, strained against his leash toward me, panting, tail wagging. I looked at him and took a small step away. We'd never had a dog, so though I liked them in theory, I hadn't had all that much experience with them. And even though I watched the reality show *Top Dog* much more than someone who didn't actually own a dog should, this didn't help when confronted with one in the real world.

"Hi, Connie," I said, already starting to edge away, hoping she'd get the hint. "Nice to see you!"

"You too," she replied automatically, but I saw her smile fade a little as her eyes traveled over my face and outfit. "You're looking a bit different today," she said. "Very . . . relaxed."

Since Connie normally saw me in my Stanwich Academy uniform—white blouse and itchy plaid skirt—I had no doubt I looked different now, as I'd pretty much just rolled out of bed, not even bothering to brush my hair, and was wearing flip-flops, cutoffs, and a much-washed white T-shirt that read LAKE PHOENIX SWIM TEAM. The shirt technically wasn't mine, but I'd appropriated it so many years ago that I now just thought of it as my property.

"I guess so," I said to Connie, making sure to keep a smile on my face. "Well . . ."

"Any big plans for the summer?" she asked brightly, apparently completely unaware that I was trying to end this conversation. The dog, maybe realizing this was going to take a while, flopped down at her feet, resting his head on his paws.

"Not really," I said, hoping that might be the end of it. But she continued to look at me, eyebrows raised, so I stifled a sigh and went on. "We're actually leaving today to spend the summer at our lake house."

"Oh, wonderful!" she gushed. "That sounds lovely. Whereabouts is it?"

"It's in the Poconos," I said. She frowned, as though trying to place the name, and I added, "The Pocono Mountains. In Pennsylvania?"

"Oh, right," she said, nodding, though I could tell from her expression that she still had no idea what I was talking about, which wasn't actually that unexpected. Some of my friends' families had summer houses, but they tended to be in places like Nantucket or Cape Cod. Nobody else I knew had a summer house in the mountains of northeastern Pennsylvania.

"Well," Connie said, still smiling brightly. "A lake house! That should be nice."

I nodded, not really trusting myself to answer, since I didn't want to go back to Lake Phoenix. I so didn't want to go back that I had snuck out of the house with practically no plan and no supplies except my sister's iPod, rather than face going there.

"So," Connie said, tugging on the dog's leash, causing him to lumber to his feet, "be sure to say hello to your mother and father for me! I hope they're both doing well, and—" She stopped suddenly, her eyes widening and cheeks reddening slightly. I recognized the signs immediately, even though I'd only been seeing them for three weeks. She had Remembered.

It was something that I had no idea how to handle, but as an unexpected upside, it was something that seemed to be working in my favor. Somehow, overnight, everyone in school seemed to know, and my teachers had been informed, though why or by whom, I'd never been sure. But it was the only explanation for the fact that I'd aced all my finals, even in classes like Trig, which I'd been dangerously close to getting a C in. And if that wasn't enough proof, when my English teacher had passed out our exams, she'd set mine down on my desk and rested her hand on it for just a minute, causing me to look up at her.

"I know that studying must be hard for you right now," she'd murmured, as though the entire class wasn't listening, ears straining for every syllable. "So just do your best, all right, Taylor?"

And I'd bitten my lip and done the Brave Nod, aware the whole time that I was pretending, acting the way I knew she expected me to act. And sure enough, I'd gotten an A on the test, even though I'd only skimmed the end of *The Great Gatsby*.

Everything had changed. Or, more accurately, everything was *going* to change. But nothing had really changed yet. And it made the condolences odd—as if people were saying how sorry they were that my house had burned down when it was still intact but with an ember smoking nearby, waiting.

"I will," I said quickly, saving Connie from having to stammer through one of the well-meaning speeches I was already sick of hearing—or even worse, telling me about some friend of a friend who had been miraculously cured through acupuncture/meditation/ tofu, and had we considered that? "Thank you."

"Take care," she said, putting more meaning in those words than they usually had, as she reached out and patted me on the shoulder. I could see the pity in her eyes, but also the fear—that slight distancing, because if something like this was happening to my family, it could happen to hers.

"You too," I said, trying to keep a smile on my face until she had waved again and headed down the street, dog leading the way. I continued in the opposite direction, but my escape no longer felt like it was going to make things better. What was the point of trying to run away if people were going to insist on reminding you of what you were running from? Though I hadn't felt the need to do it for a while now, running away had been something I'd done with real frequency when I was younger. It had all started when I was five, and I had gotten upset that my mother was paying attention only to baby Gelsey, and Warren, as usual, wouldn't let me play with him. I'd stomped outside, and then had seen the driveway, and the wider world beyond it, beckoning. I had started walking down the street, mostly just wondering how long it would take for someone to realize I was even gone. I was soon found and brought home, of course, but that had begun the pattern, and running away became my preferred method of dealing with anything that upset me. It got to be such a routine that when I used to announce from the doorway, tearfully, that I was leaving home forever and ever, my mother would just nod, barely looking at me, telling me only to make sure to be back in time for dinner.

I had just pulled out Gelsey's iPod—willing to suffer through even the Bentley Boys if it meant a distraction from my thoughts—when I heard the low rumble of the sports car behind me.

It occurred to me that I must have been gone longer than I'd realized as I turned around, knowing what I would see. My father was behind the wheel of his low-slung silver car, smiling at me. "Hi, kid," he said through the open passenger-side window. "Want a ride?"

Knowing that there was no point in even pretending any longer, I pulled open the passenger side door and got in. My dad looked across at me and raised his eyebrows. "So what's the news?" he asked, his traditional greeting.

I shrugged and looked down at the gray floor mats, still pristine, even though he'd had the car for a year. "I just, you know, felt like a walk."

My dad nodded. "Of course," he said, his voice overly serious, as though he completely believed me. But we both knew what I'd really been doing—it had usually been my father who would come and find me. He always seemed to know where I would be, and rather than bringing me right home, if it wasn't too late, we would go out for ice cream instead, after I'd promise not to tell my mother.

I buckled my seat belt, and to my surprise, my dad didn't turn the car around, but instead kept driving, turning onto the road that would take us downtown. "Where are we going?" I asked.

"I thought we could use some breakfast," he said, glancing over at me as he pulled to a stop at a red. "For some reason, all the bagels in the house seem to be sesame."

I smiled at that, and when we arrived, followed my dad into Stanwich Deli. Since the deli was packed, I hung back and let him order. As my eyes roamed over the shop, I noticed Amy Curry standing toward the front of the line, holding hands with a tall, cute guy wearing a Colorado College T-shirt. I didn't know her well—she'd moved with her mother and brother down the street from us last summer—but she smiled and waved at me, and I waved back.

When my dad made it to the front of the line, I watched him rattling off our order, saying something that made the counter guy laugh. To look at my father, you wouldn't be able to tell that anything was truly wrong. He was a little thinner, his skin tone just slightly yellow. But I was trying not to see this as I watched him drop some change into the tip jar. I was trying not to see how tired he looked, trying to swallow the lump in my throat. But most of all, I was trying not to think about the fact that we had been told, by experts who knew these things, that he had approximately three months left to live.

chapter two

"DO WE HAVE TO LISTEN TO THIS?" GELSEY WHINED FROM THE front seat for what had to be the third time in ten minutes.

"You might learn something," Warren said from the driver's side. "Right, Taylor?"

From where I was stretched out in the backseat, I pulled down my sunglasses and turned the volume up on my iPod rather than responding. Lake Phoenix was only a three-hour drive from our house in Stanwich, Connecticut, but it felt like it had been the longest car ride of my life. And since my brother drove like a senior citizen (he'd actually once gotten a ticket for driving too slowly and causing a traffic hazard) it had taken us over four hours to get there—so it was getting close to actually being the longest car ride of my life.

It was just the three of us in the old wood-paneled Land Cruiser that Warren and I shared—my parents had gone on ahead of us, my mom's car packed full with all the supplies we'd need for an entire summer away. I'd spent most of the trip just trying to ignore my siblings' squabbling, mostly over what to listen to—Gelsey only wanted to play the Bentley Boys; Warren insisted we listen to his Great Courses CD. Warren had won the final round, and the droning, English accent was telling me more than I ever wanted to know about quantum mechanics.

Even though I hadn't been back in five years, I had still been able to anticipate every turn on the drive up. My parents had bought the house before I was born, and for years, we spent every summer there, leaving in early June and coming back in late August, my father staying in Connecticut alone during the workweek and coming up on the weekends. Summers used to be the highlight of my year, and all throughout school I would count down until June and everything that a Lake Phoenix summer promised. But the summer I was twelve had ended so disastrously that I had been incredibly relieved that we hadn't gone back the next year. That was the summer Warren decided that he needed to really start focusing on his transcript and did a pre-college intensive program at Yale. Gelsey had just switched ballet teachers and didn't want to stop classes for the summer. And I, not wanting to go back to Lake Phoenix and face the mess I'd made up there, had found a summer oceanography camp (there had been a brief period when I'd wanted to be a marine biologist; this had since passed) and begged my parents to let me go. And every year since then, it seemed like there was always something happening to prevent us from spending the summer there.

Gelsey started going to sleepaway ballet camps, and Warren and I both started doing the academic-service-summer-program thing (he built a playground in Greece, I spent a summer trying—and failing—to learn Mandarin at a language immersion in Vermont). My mother started renting our house out when it became clear that we were all getting too busy to take the whole summer off and spend it together in Pennsylvania.

And this year was supposed to be no exception—Gelsey was planning on going back to the ballet camp where she was the rising star, Warren had an internship lined up at my father's law firm, and I had intended to spend a lot of time sunbathing. I was really, really looking forward to the school year ending. My ex-boyfriend, Evan, had broken up with me a month before school ended, and my friends, not wanting to split up the group, had all taken his side. My sudden lack of friends and any semblance of a social life would have made the prospect of heading out of town for the summer really appealing under normal circumstances. But I did not want to go back to Lake Phoenix. I hadn't even set foot in the state of Pennsylvania in five years. The five of us spending the summer together was something nobody would have even considered until three weeks ago. And yet, that was exactly what was happening.

"We're here!" Warren announced cheerfully as I felt the car slow down.

I opened my eyes, sat up, and looked around. The first thing I saw was green. The trees on both sides of the road were bright green, along with the grass beneath them. And they were densely packed, giving only glimpses of the driveways and houses that lay behind them. I glanced up at the temperature display, and saw it was ten degrees cooler here than it had been in Connecticut. Like it or not, I was back in the mountains.

"Finally," Gelsey muttered from the front seat.

I stretched out my neck from the awkward position I'd been sleeping in, for once in full agreement with my sister. Warren slowed even more, signaled, and then turned down our gravel driveway. All the driveways in Lake Phoenix were gravel, and ours had always been the way I'd measured the summer. In June, I could barely make it barefoot from the car to the porch, wincing every step as the rocks dug into my tender, pale feet, sheltered by a year of shoe-wearing. But by August, my feet would be toughened and a deep brown, the white of my flip-flop tan lines standing out in sharp relief, and I would be able to run across the driveway barefoot without a second thought.

I unbuckled my seat belt and leaned forward between the front seats to get a better look. And there, right in front of me, was our summer house. The first thing I noticed was that it looked exactly the same—same dark wood, peaked roof, floor-to-ceiling windows, wraparound porch.

The second thing I noticed was the dog.

It was sitting on the porch, right by the door. As the car drew closer, it didn't get up or run away, but instead starting wagging its tail, as though it had been waiting for us all along.

"What is *that*?" Gelsey asked as Warren shut off the engine.

"What's what?" Warren asked. Gelsey pointed, and he squinted through the windshield. "Oh," he said a moment later, and I noticed that he was making no move to get out of the car. My brother denied it, but he was afraid of dogs, and had been ever since an idiotic babysitter let him watch *Cujo* when he was seven.

I opened my door and stepped out onto the gravel driveway to get a closer look. This was not the world's most attractive dog. It was smallish, but not the tiny kind that you could put in your purse or might accidentally step on. It was golden brown with hair that seemed to be standing out from its body, giving it an air of surprise. It looked like a mutt, with biggish, stand-up German Shepherd-y ears, a short nose, and a longish, collie-like tail. I could see it had a collar on with a tag dangling from it, so clearly it wasn't a stray.

Gelsey got out of the car as well, but Warren stayed put in the front seat and cracked the window as I approached him. "I'll just, um, stay behind and handle the bags," he muttered as he passed over the keys.

"Seriously?" I asked, raising my eyebrows at him. Warren flushed red before quickly rolling up his window, as though this small dog was somehow going to launch itself into the front seat of the Land Cruiser.

morgan matson

I crossed the driveway and walked up the three porch steps to the house. I expected the dog to move as soon as I got close, but instead it just wagged its tail harder, making a whapping sound on the wooden deck. "Go on," I said as I crossed to the door. "Shoo." But instead of leaving, it trotted over to join me, as though it had every intention of following us inside. "No," I said firmly, trying to imitate Randolph George, the bespectacled British host of *Top Dog*. "Go." I took a step toward it, and the dog finally seemed to get the message, skittering away and then walking down the porch steps and across the driveway with what seemed like, for a dog, a great deal of reluctance.

Once the danger of the rogue canine had passed, Warren opened his door and carefully got out, looking around at the driveway, which was empty of other cars. "Mom and Dad really should have been here by now."

I pulled my cell out of my shorts pocket and saw that he was right. They had left a few hours ahead of us, and most likely hadn't driven 40 mph the whole way. "Gelsey, can you call—" I turned to my sister, only to see that she was bent over almost in half, nose to knee. "You okay?" I asked, trying to look at her upside down.

"Fine," she said, her voice muffled. "Just stretching." She straightened up slowly, her face bright red. As I watched, her complexion changed back to its normal shade—pale, with freckles that would only increase exponentially as the summer went on. She swept her arms up to meet in a perfect circle above her head, then dropped them and rolled her shoulders back. In case her bun or turned-out walk wasn't enough to tell the world that she was a ballet dancer, Gelsey had the habit of stretching, and often in public.

"Well, when you're done with that," I said, as she was now starting to bend backward at an alarming angle, "can you call Mom?" Without waiting for her response—especially since I had a feeling it was going to be something like *Why don't you do it?*—I selected the key from the key ring, turned it in the lock, and stepped inside the house for the first time in five years.

As I looked around, I let out a breath. I had been worried, after summers of renters, that the house would have changed drastically. That the furniture would be moved around, that things would be added, or there would just be the sense—hard to define but palpable—that someone had been in your space. The Three Bears had known it well, and so had I, the year I came back from oceanography camp and could tell immediately that my mother had put some guests in my room when I'd been gone. But as I took everything in, I didn't get that feeling. It was the summer house, just as I'd remembered it, like it had been waiting for me, this whole time, to finally come back.

The downstairs was open-plan, so I could see all the rooms that weren't bedrooms or bathrooms. The ceiling was high, stretching up to the top of the peaked roof, letting in swaths of sun onto the threadbare throw rugs that covered the wood floors. There was the scratched wooden dining table we never ate on, which always just became the place to dump towels and mail. The kitchen—tiny compared to our large state-of-the-art one in Connecticut—was to my right. The door off the back of it led to our screened-in porch. It looked out on the lake and was where we ate all our meals, except in rare cases of torrential rain. And off the porch was the walkway down to our dock and Lake Phoenix itself, and through the kitchen windows, I could see the glint of late-afternoon sunlight hitting the water.

Past the kitchen was a sitting area with two couches that faced the stone fireplace, the place where my parents had always ended up after dinner, reading and doing work. Beyond that was the family room, with a worn corduroy sofa, where Warren and Gelsey and I usually found ourselves at night. One section of the built-in bookcases was filled with board games and jigsaw puzzles, and we usually had a game or puzzle going throughout the summer, though Risk had been put on the highest shelf, out of easy reach, after the summer when we all had become obsessed, forming secret alliances and basically ceasing to go outside as we circled the board.

Our bedrooms were all off one hallway—my parents slept in the master suite upstairs—which meant that Warren, Gelsey, and I would all have to share the one downstairs bathroom, something I was not looking forward to experiencing again, since I'd gotten used to having my own bathroom in Connecticut. I headed down the hall to my bedroom, peering in at the bathroom as I went. It was smaller than I remembered it being. Much too small, in fact, for the three of us to share without killing one another.

I reached my room, with the ancient TAYLOR'S PLACE sign on it that I'd totally forgotten about, and pushed open the door, bracing myself to confront the room I'd last seen five years ago, and all its attendant memories.

But when I stepped inside, I wasn't confronted by anything except a pleasant, somewhat generic room. My bed was still the same, with its old brass frame and red-and-white patterned quilt, the trundle bed tucked beneath it. The wooden dresser and wood-framed mirror were the same, along with the old chest at the foot of the bed that had always held extra blankets for the cold nights you got in the mountains, even in the summer. But there was nothing in the room that was *me* any longer. The embarrassing posters of the teen actor I'd been obsessed with back then (he'd since had several well-publicized stints in rehab) had been removed from above my bed. My swim team ribbons (mostly third place) were gone, along with the collection of lip glosses that I'd been curating for several years. Which was probably a good thing, I tried to tell myself, as they all surely would have gone bad by now. But still. I dropped my purse and sat down on my bed, looking from the empty closet to the bare dresser, searching for some evidence of the fact that I had lived here for twelve summers, but not seeing any.

"Gelsey, what are you *doing*?"

The sound of my brother's voice was enough to pull me out of these thoughts and make me go investigate what was happening. I walked down the hallway and saw my sister chucking stuffed animals out of her room and into the hall. I dodged an airborne elephant and stood next to Warren, who was eyeing with alarm the small pile of them that was accumulating in front of his door. "What's going on?" I asked.

"They turned my room into a *baby's* room," Gelsey said, her voice heavy with scorn as she flung another animal—this time a purple horse that I vaguely recognized—out the door. Sure enough, her room had been redecorated. There was now a crib in the corner, and a changing table, and her twin bed had been piled high with the offending stuffed animals.

"The renters probably had a baby," I said, leaning to the side to avoid being beaned by a fuzzy yellow duck. "Why don't you just wait until Mom gets here?"

Gelsey rolled her eyes, a language she'd become fluent in this year. She could express a wide variety of emotion with every eye roll, maybe because she practiced constantly. And right now, she was indicating how behind-the-times I was. "Mom's not going to be here for another hour," she said. She looked down at the animal in her hands, a small kangaroo, and turned it over a few times. "I just talked to her. She and Daddy had to go to Stroudsburg to meet with his new oncologist." She pronounced the last word carefully, the way we all did. It was a word I hadn't been aware of a few weeks ago. This was when I'd thought my father was just having minor, easily fixed back pains. At that point, I wasn't even entirely sure what the pancreas was, and I definitely didn't know pancreatic cancer was almost always fatal, or that "stage four" were words you never wanted to hear.

My father's doctors in Connecticut had given him permission to spend the summer in Lake Phoenix under the condition that he see an oncologist twice a month to check his progress, and when the time came, that he bring in nursing care if he didn't want to go into hospice. The cancer had been found late enough that there apparently wasn't anything that could be done. I hadn't been able to get my head around it at first. In all the medical dramas I'd ever seen, there was always some solution, some last-minute, miraculously undiscovered remedy. Nobody ever just gave up on a patient. But it seemed like in real life, they did.

I met Gelsey's eye for a moment before looking down at the floor and the jumbled pile of toys that had landed there. None of us said anything about the hospital, and what that meant, but I wasn't expecting us to. We hadn't talked about what was happening with our dad. We tended to avoid discussing emotional things in our

morgan matson

family, and sometimes hanging around with my friends, and seeing the way they interacted with their families—hugging, talking about their feelings—I would feel not so much envious as uncomfortable.

And the three of us had never been close. It probably didn't help that we were so different. Warren had been brilliant from preschool, and it had come as a surprise to no one that he'd been the class valedictorian. My five-year age gap with Gelsey—not to mention the fact that she was capable of being the world's biggest brat—meant we didn't have one of those superclose sister relationships. Gelsey also spent as much time as possible dancing, which I had no interest in. And it wasn't like Warren and Gelsey were close with each other either. We had just never been a unit. I might have once wished things were different, especially when I was younger and had just read the Narnia series, or *The Boxcar Children*, where the brothers and sisters are all best friends and look out for one another. But I'd long since accepted that this wasn't going to happen. It wasn't necessarily bad—just the way things were, and something that wasn't going to change.

Just like it wasn't going to change that I was the unexceptional one in the family. It had been that way as long as I could remember—Warren was smart and Gelsey was talented, and I was just Taylor, not particularly skilled at anything.

Gelsey went back to throwing the stuffed animals into the hallway, and I was about to go into my own room, feeling like I'd spent far too much time as it was with my siblings that day, when a flash of orange caught my eye.

"Hey," I said, bending down to pick up a stuffed animal I thought I recognized. "I think that's mine." In fact, it was a stuffed animal I knew very well: a small plush penguin, wearing an orange-and-white-striped scarf. It wasn't the finest stuffed animal ever constructed—I could tell now that the felt was fairly cheap, and the stuffing was threatening to come out in several places. But the night of the carnival when I was twelve, the night I'd gotten my first kiss, the night Henry Crosby had won it for me, I'd thought it was the most wonderful thing in the world.

"I remember that," Warren said, a look coming into his eyes that I didn't like one bit. "Wasn't that the one you got at the carnival?" My brother had a photographic memory, but usually used it to memorize obscure facts, and not to torment me.

"Yeah," I muttered, starting to take a step away.

"Wasn't it the one *Henry* won for you?" Warren put a special spin on his name. I had a feeling that I was being punished for making fun of Warren's fear of small, harmless dogs. I glared at my brother. Gelsey was looking between the two of us, interested.

"Henry who?" she asked.

"You know," Warren said, a small smile starting to take form on his face. "Henry Crosby. He had a little brother, Derek or something. Henry was Taylor's *boyfriend*."

Davy, I silently corrected Warren. I could feel my cheeks get hot, which was ridiculous, and I found myself looking for an escape. If there was a way that I could have walked away from the conversation without it being totally obvious that I was uncomfortable, I would have.

"Oh, yeah," Gelsey said slowly. "I think I remember him. He was nice to me. And he used to know the names of all the trees."

"And—" Warren started, but I interrupted him before he could continue, not sure I could take any more.

"Anyway, you should get that cleaned up before Mom gets here," I said loudly, knowing even as I said it that it was highly unlikely my mother would yell at Gelsey for anything. But I tried to pretend it was true as I left with all the dignity one can muster while holding a stuffed penguin, and went to the kitchen for no reason whatsoever.

Henry Crosby. The name reverberated in my head as I put the penguin on the kitchen counter and opened and shut one of the cabinet doors. He was someone I had consciously tried not to think about too much over the years. He'd become reduced, shortened to a slumber-party anecdote when the inevitable question—*Who was your first boyfriend?*—would arise. I had the Henry story down perfectly now, so that I barely had to even think about it:

Oh, that was Henry. We'd been friends, up at my summer house. And the summer we were twelve, we started going out. He gave me my first kiss at the summer carnival. . . . This was when everyone would sigh, and if someone asked me what happened, I would just smile and shrug and say something along the lines of "Well, we were *twelve*, so it became pretty clear there weren't exactly long-term prospects there." And everyone would laugh and I would nod and smile, but really I would be turning over what I'd just said. Because it wasn't that any of those facts had been technically incorrect. But none of them—especially about why it hadn't worked out—had been the truth. And I would push thoughts of that summer out of my head and rejoin the conversation, relegating what had happened—with Henry, and Lucy, and what I'd done—back to the anecdote that I pretended was all it was.

Warren came into the kitchen a moment later and beelined for a large cardboard box sitting on the counter. "Sorry," he said after a moment, opening the top. "I was just kidding around."

I shrugged, as though I couldn't have cared less. "It's nothing," I said. "It's ancient history." Which was true. But as soon as we'd crossed the line that separated Lake Phoenix from the rest of the world, Henry had been circling around in my thoughts, even as I'd tried to turn up the volume on my iPod to drown them out. I'd even found myself watching for his house. And I had seen, to my surprise, the house that had been a soft white was now painted a bright blue, and the sign out front that had always read CAMP CROSBY now read MARYANNE'S HAPPY HOURS, decorated with a silhouette of a martini glass—all proof that new owners had taken over. That Henry wasn't

morgan matson

there any longer. I had kept my eyes on the house even as it faded from view, realizing that I might really never see him again, which the presence of Maryanne, whoever she was, seemed to cement. This realization caused a strange mix of feelings—nostalgia coupled with disappointment. But mostly I had felt the cool, heart-pounding sensation of relief that comes when you know you've gotten away with something.

Warren began unpacking his box, lining up row after row of plastic ketchup squeeze bottles on the counter in perfectly straight lines, as though there might be some sort of epic condiment battle looming on the horizon.

I stared at them. "Is Pennsylvania having some sort of ketchup shortage that I'm not aware of?"

Warren shook his head without looking up from his unpacking. "I'm just taking precautions," he said. "You remember what happened last time."

In fact, I did. My brother wasn't at all picky about food, unlike Gelsey, who seemed to live on pasta and pizza and refused to eat anything moderately spicy—but his one exception was ketchup. Warren put it on almost everything, would eat only Heinz, and preferred it chilled, not room temperature. He claimed he could tell the difference between the brands, something that he'd proved once at a mall food court when we were younger and extremely bored. So he had been traumatized five years ago, when we first arrived in Lake

Phoenix and the store had had a run on Heinz and was down to the generic brand. Warren had refused to even try it and had used my father's corporate card to have a case of Heinz shipped overnight to him, something my father—not to mention the company accountant—had not been too happy to find out about.

Now, fortified against such tragedy, Warren placed two bottles in the nearly-empty fridge and started transferring the rest into the cupboard. "Do you want me to tell you how ketchup was invented?" he asked, with an expression that I, unfortunately, knew all too well. Warren was very into facts, and had been since he was little and some probably well-meaning, but now much-despised, relative gave him *Discovered by Accident!*—a book on famous inventions that had been discovered by accident. After that, you couldn't have a conversation with Warren without him dropping some fact or another into it. This quest for useless knowledge (thanks to his equally fun obscure-vocabulary-word kick, I knew this was also called "arcana") had only grown with time. Finally, we'd complained so much that Warren no longer told us the facts, but now just told us he *could* tell us the facts, which wasn't, in my opinion, all that much better.

"Maybe later," I said, even though I was admittedly slightly curious as to the accidental origin of ketchup, and hoping it wasn't something terribly disgusting or disturbing—like Coca-Cola, which, it turned out, had been the result of a failed attempt to make aspirin. I looked around for an escape and saw the lake through the kitchen window. And, suddenly, I knew that it was the only place I wanted to be.

I pushed through to our screened-in porch, then out the side door, heading for our dock. As I stepped outside, I turned my face up to the sun. Five wooden steps led down to a small grassy hill, and below that, the dock. Even though it was directly behind our house, we had always shared it with the houses on either side of us. The dock wasn't particularly long or impressive, but had always seemed to me to be the perfect length for getting a running start to cannonball into the lake, and the water was deep enough that you didn't have to worry about hitting the bottom.

There were some kayaks and a canoe stacked on the grass by the side of the dock, but I barely noticed them as I got closer. You weren't allowed to have any motorized watercraft on the lake, so there was no roar of engines disturbing the late afternoon quiet, just a lone kayaker paddling past in the distance. Lake Phoenix was big, with three small islands scattered across it, and surrounded on all sides by pine trees. Despite the size of the rest of the lake, our dock occupied one side of a narrow passage, the other side close enough that you could see the docks across the water and the people on them.

I looked across the lake to the dock opposite ours, which had always been the Marino family's. Lucy Marino had been my best friend in Lake Phoenix for twelve summers, and there had been a time when I'd known her house as well as my own. We'd slept over at each other's houses almost every night, alternating, our families so used to it that my mother started stocking Lucy's favorite cereal. I usually tried not to think about Lucy, but it hadn't escaped my notice, especially recently, that she had been my last tell-everything-to friend. Nobody at school seemed to know how to react to the news about my father, and overnight, it was like I didn't know how to talk to anyone about it. And since I'd been thoroughly cast out of my old group of friends, I found myself, as the school year ended and preparations for our summer up here began, pretty much alone, without anyone to talk to. But at one time, I had told everything to Lucy, until we, like everything else, had fallen apart that last summer.

Out of habit, I found myself looking to the leg of her dock. Over the years, Lucy and I had developed a very intricate system of communication from our respective docks that involved flashlights and our own version of Morse code if it was dark, and a very imprecise semaphore flag system if it was light. And if one of us needed to talk to the other desperately, we would tie one of the pair of pink bandannas we both had to the leg of our docks. Admittedly, this had not been the most efficient method of communication, and we'd usually end up talking on the phone before we happened to see the lights, or flags, or bandannas. But, of course, the leg of her dock was now bandanna-free.

I kicked off my flip-flops and walked across the sun-warmed

morgan matson

planks of our dock barefoot. The dock had been walked on so much over the years that you never had to worry about splinters, like you sometimes did on our front porch. I started walking faster, almost running, wanting to get to the end, to breathe in the scent of water and pine trees, and curl my toes around the edge.

But when I was almost to the end, I stopped short. There was movement at the base of the dock. The kayak I had seen earlier was now tied up and bobbing in the water, and I could see the person who'd been in it—a guy—climbing up the ladder using one hand, holding the kayak paddle in the other. The sun was glancing off the water so that the glare was blocking his face as he stepped on to the dock, but I figured this was probably just a neighbor. He walked forward, out of the glare, then stopped abruptly, staring at me. I blinked in surprise, and found myself staring back.

Standing across from me, five years older, all grown up, and much cuter than I remembered him being, was Henry Crosby.

chapter three

I FELT MY JAW DROP, WHICH I HADN'T REALIZED UNTIL THAT moment was something that actually happened in real life. I closed it quickly, then blinked at him again, trying to regroup as my brain struggled to comprehend what all-grown-up Henry was doing standing in front of me.

He dropped the paddle on the dock, then took a small step forward and folded his arms across his chest. "Taylor Edwards," he said. He didn't phrase it as a question.

"Henry?" I asked, a little faintly, even though of course it was him. For one thing, he had known me, which some random kayaker probably wouldn't have. And for another, he looked the same—except much, much better.

He was tall, and broad-shouldered, with the same brown hair, so dark it almost looked black, and cut short. I could no longer see the freckles he'd had when we were younger, but his eyes were still the same hazel, though they looked more green than brown now. His jaw also somehow seemed more defined, and his arms were muscular. I couldn't make this fit with the last time I'd seen him, when he'd been shorter than me, and skinny, with scraped-up elbows and knees. All in all, Henry looked very cute. And very not happy to see me.

"Hi," I said, just to say something to try and mask the fact that I had been staring.

"Hello," he said, his voice cold. His voice was also deeper, and no longer cracking every other word, like it had been the last time I'd heard it. His eyes met mine, and I wondered suddenly what changes he could see in me, and what he thought of the way I looked now. Unfortunately, I'd looked pretty much the same since childhood, with blue eyes and straight, fine hair that fell somewhere between blond and brown. I was medium height, with a wiry build, and I certainly hadn't gained many of the curves I'd been so desperately hoping for when I was twelve. I now wished I'd taken the time to do anything with my appearance that morning, as opposed to just rolling out of bed. Henry's eyes traveled down to my outfit, and when I realized what I was wearing, I inwardly cursed myself. Not only was I running into someone who clearly hated me, but I was doing in it a T-shirt I'd stolen from him.

"So," he said, and then a silence fell. My heart was pounding hard, and I suddenly wanted nothing more than to just turn and leave, get in the car and not stop driving until I got back to Connecticut. "What are you doing here?" he finally asked, a hard edge in his voice.

"I could ask you the same question," I said, thinking back to only a few minutes earlier, when I'd told Warren so confidently that Henry was ancient history, sure that I'd never see him again. "I thought you'd left."

"You thought *I'd* left?" he asked, with a short, humorless laugh. "Really."

"Yes," I said, a little testily. "We passed your house today, and it was all different. And apparently owned by some lush named Maryanne."

"Well, a lot's changed in five years, Taylor," he said, and I realized it was the second time he used my whole name. Before, Henry had only called me Taylor when he was mad at me—most of the time, he had called me Edwards, or Tay. "We've moved, for one." He pointed to the house next to mine, the one so close that I could see a line of pots on the windowsill. "Right there."

I just stared where he was pointing for a moment. That was the Morrisons' house, and I'd just assumed they were still there, Mr. and Mrs. Morrison and their mean poodle. "You live next door to me?"

"We have for a few years now," he said. "But since there were always renters at your place, I didn't think you were ever coming back."

"Me neither," I admitted, "if you want to know the truth."

"So what happened?" he asked, looking right at me and startling me with the greenness of his eyes. "Why are you back, all of a sudden?"

I felt my breath catch as the reason—never far from my thoughts—crashed into the front of my mind, seeming to dim the afternoon light a little. "Well," I said slowly, looking away from him and out to the water, trying to think about how to explain it. It wasn't even like it was that complicated. All I had to say was something along the lines of *My dad's sick. So we're spending the summer together up here.* That wasn't the hard part. The hard part came with the follow-up questions. *How sick? With what? Is it serious?* And then the inevitable reaction when people realized how serious it actually was. And that what I meant, but hadn't said, was that we were spending our *last* summer together.

I didn't have a practiced explanation because I had assiduously avoided having this conversation. Word had spread around school pretty quickly, preventing me from having to explain the situation. And if I was with my mother, and we happened to run into an acquaintance in the grocery store who asked after my father, I left the task of breaking the news to her. I would look pointedly in the other direction, or wander a few steps away, as though yielding to the inexorable pull of the cereal aisle, pretending that the difficult conversation she was having had nothing whatsoever to do with me. I wasn't entirely sure I could say the words out loud—or handle the follow-up questions—without losing it. I hadn't really cried yet, and I didn't want to risk this happening in front of Henry Crosby.

"It's kind of a long story," I finally said, keeping my eyes on the calm surface of the lake.

"Yeah," Henry said, sarcastically. "I'm sure."

I blinked at his tone. Henry had never talked to me like that before. When we'd fought, it had been the kid version of fighting—arm punches, name calling, pranking—anything to get the fight over with so that we could go back to being friends. Hearing him now—and the way we were sniping at each other—felt like speaking a foreign language with someone you'd only ever spoken English to.

"So why did you move?" I asked, a little more aggressively than I meant to, as I turned to him, folding my arms across my chest. Moves within Lake Phoenix were fairly rare—on the drive up, I'd seen signs I recognized in front of house after house, the same owners still there.

Expecting an immediate answer, I was surprised to see Henry flush slightly and stick his hands in the pockets of his shorts, which had always been his tell when he didn't know what to say. "It's a long story," he echoed, looking down. For a moment, the only sound was the faint *thunk thunk* of the plastic kayak bumping up against the wooden leg of the dock. "Anyway," he said after a pause, "we live there now."

"Right," I said, feeling like we'd already established this. "I got that."

"I mean, we live there year-round," he clarified. He looked back at me and I tried to cover my expression of surprise. Though you could live in Lake Phoenix full-time, very few people did—it was

morgan matson

primarily a summer community. And five years ago, Henry had lived in Maryland. His father had done something in finance in D.C., coming up to Lake Phoenix with the rest of the fathers on the weekends, and staying in the city to work the rest of the time.

"Oh," I said, nodding like I understood. I had no idea what that meant in terms of the rest of his life, but he didn't seem like he was about to give me a detailed explanation, and I didn't feel like I had the right to ask for more information. All of a sudden, I realized there was a much bigger distance between Henry and me than just the few feet that separated us.

"Yeah," Henry said, and I wondered if he was feeling the same thing that I was—like he was standing on the dock with a stranger. "I should go," he said shortly, as he turned to leave.

It felt wrong to end this on such an unsettled note, so, mostly just wanting to be polite, as he passed me, I said, "Good to see you again."

He stopped, just a few feet from me, closer than ever, close enough that I could see that there was still a scattering of freckles across his cheeks, but so faint I could almost see each one, and connect them, like constellations. I could feel my pulse beating harder at the base of my throat, and I suddenly had a flashback to one of our early, tentative make-out sessions five years earlier—one that had, in fact, taken place on this very dock. *I've kissed you* flashed through my mind before I could stop it.

I looked at Henry, still so close, wondering if maybe he was remembering the same thing. But he was looking at me with a flat, skeptical expression, and as he started to walk away again, I realized that he had deliberately not returned my "good to see you" sentiment.

Maybe, on a different day, I would have left it at that. But I was cranky and tired and had just spent four hours listening to boy bands and facts about the energy of light, and I could feel my temper start to flare. "Look, it's not like I wanted to come back," I said, hearing my voice get louder and a little more shrill.

"Then why are you here?" Henry asked, his voice rising as well.

"I didn't have any choice in the matter," I snapped, knowing that I was about to go too far, but also knowing that I wasn't going to be able to stop myself. "I never wanted to come back here ever again."

For a second, I thought I saw a flash of hurt pass over his face, but then it was gone, and the same stony expression had returned. "Well," he said. "Maybe you're not the only one who wanted that."

I tried not to flinch, even though I knew I deserved it. We stared at each other, in a momentary standoff, and I realized that one of the main problems with having an argument on a dock is that there's really nowhere to go if the other person is standing between you and dry land.

"So," I said finally, breaking our eye contact and folding my arms over my chest, trying to indicate with my tone of voice how little I cared. "See you around."

Henry slung the kayak paddle over one shoulder like an ax. "I think that's inevitable, Taylor," he said ruefully. He looked at me for a moment longer before turning and walking away and, not wanting to watch him go, I strode to the end of the dock.

I looked out at the water, and the sun that was just starting to think about setting, and let out a long breath. So Henry was living next door to me. It would be fine. I could deal with it. I would just spend the entire summer indoors. Suddenly exhausted by the thought of all of it, I sat down and let my feet skim the surface of the water. Just then, I caught sight of something at the very corner of the dock.

We had carved it together, in the center of a crooked heart, five years ago. I couldn't believe that it was still here after all this time. I ran my fingers over the plus sign, wondering why, at twelve, I thought I'd had any concept of forever.

From somewhere behind me, I could hear the sound of tires crunching on gravel, then car doors slamming, and I knew my parents had finally arrived. I pushed myself up and trudged across the dock, wondering just how I'd gotten here.

chapter four
three weeks earlier

IT WAS OFFICIALLY THE WORST BIRTHDAY EVER.

I was sitting on the couch next to Warren, while Gelsey lay on her stomach on the floor in front of us, her legs turned out, froglike, and resting in a diamond on the carpet behind her, something that never failed to make me wince. We were all watching a sitcom that none of us had laughed at once, and I had a feeling my siblings were only there because they thought they had to be. I could see Warren sneaking glances at his laptop, and could guess that Gelsey wanted to be up in her room, which had been turned into an ad hoc dance studio, working on her *fouettes*, or whatever.

My siblings had tried to make it feel like as much of a celebration as possible under the circumstances—they'd ordered a pineapple and pepperoni pizza, my favorite, put a candle in the center of it, and clapped when I blew it out. I'd closed my eyes tightly in anticipation, even though I couldn't remember the last time I'd made a birthday wish and actually thought anything might come of it. But this was a fervent, eyes-closed-tightly wish that things would turn out to be okay with my dad, that everything that was happening was just a mistake, a false alarm, and I was imbuing this wish with as much hope in the outcome as the ones I'd made when I was little, when all I'd wanted from the universe was a pony.

The sitcom laugh track blasted through the room, and I looked at the clock on the DVD player. "What time were they supposed to be home?" I asked.

"Mom wasn't sure if they were making it back tonight," Warren said. He met my eye for a moment, then looked back at the television. "She said she'd call."

I nodded, and focused on the antics onscreen, though I could hardly follow them. My parents were at Sloan-Kettering, a cancer hospital in Manhattan, where my father was getting tests done. They'd been there for the last three days because it turned out that the back problem that had been bothering him for the last few months wasn't actually a back problem at all. The three of us had been left to fend for ourselves, and we had been doing our own chores without complaint and getting along much better than usual, none of us talking about we were all afraid of, as though by naming it, we would make it real.

My mother had called me that morning, apologizing that they were missing my birthday, and while I assured her that it was okay, I had felt a hard knot start to form in my stomach. Because it felt like, on some level, this was what I deserved. I had always been close to my dad—I was the one who went along with him on errands, the one who helped him pick out birthday and Christmas gifts for my mother, the only one who shared his sense of humor. So I should have been the one to realize something was actually wrong. I could see the signs, after all—my dad wincing as he eased himself down into the low driver's seat of his sports car, working harder than usual to lift things, moving a little more carefully. But I hadn't wanted it to be real, had wanted it to be something that would just quietly go away, so I hadn't said anything. My father hated doctors, and even though my mother could presumably see all the same things that I did, she didn't insist that he go to one. And I had been focused on my own drama at school—convinced that my breakup and its fallout was the worst thing that had ever happened to me.

I was thinking just how stupid I'd been when headlights cut through the darkness outside the window, cresting up the hill of our driveway, and a second later, I heard the hum of the garage door. Gelsey sat up, and Warren turned off the volume. For a moment, we all just looked at one another in the sudden silence.

"They're back, so that's a good sign, right?" Gelsey asked. For some reason she looked at me for an answer, and I just looked at the television, where the hijinks were winding down and everything was getting happily resolved.

I heard the door open and close, and then my mother appeared in the doorway of the TV room, looking exhausted.

"Could we talk to all of you in the dining room?" she asked. She didn't wait for us to answer, but left the room again.

As I stood up from the couch, I could felt the knot in my stomach get bigger. This did not seem to be the good sign Gelsey was talking about, and the one that I had wished for. Because if it was good news, I figured that my mother just would have told us. She wouldn't have needed to tell us in the dining room, which in itself seemed ominous. In addition to the few times it was used each year for eating fancier dinners on nicer plates than usual, the dining room was the place where things were Discussed.

I followed Warren and Gelsey through the kitchen toward the dining room, where I saw my father was sitting at his usual spot, at the head of the table, looking somehow smaller than I remembered him being only a few days ago. My mother stood at the kitchen island with a square white bakery box, and she pulled me into a quick, awkward, one-armed hug. We weren't really physically affectionate in my family, making this as worrying a sign as needing to hear news in the dining room.

"I'm so sorry about your birthday, Taylor," she said. She gestured to the white box, and I saw that the sticker keeping the box closed read BILLY's—my favorite cupcake bakery. "I brought these for you, but maybe . . ." She glanced at the dining room and bit her lip. "Maybe we'll save them for afterward."

I wanted to ask, *After what?* but I also felt, with every minute that passed, that I knew what the answer was. As my mother took a deep breath before heading in to join everyone, I looked to the front door. I could feel my familiar impulse kick in, the one that told me that things would be easier if I could just leave, not have to deal with any of this, just take my cupcakes and go.

But of course, I didn't do that. I walked behind my mother into the dining room, where she clasped my father's hand, looked around at all of us, took a breath, and then confirmed what we'd all been afraid of.

As she spoke the words, it was like I was hearing them from deep underwater. There was a ringing in my ears, and I looked around the table, at Gelsey who was already crying, and my father, who looked paler than I'd ever seen him, and Warren furrowing his brow, the way he always did when he didn't want to express any emotion. I pinched the inside of my arm, hard, just in case it might wake me up from this nightmare I'd landed in and couldn't seem to get out of. But the pinching didn't help, and I was still at the table as my mother said more of the terrible words. *Cancer. Pancreatic. Stage four. Four months, maybe more. Maybe less.*

When she'd finished and Gelsey was hiccupping and Warren was staring very hard at the ceiling, blinking more than usual, my father spoke for the first time. "I think we should talk about the summer," he said, his voice hoarse. I looked over at him, and he met

morgan matson

my eyes, and suddenly I was ashamed that I hadn't burst into tears like my younger sister, that all I was feeling was a terrible hollow numbness. As though this was letting him down somehow. "I would like to spend the summer with all of you up at the lake house," he said. He looked around the rest of the table. "What do you think?"

chapter five

"YOU HAVE GOT TO BE *KIDDING* ME." MY MOTHER CLOSED ONE OF the kitchen cabinet doors a little harder than necessary and turned to face me, shaking her head. "They took all my spices. Can you believe it?"

"Mmm," I muttered. I'd been drafted into helping my mother unpack the kitchen, but mostly I'd been organizing and reorganizing the silverware drawer, which seemed preferable to dealing with one of the large boxes that still needed to be sorted. So far, my mother hadn't noticed, since she'd been taking inventory of what was left in the kitchen. It seemed that last summer's renters had taken most everything that hadn't been nailed down—including cleaning supplies and all the condiments in the fridge. Conversely, though, they had also left a lot of their stuff behind—like the crib that had so offended Gelsey.

"I don't know how I'm expected to cook without spices," she muttered as she opened one of the upper cabinets, rising up on her toes to check the contents, her feet turned out in a perfect first position. My mother was a former professional ballet dancer, and though a tendon injury had sidelined her in her twenties, she still looked like she'd be able to reenter the studio at any moment. "Taylor," she said a little more sharply, causing me to look at her.

"What?" I asked, hearing how defensive I sounded, as I straightened a teaspoon.

My mother sighed. "Can you stop it with the pouting, please?"

If there was a sentence designed to make me pout even more, I didn't know what it was. Even though I didn't want to, I could feel myself scowling. "I'm not pouting."

My mom glanced through the screened-in porch out to the water, then looked back at me. "This summer is going to be hard enough for all of us without this . . . attitude."

I closed the silverware drawer harder than I probably needed to, now feeling guilty as well as annoyed. I'd never been my mother's favorite—that was Gelsey—but we'd always gotten along fairly well.

"I know you didn't want to come here," she said, her tone softening. "But we have to try and make the best of it. All right?"

I pulled the drawer open, then pushed it closed again. I'd been in this house for only a few hours, but already I was feeling claustrophobic. And the presence next door of an ex-boyfriend who hated me—with good reason—wasn't helping. "I just," I said, a little haltingly, "I don't know what I'm supposed to do here all summer. And—"

"Mom!" Gelsey stomped into the kitchen. "The crib is still in my room. And the lights aren't working."

"The Murphys probably took the lightbulbs, too," she muttered, shaking her head. "I'll go look." She walked out behind Gelsey, her hand resting on my sister's shoulder, but stopped at the kitchen threshold and turned back to me. "Taylor, we can talk about this later. In the meantime, why don't you or Warren go pick up a pizza? It doesn't look like I'm going to be cooking anything here tonight."

She left and I stayed in the kitchen for a few minutes longer, my eyes drawn to the plastic orange prescription pill bottles that lined the counter. I looked at them for a moment longer, then headed off in search of my dad, since I knew wherever he was, Warren would be as well.

I found them both—not that it was a very long search, in a house this small—sitting around the dining table, my father with his glasses on, a stack of papers and his laptop in front of him, Warren with a huge book that he was frowning importantly at, making notes on a legal pad as he read. Warren had gotten in early-decision to Penn, and was already planning on the pre-law track, but to look at him, you'd think that he was already an equity partner, and that law school—not to mention college—would just be a formality.

"Hey," I said, poking my brother in the back as I took the seat next to my dad. "Mom said to pick up pizza."

Warren frowned. "Me?" My father shot him a look and he got to his feet. "I mean, sure. What's the name of the place downtown?"

morgan matson

I turned to my dad, and so did Warren. My brother might have had a photographic memory, but it was my father who always remembered the important things—events, dates, names of pizza restaurants.

"The Humble Pie," my dad said. "If it's still there, that is."

"I'll find out," Warren said, straightening his polo shirt and walking to the door. He stopped after a few steps and turned to us. "You know that pizza was developed as a way to use leftovers, starting in Italy, in the fifteenth—"

"Son," my dad said, cutting him off. "Maybe over dinner?"

"You got it," Warren said, flushing slightly as he walked out. A moment later, I heard the front door slam and the sound of the car engine starting.

My dad looked at me over his computer screen and raised an eyebrow. "So, kid. Your mother really asked your brother to get the pizza?"

I tried to hide a smile as I pulled at a loose thread at the end of my T-shirt and shrugged. "She may have suggested either of us. I delegated."

He shook his head, smiling slightly as he looked back down at his papers. He hadn't stopped working when he was diagnosed, claiming that he was just going to finish up a few loose ends, but I knew that he wouldn't have been happy if he wasn't working. He'd been a partner at his law firm, specializing in appeals. He went into the office every Saturday, and most Sundays as well. It was just normal that he was only at dinner one or two nights a week, working the rest of the time. I'd gotten used to the phone ringing late at night or early in the morning. I'd gotten used to hearing the faint hum of the garage door opening and closing at four a.m. as he headed into the office early, someone's last hope at a second chance.

"What are you working on?" I asked, after he'd been typing in silence for a few minutes.

"A brief," he said, glancing up at me. "I've been working on it for a few weeks now. Would have had it done sooner, but . . ." He let the sentence trail off, and I knew what he meant. A few weeks ago—three to be exact—we'd found out what was wrong with him, which had derailed everything for a while.

"That doesn't sound so brief," I said, trying to lighten the mood, and was rewarded when my dad smiled.

"Nice," he said approvingly. My father loved puns, the more groan-inducing the better, and I was the only one who tolerated them—and, for that matter, tried to respond in kind. "I just . . ." He looked at the screen, shaking his head. "I just want to get this right. It looks like it might be my legacy."

I nodded, looking down at the scratches on the wood table, totally unsure how to respond to that. We all knew what was happening with my dad, but we hadn't really talked about it since my birthday, and I had no idea what to say.

"Well," my dad said more quietly, after a pause. "Back to it." He started typing again, and even though I'd intended to leave and start unpacking, it suddenly felt wrong to just leave my dad working alone on his last case. So I sat next to him, the silence punctuated only by the tapping of the keyboard, until we heard the crunching of the car's tires on the gravel, and my mother's voice, calling for us to come to dinner.

The bathroom wasn't big enough.

This became massively apparent when we all ended up trying to get ready for bed—what Warren called his "evening ablutions,"—at the same time.

"You didn't leave me any space," I said. I nudged past Gelsey, who was brushing her teeth with excruciating slowness, to look in the medicine cabinet. It had been filled with Warren's contact paraphernalia, Gelsey's retainer case and lip balms, and too many tubes of toothpaste to make any logical sense.

"You should have gotten here sooner," Warren said from the doorway, making the already-small space seem smaller. "Can you hurry?" he asked Gelsey, who just gave him a toothpaste-filled smile and started brushing even more slowly, which I wouldn't have believed was possible without seeing it.

"I didn't know that I would have to claim cabinet space," I snapped, as I shoved some of his boxes of contacts to the side, trying to make room for my face wash and makeup remover.

Gelsey finally finished brushing her teeth and rinsed off her toothbrush, placing it carefully in the holder. "You can keep stuff in the shower if you want," she said with a shrug as she pulled back the striped forest-green shower curtain that had been there forever. "I'm sure there's some room—" Gelsey stopped talking abruptly, and started to scream.

I saw why a second later—there was a huge spider crouched in the corner of the tub. It looked like a daddy longlegs, which, I'd learned long ago on some nature walk, were actually not dangerous. But that didn't mean that I necessarily wanted to see a spider the size of my head just hanging out in our tub. I took step back, and bumped into Warren, who was also scrambling out of the way.

"Daddy!" Gelsey shrieked, bolting for the door.

When my father appeared a few moments later, my mother behind him, the three of us were huddled around the doorway, and I was keeping my eyes on the spider in case he decided to make a break for it.

"Spider," Warren said, pointing toward the tub. *"Pholcidae."* My father nodded and took a step into the bathroom.

"Are you going to kill it?" Gelsey asked from where she was practically hiding behind my mother—which seemed a tad melodramatic to me.

"No," my father said. "I'm just going to need a piece of paper and a glass."

"On it," Warren said, hustling out and returning with one of my magazines and a water glass. He handed them across the threshold to my dad, and then the rest of us all hung back. It wasn't only arachnophobia—my father took up almost the whole of the small bathroom. He'd gone through college on a football scholarship, playing linebacker, and still was big, despite some of the weight he'd lost recently—tall, with broad shoulders and a booming voice, trained over years to carry across courtrooms to jurors' ears.

A moment later, my dad emerged from behind the shower curtain, holding the glass pressed to the magazine. The spider scrambled frantically from one end of the glass to the other, over the features of the starlet who adorned the cover. My dad grimaced as he straightened up, and my mother immediately took the magazine from him and thrust it out to me.

"Taylor, set this free outside, would you?" She took a step toward my father, and asked, her voice more quiet, "Are you okay, Robin?"

While Robin was my dad's full name, he went by Rob, and the only times I heard him called Robin was when my mom was angry or worried, or my grandfather was visiting.

My father was still wincing, and I didn't think I could stand to see it, something I'd almost never seen before—my dad in pain. Magazine and trapped spider in hand, I turned away, glad for an excuse to leave.

I headed out the front door and down the steps to the gravel driveway, where I lifted the glass. Expecting the spider to crawl away immediately, I was surprised when it stayed where it was, frozen over This Summer's Top 10 Beauty Tips. "Move," I said as I jiggled the magazine, and finally it got the message and skittered away. I shook out the magazine, and was about to go back inside, but the thought of the expression on my dad's face caused me to leave the magazine and glass on the porch and walk down the driveway toward the road.

I was barefoot, and every step made me flinch, reminding me just how long it had been since I'd been able to do this without shoes on—how long, in fact, since I'd been back here. When I was halfway down the driveway, I reached our bearbox—a wooden, weighted contraption designed to keep the bears from getting into the trash—and had to stop and give my feet a little rest, noticing the fireflies' lights starting to blink on and off in the grass. Then I practically hopped my way to the end of the driveway, and stepped onto the paved road.

Though I didn't want to, I found myself gravitating next door. The lights were on in what I now knew was Henry's house, spilling out from the windows into squares on the gravel driveway. I looked at the lighted windows, wondering if he was home, and if so, which room was his, when I caught myself and realized I was being ridiculous. I looked away and noticed, for the first time, that there was a tent pitched next to the house, a round camping one. As I stared, the tent lit up, throwing whoever was inside into silhouette. I turned and took a few steps up the street quickly, walking nonchalantly, as though I were just out for an evening stargazing session.

Which actually seemed like a pretty good idea, I decided, as I took in the moon above me, huge in the sky, sending sheets of light down onto the road. I tipped my head back to search for stars.

I'd loved them ever since I was little, and my grandfather, a naval officer, had sent me a book about constellations. I hadn't ever been good at identifying them, but the stories stuck with me. Lovers exiled to the ends of the universe, goddesses punished for vanity and hung upside down. Whenever the night was clear enough, I'd look up, trying to make out patterns in the sky, trying to see what had caused those long-ago people to tell stories about what they saw. The stars were always easier to see in Lake Phoenix, and tonight they seemed to take over the entire sky. I just stared up at them until it felt like I could breathe, maybe for the first time that day. Maybe for the first time in the last three weeks.

I really didn't know how I was going to get through the summer. It had only been a few hours, but it already felt like more than I could handle. It was like we were all just pretending that nothing was happening. We weren't even talking about the reason that we had all decamped there. Instead, we'd spent dinner listening to Warren go on about how pizza was invented.

I turned to head back to the house when I stopped short. The dog from that afternoon was sitting at the edge of our driveway, where gravel met pavement. I looked up the street, to see if there was an owner coming, leash and plastic bag in hand. The streets of Lake Phoenix were safe enough, and usually deserted enough, that people walked their dogs off the leash. The only time I'd heard about this being a problem was when the Morrisons were walking their mean poodle one night and encountered a bear, no doubt on a bearbox trash bender. Mr. and Mrs. Morrison had beat a hasty retreat, but their poodle, on the other hand—who, in addition to being mean was also apparently not too bright—seemed to think the bear was just a big dog and trotted over to say hello. At some point, the dog figured out that this was a terrible idea, and ran away, unscathed. After that, I never saw the Morrisons walking it without a leash—and a very short one, at that.

But the street tonight was quiet, no late-night walkers looking for their slightly irregular canine. I took another step, and the dog didn't get up and move, or even stiffen. Instead, its tail thumped harder, like I was just the person it had been waiting to see. I saw that the collar was a faded blue, which meant it was most likely a boy, and that there was writing on his tag. So he had a home, he just was choosing to avoid it. At that moment, I could relate.

Wherever the dog lived, though, he obviously lived somewhere, and that somewhere, despite what he seemed to think, was not our driveway. I walked around him, and headed back to the house, figuring that the dog would be able to take care of himself. I'd gone only a few steps when I heard a faint jingling sound behind me. I turned back and saw the dog following me. He froze in his tracks, then sat hastily, as though I wouldn't notice that he had moved. Feeling like I was in a bizarre game of Red Light, Green Light, I pointed back at the road. "No," I said as firmly as possible, trying to remember all the lessons from *Top Dog*. "Go."

He lowered one ear, tilting his head, and looked at me with what almost looked like a hopeful expression as his tail thumped on the ground. But he didn't leave.

As I looked closer, I could see that he looked a little mangy, some of his fur matted. But I figured that made sense—if his owners had been really on the ball, they probably wouldn't be letting their dog wander around at night on his own.

"Go," I said again, even more firmly this time. *"Now."* I kept making eye contact, like the show always advised. The dog just looked at me for a second, then his other ear dropped and he seemed to sigh. But he did stand up—which actually didn't change much, heightwise, since his legs were a little short for his body. He gave me one more long look, but I tried not to show any signs of wavering. And after a moment more, he turned and started slowly down the driveway.

The dog walked to the end of the gravel, paused, then turned left and headed down the street. And even though I'd intended to go right in, I watched the dog getting smaller and smaller, hearing the jingle of his tag growing fainter, until he finally rounded the curve in the road and disappeared from view.

chapter six

THE NEXT MORNING, I WOKE WITH A START. I BLINKED AS I LOOKED around the room, for a second not remembering where I was. Then my eyes fell on the penguin on my dresser, and it all came back to me. I groaned and rolled over again, but even as I closed my eyes, I could tell that I wasn't going to be able to get back to sleep.

I sat up and squinted out at the sunlight that was streaming in through my window. It looked like it was going to be a beautiful day, for all the good that was going to do me. I got out of bed, and after looking at the penguin for a moment, I stuffed it on the top shelf of my closet and shut the door, so it wouldn't be the first thing I saw when I woke up every morning.

I headed down the hall, throwing my hair up into a messy pony-tail as I went, noticing that the house was incredibly quiet. I glanced at the microwave clock when I reached the kitchen and realized why—it was eight a.m. In the not-so-distant past, my father would have been up for hours by now. He would have brewed a pot of cof-fee and would be halfway through answering that morning's e-mails, already settling down to work. The sight of the empty coffeemaker was enough to remind me that things had changed. That the normal I somehow kept expecting things to revert to was not going to come back again. I might have made a pot myself, but I had no idea how to make coffee—that had always been my dad's responsibility, along with remembering important information.

Not really wanting to hang out alone in a silent house, I headed outside. I would usually have gone to the dock, but after my encounter with Henry the day before, I wasn't sure I was going out to the dock ever again. So instead, I stepped into my flip-flops and walked down the driveway, figuring that maybe by the time I got back from my walk, other members of my family might be awake, and then we could . . .

I paused in the middle of the driveway, realizing that I didn't know how to complete that sentence. I had no idea what I was going to do this summer, except witness the end of my world as I'd always known it. The thought was enough to propel me forward, as though I could somehow leave it behind me, along with the house and its silent coffeemaker.

I deliberately turned and started walking in the opposite direction of Henry's house, and noticed for the first time that we appeared to have new neighbors there as well. At any rate, there was a Prius in the driveway and a sign I didn't recognize that read CUT TO: SUMMER.

Dockside Terrace, our street, was empty this early in the

morning, except for a sleepy-looking man walking an energetic golden retriever. As I walked, I found myself noticing the signs in front of all the houses, and realizing how many of them I remembered. Almost all of the houses in Lake Phoenix had names, not numbers. But our house had never had a sign, since we could never reach a consensus about a name. We used to take a vote every summer, but nothing had ever seemed to quite fit.

I'd been walking for maybe twenty minutes when I decided to head back. It was starting to get hotter out, and the more joggers and dog-walkers who appeared, all waving cheerfully to me, the more aware I was that I had literally just rolled out of bed, and wasn't wearing a bra. I was turning around when I noticed a gap in the woods that ran alongside the road. My memory was a little foggy on the details, but I was fairly certain that there was a path through here that ran almost directly back to my house.

I paused on the threshold of the woods before stepping into the gap. As soon as I did, it was like I had entered a different world. It was quieter and darker, with the sunlight filtering down to the ground in shafts and dappling the leaves of the trees. I hadn't been in the woods in years, and as I started to follow the trail, I realized how familiar it all was, the beads of dew on the moss, the smell of the pine trees, the snap of twigs and leaves underneath my flip-flops. It was the same feeling as going back into the house had been— the realization that just because you'd left something behind didn't

morgan matson

mean that it had gone anywhere. And as I walked, I found, to my surprise, that I had missed it.

Half an hour later, I was no longer feeling so warm and fuzzy toward the woods. I had lost whatever trail I thought I'd been on. My legs were scraped up from twigs, my neck had been feasted upon by mosquitoes, and I didn't even want to think about what my hair looked like. But mostly, I was annoyed at myself, and a little incredulous that I had gotten lost so close to home.

I didn't have my phone, which, with its built-in compass, not to mention GPS, would have come in handy at the moment. I couldn't see any houses around me, nothing to get my bearings, but I wasn't panicking yet. For right now, I was still hoping that if I could just find the path again, I'd be able to trace my way back. I no longer cared about the shortcut—I just wanted to go home.

Somewhere in the distance, I heard a bird caw and then, a second later, heard the sound called back—but badly, and not by another bird. A second later, the bird call repeated, slightly improved this time, and I headed in the direction I'd heard the sound come from, walking fast. If there were bird-watchers in the woods, it meant that maybe they could direct me back to the road, that maybe I wasn't completely lost.

I found them soon enough—it helped that the bird-imitation calls kept coming—two guys, one tall, one around Gelsey's height, both with their backs to me, both looking fixedly up at a tree.

"Hi," I called. I was beyond worrying about embarrassing myself.

I just wanted to go home and get some breakfast and put calamine lotion on my bites. "Sorry to bother you, but—"

"Shh!" the taller one said, still looking at the tree, in a loud whisper. "We're trying to see the—" He turned around and stopped abruptly. It was Henry, and he looked as surprised to see me as I felt.

I felt my jaw drop again, and hurriedly closed it. There was no doubt in my mind that I was blushing, and I wasn't even tan enough yet to hide it. "Hi," I muttered, crossing my arms tightly over my chest, wondering why each time I saw him, I somehow looked worse than I had before.

"What are you doing here?" he asked in the same loud whisper.

"What, am I not allowed to be in the woods now?" I asked, not quite as quietly, causing the kid next to him to turn around as well.

"Shh!" the kid said, a pair of binoculars raised to his eyes. He lowered them, and I realized with a shock that this was Henry's little brother, Davy—recognizable, but just barely, as the seven-year-old I'd last known. Now he looked a lot like Henry had at his age— except I noticed that Davy was very tan for this early in the summer and he was, for some reason, wearing a pair of moccasins. "We're trying to track the indigo bunting."

"Davy," Henry said, poking him in the back, "don't be rude." He looked over at me again, and said, "You remember Taylor Edwards, right?"

"Taylor?" Davy asked, his eyes widening, looking up at Henry in alarm. *"Seriously?"*

"Hi," I said, waving, and then immediately crossing my arms again.

"Why is she here?" Davy half-whispered to Henry.

"I'll tell you later," Henry replied, frowning at Davy.

"But why are you talking to her?" Davy continued, not really whispering anymore.

"Anyway," I said loudly, "if you could just—"

There was a flurry of wings from the tree the Crosbys had been looking at, and two birds—one brown, one blue—flew into the air. Davy scrambled for his binoculars, but even I could tell it was going to be too late—the birds were gone. His shoulders slumped, and he let the binoculars drop on the cord around his neck.

"We'll come back tomorrow, okay?" Henry said quietly to Davy, resting his hand on his brother's shoulder. Davy just shrugged, staring down at the ground. "We should go," Henry said, glancing up at me. He gave me a fraction of a nod before he and Davy started to leave.

"Um," I started, knowing it would probably be better just to get it out, rather than stalking the two of them through the woods in the hopes that they might lead me home. And what if they weren't even going to their house, and I ended up following behind them while they chased some other random bird? "Are you going back home? Because I'm a little turned around, so if you are . . ." My voice trailed off, mostly at seeing Henry's expression, which was equal parts incredulous and annoyed.

He let out a breath, then leaned down slightly to talk to Davy. "I'll meet you at home, okay?" he asked. Davy scowled at me, then took off into the woods at a run.

"Does he know where he's going?" I asked, as I watched him disappear from view. He certainly seemed to, but that's what I'd thought when I entered the woods as well.

Henry seemed to find this funny for some reason. "Davy knows these woods like the back of his hand," he said, the corner of his mouth turning up in a half smile. "He just took his shortcut—God knows how he found it. I've never even seen it, but it gets him home in half the time." Then Henry seemed to realize who he was talking to. The smile faded, and the annoyed expression returned. "Let's go," he said shortly, and headed off in a totally different direction than I'd been walking.

We tromped through the woods in silence for a few minutes, Henry not looking at me, but straight ahead. I was just counting down the minutes until I would be at home and this would be over.

"Thank you," I finally said after I couldn't take the silence any longer.

"No problem," Henry said shortly, still not looking at me.

"I just . . ." I started, not really sure where I was going with this, but feeling like I needed to explain somehow. "I didn't mean for this to happen. I was just trying to find the way home."

"It's fine," Henry said, a little less brusquely than before. "We're going to the same place, after all. And besides," he said, looking at me directly for a moment, that ghost of a smile returning, "I told you it would be inevitable."

I started to respond when I noticed that our path was blocked—there were two enormous trees down, moss already growing all over their trunks. Mixed in around the fallen trees were pieces of lumber, boards of different sizes. "What is that?" I asked. The whole thing, the downed trees and the jumbled pieces of wood made for a huge obstacle—where the pile was the highest, it reached almost up to my waist.

"Last month's storm," Henry said, already starting to walk around it. "There was a treehouse up there, it came down when the trees fell."

So that explained the lumber, and the occasional nail I could see jutting up through the beams. I started to follow him when a memory came back to me, hitting me with such force that I stopped walking. "Do you still have yours?" I asked. The second after I said it, I remembered he no longer lived in his old house. "I mean, is it still there? The treehouse?" Henry and his dad had built it together, and we had declared a younger sibling–free zone, and spent hours up there, especially whenever the weather was bad, and spending all day by the lake wasn't an option.

"It's still there," he said. "You can still kind of see it if you look down the driveway."

"I'm glad," I said, not even realizing that this was what I felt until I said it.

"Yeah," he said. "Me too."

I stared at the fallen trees as I walked around them, still a little shocked to see them on the ground, the opposite of where they should be. It seemed crazy that something so big, so seemingly permanent, could be knocked down by a little wind and rain.

Henry was already starting to stride ahead, and so, hurrying to catch up with him, I started to clamber over the downed trees. By then, I'd made it to the top of the tree, where the trunk had narrowed, and it seemed like it would be simple enough. "Ow," I muttered under my breath as yet another twig scraped my leg.

Henry turned back and squinted. "What are you doing?" he called, starting to walk toward me.

"Nothing," I said, hearing the annoyance in my voice, which I knew wasn't exactly fair, since he was helping me get out of the woods, but all I was *doing* at that moment was trying to keep him from having to wait on me.

"Don't," he said, and I could hear that he sounded equally annoyed. "That wood's rotten, it's likely to—"

With a *snap*, the trunk I'd been standing on collapsed, and I was pitching forward, bracing for the inevitable fall, when just like that, in an instant, Henry was there, catching me.

"Sorry," I gasped, feeling how hard my heart was pounding, the adrenaline pumping through my body.

"Careful," he said, as I started to step out of the trunk. "Davy twisted his ankle doing that last month."

"Thanks." I leaned on him a little bit for support as I lifted my foot out, trying very hard not to think about what kind of creepy-crawlies were probably living in a rotted-out tree trunk. It wasn't until I had both feet back on the forest floor that I realized his arms were still around me. I could feel the heat from his hands on my back through my thin T-shirt. I looked up at him—it was still so strange to have to look up at Henry—and saw how close we were, our faces just inches apart. He must have become aware of this at the same time, because he dropped his arms immediately, and took a few steps away.

"You okay?" he asked, the brusque, businesslike tone back in his voice.

"Fine," I said. I brushed off some of the wet leaves that had stuck to my ankles, mostly so he wouldn't see how flustered I was.

"Good," he said. He started walking again, and I followed behind, careful to put my feet where I saw him place his, not wanting another mishap. In what seemed like only a few more seconds, I was following Henry out of the woods, blinking in the brighter sunlight, and realizing I was just two streets away from my house. "You know your way from here?" he asked.

"Of course I do," I said, slightly insulted.

Henry just shook his head and smiled, the first real smile I'd seen since meeting him again. "It's not like you have the greatest sense of direction," he said. I opened my mouth to protest this, and he went on, "I just had to help you find your way out of the woods." He looked at me evenly for a moment, then added, "And it wasn't even the first time." Then he turned and walked away, leaving me to try and figure out what he meant.

A moment later, when he'd passed out of sight, it hit me. The first time we'd met had been in these very same woods. As I walked home, shielding my eyes against the sun, so bright after the darkness of the woods, I realized that I'd been so caught up in thinking about how things with him had ended, I'd almost forgotten how they had begun.

"Taylor, where have you been?" my mother asked when I returned, her eyes widening as she took in the scratches on my legs. I'd been trying to sneak back to my room quietly, hoping that everyone would still be asleep, but no such luck. My mom was unpacking what looked like practically a kitchenful of paper bags from the PocoMart, the closest thing to a grocery store in Lake Phoenix. There were bigger supermarkets, but they were a good half hour drive away.

morgan matson

"Just walking," I said vaguely as I glanced around the kitchen, not meeting her eye. I saw that the coffeemaker was still empty—my mother was a tea drinker—which meant that, two hours after I'd left, my father was still asleep.

"I ran into Paul Crosby at the market," she said, referring to Henry's dad. I felt my face start to get hot, and was just grateful that she'd run into him *before* his sons had a chance to report back about my getting lost in the woods. "In the dairy aisle. He said they're living next door to us now."

"Oh," I said. "How about that." I could feel my cheeks getting hotter, and I opened the fridge and stuck my head in, trying to pretend I was looking for something essential.

"You'll have to go say hi to Henry," my mother continued, as I concentrated on making sure the expiration dates on the containers of milk were all facing out.

There is only so long you can stand with your head in a refrigerator, and I had just reached that point. Plus, my ears were staring to get cold. "Mmm," I said, closing the door and leaning my back against it.

"And I suppose I should go and say hello to Ellen," my mother continued. She sounded distinctly less excited about this thought, and I didn't blame her. Henry's mother had never seemed to like kids very much unless we were quiet and out of the way. While we had always dashed full-out into my house, sometimes mid-watergun fight, when we reached Henry's door, we immediately settled down and got quiet, without even talking about it. Theirs was not a house you ever made blanket forts in. And without my mother saying anything outright, I had always gotten the sense she really hadn't liked Mrs. Crosby very much.

I pulled an apple from one of the bags on the counter, and my mother took it from me, washed it quickly, patted it dry, and then handed it back. "You and Henry used to be so close," she said.

I glanced through the kitchen window to the Crosbys' house, mostly so my mother wouldn't be able to see my expression. "I guess," I said. "But that was a long time ago, Mom."

She started to fold up the bags, and I could have helped, but instead, I leaned against the kitchen counter and started to eat my apple. "Have you called Lucy yet?" she asked.

I bit down hard on my apple, wondering why my mother always assumed she knew what was best for me. Why didn't she just ask me if I *wanted* to call Lucy, for example? Which I absolutely didn't, by the way. "No," I said, trying to stop myself from rolling my eyes. "And I don't think I'm going to."

She gave me a look that told me plainly that she thought this was a mistake as she put the paper bags away where we'd always kept them, under the sink. "Your childhood friends are the ones you should hang on to. They know you in a way that nobody else does."

After this morning's encounter with Henry, I wasn't convinced this was a good thing. I watched as my mother crossed to the fridge with the summer calendar. The Lake Phoenix association made them every year, and one had been on the fridge up here for every summer that I could remember. They were designed to hang vertically, so that you could see all three months of the summer at once, each month flanked with pictures of smiling kids on sailboats, happy couples relaxing by the lake, and seniors taking in a sunrise. My mom attached it to the fridge with the mismatched magnets we'd always had and that I was suddenly glad the Murphys hadn't taken, and I leaned closer to look at it, at all those empty squares that represented the days of summer ahead.

This calendar had always been a way, especially this early in the season, to revel in how much time was still left in the summer. In years past, the summer had just seemed to stretch forever, so that by the time August rolled around, I'd had my fill of s'mores and popsicles and mosquito bites, and was actually looking forward to fall— to cooler weather and wearing tights and Halloween and Christmas.

But as I stared at it now, and started to do the math, I got a panicky feeling in my chest, one that made it harder to breathe. On my birthday, three weeks ago, the doctors had told my dad that he had four months. Maybe more . . . but maybe less. And three weeks of those months had already passed. Which meant . . . I stared at the calendar so hard, it got a little blurry. It was the middle of May, so we still had the rest of the month and all of June. And then all of

July. But then what? I looked at August, at the picture of the older couple holding hands as they watched the sun rise over Lake Phoenix, and realized I had no idea what would be happening then, what my world would look like. If my dad would still be alive.

"Taylor?" my mom asked, her voice concerned. "You okay?"

I wasn't okay, and this normally would have been when I would have hit the road—gotten in my car and driven somewhere, gone for a long walk, anything to avoid the problem. But as I'd learned this morning, going outside certainly didn't seem to help things—and in fact, made them worse.

"I'm fine," I snapped at her, even though there was a piece of me that knew she didn't deserve it. But I wanted her to know what was wrong without having to ask. And what I really wanted her to do was what she hadn't done, now that it mattered the most—I wanted her to fix it. But she hadn't fixed it, and she wasn't going to be able to. I threw away my half-eaten apple and left the kitchen.

Finding the bathroom miraculously empty, I took a long, hot shower, washing the dirt from the scratches on my legs and staying in there until the hot water in our tiny hot water heater started to run out.

When I came back into the kitchen, it was filled with the smell of coffee. The coffeemaker was burbling and hissing and there was half a pot already brewed. I could see my dad sitting on the screened-in porch, laptop in front of him, steaming mug in hand, laughing at something my mom was saying. And even though I knew what the calendar on the fridge said, I somehow couldn't get it to make sense, not with my dad sitting in the sunlight, looking totally healthy, unless you knew otherwise. I walked to the doorway of the screened-in porch, leaned against the door frame, and my dad turned to look at me.

"Hi, kid," he said. "What's the news?" And before I could get the words around the lump that had formed in my throat, to begin to answer, he looked out to the view of the lake, and smiled. "Doesn't it look like a beautiful day out there?"

Metamorphosis

chapter seven

A THIRTEEN-LETTER WORD FOR "CHANGE." I GLANCED DOWN AT the *Pocono Record*'s crossword puzzle and tapped my pencil on the empty squares of 19 across. Trying to concentrate, I looked through the screened-in porch and out to the lake. I wasn't exactly in the habit of doing crosswords, but I was getting a little desperate for entertainment. After five days in Lake Phoenix, I was officially bored out of my mind. And the worst part was that in this situation, unlike family vacations or Gelsey's dance recitals, I couldn't complain to anyone that I was bored out of my mind and know they were feeling the same way. Because I wasn't supposed to spend this summer being entertained. It wasn't supposed to be *fun*. But that didn't change the fact that I was, in fact, incredibly bored. And suffering majorly from cabin fever.

I heard the now-familiar sound of the FedEx truck's tires crunching on our driveway and jumped up to intercept the daily package, just to have something to do. But when I stepped outside, I saw that my dad was already holding the white box in his hands, nodding at the driver—who, after daily deliveries, was getting to be pretty familiar.

"You're keeping me busy in this neck of the woods," the driver said, flipping down his sunglasses. "You're just about the only delivery I get around here."

"I believe that," my dad said, pulling open the tab on the box.

"And if you guys could keep your dog tied up, I'd appreciate it," the driver said as he settled into the front seat. "I almost hit him this morning." He started the truck and backed down our driveway, beeping once as he turned down the road.

My dad turned to me, eyebrows raised. "Dog?"

"Oh, my God," I said. I leaned over the front porch railing and saw, sure enough, the same dog loitering by the edge of our driveway. "Shoo!" I yelled at him. "Get out of here!" He glanced at me, then trotted past our driveway and out of sight, but I had a feeling he'd be back before too long. "It's just this dog," I said, as the jingling of his tags grew fainter and fainter. "He thinks he lives here."

"Ah," my dad said, still looking a little puzzled, and I could see that I hadn't really clarified anything. He crossed the driveway and climbed the stairs, leaning a little bit on the railing. "Well, just don't let your brother see him."

"Right," I said, and followed my dad to the screened-in porch, where he shook out the box's contents, a thick sheaf of papers, many marked with brightly colored flags. He'd gotten a similar delivery

morgan matson

from his law firm every day so far, all apparently pertaining to a case that he'd been working on. When I'd asked why his firm couldn't just e-mail the documents, instead of sending a FedEx truck through the mountains of Pennsylvania every day, he'd told me that it was due to security issues.

I slumped down in the chair across from him and sighed, all the while aware that I wasn't even managing to do the one thing my dad had asked of us—that is, stop hanging around the house.

On our first full day, it quickly became obvious that Warren and Gelsey and I had no idea what to do with ourselves. And so, the three of us spent the first two days simply following my dad from room to room, in case he wanted to bond or something. After the second straight day of this, we'd been sitting around the table on the screened-in porch while my father worked. Gelsey had her battered copy of *Holding On to the Air*, the ballerina Suzanne Farrell's autobiography, I had my magazine, now with the spider-tainted cover removed, and Warren had a textbook in front of him. We were all reading, kind of—except every time my dad would glance up from his work, we would look up too, and Warren would smile unnaturally, all of us waiting for some cue, someone to tell us how to act. But it was becoming very clear to me that it was called *quality* time for a reason—by definition, it didn't mean spending every waking minute together.

And in summers past, we'd certainly never spent much time inside unless it was raining. As its name implied, Lake Phoenix was a summer community on a lake, and the lake—and its beach—was pretty much the main attraction. There was also a pool, complete with a waterslide that I'd spent a lot of time at when I was younger, plus tennis courts and a golf course. It was like a strange combination of a country club and camp—except that it wasn't at all fancy. There were no million-dollar houses or estates, but you did have to buy a membership to be able to go to the beach and pool. And because it was so far removed from everything, and such a small community, Lake Phoenix was incredibly safe, and I'd basically had free run of the place from when I was about seven. There was a bus for kids, the shuttle bus, that ran from the Recreation Center around to the pool and beach. But I'd taken it only rarely. Most of the time, I'd ridden my bike everywhere.

When we'd been up here before, my mother would spend her time either at the beach or playing tennis, my father would be working outside or playing golf, and my siblings and I were either at the tennis and golf lessons our parents had forced us to take, or at the beach or pool. We would all come back for dinner and eat together on the screened-in porch, everyone a little more tan than when we'd left that morning. But we'd never just stayed home, all day, when it was gorgeous and sunny out.

"Enough is enough," my dad said, after he'd glanced up to find us all looking—and Warren still smiling—at him. "You three are driving me crazy."

I looked at my brother, who shot me a questioning look back. I really wasn't sure what my father was talking about—especially since I had been so careful *not* to do anything that might drive him crazy. "Um," I finally said after a moment, when it became clear my siblings weren't going to jump into the breach, "what are we doing?"

"You're not doing anything," he said, sounding aggravated. "And that's the problem. I don't need the three of you staring at me all day. It makes me feel like I'm in some kind of science experiment. Or—even worse—some kind of reality show."

I saw Warren open his mouth to respond, but then close it again—further proof that none of us were acting like we normally did. I had never seen Warren back down from an argument.

"Look," my dad said, his tone softening a little, "I appreciate what you are all trying to do. But while we still can, I would like to have as normal a summer as possible. Okay?"

I nodded, even though I wasn't sure what a "normal" summer was. In a normal summer, or at least what they'd looked like over the last few years, we wouldn't have been together.

"So," Gelsey said, and I noticed she was sitting up a little straighter, a glint coming into her brown eyes, "what should we do with our time, then?"

"Whatever you want," he said, spreading his hands open. "Just so long as it doesn't involve just hanging around the house all day. It's summer. Go have fun."

That seemed to be all the impetus my sister needed. She bolted from the table and ran into the house, yelling for my mother, asking if they could do a barre. My father watched her go, smiling, then turned back to me and Warren, who still hadn't moved.

"I mean it," he said, waving us away with his hands. "In addition to this case, I have to start work on a very important project soon, and I'd like some peace to do it in."

"Project?" Warren asked. "What kind?"

"Just a project," my dad said vaguely, looking down at the papers in his hands.

"So," Warren said, and I could tell he was trying a little too hard to sound casual, the way he always did when his feelings were hurt and he didn't want to show it. "You don't want us to spend time with you?"

"It's not that," my dad said, and he looked pained for a moment. "Of course I want to spend time with you. But this is just weird. Go enjoy your summers." Warren took a breath, probably to ask my dad to qualify what, exactly, that meant. Maybe sensing this, my dad went on, "You can do whatever you want. I just want you to do *something*. Get a job. Read the collected works of Dickens. Learn to juggle. It doesn't matter to me. Just stop lurking about, okay?"

I nodded, even though none of these seemed like actual possibilities for ways to spend my time. I'd never had a job, had zero interest in juggling, and had pretty much written off Dickens after freshman year English. He'd lost me from page one of *A Tale of Two Cities*, when I'd been unable to grasp how something could simultaneously be the best of times *and* the worst of times.

Warren and Gelsey, in contrast, had no such problems figuring out what to do. Gelsey was going to do a barre with my mother every day, working on her technique so that she didn't fall too far behind in her ballet training. My mom had also gone over to the Lake Phoenix Recreation Center and somehow convinced the people running it to let Gelsey use one of their rooms—when it was empty and the seniors weren't using it for yoga—to practice in a few times a week. And as a compromise with my mother, Gelsey had also agreed to take tennis lessons. Warren had blissfully thrown himself into reading what seemed like his entire freshman course-load, and could usually be found on the porch or the dock, merrily highlighting away. The whole situation was yet another reminder of my siblings' exceptionalism—as ever, they had something to do, the thing they'd always done, the thing that they seemed to know from birth that they were best at. Which left me, as usual, alone and far behind as they pursued their paths to greatness.

So for the past five days, I had mostly been wandering around and feeling in the way. I had never been so aware of just how small the house was, and how few places there were to hide in it. And ever since the *two* embarrassing Henry encounters, I was avoiding both the dock and the woods, and had pretty much stopped going outside, except for my nightly excursion to take the trash out to the bearbox (which had somehow become my job) and shoo away the dog who seemed to have no intention of leaving. My mother had also reported that when she'd stopped by to bring a planter of geraniums to Henry's mother, she wasn't there, but that a blond girl, around my age, had answered the door.

I had tried very hard not to think about this too much, and certainly wasn't letting it bother me. After all, what did I care if Henry had a girlfriend? But it somehow, retroactively, made those two encounters with him even more humiliating, and I had been careful to avoid looking at the house next door, not letting myself wonder if he was home.

As I sat at the table now and watched my dad flip through his papers, I started to get the claustrophobic feeling that I was getting more and more lately—like I needed to get out but had absolutely nowhere to go.

"How are you doing on that?" my father asked, and I noticed him trying to read my crossword puzzle upside down.

"I'm stuck on this one," I said, tapping my finger on the empty boxes. "A thirteen-letter word for 'change.'"

"Hmm," he said. He leaned back in his chair, frowning, then shook his head. "I've got nothing," he said. "But maybe it'll come to me. I'll keep you informed." He pushed himself back from the table and stood up. "I'm going to run some errands in town, kid," he said. "Want to come?"

"Sure," I said, automatically. It definitely sounded like more fun than pointlessly surfing the Internet, which was what had pretty much been on my afternoon agenda now that trailing behind my father was no longer an accepted option. I headed inside to get my shoes.

When I met him out on the driveway, my dad was standing by the driver's side and tossing the Land Cruiser keys in his hand. I walked across the gravel, feeling the rocks through the thin rubber of my flip-flops, and stopped in front of the hood.

"All set?" my father asked.

"Sure," I said slowly, adjusting the canvas bag over my shoulder. I couldn't help but think about the pill bottles that were lined up on the kitchen counter. I had no idea what they were for—or what the side effects were. My dad hadn't driven, as far as I knew, since the morning we left, when he showed up to get me and took me for bagels. "Do you want me to drive?" I asked, realizing I didn't know how to phrase the question I wanted to ask. My father waved this away and started to open the door. "I mean . . . ," I started. I could feel my heart beating fast. Criticizing my father—or questioning his judgment—was something I had absolutely no experience doing. "Is it okay for you to be driving?" I said it quickly, just trying to get the words out.

The sentence hung between us for a moment and when my father looked across the hood at me, his expression told me that I had overstepped. "I'm fine," he said a little shortly. He pulled open the driver's side door, and I walked around the hood to the passenger side, feeling my face get hot.

We drove in silence down our street for several minutes before I broke in. "So what are these errands?" I asked. I could hear how my voice was unnaturally cheery, not really sounding like me, and I realized it was probably the vocal equivalent of Warren's strained smile.

"Well," my father said, and I could tell by the way he glanced over at me with a quick smile before rolling to a stop at a stop sign, that he'd gotten past my comment and wanted to move on as well, "your mother has requested some fresh corn for dinner tonight. I need to pick up the mail. And . . ." He paused for a moment, then looked back at the road. "I thought you might want to stop by the Clubhouse. Maybe apply for a job."

"Oh," I said. "A job." I looked out the window, feeling embarrassment wash over me. So he'd noticed that, unlike Warren and Gelsey, I had no talents to occupy my time with. Unfortunately, I also had no work experience—I'd spent the most recent summers doing things like service projects, language immersions, and going to camps in which I had to dissect things.

"You certainly don't have to," he said as we got closer to Lake Phoenix's main street—called, creatively, Main Street. "It was just a thought."

I nodded, and as my dad made the right turn onto Main and swung into a parking spot, I turned over his words in my head. I knew I couldn't just keep hanging out at home with nothing to do. And, frankly, I didn't see many other options. "Okay," I said, shouldering my bag as we got out of the car. I shut my door and I tipped my head toward the Clubhouse building, where the Lake Phoenix administrative offices were. "I'll give it a shot."

My father smiled at me. "That's my girl," he said. I smiled back, but even as I did, I could feel an immediate, almost panicky reaction. I wanted to freeze this moment, keep it from moving on, dip it in amber somehow. But just as I thought this, my dad was already looking away, starting to walk up the street. "Shall we reconnoiter in thirty?" he asked.

I glanced down at my watch. Back home, I almost never wore one, because I always had my phone with me. But aside from a few awkward text exchanges with acquaintances that I'd resorted to in extreme loneliness, my cell had been quiet. And since I hadn't felt I needed constant proof that nobody was calling me, I'd taken to leaving it in my room, which meant that I needed some other way to tell the time. "Thirty," I echoed. "Sure." My dad gave me a nod before walking up the street to Henson's Produce, no doubt on a mission to get my mother her corn.

I turned and headed toward the Clubhouse building, wishing that I'd straightened myself up a little more that morning. I was wearing what had, after only a few days, become my de facto summer uniform—cutoff jean shorts and a tank top. I was worried that this outfit, coupled with the fact that I had never held a job before, might seriously impair my chances of getting hired. But as I stood in front of the wood-paneled building, with the painted Lake Phoenix design (a phoenix rising from the lake, water dripping from its wings while the sun rose—or set—behind it) on the window, I realized that there was nothing to do but to give it a try. So I straightened my shoulders and pulled open the door.

Fifteen minutes later, I had a job. I stepped back out into the sunlight, blinking at it before I slipped my sunglasses back on, feeling a little bit dazed. I now had three white Lake Phoenix employee T-shirts (the cost of which would come out of my first paycheck), an employee handbook, and instructions to show up for work at the beach in three days. Jillian, the woman who was in charge of the hiring, had told me repeatedly, even as she looked over my application and scrolled through the options on her computer, that I was much too late in the application process to expect anything great—or, for that matter, anything at all.

The Lake Phoenix administrative offices were bigger than I'd expected—I'd never spent much time in the Clubhouse, except for when we'd occasionally gone for brunch on Sundays, Warren and I staying put for what felt like hours before getting permission to leave and running for the beach. I finally located the employment office, which placed the teenagers of the summer community in jobs around Lake Phoenix—lifeguarding, working at the beach or pool snack bar, teaching seniors yoga. Most of the kids I had known had gotten their first job—usually doing something low on the seniority ladder, which always seemed to mean cleaning bathrooms—at fourteen, and the jobs got better the older you got. If I'd continued to come to Lake Phoenix in the summers, I probably would have had my first job years ago. Instead, the "work experience" section of my application had been embarrassingly empty.

But Jillian had finally come up with a job—there was an opening at the beach. The job description had been very general, which was slightly worrying to me, but Jillian said that since I didn't have lifeguard training or much sailing experience, it would most likely be at the snack bar. And since she hadn't mentioned that cleaning bathrooms was in any way a job requirement, I'd accepted. I'd filled out my payroll and tax forms, and had gone from having no plans for the summer to discovering that employment comes with T-shirts.

Now, standing out in the early afternoon heat of Main Street, I realized I had some time to kill before I had to meet my father. I stopped into the tiny Lake Phoenix library, renewed my card, and checked out three paperback mysteries. I was tempted just to hang out there for a bit, soaking up the air conditioning, but also wanted a chance to wander up Main Street.

Lake Phoenix's commercial district was pretty small, just the length of one street. There wasn't even a movie theater. To see movies, you had to drive twenty minutes to the next town, Mountainview, and the Outpost, a combination movie theater/miniature golf course/arcade that we'd gone to whenever it had rained. But Lake Phoenix only had a single stoplight, a gas station, and handful of stores. There was The Humble Pie, and next to it, Henson's Produce. There was Sweet Baby Jane's, the ice cream parlor where Gelsey had never ordered anything except a strawberry shake, and a hardware store. There was the Pocono Coffee Shop, which everyone always just called "the diner," and a store, Give Me A Sign, that specialized in personalized signs for houses.

As I continued up the street, I found myself automatically noticing the new stores, every time one didn't fit with what I expected to be there—but then I would also find that I couldn't remember what had been there before. A pet store/dog grooming parlor, Doggone It!, was definitely new, but looked pretty empty, except for a red-haired girl behind the counter, turning the pages of a magazine. I had made it almost to the end of Main Street when I found myself in front of another new store, Borrowed Thyme. It looked like it was a bakery—there were loaves of bread stacked in a display in one of the plate-glass windows, and a beautiful layer cake in the other. My stomach rumbled just looking at them, and I was peering past the cake to see farther into the shop when I became aware of someone

morgan matson

clearing their throat behind me. I turned and saw a peeved-looking older man, wearing an overlarge Phillies baseball cap and a scowl.

"Going in?" he barked, nodding at the door that I now realized I was blocking.

"Oh," I said. "Right." I pulled the door open, holding it for the man, who grunted in response as he made his way inside. I was about to just close the door and head back to meet my dad when curiosity got the best of me. Also, I could feel the air conditioning from the doorway and smell that wonderful bakery smell—freshly baked bread and buttercream icing. I stepped inside, letting the door slam behind me.

It was cool and darker inside, and it took a moment for my eyes to adjust after the brightness of the street. I could see, as things came into focus, two small wooden tables with matching chairs by the windows, and a glass-topped counter that ran almost the width of the shop. Pastries and cookies were displayed beneath it, and behind the counter was a baker's rack stacked with the bread that I had been able to smell from the street. My stomach grumbled again, and I started thinking that maybe I would get something small, just to tide me over until lunch.

There was nobody behind the counter, and the man in the Phillies cap didn't seem too pleased about that, as he kept whacking the small silver bell on the counter loudly, in between mutterings about shoddy service. I took a step closer to check out what looked like a raspberry coffee cake, when I noticed, lying on the glass-topped counter, a pencil across it, that morning's *Pocono Record*, folded to the crossword section. I took another step closer, trying to see if this person had had any more luck that I had with 19 across. As I leaned over, the man whacked the bell once more, hard, and a voice came from the back.

"Just a moment!" the voice called. "Be right with you."

"I won't hold my breath," the man muttered, turning to me for agreement. But I had frozen in place. It was a voice I recognized. I glanced at the door, wondering if I had enough time to make it out without being spotted. I was thinking that I just might, when the metal door behind the counter swung open and Henry stepped out.

chapter eight

HENRY JUST STARED AT ME, AND I LOOKED BACK INTO HIS GREEN eyes, feeling the sudden urge to break into hysterical laughter, because it was beginning to seem like I couldn't turn around in Lake Phoenix without running into him. The man looked between us, frowned again, and whacked the bell once more.

This seemed to snap Henry into action. "Sorry about that," he said quickly, as the man harrumphed. "What can I get you?"

"Been waiting out here," the man grumbled. Now that he had someone to wait on him, rather than ordering, he appeared to want to use his time to complain about the lack of service.

"Sorry about that," Henry repeated, with the exact same inflection, and I could feel myself start to smile. To hide this, I bent down to look in the case, where there were rows of small iced cookies, cannoli, and brownies. But only half my attention was on the (admittedly delicious-looking) desserts. I snuck a glance at Henry as he nodded, appearing to listen as the man vented at him. He was wearing a light green T-shirt with his jeans. It had the Borrowed

Thyme logo in black across the front and a dusting of flour on one shoulder. I realized I was surprised to see him working there, which was fairly ridiculous, since I clearly knew nothing about him now. But when I'd known him before—and seeing him in the woods had confirmed this—Henry had always seemed most comfortable outside. And on the rare occasions over the last few years when I let my thoughts drift back to Lake Phoenix and the people I'd left up there, I'd always imagined Henry doing something outdoors.

The *ding* of the register brought me back to the present, as Henry handed the man his change and slid a green bakery box across the counter. "Thanks," he said, his tone still blandly professional. "Have a nice day."

"Yeah," the man grumbled, taking the box and heading out of the shop. It wasn't until I turned back to the counter that I realized it was just me and Henry, alone in the bakery.

I looked at him, then down at my outfit, wishing for the second time that day that I had pulled myself together a little bit more. But then I dismissed the thought. He'd already seen me straight out of bed, scratched up in the woods. And anyway, it seemed like Henry had some blond girlfriend. Not that I cared about that.

"So," Henry said, shaking his head. "I think we should stop meeting like this."

"Do you work here?" I asked, then immediately cursed myself for my stupidity. Of *course* he worked there. Otherwise, he wouldn't be standing behind the counter, waiting on irascible Phillies fans. "I mean," I corrected immediately, trying to make it sound as little like a question as possible, "you work here."

"I do," Henry said, and I could see a smile playing around the corners of his mouth. Clearly, my attempts at correcting my blunder syndrome had not been successful. "It's my dad's bakery."

"Oh," I said, not quite able to conceal my surprise in time. Henry's father, from what I remembered, had been like mine, one of the many fathers in suits getting off one of the buses on Friday nights, briefcase in hand. I glanced around the bakery, trying to reconcile these two things, and failing. "But," I started after a moment, "I thought he used to do something with banking?"

"He did," Henry said, his tone clipped and final, and I immediately regretted asking my question. His father had probably lost his job, and Henry didn't need me to point this out. "He says it's the same principle," Henry added after a moment, his tone softening a little. "Still trying to get the dough to rise." I groaned at that—it was the kind of joke my father would make—and Henry gave me a tiny smile in return.

Silence fell between us, and then Henry stuck his hands in his pockets and cleared his throat. "So what can I get you?" he asked, back to sounding detached and professional.

"Right," I said quickly, realizing that I was a customer in a shop, and the fact that I was supposed to know what I wanted should not have been such a shock to me. "Um . . ." I saw a platter of cupcakes with multicolored pastel icing, and I immediately looked away from them. Cupcakes reminded me all too much of my birthday, the slapdash celebration, the news about my dad. Searching for something—anything else—I tapped on the case in front of the next thing I saw. "A dozen of these." I looked closer and saw that what I'd just pointed to were, unfortunately, oatmeal raisin cookies. I hated oatmeal in all forms, but especially when people tried to dress it up as a dessert; Gelsey refused to eat raisins, and none of the rest of my family had ever been huge fans. I had just ordered a dessert that nobody at our house would most likely eat.

"Really." Henry didn't exactly phrase it as a question, and he raised his eyebrows at me. "Oatmeal?"

I just stared at him for a moment. There was no way Henry remembered that, five years ago, I hated oatmeal cookies. It just wasn't possible. "Yeah," I said slowly. "Oatmeal. Why?"

"No reason," he said as he took down another green bakery box from the shelf behind him and began transferring in the cookies two at a time. "I just didn't think you liked them."

"I can't believe you remember that," I said, as I watched the bakery box slowly fill with the World's Worst Cookies.

"My dad calls me the elephant." I just looked at him, not at all sure what to say to this, when he explained, "They're supposed to have really long memories." He reached toward the front of the

morgan matson

tray to get the two remaining cookies. "I don't really forget a lot," he added quietly.

I was about to nod when the double meaning of this hit me. Henry hadn't forgotten the kind of cookies I hated five years ago, but that also meant he hadn't forgotten the other things that I had done.

He'd put all the oatmeal cookies into the box, and he straightened up and looked at me. "Only had eleven," he said. "Can I give you one chocolate chip instead?"

"Yes!" I said, probably a little too eagerly. I thought I saw him smile as he bent down again and placed the lone chocolate chip in the box, tucked in the lid, and pushed it across the counter to me. He rang me up, and I noticed when he gave me back my change, he held the bills at the very ends and dropped the coins into my palm, as though he was trying to make sure that we didn't make any accidental contact. "Well," I said, when I realized there was nothing to do except take my bakery box and leave, "thanks."

"Sure," he said. His eyes focused on my shoulder, and he frowned slightly. "What's with the shirt?" he asked, and I saw he was looking at my canvas bag, which had one of my new employee T-shirts peeking out of the top.

"Oh," I said, pushing it down a bit farther, "I just got a job. Beach snack bar."

"Really?" he asked, sounding surprised. It was definitely a question this time.

"Yes," I said, a little defensively, until I realized that he would have no idea that I'd never had a job before and would therefore be somehow unqualified. "Why?"

Henry took a breath, about to answer, when the shop door opened and two women who looked around my mother's age came in, both wearing caftanlike cover-ups and sandals. "Nothing," he said, shaking his head. "Never mind."

The women were now standing behind me, peering into the bakery cases, and I knew that it was time for me to leave. "See you," I said, picking up the green box.

"Stay out of the woods," he replied, smiling faintly.

I met his eye for a moment, and I wondered if this was an opening, if I should just bite the bullet and apologize for what I'd done. Not that we'd ever be friends again, but we were neighbors. And it might make things a little less strained—or at least allow me to feel like I could venture out to the dock again.

"Was there something else?" Henry asked, but not unkindly. I could feel the women's eyes on me, waiting for my answer. But I had been a coward then—it was what had caused the whole mess—and it seemed that I was a coward still. "No," I said, as I stepped aside to let the women order the coffee cake they had been debating about. "Nothing else." I turned from the counter and left, walking back into the heat of the afternoon.

My father was leaning against the Land Cruiser when I reached him, a paper Henson's Produce bag between his feet and a plastic bag of licorice bits in his hand. They were for sale by the register, and whenever my father was in charge of picking some produce up—or able to intercept one of us before we went—he put in his order for a bag, the black licorice only. His particular views on this had only become more deeply entrenched when Warren had told him the fact that red licorice isn't technically licorice at all, as it's not made from the licorice plant.

"Hey, kid," he said as I approached, smiling at me. "What's the news?" His eyes landed on the bakery box, and he smiled wider. "And what did you get?"

I sighed and opened the box. "Oatmeal cookies," I said a little glumly.

"Oh." He peered down into the box, his brow furrowing. "Why?"

"It's a long story," I said, not wanting to admit that it was because my ex-boyfriend had flustered me. "But the news is that I got a job. I start tomorrow at the beach snack bar."

My father's smile returned, real and genuine and happy. "That's great, kid," he said. "Your first job! It's a milestone. I can remember—" He stopped short, his eyes squeezing shut as a spasm of pain flashed across his face.

"Dad?" I asked, stepping closer, hearing the fear in my voice. "Daddy?"

My father's face twisted again, and he grabbed his back with one hand, the bag of licorice bits falling and spilling onto the ground. "I'm okay," he said through clenched teeth. I didn't believe him—his eyes were still tightly closed and I could see perspiration beading on his forehead. "I just . . . need a second."

"Okay," I said. I gripped the bakery box tightly, looking around the street for someone who might help us somehow or tell me what I should be doing. I could feel my heart pounding, and wished that my mother was here, that I wasn't alone with this.

"You all right?" The redhead I'd seen through the window was standing in the doorway of Doggone It!, watching my father, her expression concerned. She held a cordless phone in her hand. "Do you need me to call someone?"

"No," my father said, his voice a little strained. He opened his eyes and took a folded white handkerchief from his back pocket, passing it quickly over his forehead. My father was never without one; they got washed with the rest of his laundry, and when I was really stumped for gift ideas—or really broke—they were what I gave him for Father's Day. He returned the handkerchief to his pocket and gave the girl a smile that didn't quite reach his eyes. "I'm fine."

"Okay," the girl said, nodding. But she didn't move from where she was standing, instead keeping her eyes on my father.

My father turned to me, and I noticed he looked much paler than he had only a few moments ago, and his breathing was labored. "Didn't mean to scare you, kid," he said.

I nodded, and swallowed hard, not sure what exactly had happened, or how to address it. "Are you," I started, then heard my voice falter. "I mean . . ."

"I'm fine," my father said again. He reached down to pick up the Henson's bag, and I noticed that his hands were shaking. He took out the key ring and headed to the driver's side, the keys jangling against one another in his trembling hand. Without realizing I was going to do it, I took a step closer to him and reached out for the keys. He looked at me, and a terrible, resigned sadness swept over his face before he looked away.

He let me take the keys from his hand, then walked around to the passenger side of the car without a word. As I unlocked the car, I looked down and saw the scattered licorice bits at my feet, the plastic bag trapped under the tire of a minivan two parking spots away. I climbed into the car and reached over to open the passenger door. I caught a glimpse of the girl, still standing in the door of the pet shop. She raised a hand in a wave, and I nodded back, trying not to notice that she still looked worried.

My father settled himself into the seat a little more gingerly than he had only an hour ago. I dropped the bakery box and my bag in the backseat and moved my seat way up—even though I knew how tall my father was, this never seemed as clear as when I was attempting to drive a car he'd been in before me, and my feet couldn't even reach the pedals. I started the car, and we drove in silence most of the way home, his head turned to the window. I didn't know if he was still in pain. But for whatever reason, I couldn't seem to form the words to ask him. After we'd had the dining room conversation on my birthday, we had talked very little about the realities of his illness. And I hadn't really tried. He clearly wanted to pretend that things were just normal—he'd said as much—but in moments like this, everything that we hadn't said seemed to prevent me from saying anything at all.

"Did you see the name of the pet store?" I asked after driving in silence for as long as I could stand it. I glanced over and saw the corner of my father's mouth twitch up in a small smile.

"I did," he said, turning to look at me. "I thought it was a little *ruff.*" I groaned, which I knew he expected, but I was also feeling a wave of relief. It seemed like the air in the car had become less heavy, and it was a little easier to breathe.

"Wow," I said as I made the turn onto Dockside. "You came up with that one without taking a *paws.*" My father let out a short laugh at that, and gave me a smile.

"Nice," he said, which was the very highest compliment he gave, pun-wise.

I pulled the car in next to my mother's and shut off the engine, but neither of us made a move to get out of the car.

"It really is good news about the job," my father said, his voice sounding tired. "Sorry if that got lost in . . ." He paused, then cleared his throat. "Everything."

I nodded, and ran my finger over a spot on the steering wheel where the leather was cracked and could probably be coaxed to come off, if I worked hard enough at it. "So," I started, hesitantly. "Should we ... you know ... talk about it?"

My father nodded, even as he grimaced slightly. "Of course," he said. "If you want to."

I felt a flare of anger then, as sudden and unexpected as if someone had set off a firecracker. "It's not that I want to," I said, hearing the sharpness of my tone, regretting it even as the words were spilling out of me. "It's just that we're all here, we're all up here, and we're not talking, or ..." I seemed to run out of words and anger at the same time, and was left with only a sinking feeling in my stomach, since I knew that the last thing I should be doing was yelling at my father. I started to take a breath, to apologize, when my father nodded.

"We will talk," he said. He looked away from me, straight into the screened-in porch, as though he could see the time in the future when this would be happening. "We'll say ... all the things that we need to say." I suddenly found myself swallowing hard, fighting the feeling that I was on the verge of tears. "But for now, while we still can, I just want to have a little bit of a normal summer with all of you. Sound good?" I nodded. "Good. The defense rests."

I smiled at that—he used the legal expression whenever he wanted to declare a subject closed—but I couldn't push away the question I'd had ever since he'd been diagnosed, the question that I somehow never felt I could ask. "I just . . ."

My father raised his eyebrows, and I could see that he already looked better than he had a few minutes earlier. And if I hadn't known, if I hadn't seen it, I might have been able to pretend that it hadn't happened, that he was still fine. "What is it, kid?"

I felt myself smile at that, even though I still felt like I might start crying. This was my dad's name for me, and only me. Gelsey was always "princess," Warren was "son." And I had always been his kid.

As I looked back at him, I wasn't sure I could ask it, the thing that I'd been wondering the most since he'd told us, sitting at the head of the dining room table. Because it was a question that went against everything I'd always believed about my father. He was the one who checked for burglars when my mother was sure she heard a noise outside, the one we yelled for when confronted with a spider. The one who used to pick me up and carry me when I got too tired to walk. The one I'd believed could vanquish dragons and closet-dwelling monsters. But I had to know, and I wasn't sure I'd get another chance to ask. "Are you scared?" I asked, my voice barely a whisper. But I could tell from the way that his face seemed to crumple a bit that he had heard me.

He didn't say anything, just nodded, up and down one time.

I nodded as well. "Me too," I said. He gave me another sad smile, and we sat there together in silence.

The shuttle bus rumbled up the street and passed our driveway, coming to a stop in front of the house next to ours, the CUT TO: SUMMER house. A dark-haired girl in an all-white tennis outfit got out, looking, even from this distance, fairly disgruntled as she stomped off the bus and up her driveway, soon obscured by the trees that separated our houses.

"Was that it?" he asked, after the girl had disappeared from view and the shuttle bus had moved on.

"That's it," I said. Then he'd reached out and ruffled my hair, resting his hand on the top of my head. And though we were certainly not a touchy-feely family, without even thinking about it, I leaned closer to my father, and he wrapped his arm around my shoulders, pulling me into a hug. And we stayed like that for just a moment before we both moved apart, almost at the same time, as though we'd agreed upon it beforehand. I slid out of the driver's side, opening the back door to retrieve my bag, the bakery box full of unfortunate cookies, and the Henson's Produce bag, which my father let me take.

We were heading up the steps to the house, my father leaning on the railing when he stopped and turned back to me, a smile starting to form that made him look less tired. "Metamorphosis," he said.

I frowned, trying to make this make sense. "A thirteen-letter word for change," he continued. He raised his eyebrows at me, pleased with himself.

"Maybe so," I said. I saw the abandoned crossword lying on the table, and I wanted to run over to it, see if it was the answer I'd been looking for. "Let's find out."

chapter nine

"GELSEY!" I YELLED IN THE DIRECTION OF THE house. "LET'S GO!" I was standing in the driveway, keys in hand, where I had been for the last ten minutes. I checked my watch and saw that I really should have left by now. Though I had no actual job experience, I had a feeling that that showing up late on your first day of work was probably frowned upon. The plan had been for Gelsey to bike to her first tennis lesson this morning. But her bike (technically, my old bike that was now too small for me) turned out to have a flat tire, and then Gelsey had some sort of meltdown, so it had fallen to me to drive her.

The front door slammed and she stepped out onto the porch, my mother right behind her. I noticed my mother stayed in front of the door, almost like she was blocking it, lest Gelsey try to make a break for it and run back inside. "Finally," I said. "I'm going to be late."

"You'll be fine," my mother said. Gelsey just glowered at me, as though I was somehow responsible for all this. My mother smoothed down Gelsey's hair and straightened the sleeves of her white tennis dress, one that had been mine when I was her age.

"Are you ready?" Gelsey asked, as if it had been me who had been holding us up all along. She pulled herself away from my mother and stomped down to the driveway.

My father, shielding his eyes, came forward a few steps from the garage, where he'd been fixing up our bikes since most of them hadn't been in a fit condition to ride. "Have a good first day, you two," he called. "And when you come back, I'll have the bikes all ready. So you both should be able to ride tomorrow."

"Great," I said, trying to sound enthusiastic about this while also trying to remember how many years it had been since I had ridden a bike.

"Have fun," he called. "Do great things." I turned back to wave, but he was already heading for his workbench, reaching for an air pump, humming tunelessly to himself.

"Can we leave already?" Gelsey asked, her voice heavy with disdain. I was about to throw disdain right back at her—maybe paired with a lecture about how it was *her* fault we weren't leaving until now—when I realized we probably didn't have time.

"Good luck," my mother called from the doorway, smiling at me. I wasn't sure if she was talking about my first day of work or about me getting Gelsey there in one piece, but I gave her a half-hearted smile back, then opened the driver's door and climbed into the car.

I started the engine, trying not to panic when I saw that I had

morgan matson

only seven minutes to drop my sister off at the Rec Center and get myself to the beach—not to mention that I'd received only the vaguest instructions from Jillian as to who I was supposed to talk to when I got there. So as soon as I'd reached the end of the driveway and passed out of sight of my parents, I stepped hard on the gas, now driving much faster than the WE LOVE OUR CHILDREN . . . PLEASE DRIVE SLOW! signs that dotted the road recommended.

Gelsey looked over from where she had been glaring out the window and glanced at my speedometer. "Speed much?" she asked, eyebrows raised.

"I wouldn't have to if you'd been ready on time," I said, hugging one of the curves as we barreled down Dockside Terrace. "I was about to leave without you."

"I wish you had," Gelsey said as she slumped back in her seat. I came to an abrupt stop that jolted us both forward, then picked up speed again as I headed toward what we had always called Devil's Dip. It was a huge hill that dropped sharply, then went up again just as sharply on the other side, creating a giant *U* shape. The Dip had been my Waterloo when I'd been learning to ride a bike, and it hadn't gotten any less steep with time. "I really thought Mom was bluffing. I can't believe she's making me do this."

"Tennis isn't so bad," I said as we coasted down the hill and then back up the other side, while I tried to remember my own long-ago lessons. I had never loved it like my father and Warren, and hadn't ever hung around the Tennis Center, working on my backhand on the practice wall the way that other kids had.

"Really," Gelsey said flatly.

"Really," I said, remembering how Lucy and I had spent very little time playing tennis, and most of our time talking. "It's mostly just hanging out with your friends, with a little tennis mixed in."

"Friends," she repeated softly, looking out the window again. "Right."

I glanced over at my sister before looking back at the road, regretting my word choice. Gelsey had never made friends easily, and had never had a best friend that I'd been aware of. It probably hadn't helped that she had spent all of her waking hours, until now, in the dance studio. But Gelsey also didn't do herself any favors, especially because whenever she got nervous, she masked it with haughtiness or disdain. "Look," I started, a little uncertainly, glancing over at her, "I know it might be hard at first, but—"

"Taylor!" Gelsey's voice was suddenly sharp. I glanced back at the road and then slammed on the brakes, hard, causing a loud screeching noise.

There was a girl on a bike directly in the middle of the road. She was riding fast, steering with one hand, the other holding a phone to her ear.

"Jesus," I muttered, my pulse pounding hard, as I checked the other lane, then gave her a wide berth. As we passed her, Gelsey leaned over and honked my horn. "Hey!" I said, pushing her hand away. The girl swerved, her bike wobbling dangerously for a second before she righted it and glanced at the car. In an impressive move, she transferred her phone to her ear and gripped the handlebars with her opposite hand, so that the hand closest to my car was free to give us the finger. Her face was obscured by a curtain of dark hair, but there was no question as to how she felt about us at that moment. As we drove past, I looked back and saw her in my rearview mirror, becoming reduced to a dot in a purple T-shirt.

"Don't do that," I said as I swung into the recreation complex parking lot.

"She was taking up the whole road," Gelsey said. But her voice didn't sound nearly as confident anymore as I pulled to a stop in front of the main entrance. The building looked exactly the same, a tall wooden structure with LAKE PHOENIX RECREATION CENTER carved into the awning. Just beyond the entrance, you'd have to show your badge to the employee inside to access the pool and tennis courts.

I looked at my sister and saw that her hands were gripping the straps of her tote bag so hard that her knuckles had turned white. She glanced over at me and I realized that she was scared. I knew it was probably up to me to say something, something encouraging and big-sisterly, but I had no idea what that would be.

"I should go," Gelsey said after a moment, taking a deep breath and pushing open her door. "I'll call Mom for a ride home, or walk, or something."

"Okay," I said. "Have fun."

Gelsey rolled her eyes hugely at that, got out of the car, and walked up to the entrance stiffly, like she was facing a firing squad and not a tennis lesson. I looked down at the clock, cursed, and put the car into gear. I peeled out of the parking lot, now officially five minutes late for my first day of work.

I hadn't gone to the beach since I'd been back, but as I got out of the car, I could see it hadn't changed much. There were picnic tables and benches on the grassy area nearest to the parking lot. A small incline (there was a set of steps if you didn't want to roll down the hill, as I'd been fond of doing when I was around eight) led down to the sand. The beach wasn't very full—there were only a handful of towels and blankets spread out, with some families and sunbathers staking their claims. A few ambitious kids were already mid–sandcastle construction, but the water was free from swimmers. When I saw the tall white lifeguard's chair perched at the edge of the water was empty, I realized why there was nobody swimming—the lifeguard wasn't on duty yet. The far right side of the beach was the marina area, with sailboats up on their wooden pallets, and kayaks and canoes stacked in wooden structures. The lake was the main feature, stretching out almost as far as you could see. A large wooden raft, complete with ladder, was anchored beyond the roped-off swimming section that kids weren't supposed to go past, and the bobbing round yellow buoys by the raft demarcated where adults were supposed to stop. The lake was bordered on all sides by pine trees, and the three islands scattered across it were also covered in them. The sky above the lake was clear and a bright blue, with wispy clouds streaking across it. Looking back, it sometimes seemed like I had spent all my childhood summers at this beach. The pool had never held as much charm for me, with its rough concrete and smell of chlorine. The beach had always felt like home.

"Are you Taylor?" I turned around and saw a short man with a very red face, in his forties or thereabouts, wearing a Lake Phoenix polo shirt and squinting at me.

"Hi," I said, hurrying over to him, trying to simultaneously smooth down my hair and come up with an excuse for why I was late for my first day of work. "I mean, yes." I held out my hand to shake his—the night before, Warren had given me a tutorial on making a good first impression, and he seemed to rank a strong handshake very highly—but the man was already turning and walking down the steps toward the snack bar, gesturing for me to follow him.

"Fred Lefevre," he said over his shoulder. "This way." The snack bar was in the building that was adjacent to the Clubhouse, where the bathrooms, equipment rooms, and administrative offices were, and Fred headed through this building's open doorway and to an office marked BEACH DIRECTOR. He pushed the door open and motioned me in, but as soon as I crossed the threshold, I stopped short.

There were fish everywhere. None alive, but stuffed and mounted fish were affixed to most of the available wall space, and a fishing calendar hung behind the desk, the surface of which was covered with framed pictures of Fred holding up huge trophy fishes. There were tackle boxes and fishing poles scattered all over, and as Fred took the seat across from me, behind his desk, I noticed that he had the permanently sunburned look of someone who spent most of his time outside. Fred leaned back in the squeaky leather chair, the kind on wheels with casters, and looked across the desk at me. I immediately sat up straighter on the metal folding chair that was cold against the backs of my legs. "So," he said. "You're our late hire."

I wasn't sure if he meant that I had been hired late, or if he was talking about the fact that I'd been late for work today, so I just nodded. Fred picked up the frame closest to him and gazed at it for a moment before turning it to face me. In the picture, Fred held up on his line a fish that looked almost as tall as he was. "Know what that is?" he asked. My knowledge of fish was pretty much limited to what I got on seafood menus, so I just shook my head. "It's a threespine stickleback," he said wistfully. "Isn't she a beauty?"

"Mmm," I said with as much enthusiasm as possible.

"That was two years ago," he said, setting the picture down, continuing to stare at it. "I haven't caught one as big since. And that's why you're here."

I blinked at him for a moment, then glanced at the picture of the large, disgruntled-looking fish, as though it would somehow help me out here. "Um, what?" I asked.

"I like to fish," Fred said, tearing his eyes away from the stickleback and looking at me. "And June and July are my peak fishing months. And I can't put in my time on the lakes if I have to be micromanaging this place."

"Okay," I said, still waiting for an explanation of how I fit into all this.

"So I put in a request with Jillian for one more employee," he said. "Someone here who can do what needs doing. Mostly the snack bar, but I also need someone to help figure out the movie-on-the-beach nights. Last year, they were . . ." He paused for a moment. "Not a success," he finally concluded. "Basically, I need to be able to be away from this place and know that everything is going to be covered. So that'll be you. Sound good?"

"Well," I said, turning over my job description in my head. It wasn't that it sounded bad—it was only that I wasn't sure I was qualified to do any of it. "It's just—"

"Good!" Fred said, standing up, this meeting apparently now over as far as he was concerned. "Let's say four days a week. I'll let you work out the schedule with the others, figuring out where the holes are."

I stood up as well, out of instinct, since he was looming over me and clearly wanted me to leave his fish-bedecked office. "But—"

"The job's very easy, Taylor," he said, coming around to join me on the other side of his desk, and then opening the door for me, in case I still wasn't getting the hint that I was supposed to leave. "Just make my life simple. I want to fish. And I want to fish undisturbed. So if you can help me make that happen, you'll be doing great work. Okay?"

"Okay," I said, taking a step out of his office, then another one, as he began to ease the door shut. "But where should I—"

"Start at the snack bar," he said. "See what needs doing. Welcome aboard!" With that, he shut the door firmly in my face.

I looked around, and seeing no other options, headed to the snack bar. I had only ever approached it from the front, after scrounging quarters and pennies, or finding a crumpled, sandy dollar bill in my beach bag, usually to get a Cherry Coke or a frozen Milky Way to split with Lucy. But down the hall from Fred's office there was a door clearly marked SNACK BAR EMPLOYEES ONLY, so I took a breath and pushed it open, hoping someone in there could tell me exactly what I was supposed to be doing, preferably without fish anecdotes.

From the other side of the counter, the snack bar was fairly small and cramped. The soda fountain lined the one wall, along with a large silver refrigerator and two freezer cases. Behind that was a grill and fry station. There were shelves displaying the chip options and posters showing the ice-cream bars available, and there were individually wrapped pieces of candy, on sale for a quarter, on the counter.

"Don't. Move," a voice from behind me said. I whirled around and saw a guy sitting on the counter, perfectly still, a rolled-up newspaper raised above his head.

I had thought I'd been alone in the snack bar, and my heart was beating hard from the shock that I wasn't. "Hi," I stammered when I'd gotten some of my composure back. "I'm—"

"Shh," he hissed, his voice low and steady, still not looking at me. "Don't scare it away."

I froze, and tried to see to what he was raising his newspaper at, but could only see the empty counter. I suddenly had a horrible fear that made me not only want to move—and fast—but also jump up on the counter with him. "Is it a mouse?" I whispered, feeling my skin begin to crawl. If it was, I didn't care about what he said, I was getting out of there as soon as possible.

"No," the guy murmured, concentration still on the counter. "It's a fly. He's been taunting me all morning. But I will have my victory."

"Oh," I said quietly. I shifted from foot to foot, wondering how long this was going to go on—and also what we were supposed to do if any customers came. In the silence that soon fell between us, all his concentration focused on the fly, I took the opportunity to look at the guy. Something about him was ringing long-ago bells of recognition. It was hard to tell because he was sitting, but he looked short and somewhat stocky. He was wearing nerdy-cool glasses and had close-cropped brown hair. "I've almost got him," the guy suddenly whispered, leaning forward, newspaper poised. "Just don't move, and—"

"Oh, my *God!*" The door to the employee entrance was flung open with a bang, causing both me and the guy to jump, and the fly presumably to make his escape. A girl breezed past me and the guy, hanging her purse on a hook around the corner, talking loud and fast. I caught a glimpse of long dark hair and a purple T-shirt, and a feeling of dread crept into my stomach. "You are not going to *believe* what happened to me this morning. I was just riding into work, minding my own business, when this absolute *idiot*—" The girl came back around the corner to face us, and froze when she saw me.

I did the same. Standing in front of me was the girl in the purple shirt, the one whom I'd almost run off the road this morning, the one who'd given me the finger.

Who also happened to be Lucy Marino, my former best friend.

chapter ten

I just stared at Lucy. As with Henry, it took my mind a second to reconcile her twelve-year-old appearance with the current version. Lucy and I had been around the same height when we were kids, but it seemed like she hadn't grown nearly as much as I had, because she was now a good four inches shorter than me, and curvy, like we'd both once hoped to be. Her hair was still dark brown and shiny, but what had been an unruly mass of curls was now sleek and straight. Her olive-toned skin was already tan, and she was wearing expertly applied makeup, clearly at some point in the last five years having moved on from our clumsy first attempts at eyeliner.

Lucy blinked at me, then narrowed her eyes and crossed her arms over her chest. "What the hell are you doing here?" she asked, sounding equal parts baffled and angry. The guy on the counter looked to me and raised his eyebrows.

"I . . . um," I started. I gestured behind me in the direction of Fred's office. "Fred told me to come in here. I'm working here now."

"Really." Lucy didn't phrase it as a question.

"Really?" The guy on the counter did. He hopped off and relinquished his weapon, dropping the newspaper on the counter.

"Yes," I said, without as much conviction as I would have preferred, since I was beginning to wonder if this was really such a good idea. And it hit me a moment later that Lucy's presence at this job explained Henry's hesitation when I'd told him I was working here.

"Excellent," the guy said. "Reinforcements." He held out his hand and shook mine a little too firmly, maybe having read the same book as Warren. "I'm Elliot."

It clicked into place then. I could suddenly see him, at ten, even stockier and shorter, with glasses that weren't nearly as fashionable, hanging out by the pool snack bar, one of those kids who always had a deck of cards and was constantly trying to get some kind of game going. He'd been primarily Henry's friend, but sometimes the three of us would hang out, especially when it was raining and there was nothing else to do.

"Taylor," I said. "Do you . . . ?" I paused, suddenly realizing how pathetic it was to have to ask someone if they remembered you.

"Oh," Elliot said, eyebrows flying up. *Taylor.* " He glanced at Lucy, then back to me. Lucy was looking straight ahead, glaring out at the water, as though even the sight of me was too much for her to take. "Sorry I didn't recognize you. It's been a while, huh?"

I nodded. "It really has," I said. Silence fell among us all, and then Elliot cleared his throat.

"Welcome," he said. "Are you going to be working the snack bar?"

"Kind of," I said. I looked over at Lucy, catching her eye for a second before she looked pointedly away again. "Also doing something with the movies . . ." My voice trailed off, and I realized just how little I knew about what this job would entail.

"I guess Fred finally got his fishing employee," Elliot said. Lucy only shrugged, and Elliot turned to me. "He's been trying for years. But rumor is that he started dating Jillian in the office, which I guess gave him some kind of pull."

"Don't you have a lesson?" Lucy asked, glancing up at the round wall clock hanging crookedly above the microwave.

Elliot looked down at his watch, which I saw now was big and plastic and practically took up his whole wrist. It looked like a diver's watch, and like it would be capable of withstanding much greater depths than Lake Phoenix. "In ten," Elliot said with a sigh. "Unfortunately."

"Lesson?" I asked. In my peripheral vision, I saw Lucy roll her eyes. But since my introduction to this place had been so vague, I was desperate to get what information I could from the one person in the snack bar who seemed willing to talk to me.

"I teach some sailing lessons, plus working snack bar," Elliot said to me. "We all kind of overlap here. And today is my day for the advanced beginners, who seem to be allergic to retaining any sort of knowledge." He started to head out the door, then stopped and turned back to us. "If you see the fly," he added gravely, "avenge me. Okay?"

Lucy nodded in a distracted way that made me think he said things like that a lot. When Elliot stepped back out and the door slammed behind him, Lucy turned to face me, arms still folded, her face inscrutable. "So," she said after a long moment. She leaned against the counter and studied me in silence. "You're back."

"I am," I said, my voice sounding a little shaky. I was feeling off-balance, and had realized that no matter what I might look like now, some things were still the same. I still hated confrontation. And Lucy thrived on it. "Just . . . recently."

"I heard," she said. I blinked, and was about to ask from whom, but something in her expression stopped me. I realized that it could have been from any number of sources, Jillian included. Lake Phoenix was small enough that news tended to travel fast. "I just didn't think I'd see you," she continued, arching one eyebrow at me, something she'd always been able to do and that I could never get the hang of. It used to make me incredibly envious, since whenever I tried to do it I just looked like I was in pain. "And I certainly didn't think I'd see you here."

I stuck my hands in the pockets of my shorts and looked down at the scratched wooden floors. I could feel the restlessness in my legs that was my body's way of telling me to get out. I glanced to the

morgan matson

door for just a second, considering it. "If it's going to be a thing," I said after a moment, "I can leave. See if I can get placed somewhere else."

I looked up at Lucy and saw a flash of hurt cross her face before her more blasé expression returned. She shrugged and looked down at her nails, which I noticed now were painted a dark purple, and I wondered if she'd matched them to her shirt. The Lucy I'd known certainly would have. "Don't do it on my account," she said, her voice bored. "I don't really care."

"Okay," I said quietly. I took a breath and started to say what I probably should have said right away—what I should have said to Henry as soon as I saw him. "Lucy," I started, "I'm really—"

"Can I help you?" Lucy hopped off the counter, and I turned and saw a customer at the window, a harried-looking mother with a baby on her hip. The top of the kid's head just cleared the wooden counter, his eyes fixed on the bowl of individually wrapped Starbursts and Sunkist Fruit Gems.

"Yes," she said. "I need two waters, an order of fries, and a Sprite with no ice."

Lucy punched the total into the register and turned back to look at me. I moved uncertainly over toward the cups, my hand hovering near them, but otherwise totally unsure what to do. "Go get Elliot," Lucy said, shaking her head. "You don't know what you're doing." She turned back to the woman and deftly moved the candy bowl away just as the kid made a grab for it. "Nine twenty-nine," she said.

I pushed open the door and closed it fast behind me, stepping into the hallway. The whole interaction had shaken me. For some reason, I felt like I was on the verge of bursting into tears, so I was glad to have a minute to walk it off. I knew Elliot had ten minutes before his lesson, so I didn't have long to find him. I started by looking for Elliot in the few rooms in the building—but I found only an equipment shed, piled high with life preservers and buoys, and a supply cupboard with plates and cups and syrup bags for the soda machine. Fred's door had a GONE FISHIN' sign attached to it—no help there. I was beginning to panic, knowing the longer I took, the madder Lucy was getting, when I saw Elliot sitting on the grass near the bike racks, next to a curly-haired guy playing guitar. There were about ten life preservers arranged in a circle, but no kids there yet. Incredibly relieved, I hurried over and started speaking before I'd even reached him. "Lucy needs your help in the kitchen," I said, as Elliot looked up at me and the guy with the guitar paused mid-chord. "I don't really know what I'm doing yet."

Elliot raised his eyebrows. "But she can show you, right?" he asked. "Luce is great at training. She taught me everything I know."

"Oh," I said, glancing back to the stand, thinking about how she'd hustled me out, clearly ready to be rid of me. "Well," I said, "I don't think that she really . . . um . . . wanted to."

"Right," Elliot said, nodding. He gave me a sympathetic smile

morgan matson

and pushed himself to his feet. "Well, I guess you can't blame her, right?" He started to head toward the snack bar before I could formulate a response. "Oh," he said as he turned back to me for a second, pointing at the curly-haired guy, "Taylor, that's Leland. Leland, Taylor. She's new." With that, he hurried toward the building, and a moment later, I heard the door bang shut.

Leland looked tall, with pale, freckled skin and sun-bleached hair that seemed like it might not have been combed too recently. He strummed another chord and then glanced up, giving me a sleepy smile. "Hey," he said. "You a lifeguard too?"

"No," I replied. "Snack bar."

"Cool," he said as he strummed a few more chords, lingering over the last two strings. As I watched him play, it seemed a little incongruous that this guy, with his chill, spaced-out vibe, was a lifeguard. It wasn't what I had expected.

"Speaking of," Leland said, unfolding his long legs and standing up, "I'd better get to work. I'm sure I'll see you around." He shuffled down toward the beach, not seeming like he was in any particular hurry.

I looked back toward the concession stand, then over to my crookedly parked car. There was a piece of me, a big one, that just wanted to get in and drive, not stopping until I was miles and states away from here. But there was something about quitting twenty minutes into your first day that just seemed pathetic. And I knew that if I left now, it would confirm everything that Lucy already thought about me. So I made myself walk toward the concession stand, suddenly with a lot more sympathy for my sister and what she'd had to face this morning. I took a deep breath before I pulled open the employee door, feeling a little bit like I was going to face a firing squad myself.

The rest of the workday did not exactly go well. Lucy barely spoke to me. She either spoke to me through Elliot, when he was around between lessons, or simply ignored me, leaving several times to make calls on her cell. After the lunch rush, she'd sent me to organize the equipment and supply rooms. It was mind-numbing work—counting and straightening the piles of life jackets, then doing inventory of the supply closet—but at least I was alone, with no uncomfortable pauses or waves of irritation being sent my way. I'd spent my lunch hour sitting on the beach alone, off to the side, in the shade of one of the pine trees. There were groups of kids playing in the water, having the kind of raft-tipping fights that I remembered well. I could see Elliot, out on the lake in a kayak, directing a sailing class around a buoy course, and retrieving one boat when it seemed in danger of floating out toward Delaware. When I returned to the supply room after my break and began counting the cups again, time seemed to crawl, the hours passing with excruciating slowness. When five o'clock finally arrived and I closed up the supply closet,

I was exhausted. I smelled like fryer grease and the mayonnaise I'd accidentally spilled on myself, my feet were killing me, and all I wanted was to crawl into bed and not have to go back to this job ever again.

I met Lucy and Elliot outside, as Lucy pulled a metal gate down over the front of the concession stand and locked it. I saw Leland striding up from the beach, guitar over his shoulder, and was surprised to see that there were still some swimmers in the water, a few lone people still bobbing in their rafts. "So," I said, as Elliot approached me and Lucy yanked on the lock twice, testing it, "what happens if there's no lifeguard?"

"A sign goes up," Elliot said. He nodded at Leland, who was loping over to us. "Lifeguard's only on duty from nine to five. There's a sign on the chair the rest of the time that it's swim at your own risk."

I nodded as Lucy came over, her phone clutched in her hand. She smiled at Leland, then dropped the friendly expression as soon as she saw me. "So we should figure out schedules," she said, her voice cold and clipped. "I'll talk to Fred and then call you. What's your cell?" I told her, and she punched it into her phone, pressing each button a little harder than necessary. "Okay," she said, when she'd saved it. She gave me a long look, and as I took in the rest of the three of them standing closer together, I realized that they were probably going to be making plans to hang out. Plans that I, without question, wasn't a part of.

"Oh," I said, feeling my face get hot. "Right. Great. So just . . . call me about the schedule, and I'll . . . be here then." I could hear that I sounded like an idiot, but the words were out before I could stop them. I gave everyone a nod, and power-walked to my car as fast as possible.

As I opened the door, before I got inside, I looked back and saw Lucy watching me. She didn't look away immediately, like she had all day, and her expression seemed more sad than angry. But then she turned away again, and I was reminded of what Elliot had said. He was right—I couldn't blame her. Because it was exactly what I deserved.

chapter eleven
five summers earlier

I STARED ACROSS THE DOCK GLUMLY AT LUCY. "THIS STINKS." I separated out the purple Skittles from the pile in front of me, and pushed them toward my best friend. Lucy frowned down at her own pile, then selected all the greens and pushed them to me. We divided all our candy this way, our color preferences so ingrained that we never had to ask. When it came to things like Snickers or Milky Ways, we preferred them from the beach snack bar, frozen. We would get one, along with a plastic knife, and Lucy would divide the candy bar with a surgeon's precision. We shared everything, fifty-fifty.

"I know," Lucy agreed. "It *sucks*." I nodded, secretly impressed and a little jealous. My mother yelled at me whenever I said that word, and Lucy's mother had as well, until recently. But, as Lucy was always pointing out, divorce meant that you could get away with tons of things that used to be off-limits.

Unfortunately, divorce also meant that Lucy wasn't going to be here for most of the summer, a fact that I was still having trouble getting my head around. Summers in Lake Phoenix meant Lucy, and I had no idea what I was supposed to do without her. We had even gone before my parents, sitting them down on the screened-in porch one night to make our case: Lucy could just live with us this summer while her parents were in New Jersey, dealing with lawyers and meetings and "mediation," whatever that was. This way, Lucy would be able to take advantage of the Lake Phoenix fresh air, and not be in her parents' way. She could share my room—we'd even worked out a system where we'd alternate who would get the real bed, and who would get the trundle bed.

But my parents hadn't agreed, and now, after only two weeks here, Lucy was leaving. I was supposed to be saying good-bye, and even though I said good-bye to Lucy at the end of every summer, this was different.

"Look," Lucy said, carefully smoothing her bangs down. I loved Lucy's bangs and was incredibly jealous of them. But when I'd gotten my own cut the fall before, they hadn't hung even, straight, and thick, like Lucy's did. They had been wispy and flyaway, always parting in a cowlick in the center and causing my mother to have to buy me a lot of headbands. My hair had grown out by the time summer came, and I never had to tell Lucy that I'd copied her. "My mom said if she gets the house and things work out, I'll be able to come up here soon. Maybe even in a month." She tried to put a positive spin on the last word, but I could hear how hollow it sounded. What was I supposed to do for a month without Lucy?

"Right," I said, trying to be cheerful too, even though I didn't mean it at all. "It'll be great." I gave her a big, fake smile, but Lucy just stared at me for a moment, and we both started cracking up.

"T," she said, shaking her head. "You are the worst liar ever."

"I know," I said, even though I couldn't remember a time when I'd ever needed or wanted to lie to Lucy.

"But at least you aren't going to be all alone in New Jersey, like I am," Lucy said with a dramatic sigh. "I'm going to be *so bored*."

"I'm going to be bored too," I assured her. "Who am I going to hang out with?"

Lucy shrugged, and for some reason didn't meet my eye when she said, "Your friend Henry, maybe?"

Even though I knew it wasn't fair to Henry, I groaned in response. "It's not the same," I said. "All he wants to do is go into the woods and look at rocks. He's a huge dork." This wasn't exactly true, and I felt bad after I said it, but I was trying to make Lucy feel better.

"Lucy!" Mrs. Marino yelled from the house, and as I turned to look, I could see her standing in the driveway, where the car was packed up and ready to go.

Lucy let out a long sigh, but both of us seemed to realize it was time to leave. We scooped up our Skittles and walked toward the house. In her driveway, we did the hand-slap pattern we spent most of last summer working out (it involved a double spin) and then said good-bye and hugged quickly when Lucy's mom started complaining about how if they didn't get started soon, they weren't going to beat the traffic.

I stood with my bike at the side of Lucy's driveway and watched the car pull away, Lucy leaning out the window, waving until I couldn't see her any longer. Then I got on my bike and started to pedal slowly in the direction of home. I didn't necessarily want to be there—it was hours until dinnertime—but I didn't know what else to do. It seemed incredibly lame to go to the beach or the pool by myself.

"Hey, Edwards!" I looked over, but I knew it was Henry, skidding to a stop next to me. He'd been going through a phase recently where he was calling everyone by their last names. And even though I knew he wanted me to, I refused to call him "Crosby."

"Hey, Henry." I stepped down to the ground and kicked at my pedal, setting it spinning. Henry, on the other hand, kept riding, looping in circles around my bike.

"Where's Marino?" he asked, as he circled me. I kept having to turn my head to look at him, and I was starting to get dizzy.

"Lucy's gone for the summer," I said, feeling the impact of the words. "Most of it, anyway."

Henry stopped circling me and dropped one bare foot to the ground. "That's a bummer," he said. "Sorry to hear that."

I nodded, even though I wasn't sure Henry meant it. He and Lucy had never gotten along that great. I knew he thought she was

morgan matson

too girly, and she thought he was a know-it-all. The few times the three of us had tried to hang out together, I'd felt like I was a referee, constantly trying to make sure everyone was getting along, and it had been exhausting. So I tended to hang out with them separately, which worked out better for everyone.

"So," Henry said, getting back up on the bike's pedals, "I was going to the beach. Want to come?"

I looked at him and thought about it. Hanging out with Henry would definitely be better than going home—even if he did call me Edwards and was always trying to get me to race him or see who could eat more hot dogs. "Okay," I said, spinning my pedal back and standing on it. "Sounds fun."

"Awesome." Henry smiled at me, and I noticed that his teeth were no longer crooked in front, like they'd been when I first met him. And his smile was really nice. Why hadn't I ever noticed that before?

"Race you to the beach?" he asked, already ready to ride, his hands gripping the handlebars.

"I don't know," I said, as I pretended to fuss with my gears, all the while getting into position. "I'm not sure if I—Go!" I yelled the last word and started pedaling as fast as I could, leaving Henry to catch up. I laughed out loud as I started to fly down the street, the wind lifting my ponytail. "Loser buys the Cokes!"

Lost & Found

chapter twelve

THE WAITING ROOM IN THE ONCOLOGY DEPARTMENT OF THE Stroudsburg hospital seemed like it had given up on any attempts to be cheerful. The walls were painted a dull peach, and there weren't any encouraging posters about managing your cold or proper hand-washing techniques, like I'd been used to seeing in my doctor's office. Instead, there was only a single badly painted landscape of a hill dotted with either sheep or clouds, I wasn't sure which. The chairs were overstuffed, making me feel like I was slowly sinking down into them, and all the magazines were months out of date. Two of the celebrity marriages trumpeted on the glossy covers had since imploded in messy divorces. I flipped through the closest magazine at hand anyway, realizing how different these happily-ever-after stories seemed when you were aware of what the outcome was going to be. After a few minutes, I tossed it aside. I glanced down at my watch, and then at the door my father had gone through to meet with his doctor. This was not exactly how I'd imagined spending my day off.

I had planned on quitting the snack bar after the first disastrous day, seeing no reason to spend the summer with people who disliked me and made no secret of it. But at dinner that night, as we'd feasted on corn on the cob, French fries, and hamburgers cooked on the grill—what felt like our first real summer meal—my plan hit a snag.

Gelsey, it seemed, hated tennis. While she complained about how stupid the sport was, and how all the people in her tennis class were equally stupid, and Warren was simultaneously attempting to tell us that tennis had been invented in twelfth-century France and popularized in the court of Henry the Eighth, I'd just sat there, enjoying my corn, waiting for the moment that I could jump in and explain that while I was sure that there were merits to working at the snack bar, I felt that my time might be better utilized this summer by doing something else. Anything else. I was working out my explanation in my head, and so wasn't really paying attention to the conversation around the table. It was only when I heard my name that I snapped back to attention.

"What?" I asked, looking at my father. "What was that, Dad?"

"I was just saying," my dad said, mostly to my sister, who was glowering down at her plate, "that you also had a new, challenging experience today. But unlike your sister, you are taking it in stride."

Crap. "Um," I said, glancing at Warren, trying to see if I could silently communicate with him, and get him to distract everyone, or tell us how something else was invented. But Warren just yawned and helped himself to more fries. "Right. About that . . ."

morgan matson

"Taylor's not quitting," my father said. I cleared my throat, hoping that I could get him to stop somehow without looking like the flakiest person on earth. "And I'm sure her day wasn't easy. Was it?"

He turned back my way, and everyone in my family looked at me, Warren's fry raised halfway to his mouth. "No," I said honestly.

"There you go," my dad said, giving me a small wink, making me feel terrible about what I was about to do. But then I thought of Lucy's face when she'd realized I was working there, and how lonely it had been, eating lunch by myself.

"Look," I said, realizing that this might be my best chance to extricate myself from a situation that, I was sure, was only going to get exponentially worse as the summer went on. "It's not that I don't want to work. It's just that the snack bar wasn't . . . um . . . exactly what I expected." My mother glanced over at me, her expression indicating she knew exactly what I was about to say. I looked away from her as I continued. "And, given my academic workload next year, I think I should use this summer to—"

"I don't care!" Gelsey wailed, sounding on the verge of tears. "I don't want to play tennis and I shouldn't have to. It's . . . not . . . fair!"

Warren rolled his eyes at me across the table, and I shook my head. This was what came of being the baby of the family. You got to throw tantrums years after you were officially much too old to do so. Gelsey started to sob into her dinner napkin, and I realized that the moment to announce that I was quitting my job had probably passed.

So I'd suffered through two more shifts at the snack bar, mostly just so that I could quit and still save a little bit of face with my dad. They were pretty much the same as my first day—Lucy barely spoke to me, and I spent the entire workday counting down the minutes until I could go home, more convinced with each passing hour that this was not worth the minimum wage. I'd planned on taking my day off to go down to the clubhouse, tell Jillian, leave a message for Fred (who would undoubtedly be fishing), and then tell my family once it was a done deal. But that afternoon, as my dad set aside his work and prepared to go to Stroudsburg for his doctor's appointment, my mom called me out to the porch.

She was sitting on the top step, combing my sister's hair. Gelsey was one step below her, a towel around her shoulders, her head tilted back slightly as my mother pulled a wide-tooth comb through her damp auburn curls. This was a ritual the two of them had. They didn't do it all the time, just when my sister had a bad day or was upset about something. As I watched her getting her hair combed now, I wondered if this was because of the trauma she'd suffered at her tennis lessons (which she hadn't been allowed to quit) or something else. Years ago, I'd wanted my mother to do this for me, when I was much younger. I'd eventually realized, though, there was probably no point to it. My mother and Gelsey had the same reddish-brown hair— long, thick, and curly. And I had fine, pin-straight hair that never got tangled and that I barely needed to comb myself. But still.

morgan matson

"What?" I asked. Gelsey made a face at me, but before I could respond in kind, my mother turned her head back so I could only see her profile.

"Would you go to Stroudsburg with your dad today?" my mom asked.

"Oh," I said. This was not what I had been expecting. "Is he okay?"

"He just has his doctor's appointment, and I was hoping you could go with him," my mother said, her tone even, as she drew the comb from the crown all the way down to the ends that were already starting to curl into ringlets. I looked at my mother closely, trying to see what she meant by this, if there was anything truly wrong, but my mother could be inscrutable when she wanted to be, and I couldn't tell anything. "You're all set," she said, smoothing her hand down Gelsey's hair, then whisking the towel off her shoulders.

Gelsey stood and headed inside, crossing to the door in a series of fast twirls. I stepped aside to let her pass, totally used to this, since for several years now, when she was in the mood, Gelsey would seldom walk when she could dance.

"So?" my mother asked, and I turned back to see her plucking the loose hairs from the comb. "Will you go with your dad?"

"Sure," I said, but still felt like there was more to this than she was telling me. I took a breath to ask when I noticed that my mother was tossing the stray hairs into the air, where they were lifted by the faint breeze that had been ruffling the trees all afternoon. "What are you doing?"

"It's why you should always comb your hair outside," she said. "This way, mother birds can weave the strands into their nests." She looked down at the comb, then started to head inside, folding the towel as she went.

"Mom," I said, before she reached the door. She looked at me, eyebrows raised, waiting, and I suddenly wanted nothing more than to be able to talk to her like Gelsey could, and tell her what I was really afraid of. "Is Dad okay?"

My mom gave me a sad smile. "I just want him to have some company. Okay?"

And of course I had agreed, and my dad and I drove the hour into Stroudsburg together, my father behind the wheel—I felt like I'd learned my lesson as far as questioning him about that. My dad seemed to be treating this excursion, brief as it was, like a real road trip. He stopped at PocoMart for honey-roasted peanuts and sodas for us, and put me in charge of radio duties as we headed out of town. This was perhaps the most unexpected part of the afternoon, since whenever we'd been in the car together before, he was always either on the Bluetooth talking to his office, or listening to the financial report.

When we'd arrived at the hospital, my dad led the way up to the oncology wing, and as he headed into his appointment, he promised me it wouldn't be too long. But it had been twenty minutes now, and I was starting to get restless.

I bypassed the elevator and took the stairs down to the lobby, feeling the need to move. The lobby didn't offer all that much distraction—just oil paintings of the founders and plaques commemorating big donations. There were also a surprisingly large number of people smoking outside the building's entrance, considering that this was a hospital. I ended up in the gift shop, walking around the aisles, taking in the bouquets of flowers for purchase, the cheerful, bright-colored teddy bears emblazoned with GET WELL SOON! across their stomachs. I wandered into the card aisle, looking through the racks of Thinking of You and Get Well Soon options. I moved past the sympathy section, not even wanting to know what was inside the somber-looking cards that mostly seemed to feature a single flower, a bird in flight, or a sunset.

Since there was nothing I wanted, I just bought a pack of gum, tossing it onto the counter as I dug in my purse for change. As I did, I noticed a large flower arrangement on the counter, made up of summer flowers, all bright purples and oranges. It looked vibrant and healthy, and seemed to smell like sunshine even in the sterile, fluorescently lit gift shop. Looking at it, I got, for the first time, why people would bring flowers to sick people, stuck inside the hospital with no way to get outside. It was like bringing them a little bit of the world that was going on without them.

"That it?" the woman behind the counter asked.

I started to reply, but my eye was caught by the preprinted card in the arrangement, displayed on a long plastic holder that poked out of the flowers. JUST TO SAY I LOVE YOU, it read.

"Did you want something else?" she asked.

I looked away from the card, embarrassed, and handed her a dollar. "That's it," I said, as I pocketed the gum and then dropped my few cents change into the penny cup.

"Have a good day," she said, then cleared her throat. "I hope everything . . . turns out all right."

I looked up at her then, and saw that she was older, closer to my grandmother's age, wearing a name tag and a sympathetic expression. It was different from the expressions of pity and premature sympathy that I'd hated so much in Connecticut, and I realized I didn't mind. It struck me that she must see, all day long, people coming through the shop who also didn't want to be in the hospital, who were looking for something they could buy, some cheap teddy bear or arrangement of flowers, that would seem to make things better.

"Thanks," I said. I let my eyes linger on the card for a moment longer before I headed out to the lobby. I skipped the stairs and took the elevator to the oncology wing. The card had made me uncomfortably aware of something—I couldn't remember the last time I'd told my father I loved him. I searched my memory as the elevator rose silently through the floors. I knew I'd said it a lot when I was younger, as our home-movie collection attested to. And I'd sign his birthday and Father's Day card every year with a scrawled *love, Taylor*. But had I ever said it to him? Out loud, and in recent memory?

I couldn't remember, which made me pretty sure that the answer was no. This fact weighed heavy in my thoughts, to the point where once I got back to the waiting room, I didn't even bother picking up one of the outdated magazines. And when my father finally appeared, and asked me if I was ready to go home, I agreed without a second's hesitation.

In contrast to the trip there, our ride home was pretty silent. My dad looked so worn-out after his appointment, he hadn't even tried to drive; instead he just tossed me the keys once we made it to the parking lot. We had kept up a conversation for the first few miles, but then I noticed the pauses in my dad's responses getting longer and longer. I'd look over and see that his head was resting against the seat, his eyelids fluttering closed before opening once again. By the time we got on the highway that would take us back to Lake Phoenix, I glanced over to change lanes and noticed that my dad was fully asleep, his eyes closed and head tipped back, mouth slightly open. This was unusual to the point of being shocking, because my father wasn't a napper. Though I knew he'd been sleeping more than normal lately, I couldn't remember a time when I'd seen him nap—especially not like this, not in the afternoon. It made me feel panicky, somehow, even though I couldn't have said why, and I wanted more than anything to put on some music, drown this feeling out a little. But, not wanting to wake my dad, I hadn't turned on the radio, and had just driven in silence, punctuated only by my father's low, even breathing.

As we crossed into Lake Phoenix, my dad's cell phone rang, startling both of us, the sound of his ringtone suddenly very loud in the quiet car. My dad jerked awake, his head snapping forward. "What?" he asked, and I hated to hear the confusion in his voice, the vulnerability in it. "What's that?"

I reached down for the phone in the cupholder, but he got there first, answering the call and smoothing his hand over his always-neat hair, as though trying to make sure he hadn't gotten too unkempt while he'd been sleeping. I could tell in a second that it was my mother, and after their brief conversation, my dad seemed more composed, and much more himself, his voice no longer thick with sleep when he hung up and turned to me.

"Your mother requested we pick up a few things for dinner tonight," he said, "and I just realized that we haven't been to Jane's this year. I for one feel like we've been skimping on the dessert this summer." There were still eleven oatmeal cookies in the fridge, but I didn't mention those. The one chocolate chip had been divided into five equal pieces among us, and the rest had sat untouched.

I glanced at the clock and saw that it was almost four, definitely verging into what my mother would consider the dinner-spoiling hour. But my dad and I had a tradition of getting ice cream and keeping it a secret—like when I was younger and he would pick me up from wherever I'd tried to run away to. "Really?" I asked, and my dad nodded.

"Just don't tell your mom," he said. "Otherwise, I'll be facing a *rocky road*."

I couldn't help laughing at that. "I don't know," I replied, as I pulled into a spot along Main Street. "She might be in a *good humor* about it."

My dad smiled in appreciation. "Nice," he said.

We parted ways as he headed to PocoMart and Henson's Produce, and I walked toward Sweet Baby Jane's. It was a tiny shop with a sky-blue awning, the name printed across it in curly white type. There were two benches on either side of the entrance, a necessity because the space had only room for the counter and a single table. Maybe because of the in-betweenness of the hour, Jane's didn't look very busy. There were just two boys who appeared to be around Gelsey's age, eating cones on one of the benches, their bikes tossed in a heap to the left of them. It was rare to see Jane's this deserted— at night, after dinner, the benches would be packed, the crowd spilling out along Main Street.

As I pulled open the door and stepped inside, a blast of air-conditioning and nostalgia hit me. The store hadn't changed much from what I remembered; same single table, same painted signs listing the flavors and toppings. But apparently time hadn't totally passed Jane's by, as there was now a list of frozen yogurts, and many more sugar-free options than I had remembered before.

I didn't need to ask what my father wanted. His ice cream order had never changed—a cup with one scoop of pralines & cream and one scoop of rum raisin. I got one scoop coconut and one scoop raspberry in a waffle cone, which had been my ice cream of choice the last time I'd been there. I paid and, finding my hands full with the cup and cone, was pushing open the door with my back. I was about to take my first bite when I heard someone say, "Hold on, I've got it." The door was held open for me, and I turned and suddenly found myself looking right into the green eyes of Henry Crosby.

By this point, I should have just been expecting it. It probably would have been more surprising if I *hadn't* bumped into him. I smiled and, before I could stop myself, I was quoting something I'd heard my father say, a line from his favorite movie. "Of all the gin joints, in the all the world," I said. "You walk into mine." Henry frowned, and I realized in that moment that of course he didn't know what I was talking about. I barely knew what I was talking about. "Sorry," I explained hurriedly. "It's a quote. From a movie. And I guess I should have said ice-cream parlors. . . ." I heard my voice trail off. I wasn't entirely sure what a gin joint even was. Why had I felt the need to say anything at all?

"It's okay," Henry said. "I got what you were going for." His dark hair was sticking up in the back, and he was wearing a faded blue T-shirt that looked so soft I had a sudden impulse to reach out and rub the cotton between my fingers. I didn't do this, of course, and took a small step back, just to remove the temptation.

"So," I said, grasping for something to say, but not coming up with much. "Ice cream, huh?" I felt my cheeks get hot as soon as I said it, and I glanced toward the car, wondering if my dad was finished at Henson's and I'd be able to use this as an excuse to leave.

"Don't tell me," Henry said, nodding at my rapidly melting cone. "Raspberry and coconut? Still?"

I stared at him. "I can't believe you remember that."

"Elephant," he said. "I told you."

"Ah," I said. I felt the first cold drip hit my fingers clutching the cone. My ice cream was melting fast, and since I was holding my dad's ice cream in my other hand, I couldn't do anything to stop it. But somehow, I felt weird about licking my cone in front of Henry, especially since he didn't have any ice cream himself. "So," I said, trying to ignore the second, then third drips, "how did that even start? Who first thought that elephants would be good at remembering things?"

"I don't know," Henry said with a shrug and a small smile. "Who decided owls were wise?"

"My brother could probably tell you that," I said. "I'll ask him."

"Great," Henry said with a small laugh. "Sounds like a plan." He stuck his hands in his pockets, and I felt my eyes drawn to his arm, and sure enough, I could see it—the faint white scar by his wrist. I knew it well—he'd scraped it against the daggerboard when he'd swum under my boat, in the boys vs. girls tipping war that had raged the summer we were eleven. I'd touched it the first time he held my hand, in the darkness of the Outpost's movie theater.

With this memory flooding through me, I looked at him, and took a breath to say what I should have said right away. That I was sorry, that I had never meant to hurt him, that I shouldn't have left with no explanation. "So," I said, as my heart started to beat a little harder and my sticky hand gripped my cone, "Henry. I—"

"Sorry about that! Parking took forever." A very pretty blond girl, about my age, was walking up to Henry. Her hair was up in one of those perfectly messy knots, and she was already deeply tan. I suddenly realized that this must have been the blond girl my mother was talking about. Henry's girlfriend. I knew that there was absolutely no logic in me feeling proprietary toward someone who I had dated when I was twelve. But even so, I felt a hot stab of jealousy in my chest as I watched her hand the car keys to him, their fingers brushing briefly.

"I want moose tracks!" Davy Crosby was running up, wearing the same moccasins I'd noticed in the woods. He spotted me and his exuberant expression turned sullen. Clearly, he was still holding a grudge about the bird-scaring.

The girl smiled at Davy and rested her hand on his shoulder

before he wriggled away. I watched this interaction, trying to keep my expression neutral. So she was close with Henry's brother, too. Not that I cared. Why should I?

"Did you know your ice cream's melting?" Davy asked me. I looked down at my cone and saw that, in fact, things were getting a little dire, and melted raspberry—of course, it really *couldn't* have been the coconut—was covering my hand.

"Right," I said, lifting up the cone, which actually just let the ice cream run down my wrist. "I caught that, actually."

"Sorry, Taylor—were you saying something?" Henry asked.

I looked at him and just thought about doing it now, saying I was sorry and getting it over with. Since we'd come back, I was feeling guilty about that summer in a way I'd never really had to face when we were in Connecticut. I'd even had to turn the stuffed penguin around in my closet, since it always seemed to be looking at me accusingly. "I was just going to say that . . . that I was really . . ." I trailed off, well aware that I had two extra audience members. I tried to go on, but found that I'd lost my nerve. "Nothing," I finally said. "Never mind." I felt the girl's eyes on me, and I saw her gaze travel to my arm, where the drips had gotten even worse, forming a small puddle next to my feet where they were landing on the ground. "I should go," I said, not waiting—or wanting—to be introduced to this girl who was clearly with Henry, and who was probably wondering why I was intruding on their time.

Henry took a breath, like he was about to say something, but then just glanced at the girl and remained silent.

"I'll see you," I said quickly, and to nobody in particular. I walked away from Jane's fast, not meeting Henry's eye, and headed down the street toward the car. I hadn't made it very far when my dad came out of Henson's and started down the street toward me, a paper sack under one arm.

"Hey," he said when we got within earshot of each other. "I thought I was meeting you there."

"No," I said quickly, since the last thing I wanted to do was eat ice cream on the Jane's benches next to Henry and his girlfriend and his brother, especially after I'd so thoroughly embarrassed myself. "Why don't we eat it in the car? Jane's is pretty busy right now."

My dad glanced over at Jane's—which couldn't have been more obviously empty —and then at me, where I saw him taking in the dripping mess I had turned into. "I've got a better idea," he said.

We ended up at the beach, which was only a few minutes' drive from Main Street, sitting at one of the picnic tables, and looking out at the water. I'd cleaned myself up with the paper towels in the backseat of the car, and some hand sanitizer I found in the glove compartment, and now I no longer looked like I was going to pose an ice-cream hazard to everything I came in contact with. Despite the fact it was getting late, the beach was crowded, a line forming at the snack bar.

As I looked over, I found myself wondering if it was just Lucy working, or if Elliot was on duty as well. As though sensing this, my dad rotated his cup, searching for the ideal bite, as he asked me, "How are you liking it, working here?"

I realized this was my opening, the moment to tell him that while I'd really given it a shot, it just wasn't going to be a great fit. And maybe after I mentioned it to him, I could go over to the administrative offices, quit, and have this whole thing resolved before dinner. "So here's the thing," I said. My dad raised his eyebrows and took a bite of his (nearly finished) ice cream. "I'm sure that working at the beach is a great experience. But I just don't think it's necessarily the right fit for me now. And maybe, like Warren, I should really be focusing on academics. . . ." I trailed off as I ran out of excuses and realized that I didn't have any siblings or distractions to interrupt me—just my dad, looking at me with a level gaze, like he was seeing right through me.

"Tell me, kid," he said after finishing his last bite and setting his cup aside, "did I ever tell you how much I hated law school when I first started?"

"No," I said, not even having to think about it. My dad rarely talked about himself, so most of the personal stories I'd heard either came from my mom, or my grandfather, when he was visiting.

"I did," he said. He reached across with his spoon for what was left of my ice cream, and I tilted my cone toward him. "I'm not like your brother. Things didn't come so easily to me in school. I had to work like hell just to get in to law school. And once I was there, I thought I'd made the biggest mistake of my life. Wanted to get out of there as soon as possible."

"But you stuck it out," I said, feeling like I knew where the story was going.

"I stuck it out," he confirmed. "And it turned out I really loved the law, once I stopped being scared I was going to make a mistake. And if I hadn't stayed with it, I never would have met your mom."

That was one story I did know—how my parents had met at a diner on the Upper West Side of Manhattan, my dad a third-year student at Columbia Law, my mom having just finished a performance of *The Nutcracker*.

"Right," I said, feeling like my window to get out of the job was rapidly closing. "But in this case . . ."

"Is there something wrong with the job? A real problem you have with it?" My dad reached toward the cone with his spoon again, and I just handed it to him to finish, having lost my appetite for ice cream. It wasn't like I could really tell my dad that it was because my former BFF was being mean to me.

"No," I finally said.

My dad smiled at me, his blue eyes—the ones I'd gotten from him, the ones nobody else in our family had—crinkling at the corners. "In that case," he said, like the matter had been decided, "you'll

morgan matson

stick it out. And maybe something good will come of it."

I doubted that entirely, but I also knew when I'd been beat. I looked at the snack bar for a moment, dreading the fact that I'd now have to return there tomorrow. "Maybe so," I said trying to sound as enthusiastic as possible—which, even I could hear, wasn't all that enthusiastic.

My dad laughed and ruffled my hair with his hand, the way he always used to do when I was little. "Come on," he said. He stood up, wincing slightly, and tossed away the ice-cream cup. "Let's go home."

After dinner, out of nowhere, it started to rain. It caught me off guard, and seeing the world that had only been sunny and warm transformed by a sudden thunderstorm was jarring, a reminder of just how quickly things could change.

I ducked under the screened-in porch gratefully, wiping the droplets from my face and kicking off my flip-flops in the pile of sandals that inevitably accumulated by the door. I had taken the trash out to the bearbox, thinking that with an umbrella I wouldn't get too wet, only to have the rain pick up in intensity and the wind pick up in speed the second I stepped outside.

"You okay?" Warren asked from his seat at the table, looking up from his book at me.

"Just half-drowned," I said, taking the seat across from him. It was the two of us on the porch. My parents were inside reading, and

Gelsey, who always denied emphatically that she was afraid of thunderstorms, had nevertheless left for her bedroom at the first crack of thunder and was apparently in for the night, wearing my dad's noise-canceling headphones that were much too big for her.

Warren went back to his book and I pulled my knees up, hugging them as I looked at the rain coming down in sheets. I'd never minded thunderstorms, and had always liked watching them from the screened-in porch—you were inside but also outside, able to see each flash of lightning and hear each crack of thunder, but were also dry and covered. As I listened to the rain on the roof, I suddenly worried about the dog, who I hadn't seen in a few days. I hoped that he was back where he belonged, and if not, that he'd had the sense to take shelter from the rain. Somehow I doubted it. I'd gotten used to the little dog, and I didn't like to think about him caught out in a storm.

"Mom said that the Crosbys are living next door," Warren said, carefully highlighting a passage and looking up at me. "Henry and Derek."

"Davy," I corrected automatically.

"You didn't *mention* that," Warren said, his tone of voice singsong, designed, I knew, to bait me. I was suddenly very envious of Gelsey and her noise-canceling headphones.

"So?" I said, as I crossed and then uncrossed my legs, wondering why we were even talking about this.

"Have you seen him yet?" Warren was continuing to highlight, and if you didn't know him, you'd think he had no idea that he was torturing me, and enjoying it, which he absolutely was.

"A couple times," I said, raking my fingers through my wet hair. "I don't know. It's been weird," I said, thinking of all our encounters, not one of them suited for a real conversation or an apology.

"Weird?" Warren repeated. "Because you two dated when you were . . . twelve?" He smirked, shaking his head.

"Because—" I started. A huge crash of thunder sounded, making both of us jump. Warren dropped his highlighter, and as it rolled across the table, I reached out and grabbed it, twirling it between my fingers.

"Because?" Warren prompted, glancing over at me. He motioned for me to give him his highlighter back, and I pretended not to see.

"I don't know," I said, a little irritably. I didn't want to talk about this. And I certainly didn't want to talk about it with my *brother*. "Why do you even care?" I finally asked. "And since when do we talk about stuff like this?"

"We don't," Warren said. He shrugged, and in a patronizing voice, he continued, "It's just obviously an issue for you, so I was giving you an opening. That's all."

I knew that there was probably no point to this. I should just walk away and let it go. But there was something in my brother's expression that seemed to indicate that he knew *so* much more than me. And about some—if not most—things, this was true. But not everything. Warren had never had much of a social life, preferring to spend weekends studying and working on his various projects. He'd never had a girlfriend, that I had been aware of. He had gone to his senior prom, but with his study partner, who was pretty much the female version of Warren. They'd said they wanted to examine the ritual as a cultural experiment. After the prom, they had had cowritten a paper on it for their A.P. Psychology class that had won a national award.

"You don't know what you're talking about," I said. My brother's head swiveled over to me, probably because this was a sentence he was so unused to hearing. I knew I should stop, but even as I recognized this, I heard myself keep going, my voice with a snide edge to it that I hated. "You have to have been in a relationship to have a breakup."

Even in the dim lighting of the screened-in porch, I could see my brother's face flush a little, and, like I knew I would, I regretted saying it.

"I'll have you know," Warren said stiffly, flipping the pages in his textbook much faster than he could read them, "that I have been putting most of my focus into my academics."

"I know," I said quickly, trying to smooth this over, wishing I hadn't said anything.

"There's no need to get involved with people who aren't going to turn out to matter," he continued in the same tone of voice.

I had been about to agree and head inside, but something that

Warren had just said was bothering me. "But how do you know?" I asked.

He looked up at me and frowned. "Know what?"

"You said you didn't want to waste your time on people who aren't going to matter," I said, and he nodded. "But how do you know they're not going to matter? Unless you give it a shot?"

Warren opened his mouth to reply, but nothing followed. I could practically see his brain working furiously, his future-lawyer logic churning through answers. He took a breath to say something but then let it out. "I don't know," he finally said.

I had planned on going in, but I changed my mind as I looked at my brother, sitting in the semidarkness, reading books he wouldn't even need for months or years. I slid the highlighter back across the table at him and he gave me a brief smile before picking it up. I settled back into my seat as he started slowly going through the book again, highlighting the relevant passages, making sure that he wasn't missing anything important, as all around us, the rain continued to fall.

chapter thirteen
five summers earlier

IT WASN'T A DATE. THAT WAS WHAT I'D BEEN TELLING MYSELF EVER since Henry had asked me, the day we'd walked our bikes home from the pool with our wet towels slung around our shoulders. We were just seeing a movie together. It was not a big deal.

Which didn't explain why I was so nervous now, sitting next to him in the dark of the Outpost theater. I was barely paying attention to the movie at all, because I was fully aware of his presence next to me, every time he shifted in the red velvet seat, every time he took a breath. I was more conscious than I ever had been in my life of the movie theater armrest between us—wondering if I should rest my arm on it, wondering if he would, wishing that he would reach across it and take my hand.

The summer without Lucy was turning out to be less painful than I'd expected, mostly because of Henry. We'd spent the first few weeks hanging out, long afternoons together at the beach or the pool, or in the woods, when Henry needed to show me some rock or insect that he promised would "blow my mind." Whenever it rained, and nobody was willing to take us to the Stroud Mall, or bowling at Pocono Lanes, we would hang out in his treehouse. Sometimes Elliott would come, and we'd play the three-person poker game he'd invented. I didn't do as well at this as with other card games, because Henry, for whatever reason, always seemed to know when I was bluffing, and wouldn't even reveal to me what my tell was. Unlike with Lucy, being friends with Henry meant that there wasn't any makeup-swapping, watching of cheerleading movies, or candy-sharing going on. (Henry, I'd discovered, was ruthless, and claimed not to be able to taste the difference among any of the Skittle colors.) I also no longer had anyone to endlessly pore over the library's back issues of *Seventeen* magazine with, studying each page carefully. Despite that, Henry and I had been having fun.

But something had started to change last week, on the lake's wooden float. It was big enough across that almost ten people could be on it at once (although the lifeguards blew their whistles when more than five people were on it at a time, and always if you tried to push people in). We'd been challenging each other to races that had gotten more and more complicated as the afternoon went on. The last one—swim from the raft to shore, run across the beach, around the concession stand, back across the beach, and swim back to the raft—had left us both exhausted. We'd been lying on the raft, getting our breath back, but now I was pretty sure that Henry had fallen asleep.

To check, I'd been squeezing out the water from the bottom of my braid on him, trying to get him to wake up. And either he really was asleep, or he was really good at pretending, because he wasn't moving. Since my braid was pretty well wrung out, I dipped my hand into the water and started letting the drops fall from my fingers onto him, but Henry didn't even flinch. Figuring he must actually be sleeping, and feeling a little bad for tormenting him, I started to brush some of the water droplets off his face. I was brushing one off his forehead, when his eyes opened and he looked at me. We just froze that way for a moment, looking at each other, and I noticed for the first time what nice eyes he had. And suddenly, out of nowhere, I wanted him to kiss me.

The thought was so unexpected that I immediately moved away from him on the raft, and we started talking—both of us a little too loudly—about other things. But something had shifted, and I think we both felt it, because a few days later, walking our bikes home, he'd asked me if I wanted to see a movie, just me and him.

Now, sitting in the darkness of the theater, I concentrated on facing forward, trying to take deep breaths and calm my racing heart. Even though I hadn't been following the story in the least, I could tell that things were beginning to wind down. Just when I could feel my disappointment start to take hold, the stomach-plunging sadness that I'd gotten so excited for nothing, Henry reached across the armrest and held my hand, intertwining his fingers with mine.

In that moment, I knew that things had changed. Henry and I were, in fact, on my very first date. And we were no longer just simply friends.

chapter fourteen

"I'LL HAVE . . ." THE WOMAN IN THE BRIGHT PINK VELOUR HOODIE paused, squinting up at the snack bar menu. She drummed her fingers on the counter, deliberating. Even though it was cloudy and overcast and had been all morning, she had a bright white line of sunblock covering her nose. "A Diet Pepsi, small fries, and a cup of ice," she finally said.

I turned back to where Elliot was standing by the grill, the spatula hanging slack by his side, all his attention focused on a thick paperback in his hands. "Fries!" I yelled back at him, and he nodded, setting the book aside. As I punched the woman's order into the register, I explained, "We only have Diet Coke. And there's a fifteen-cent cup charge for ice."

She shrugged. "Fine."

I glanced down at the register for a second, making sure I'd remembered to add the tax, which I hadn't done for the first three days on the job. When Fred found out, he'd turned even redder than normal, and had to spend a day away from the fish, going over the receipts in the office and muttering. "Five ninety-five." The woman handed me six, and I placed it in the register and slid a nickel across the counter to her, which she dropped in our nearly empty tip jar. "Thanks," I said. "Should be ready in five."

I turned to the soda jets behind me and started filling her cup, waiting until the foam died down before hitting the button again. I'd only been at the job about a week, but I seemed to have gotten the basics down.

I had decided that I would rather suffer Lucy's wrath than disappoint my father, and was trying to make the best of the job. I got the hang of the scary industrial coffeemaker, essential for the senior-citizen power walkers who stopped by the beach at nine thirty sharp for decaf after their "workout." Through trial and error, I figured out the fryer—and, as a result, now had a series of small burns on my arm, from where the grease splattered until I learned to avoid it. I learned the basics of the grill, but hadn't had much chance to test them out yet.

"It's the beach," Elliot told me on my third day, when there was a lull in customers and he was showing me how the grill worked. "And the thing about food at the beach is that sand gets everywhere. And who wants sand in their cheeseburger?"

I thought about it, and made a face. "Not me."

"Not anybody," he said. "Trust me." After working with Elliot for a few days I'd found, to my surprise, that I liked him. I'd been worried that he would side with Lucy, shunning me out of loyalty to her. But he wasn't taking sides, which I was grateful for. He was patient with me when showing me the ropes, and was easy to talk to, even if he could be a little intense, especially about what he called "hard sci-fi." Already I'd heard far more than I ever wanted to know about some show that seemed to feature an evil Muppet as the villain.

"See that?" he asked, flipping a burger with a large metal spatula, then twirling it in a way that made me think he may have watched *Cocktail* recently. I tried to give him what I hoped was an impressed smile. "People will get fries, because they're protected in their little fry container. But we serve the burgers on plates. And if you're going to set your plate down on your towel, you're going to get sand in your burger. It's a given."

So I learned how to make burgers, even though I probably wouldn't need to do it that often. I learned how much ice to put in the fountain sodas, and how to work the register, and how to open the snack bar in the morning and close it at night. But the biggest thing I learned was that Lucy could still hold a grudge.

I'd known this about her back when we were friends, of course. She had famously been on the outs with Michele Hoffman for years before someone asked them point-blank what they were fighting about and neither one had been able to remember. Lucy had always had a very distinct sense of right and wrong, but for the first time,

morgan matson

I was on the "wrong" side of things. She pretty much ignored me, giving me instructions, when she had to, through Elliot.

It also became clear after a few shifts that she had gone a little boy-crazy. She flirted outrageously with every passably cute male customer, and had collected more guys' numbers than I would have believed possible, had I not been a silent witness to it. Back when we'd been friends, Lucy and I had both been tongue-tied and awkward around boys. And despite the few relationships I'd had, I still sometimes felt that way. But Lucy had clearly gotten over any hint of shyness sometime in the last five years. Her camaraderie with Elliot and her friendliness toward the (particularly male) customers made our silent standoff all the more apparent. When it was just the two of us working, there was total silence, as she didn't speak to me unless absolutely necessary. She either busied herself with her phone or read magazines, angling them away from me so that I couldn't read over her shoulder or see what she put down as her answers on the *Cosmo* quiz.

And I'd just wipe down the already-clean counters and look up at the clock, trying to calculate how much time was left before I could go home. But there was something sad about the silence that was between us whenever we worked together, especially considering that when we were younger, when she'd been my friend, we had never run out of things to say to each other. If my mother would comment on how chatty we were, Lucy would always say the same thing—that we didn't see each other for most of the year, and that we had nine months' worth of stuff to catch up on. And now, in contrast, there was silence. Silence so palpable, it was like you could feel it in the air. When I worked with Lucy, I'd find myself so desperate for conversation that I'd go down to the lifeguard chair on my breaks to try to talk to Leland. And Leland wasn't exactly the world's finest conversationalist, as most of his responses—no matter what you said—usually consisted of some variation of "totally," "no way," and "I hear that noise."

There were two other lifeguards, Rachel and Ivy, who rotated shifts with him. But they were both in college, and tended to hang out mostly with each other, stopping by the snack bar only when they wanted a bottle of water or a Diet Coke. Even though they weren't overly friendly, their presence was reassuring, because I was still not convinced that someone as spacey as Leland ever should have been put in charge of guarding people's lives.

I placed the woman's diet soda, still fizzing, on the counter in front of me, and snapped on the plastic lid. I put the cup of ice next to it and slid them both across the counter from her just as Elliot dinged the bell to let me know the fries were ready. I picked up the container, warm, with that hot-fry smell that made my stomach rumble, even though it was only eleven in the morning, salted them generously, and placed them next to the woman's drink. She was talking on her cell as she picked them up, but she nodded and mouthed *Thanks* as she headed back to her towel.

I looked out at the mostly empty beach and shifted from foot to foot, trying to get some warmth back into my extremities. It was a cloudy, overcast day, and we'd had only about three customers so far. Lucy was working as well, but had left to make a phone call about half an hour before and hadn't come back yet. I ran my hands up and down my arms, wishing that I'd worn a sweatshirt over my uniform T-shirt that morning, like Elliot, Lucy, and even Leland had been smart enough to do.

If I'd been biking to work, like Elliot and Lucy did, I undoubtedly would have worn a sweatshirt. But I was still coming to work by car, despite the fact that my mother had told me repeatedly that it was inconvenient to have one car stranded at the beach parking lot all day long. And even though my dad had gotten my mother's old bike ready for me to ride, I'd left it so far to sit in the garage. I wasn't sure if it was possible to forget entirely how to ride a bike, but I was in no hurry to find out.

"Cold?" I looked over and saw Elliot pushing himself up to sit on the counter next to me.

"Just a little," I said. I took a sip of the hot chocolate I'd made for myself that morning, but found it was no longer warm enough to really help.

"There's probably something in there," Elliot said as he pointed under the counter.

"I don't know," I said doubtfully as I pulled out the lost and found box. I'd become quite familiar with the box in the week I'd been working there. Even though it was still early in the summer, the cardboard box was already full to the gills. I looked through it, a little amazed at the things that people left behind. I mean, how could you leave the beach and not realize you were no longer in possession of your bathing suit top? Or your left, men's size eleven, flip-flop? The only warm thing I found in the bin was a hideous white sweatshirt that read, *Teachers Do It With Class!* across the front in green script.

Elliot nodded approvingly. "Nice," he said.

It was the opposite of nice, but at that moment the wind picked up, and two of the remaining beach stragglers got to their feet and started folding up their blanket. I shivered again, then pulled the sweatshirt over my head.

"So I heard you saw Henry," Elliot said.

I froze, wondering if it would be possible to just stay like that, until I figured out what to say. I didn't think I could hide inside a sweatshirt, though, without appearing totally crazy. I pulled my head through the neck hole and smoothed my hair down, willing myself not to blush but feeling that I nevertheless was. I don't know why it hadn't occurred to me that Elliot and Henry would still be friends. I wondered which of the embarrassing encounters he'd told Elliot about—or if he'd given him the complete rundown. "Um, yeah," I said, busying myself with putting the lost and found box back under the counter. "A couple times."

I looked at Elliot, willing him to tell me what Henry had said about these meetings without having to ask him. "So . . ." I started, then stopped when I realized I had no idea how to ask this without sounding needy or pathetic—and with the added knowledge that this conversation might make its way right back to Henry. "Never mind," I muttered, leaning back against the counter and taking a big sip of my now-cold chocolate.

"I think you've thrown him for a loop," Elliot said, shaking his head. "And that is a guy who does *not* do well when thrown for a loop."

I nodded as though this was perfectly understandable, all the while wondering what, exactly, this meant, and wishing I could ask Elliot more directly. Before I could say anything, though, two things happened almost at the same time—Lucy breezed in through the employee door, and Fred's red face appeared at the window.

"My God," Lucy said. "I'm *freezing!*" She glanced at me, then looked at my sweatshirt and raised her eyebrows just as Fred dropped his tackle box on the counter, loud enough to make us all jump.

"Hi, Fred," Elliot said, as he scrambled off the counter (where we weren't supposed to sit) and, maybe in an attempt to look busy, started straightening the display of chips.

"Hi," Lucy said, sliding her phone into the back pocket of her jeans and leaning casually against the counter, as though she'd been there all along. "How's the fishing?"

"Not so good," Fred said with a sigh. "I think they're onto me." He pointed at me. "Are you ready for Friday?"

I just stared at him, waiting for these words to make sense. "Friday?" I finally asked.

"Movies Under the Stars," Fred said, and I could hear the capital letters in his voice as he said it. "I told you on your first day. You'll be running it. First one's this Friday." He dropped a stack of posters on the counter. Movies Under the Stars were movies shown on the beach once a month, with a large screen set up at the water's edge on the sand. People brought blankets and chairs and, like the name suggested, watched movies under the stars. I'd gone a few times when I was younger, but usually they were old movies that I'd had very little interest in.

I looked down at the poster for longer than it took for me to read the title of the movie—*What About Bob?*—and the date and time. Fred had mentioned that I'd be doing something with this, but I had expected that I'd have more of a heads-up than three days. "Okay," I said slowly. "So, what exactly do I have to do?"

"Well, we're in a little bit of a situation after last summer," Fred said, and both he and Lucy looked at Elliot, who turned bright red.

"You let me pick the movies," he said, defensive. "If you had wanted specific movies, you should have let me know."

"Attendance was very, very low by the end," Fred said. "*Very* low. So we're looking for movies that will bring in a crowd. *Family-friendly* movies," he said, glaring at Elliot. "The first one's already set, but you'll pick the next two. And help put up posters around town. Everyone can help with that," he added, as he pushed the stack across the counter.

"Oh," I said. This didn't sound so bad. "Sure."

"Good," Fred said, picking up his tackle box. He looked out at the nearly empty beach and shook his head. "We certainly don't need three people working when there's no customers. Two of you can go home, if you want. I'll leave it to you to choose." He nodded at us, then turned and headed toward the parking lot.

As soon as he was gone, Lucy turned toward me and Elliot. "Not it," she said, quickly.

Before I could even draw breath, Elliot echoed her. "Not it."

I shrugged. "I guess that means I'm staying." I actually didn't mind, since working by myself would basically be the same as working with Lucy—just as silent, but less stressful.

"Don't sweat the movie thing," Elliot said as Lucy passed him, heading toward the row of hooks where we all kept our things. "I promise it's no big deal."

"I won't," I said. "It sounds doable. But, um, what happened last year?"

Elliot blushed again, and Lucy returned, looking at her phone as she said, "Fred put Elliot in charge of choosing the movies." This was the most direct thing she'd said to me since our initial confrontation, and so I just nodded, not wanting to upset whatever delicate balance had brought this about.

"He said 'summer movies,'" Elliot said, his voice becoming defensive again. "He said 'beach-themed.' So . . ."

"He picked *Jaws*," Lucy said, still looking at her phone and not me, shaking her head. "To be shown at the beach, right near the water. One kid had to be carried out, he was crying so loud."

Elliot cleared his throat. "Anyway," he said loudly, "the point is that—"

"And then," Lucy continued, glancing at me only briefly before looking at her phone again, "he picks some horrible sci-fi that nobody's ever heard of. . . ."

"*Dune* is a classic," Elliot said hotly, though I noticed that he was blushing more than ever. "And there are no sharks it in, which was all Fred specifically requested."

"Sand monsters," Lucy said flatly. "Again . . . we were on a beach. Again, children carried out crying."

"But the lesson we can glean from this," Elliot started. "Is that—"

"And movie number three?" Lucy said, shaking her head. "To show to an audience of kids and their parents?"

"Listen," Elliot said, turning to me, as though pleading his case, "since my last two choices were apparently unacceptable, I went online, looking for the most popular summer movie. And still, apparently, it didn't work."

I turned to Lucy, who was shaking her head again. *"Dirty Dancing,"* she said. "It didn't go over too well with the mothers of the six-year-olds."

"So," Elliot said, with the air of someone who very much wanted to change the subject, "when you have to pick, just check with Fred first. And keep your intro short, and you should be fine."

"Intro?" I asked. I could feel my palms start to sweat. "What do you mean?"

"See you," Lucy called, giving a backward wave to the snack bar in general as she slung her purse over her shoulder and headed out the door. Elliot watched her leave, and then continued watching the door for a moment after she'd gone.

"Elliot?" I prompted, and he turned back to me quickly, adjusting his glasses, something I'd noticed he did when he was flustered or embarrassed about something. "What intro?"

"Right," he said. "I promise it's no big deal. Just stand up before it starts, say a few things about the movie, tell people how long the snack bar is open. Easy."

I nodded and tried to smile at him when he left, but my heart was pounding hard, and I wondered if this would finally give me the loophole I needed to quit. I'd hated public speaking for as long as I could remember. I was fine speaking to one or two people, but as soon as the numbers got big, I turned into a wreck—stammering, sweating, shaking. As a result, I tended to avoid it whenever possible. I really didn't know how I was going to get up and talk in front of a group of people just three days from now.

The rest of the afternoon crawled by, with only two more customers, both of whom wanted hot beverages. When the hand on the clock above the microwave started hovering near five, I began the routine of shutting the snack bar down for the day—wiping down the counters, totaling the register and collecting the receipts, cleaning and turning off the coffeemaker. I was just about to pull down the grate and lock it when I heard, "Wait! Are you still open?"

A moment later, a red-faced (though not in Fred's league) middle-aged man came running up to the counter, carrying a little boy piggyback. "Sorry about that," he wheezed, as he set his son down and leaned on the counter for a moment, taking a breath. "We were trying to get here before five." The kid, his head just clearing the top of the counter, regarded me solemnly. "Curtis is missing his shovel, and I think you keep the lost and found here?"

"Oh," I said, a little surprised but nonetheless relieved that they didn't want me to turn all the equipment back on and make a milk shake or some fries. "Sure." I pulled the box out and set it on the counter.

The father and son sifted through the items, and, as I watched, the kid's face broke into a huge smile as he triumphantly lifted a red plastic shovel from the box. "Thanks so much," the dad said to me as he easily slung his son up on his back again. "I don't know what he was going to do without it."

I just nodded and smiled as they went, glancing into the box once more as I put it away. It struck me that each of these items, discarded and left behind, had once been special, important to the people that they belonged to. And even though I couldn't see it, all it would take was for someone to find them again for them to be restored. I took off the *Teachers Do It With Class!* sweatshirt and folded it carefully before placing it back in the box and closing up for the night.

chapter fifteen

"I CAN'T DO THIS." I STOOD OUTSIDE THE SNACK BAR, NEXT TO Elliot, staring at the crowds of people who had assembled on the beach, facing the screen at the water's edge, spreading out blankets and towels in the fading light. Overhead, the stars were beginning to emerge, and the moon was almost full, hanging over the lake and doubling itself in the reflection. It would have been a perfect night to see a movie outdoors. But, instead, it appeared that I was going to have an aneurysm.

"You'll be fine," Elliot said, in what I'm sure he thought was a reassuring voice, but was actually just his regular voice, only deeper. He turned to Lucy, who was frowning at the popcorn machine we were using for the night. "Won't she?"

"Okay, I have no idea how to work this," Lucy said, poking at the metal contraption at the top. She looked at Elliot. "Do you?"

"Seriously," I said, and I could hear that my voice was a little strangled. I leaned back against the counter for support, and even though I could practically feel Lucy rolling her eyes at me, I no longer cared. I was pretty sure I was about to pass out. Which didn't seem like a bad idea, considering the circumstances. If I passed out, I wouldn't have to introduce the movie.

"Are you okay?" Elliot asked, peering at me. "You look a little green."

"Taylor!" I looked across the sand to see my mother waving at me. She had set up camp right in the center of the beach, on our enormous white beach blanket. Gelsey was talking to my dad, who was sprawled out on the blanket—he believed that beach chairs were for wimps and the elderly. Warren was next to him reading a book, aiming a flashlight at the text. They had all insisted on coming, even though I had tried to dissuade them. It was actually a little embarrassing to hear my mom going on about it, and it only served to highlight how few opportunities I'd given my parents to brag about me. We'd all been going to Gelsey's dance recitals forever, and it seemed like we were always attending some mock trial competition or ceremony where Warren was winning yet another award for excellence. But aside from the mandatory stuff, like junior-high graduation, I'd never really had an event of my own.

I waved back, wondering how much it would cost to bribe Warren to do this for me. He had no problem speaking in front of people, and had given his valedictorian address without even breaking a sweat.

"Did it come with instructions?" Elliot asked, leaning over to examine the popper that Lucy was still looking at dubiously.

"Can you do this for me?" I asked him, now desperate. "Because I think I'm about to collapse."

"No," Lucy said quickly, shaking her head. "Fred doesn't want him out there. In case, you know, people remember him from last summer and leave."

Since Fred was on a fishing trip, I didn't think he had to know about it, but I didn't mention that. I wasn't about to ask Lucy—I knew she would say no—so I just nodded and tried to swallow as I looked down at the note cards in my hands. I'd found out as much as I could about the movie online, but the neatly written, bullet-pointed list of facts no longer seemed very helpful.

Leland, our projectionist for the evening, ambled over. "So what's the plan?" he asked. "We ready to do this?"

I looked at the snack bar clock in a panic. I thought I had more time to figure out what I was going to say, and also remember how to breathe. But it was almost eight thirty. I caught Lucy's eye and she arched an eyebrow at me, her expression a challenge.

"Okay," I said, and part of me was wondering why I was saying that, since I really felt like at any moment I might throw up.

"Sweet," Leland said as he loped off to the makeshift projection booth at the other end of the beach.

"Good luck," Elliot said. He came with me as I started my slow walk across the beach. "Don't forget to tell people when the next

morgan matson

one is. And that the concession stand will only be open for another half an hour. Oh, and that they should turn all cellular devices off."

"Right," I murmured, my head swimming, and my heart pounding so hard that I was sure the people in the front row would be able to hear it.

"Go for it," Elliot prompted, giving me a small nudge when, a moment later, I still hadn't moved.

"Right," I repeated. I took a big breath and forced one foot in front of the other until I was standing in the center of the projection screen. "Hi," I started. But not many people were looking at me. I would have thought this would be reassuring, but it wasn't, because I knew it meant that I was going to have to keep talking, and more loudly. "Hi," I repeated, louder this time, and I saw heads turn toward me, expectant. From the center of the crowd, I saw my brother switch off his flashlight. "Um, I'm Taylor. Edwards. And I work at the snack bar." I looked down at the notes in my hands, which were shaking slightly, and I could feel panic start to rise, as I heard the silence stretch on. "Welcome to the movies. Under the stars," I finally managed to say. I looked up and saw just a sea of eyes staring back at me, and my panic increased. I could feel beads of sweat start to form on my forehead. "It's *What About Bob*, tonight. Which . . . Bill Murray," I said, seeing some of my bullet points and grabbing onto them. "1991. Old school. Comedy. Classic." I wanted nothing more than to flee, but for some horrible reason, I was also feeling like I was glued to the spot. From the direction of the snack bar, I could hear a faint *pop-pop-pop* and realized, somewhere in the part of my brain that was still functioning, that Lucy must have figured out the popcorn machine.

"So . . ." I looked at the crowd again, many of whom were now regarding me with skepticism, my family with alarm. And I saw, in the back near the projection booth, as clearly as if they had a spotlight shining on them, Henry and Davy. Henry was looking at me with an expression of pity that was somehow worse than Warren's look of horror. I looked down at my notes again, my vision blurring. I couldn't seem to make any words out, and I could feel the silence stretching on and on, and my panic growing, until I was pretty sure I was about to cry.

"So thanks so much for coming!" Miraculously, Elliot was by my side, smiling at the crowd like nothing was wrong. "Snack bar's only open for another thirty minutes, so don't forget to stop by for popcorn. And please turn off your cell phones. Enjoy the show!"

There was a faint smattering of applause, and a moment later, the FBI warning was flashing blue on the screen. Elliot pulled me away, toward the snack bar, and my legs were shaking so hard, I felt like I was about to fall over.

"I guess I should have listened to you when you said you weren't good at public speaking," Elliot said, shooting me a sympathetic look that was meant to make me feel better but somehow made everything worse. I knew I should be able to move on, laugh it off, at least let him know how grateful I was for the rescue. But instead, I could feel the shame creeping over me, and his acknowledgement of how terrible I had been wasn't helping.

"Thanks," I muttered, avoiding his gaze. I knew I needed to get out of there, and as fast as possible. "I just have to ... I'll be right back."

"Taylor?" I heard Elliot call after me, sounding puzzled, but I didn't care. I speed-walked past the people who were now laughing at Bill Murray's antics and headed straight for the parking lot. I'd just drive myself home, and in the morning, I would call Jillian and quit.

"Going somewhere?" I whipped around and saw Lucy standing by the Dumpsters, a garbage bag in her hand. She tossed the bag into the trash and then turned to face me, arms folded across her chest.

"No," I stammered, wondering why I felt so caught out, since I was going to quit in the morning. "I just ..."

"Because it would be a really shitty thing to do if you just left me and Elliot. Plus, isn't your family here?" Lucy was staring right at me, as if daring me to deny any of this. I couldn't help noticing that whenever she did decide to talk to me, it was generally to point out what a horrible person I was being. "But I'm sure that you were probably getting something from your car," she continued, dropping the lid of the Dumpster and letting it fall with a bang. "Otherwise, it would be awful if you took off and left, with no explanation, when people were waiting for you." Even in the dimness of the parking lot—

it was almost totally dark now—I could see the hurt in Lucy's expression, and I knew what she meant, and that she was no longer talking about what was happening now.

"I . . ." I started, and it was like every word was a challenge, like speaking them was going through an obstacle course. "I did a really bad job," I finally managed to say. "I don't know how I can go back there."

Lucy let out a long breath, and shook her head. "Taylor, it's okay," she said, and her voice was gentler than I'd heard it yet this summer. "Nobody cares. Nobody will even remember." She gave me a small smile, and then turned and strolled back to the concession stand. I looked at my car for a moment, but leaving no longer seemed like it would make me feel any better. In fact, I had the distinct impression that it would make me feel worse.

So I turned and walked back to the concession stand, ducking through the employee entrance. Elliot was ringing someone up for two sodas and a popcorn, and he smiled when he saw me. I busied myself straightening the cups, but it didn't seem like the customers even noticed me—never mind remembered me as the girl who thoroughly messed up the movie's introduction.

Lucy met my eye across the concession stand, where she was manning the popcorn machine, and she gave me a small nod, almost imperceptible unless you were watching for it.

· · ·

Half an hour later, we were locking up the snack bar, and all the people on the beach seemed to be having a good time. The picture had only slid out of focus twice so far, which Elliot told me was much better than Leland's track record the previous summer.

Lucy had disappeared a few minutes before, and now emerged from the bathroom wearing a jean miniskirt and even more eyeliner than usual. "Wow," Elliot said, as I yanked on the padlock to make sure it was clicked into place. "I mean, you know. Where are you, um . . . going?"

"Hot date," Lucy said, as her phone beeped. She pulled it out and smiled so wide at what she saw, she flashed the dimple in her cheek. "I'll see you guys," she said, meeting my eye for a moment before she turned and headed toward the parking lot, and I registered that I had been included, for the first time, in this farewell.

Elliot was still staring after Lucy, his expression wistful, and I yanked on the lock once again, even though it was clearly secured. "Are you going to stay and watch the rest of the movie?" I asked, and he turned back to me, adjusting his glasses hurriedly.

"No," he said. "I like to see a movie from the beginning. And I think I've missed too much."

I held up my note cards. "I have the plot here if you want to be filled in. Straight from Wikipedia."

Elliot gave me a faint smile at that. "Thanks anyway. I'll see you tomorrow, Taylor."

I nodded, and as I watched him go, realized that I would. That I was staying, that maybe for the first time ever, I hadn't gone running away when things got hard.

I held my flip-flops in my hand as I picked my way across the beach, ducking low to try and avoid blocking people's views. I reached my family's blanket and settled down into the spot next to my dad. My mom was sitting toward the front of the blanket, her back to me, next to Gelsey, who was stretching while she watched. Warren's book was forgotten next to him and he appeared utterly absorbed, his mouth hanging slightly open, his eyes glued to the screen. I dropped my shoes on the sand, and then sat down, brushing my hand over the blanket to make sure I hadn't tracked any sand onto it. When I had run out of stalling techniques, I looked over at my dad, his face illuminated by the moonlight and by the flickering light from the screen. But it wasn't judgmental or disappointed or any of the things I'd been afraid that I would see.

"You'll get 'em next time, kid," he said as he reached out and ruffled my hair. He nodded at the screen and smiled. "Have you seen this before? It's pretty funny." He turned back to the movie, laughing at the sight of Bill Murray strapped to the mast of a ship.

I leaned back against my hands and stretched out my legs in front of me, and turned my attention to the film. And by the time things were winding down, I was laughing out loud, along with everybody else.

morgan matson

chapter sixteen

"TAYLOR. RISE AND SHINE. UP AND ADAM."

I groaned, not only at my father's bad joke—when I was younger I'd misunderstood the phrase "up and at 'em" and had asked my father who this "Adam" character was, to his lasting enjoyment—but because it was a Sunday morning, it was my day off, and I wanted to spend it sleeping in. "No," I mumbled into my pillow.

"Come on," my father said, and I heard the rasp of metal on metal as he pushed open my curtains, the decorative rings sliding on the iron bar, and it suddenly got a lot brighter in my room. "Time to get up."

"What?" I asked, squeezing my eyes tightly shut, not understanding what was happening. "No. Why?"

"Surprise," he said, and then he tickled the bottoms of my feet, which were sticking out from under the sheet. I felt myself giggling uncontrollably—that had always been my most ticklish spot. I yanked my feet under the covers as I heard my father leave the room. "Meet you outside," he called. "Five minutes."

I tried to keep my eyes shut, and attempted to return to the dream that now seemed very far away—but I knew it was futile. Between the light streaming into the room and the tickling, I was now wide awake. I opened my eyes, sat up, and checked my watch. It was nine a.m. So much for a day off.

I had gone back to work yesterday following the movie debacle, and it had been fine—Lucy continued to be slightly more cordial to me, and nobody brought up how terrible I had been. But I was still happy to have a day away from the site of my most recent humiliation, and had planned on spending it sleeping until noon, and then maybe sunbathing out on the dock while reading a magazine. But that was clearly not going to happen.

Ten minutes later, I walked through the kitchen, glancing briefly at the calendar as I went, looking at the days that had been crossed off, a little unable to believe that it was June already. My dad was on the porch, pacing around, and he appeared entirely too awake for how early it was, especially considering that he'd been sleeping in lately, and usually hadn't been up when I'd left for work.

"What's the surprise?" I asked, as I joined him on the porch and looked around. I saw nothing except my father and the cars in the driveway. I was slowly getting the feeling that I'd been duped.

"Well," my dad said, rubbing his hands together and smiling. I noticed that his clothing had relaxed very slightly—rather than a button-down shirt, he was wearing a polo shirt with his khakis, and

　　　　　　　　　　　　　　　　morgan matson

ancient boat shoes. "It's not so much of a surprise, per se. It's more of an outing."

I looked at him. "An outing."

"You got it," he said. "We're going to get breakfast." He looked at me, clearly waiting for a reaction, but all I was thinking was that it was very early, and I was awake when I didn't want to be, and had been promised a surprise. "You need a good breakfast," he said in his best persuade-the-jury voice. "It might be a big day." When I still didn't move, he smiled at me. "My treat," he added.

Twenty minutes later, I found myself sitting across from my father at the Pocono Coffee Shop, aka the diner, at a table by the window. The diner did not seem to have changed at all in the time I'd been gone. It was wood-paneled, with red booths covered with cracked leather. The cream on the tables was in squeezy syrup bottles, something that had provided endless entertainment for me and Warren when we were younger. There were framed pictures of Lake Phoenix though the ages covering the walls, and the one next to us showed a beauty pageant of some sort, girls with forties hair and sashes across their bathing suits, smiling at the camera as they lined up along the beach, all in high, stacked heels.

"What looks good?" my father said as he opened his large, plastic-covered menu. I opened mine as well, and saw that nothing on the menu seemed different since I'd last seen it, even though I was pretty sure that in the past five years, there had been some important discoveries about cholesterol and saturated fats. But maybe the management figured that adding healthier options would hurt their reputation—after all, the sign by the door read WALK IN. ROLL OUT.

"Everything looks good," I said honestly, my eyes scanning down all the egg-and-meat combination options. I had been running so late for work every day this week, I'd usually been eating a granola bar as I drove.

"You folks set?" A middle-aged waitress, glasses on a chain around her neck, approached our table, her pencil already poised above her order pad. She was wearing a name tag on her red uniform T-shirt that read ANGELA.

My father ordered a short stack of the blueberry pancakes and a side of bacon, and I got what I'd always ordered, the Pocono Omelet, which was distinguished by the fact that it mostly contained eggs and different kinds of meat and cheese, without any vegetables whatsoever.

Angela nodded and wrote down our order as she walked away. And I looked across the table at my dad and felt suddenly on the spot.

It wasn't that my father and I had never eaten together, just the two of us. We had certainly gotten ice cream together more times than I could count. But it was rare for it to be just the two of us at a meal, and, frankly, to have his undivided attention at all—no siblings, no BlackBerry constantly buzzing. I wondered if this was the time to do what I'd been thinking about ever since I'd gone with him to the hospital—the moment that I should tell him I loved him. But just as I thought this, Angela reappeared with her coffeepot and poured cups for both of us, and I felt that the opportunity had passed.

My dad took a sip of his coffee and made a face after he swallowed, widening his eyes and raising his eyebrows at me. "Wow," he said, deadpan. "So I don't think I'll be sleeping for the next week or so."

"Strong?" I asked. I squeezed some cream into it and stirred in some sugar as my dad nodded. I liked coffee, as long as I could get it to taste as little like coffee as possible. I took a tentative sip, and even with my additions, could taste how strong the coffee was. "Well, now I'm awake," I said, adding in some more cream, partially to make it less strong and partially because the squeezy bottle just made it fun.

Silence fell between us for a moment, and I found myself racking my brain for conversation topics. I glanced down at my paper placemat and saw that it was printed with ads for local businesses, and in the center was something billed as the *Diner's De-Lite!* It had a word scramble, a Sudoku puzzle, and a five-question quiz. I looked at the quiz more closely and realized it wasn't asking trivia questions. Instead, it was called *The Dish!* and was a list of personal questions—What did you want to be when you grew up? What's your favorite food? What's your best memory? Where's your favorite place to travel? It seemed like it was a get-to-know-your-table-companion game. Or maybe you were supposed to guess the answers for the other person and compare—there weren't any instructions.

I looked up and saw that my dad was also reading his placemat. "What do you think?" he asked, nodding down at it. "Should we give it a whirl?"

By the time our food arrived, we'd solved the word scramble and the Sudoku puzzle. My dad dug into his pancakes as I took a bite of my omelet. I tried to concentrate on the cheese-and-meat extravaganza I was currently experiencing, but my glance kept returning to the five-question quiz. As I read the questions again, I realized I didn't know any of my father's answers. And even though he was sitting across from me, adding more syrup to his blueberry waffles and tapping his coffee cup for a refill, I knew—even though I hated to know it—that at some point, some point soon, he wouldn't be around to ask. So I needed to find out his answers to these questions—which seemed somehow both utterly trivial and incredibly important.

"So," I said, pushing my plate a little off to the side and looking down at question one, "what is your favorite movie?" I realized I knew the answer to that as soon as I'd asked it, and together we said, *"Casablanca."*

"You got it," my dad said, shaking his head. "I can't believe that none of my progeny have seen it. It is, from first frame to last, a perfect movie."

"I'll see it," I promised. I'd said this to him a lot in the past when he'd started giving me a hard time for not having seen it. But I meant it now.

"Although," he said thoughtfully, "it's probably better to see it on the big screen. That's what I've always heard. Never gotten the chance to see it that way, myself, though." He raised his eyebrows at me. "You know the plot, right?"

"Sure," I said quickly, but not, apparently, fast enough.

"So it's the dawn of World War II," he said, settling back in his chair, "and we're in unoccupied French Morocco. . . ."

By the time we turned down Dockside, I was thoroughly full and had heard most of the plot of *Casablanca*. He was now waxing nostalgic about the music when something at the foot of our driveway caught my eye. "Dad!" I yelled, my voice sharp, and he stepped on the brake, slamming me forward against my seat belt and then back against the seat again.

"What?" he asked, looking around. "What is it?"

I looked down from my window and saw the dog, who was basically doing the canine equivalent of stalking, sitting in the middle of our driveway. "It's that dog," I said. I got out of the car and shut my door. He looked particularly mangy in the bright sunlight, and I wondered, for the first time, collar notwithstanding, whether he actually had a home to go to. He wagged his tail as I approached, which surprised me, since the only interactions I'd had with him had not been friendly ones. Maybe this dog had an amazing capacity for forgiveness—or, more likely, a really short memory.

I reached my fingers under his collar and pulled him aside, out of the way of the car, and my father drove on past us.

"Is that the same dog from before?" my dad asked, and I nodded as I walked toward the house. As I'd been expecting, the dog followed, looking so thrilled to find himself on the promised land, the *driveway*, that he was practically high-stepping.

"Yeah," I said. The dog stopped when I stopped, sitting at my feet, and I bent down and looked at his tag. I was hoping the scratched gold disk might give me an address or phone number where I could finally deposit him. But the tag read only MURPHY. This rang a bell with me for some reason, but I couldn't remember why. "Same one."

"No tags?" my father asked, bending down slowly and wincing a little as he did so, until he was crouched in front of the dog.

"No address or owner," I said, "just a name. Murphy." Upon hearing this, the dog stopped scratching himself and sat up at attention, tail thumping on the ground again.

"Hey there," my dad said softly. He rested his hand on the dog's head and scratched him between the ears. "Between you and me," he said, almost confidentially to the dog, "you don't smell too good."

"So what should we do?" I asked. I knew, vaguely, mostly from

TV shows, about shelters and vets' offices, but had never had any experience with them myself.

"Well," my dad said, pushing himself to his feet a little unsteadily, "I think the first thing is to talk to the neighbors, make sure he's not just someone's pet who wandered away. And then if nobody claims him, I think there's an animal shelter in Mountainview."

"What's going on?" Gelsey asked as she stepped onto the porch, not wearing her tennis or her dance clothes, but instead, a pink sundress with sandals, her hair loose and hanging around her shoulders. Her eyes widened when she looked at the dog. "Did we get a dog?" she asked, her voice raising excitedly on the last word, making her sound actually twelve for once, and not twelve-going-on-twenty-nine.

"No," my father and I said together.

"Oh," Gelsey said, her face falling.

"I should get to work," my father said, turning to head inside. He was still working on his case, the FedEx truck still arriving with files from his office. The deliveries were no longer happening every day, but had gone down to two or three times a week. My dad had also taken to closing his laptop screen if any of us leaned in for a look, fueling Warren's speculation that he was also spending a lot of time of this mystery project of his. "Can you handle this, Taylor?" he asked, nodding down at the dog. The dog was now scratching his ear with his back paw, seemingly oblivious to the fact that his fate was being discussed.

"Sure," I said, even though I would have very much preferred someone else handle it, as my experience with dogs had been pretty much limited to watching *Top Dog*. I started to leave, to begin the process of talking to the neighbors, when I caught a glimpse of my sister still standing on the porch. When I was her age, I rarely just hung around the house. I always had something going on with Henry or Lucy. But, in fairness, Gelsey hadn't been here since she was little, and she wasn't the greatest at making friends. I glanced at the house next door and remembered the girl I'd seen. "Gelsey, come with me," I called to her. "And bring the cookies."

chapter seventeen

WE HEARD THE ARGUMENT BEFORE WE MADE IT TO THE FRONT steps. It was impossible not to hear it—there was just a screen door, and the words carried all the way out to the gravel of the driveway, where Gelsey, the dog, and I all paused.

"You knew what this would do!" a woman's voice, shaking with anger, rang out. "I told you back when we were undercover. You've killed Sasha with this, you heartless bastard!"

I looked at the front door again, then took a small step in front of my sister. *Undercover?* Who had ended up next door to us? "I'm not sure," I said quietly, starting to take a step away. "Maybe—"

"You can't blame this on me!" a man's voice rang out, sounding equally angry. "If you'd done what you were supposed to in Minsk, we wouldn't be here!"

The woman gasped. "How *dare* you bring up Minsk!" she yelled. "It's just . . ." Silence fell, and then, sounding perfectly calm, she said, "I don't know. It's a little too much, I think."

Gelsey frowned at me, and I just shook my head, totally lost, but thinking that there might be a better time for us to ask these people if they were missing a dog. And we didn't even have the oatmeal raisin cookies with us. When we went to bring them, my mother had told us she'd tossed them out after a week when it became clear they were never going to be eaten. "Let's come back later," I said, taking another step away. Gelsey tugged on the dog's collar, using the makeshift leash—a length of pink satin ribbon, the kind she used for her pointe shoes.

"Hey there!" I glanced up and saw a woman standing in the doorway on the front porch. She looked like she was in her mid-thirties, and was dressed casually, in jeans and a T-shirt that read IN N OUT. She had long, pale blond hair and shielded her eyes from the sun. "What's up?"

"What's going on?" a guy came to stand next to her, smiling when he saw us and raising a hand in a wave. He was African-American and looked around the woman's age. He was dressed almost identically, except that his T-shirt read ZANKOU CHICKEN.

"We, um," I said, taking a step forward, looking at them closely, still trying to make sense of the argument I'd heard. They didn't look like spies. But really good spies probably didn't. "Had a question. But if this isn't a good time ..." They just stared at me, looking blank. "It sounded like you might have been in the middle of something," I tried to clarify. "I didn't want to disturb." They still were just staring, so I prompted, "Minsk?"

morgan matson

"Oh!" The woman burst out laughing. "I hope you didn't think that was real. We were just working."

"Working?" Gelsey asked, finding her voice and taking a tiny step forward. "Are you actors?"

"Even worse," the guy said, shaking his head. "Screenwriters. I'm Jeff Gardner, by the way."

"Kim," the woman said, waving, a ring on her left hand flashing at me in the sun.

"Hi," I said, incredibly relived that there was not international espionage going on next door. "I'm Taylor, and this is my sister Gelsey. We live right there," I said, pointing through their tree hedge to our house.

"Neighbors!" Jeff said with a big smile. "So nice to meet you, Taylor, and ..." He paused, looking at my sister. "Did you say Kelsey?"

This happened a lot with her name, and when it did, it was the one time I was grateful to have a name everyone knew and had no problems spelling. My mother hadn't thought it would be a problem—when she'd named my sister for a famous ballerina, she obviously thought a lot more people would be familiar with it. "Gelsey," I repeated, louder. "With a *g*."

"It's great to meet you both," Kim said. Her eyes lingered on my sister for a moment, and she smiled before she turned her head and called into the house, "Nora!"

A second later, the screen door banged open and the girl I'd seen a few days before stepped out onto the porch. She had black curly hair and skin the color of my coffee after I'd added enough milk to make it drinkable. She was also glowering, which was in direct opposition to her parents, who both seemed thrilled to have met us. "This is our daughter, Nora," Kim said, nudging her until Nora was standing by her side. "These are two of our neighbors," she said. "Taylor and Gelsey."

In succession, Nora frowned at me, at Gelsey, and at Murphy. "What's wrong with your dog?" she asked.

Gelsey frowned right back at her, pulling the ribbon, and the dog, a little closer to her. "Nothing," she said. "What do you mean?"

Nora just nodded at him, wrinkling her nose as though it should be obvious. "It's all matted," she said.

"That's actually why we're here," I said quickly, trying to head off Gelsey, who had just taken a breath as though to launch into an argument about the merits of the dog's grooming habits. "We've noticed this dog wandering around recently. There's no address on the tag, so we didn't know if he might be yours."

Jeff shook his head. "Not us," he said. "Have you tried the house on the other side?"

Also known as Henry's house. "Not yet," I said brightly. "I guess we'll ask them next." We all just stood around for a moment, nobody really quite sure what to say. I saw Kim glance back into the house and realized that she probably wanted to get back to work. "So," I said, as the silence was starting to edge toward uncomfortable, "screenwriting, huh? That's cool." I didn't know much about screen-writing except for what I'd seen in, ironically, the movies, where writers seemed to be either going out to power lunches or throwing balled-up pieces of paper against the wall.

"Well, I don't know about that," Jeff said, laughing. "But it pays the bills. We're in Los Angeles most of the year. It's our first sum-mer up here."

I nodded, but was really looking at Gelsey, who was looking down at Murphy, who was scratching his ear again. I no longer knew anything about how twelve-year-olds made friends, and I frankly had never seen Gelsey make a friend, but I figured that in terms of trying to help her, I had done my best. "Okay," I said, raising my eyebrows at my sister, "we should probably get—"

"Microchipped!" Kim said, snapping her fingers, as she looked down at the dog. "Maybe he's microchipped. Have you checked it out?"

"No," I said. I hadn't even thought about it. "Do you know where they can find that out?"

"Animal shelters, vets' offices," Jeff said. "And they do it at the pet store in town. Doggone something or other."

Kim turned to him, eyebrows raised. "How do you know that?"

"I went in the other day while I was picking up the pizza for dinner," he said. "I was talking to the girl who works there."

Now Nora turned to look at her father as well. "Why?" she asked.

"I was thinking," Jeff said, even more energy coming into his voice, "that it could be a great character. Maybe for a TV pilot—think of all the different people she'd come into contact with."

Kim was nodding excitedly, her words overlapping his. "I like it," she said. "And what if she's also a detective? Righting wrongs, solving mysteries on the side."

Jeff turned to her, and they now seemed to be talking only to each other. "And the animals play a part," he said. "They help her solve the crimes." They looked at each other and smiled, then turned back to us.

"It was great to meet you," Kim said. "Good luck with the search." Jeff waved and then they both practically ran inside. A moment later, I could hear the clacking of the keys from two keyboards.

"Come on, Gelsey," I said, as I turned to go. "Nice to meet you," I called to the very unfriendly Nora, who still had her arms crossed, and who hadn't once lost her glower. It was behavior I recognized, but I didn't remember acting like that until I was at least fourteen. Maybe things just moved more quickly when you grew up in Los Angeles.

"So," Nora said, grudgingly, when we'd taken a few steps away. Gelsey turned back, crossing her arms in an identical manner. "Do you like the beach?"

"I guess so," Gelsey said, with a shrug. "My sister works there,"

morgan matson

she said, a note of unmistakable pride in her voice that surprised me.

Nora glanced over at me, unimpressed, then back to Gelsey. "Want to go over there?" she asked. "I'm totally bored."

"Me too," Gelsey said, the morning's adventure of finding a home for a lost dog apparently now forgotten. "There's *nothing* to do here. My mom's even making me take tennis."

Nora's eyes widened. "Me too!" she said. "It's so stupid."

"I know, right?" Gelsey replied.

"Totally," Nora said.

I had a feeling I knew what the rest of the conversation was going to be like, so I just took the ribbon from Gelsey, who surrendered it easily. "I'll see you later," I said. Gelsey waved at me over her shoulder and continued her conversation, not even looking back.

I pulled Murphy, who was far too interested in sniffing every rock on the Gardner driveway, back to the road. I couldn't help taking a little bit of satisfaction in the fact that Gelsey seemed to be on the road to making a friend, that my plan had been a tiny bit successful. I walked with the dog to the edge of the Crosby driveway, but the house had the look about it that indicated all the occupants were elsewhere—no cars or bikes in the driveway, nobody in the tent, the curtains drawn.

I steered the dog back toward our house, wondering what I would have done if it looked like people had been home. I wanted to think that I would have gone up and rung the bell, but I wasn't quite sure. I did know that ever since the ice-cream parlor, I had been thinking about Henry more than I probably should have, since he was still mad at me (with good reason) and had a girlfriend. But I couldn't help it.

When we reached the driveway, Murphy no longer needed to be pulled. Instead, he started running ahead, straining on the make-shift leash. I tied him up to the porch steps and walked into the screened-in porch, where my father was sitting in his normal dinner spot, frowning at his laptop, and Warren was reading a textbook, his legs extended in front of him on a second chair.

"Hey," Warren said, looking up from his book after carefully marking his place with a sticky flag. He half-stood and peered out to the driveway. "What is that?" he asked, and I could hear a note of panic in his voice. "Why is there a dog there?"

"It's nothing to worry about," I assured my brother, as my dad shot me a tiny smile, then looked back at his laptop before Warren could see. "He's pretty much the world's least frightening dog. Seriously."

"Right," Warren said, nodding like this was no big deal, but I noticed he was keeping an eye on the porch. He shifted his chair a few feet away from the door, in a move I'm sure he thought was nonchalant. "Sure."

"No owner?" my dad asked.

"Not next door, at least," I said. "But we met the neighbors. There's a girl there Gelsey's age."

"Wonderful," my dad said with a smile. "But what about the canine?"

"I was going to bring him to the pet store," I said. "See if he's microchipped."

"Good thinking," he said with an approving nod, and I wondered if I should actually tell him it was our screenwriter neighbor's idea, but decided to just let it go. "Son," he said, turning to Warren, "didn't you say that you wanted to go to the library?"

Warren cleared his throat and cast another glance at the porch. "I did mention that," he said. "But upon further consideration, I think that I can—"

"Oh, just come," I said. "I'll keep the dog away from you. I promise."

"It has nothing to do with that," Warren muttered, nevertheless turning a bright red that nearly matched his polo shirt. "I'll just go and get my wallet." He headed into the house and my dad smiled at me over his laptop.

"You see?" he asked. "An excursion. I told you it was going to be a big day, kid." He hit a few keys, then leaned back in his chair. "You know, if you're going into town, you'll be by Henson's. And if you wouldn't mind picking me up some licorice . . ."

Ten minutes later, Warren, Murphy, and I arrived at Doggone It!, Warren staying a good three steps behind us. Despite the fact that I could lift Murphy with one hand—not that I wanted to; my father had been right about his smell, and we'd had to drive with all the windows down—Warren still didn't seem convinced that he wasn't going to turn into a murderous beast at any moment.

The store was fairly small, with birds in cages, a large aquarium full of fish, kittens in a pen along one wall, and the rest devoted to pet accessories. It looked like there was a grooming station to the back, behind the register. There was nobody behind the counter, and no helpful bell to ring, like there had been at Borrowed Thyme. I looked around for a moment, but the only sound in the store was one of the birds chirping loudly, in what I was pretty sure was an imitation of a car alarm going off.

"Hello?" Warren called, causing the bird to chirp even more loudly.

"Coming, coming, so sorry!" a voice called out from the back. The door opened, and the girl I'd seen before—the one who'd offered to make the phone call for my father—came out, wiping her hands on a red DOGGONE IT! apron that covered up a white T-shirt and jeans. Upon seeing her closer, I could tell she was about my age, with blue eyes, a sweet-looking, heart-shaped face, and long red hair in braids that reached past her shoulders. She glanced from me to Warren, smiling. "What can I do for you?" I noticed that the stitched embroidery on her apron read *Wendy*.

"Well," I started, when I heard my brother make a strange throat-clearing noise. Warren was staring at Wendy, his mouth

morgan matson

hanging open slightly, and he was apparently trying to form words, without much luck. "We found this dog," I said as I lifted Murphy up to the counter, where he sat immediately, looking around, seeming to enjoy the elevated view. To my surprise, my brother didn't immediately move away, but stayed right where he was, in close dog proximity. "And we didn't know where he'd come from," I said. "I heard you can check for microchips here?"

"Right," Warren said, jumping in a moment too late, recovering the power of speech. "Microchips."

"Are you lost, buddy?" Wendy asked. She reached forward and scratched just behind Murphy's ears, not seeming to care about how he smelled. He closed his eyes and his tail thumped on the counter, onto a stack of pamphlets about flea collars. "Well, we can check for that, no problem." She reached under the counter and pulled out a device that looked a little bit like a remote control, with a screen taking up the top half. She ran it slowly over the dog's back while scratching his ears with her opposite hand. When she passed a spot just below his shoulder blade, the device beeped. "There you go!" she said, smiling at Warren and me. I noticed Warren smiled back, but not in time, because she was already sitting down and wheeling her chair over to the computer.

"So do we know who he belongs to?" I asked, leaning over the dog on the counter to try to see what she was looking at.

"Not yet," she said. "That only gave us the microchip number. I just have to check the database and it should tell us where this little guy lives."

"Or girl," I said, since we still didn't have confirmation on this, and I was pretty much going off the fact that his collar was blue. Wendy stopped scrolling through her screen and stood up again, lifting the dog's front paws up.

"Nope," she said. "Definitely guy." She sat back down again, and started typing.

"Did you know that the name Wendy came into usage in 1904?" Warren asked suddenly, all in a rush. "Through J.M. Barrie, in his play *Peter and Wendy*, which later became *Peter Pan*."

Wendy looked at Warren quizzically, and I felt myself do the same. I was about to interject, say that my brother had had too much sun today or something, when she smiled wide. "I never knew that," she said. "Thanks."

Warren nodded, then said, in a voice that sounded like he was trying very hard to be casual, but failing miserably, "Have you, um, worked here long?"

"About a month now," she said, giving him a quick glance before returning to the computer. "Just making some extra money before starting school in the fall."

"Oh?" Warren was practically eye-to-eye with the dog, he was leaning so far over the counter to continue this conversation. The dog took advantage of this opportunity and licked his ear and Warren, to his credit, only flinched slightly. "Where are you going?"

"Stroudsburg State," she said, still looking at the computer. "They've got a great veterinary program."

"Great," Warren said, trying to disengage himself from the dog, who had now moved on to enthusiastically licking his face. "That's great."

I turned and stared at my brother, trying to contain my astonishment. Warren had always been a college snob, but it had just gotten worse since he'd gotten into an Ivy. I'd heard him refer to Stanford as his "safety." The fact that he was talking positively about a school I was fairly sure he'd never heard of five minutes ago was so out of character that it was shocking. But then again, I'd never seen Warren this way around a girl before, ever.

"Okay," Wendy said as she leaned closer to the screen, "it looks like we have a match!"

"Excellent," I said, wondering what the next step was—if she would contact the owners, or if we would have to. Either way, as friendly as this dog seemed, I was ready to send him back where he belonged.

"And," she said, scrolling down her screen, "it looks like the microchipping was actually done here, so he's local. Which is a good thing. His address is . . ." She paused, then said, "84 Dockside Road in Lake Phoenix." She looked at us and smiled, and I just stared back at her, sure that I'd heard wrong. "It's not too far from here," she added after a moment. "I could print out directions."

"I know where it is," I said, staring down at the dog. I now understood why he was so eager to make it up our driveway. "That's our house."

Two hours later, Warren, Murphy, and I returned home. The dog had gotten a thorough cleaning, and now smelled faintly of chemicals. The groomer must not have cared that Murphy was a boy, because there was a pink polka-dot ribbon tied into his wiry hair, just between his ears. We had a bag full of supplies, including a dog dish, water bowl, bed, leash, and food. I hadn't been under the impression that we were keeping him, but once Wendy had started picking out "the basics we'd need," Warren had trailed her around the store, nodding at everything she selected, not stopping to consult me about the situation. It wasn't until we were in the car driving home, just the three of us, Murphy panting happily out the window, his breath now much improved, that I turned to Warren and said, "I can't believe this."

"I know," Warren said, shaking his head. He must have been attempting to look serious—his default expression—but it kept slipping into something a little more dreamy. "It must have been the renters last summer, right?" he asked. "Wendy said that that's when the microchip information was entered."

"And that's their name," I said. "Pretty conclusive evidence."

I paused at a stoplight, noting the fact that my brother had pronounced Wendy's name in the tone of voice he usually reserved for facts about tollbooths and lightbulbs. "So what happened?" I asked, speeding up again, even though I knew my brother, who had all the answers, wouldn't know this one. "They left him at the end of the summer?" I asked. I could feel my anger rising as I said it, getting furious at these heartless, spice-stealing renters, treating the dog that way. "They just abandoned him at the house?"

Warren shrugged. "Or perhaps he ran away," he said, his tone becoming, finally, one that I recognized—measured, careful, weighing all the facts. "We don't know the situation. We'll tell Mom, and she can contact them. Maybe this is all a misunderstanding."

"Maybe," I said, but not really believing it. I turned down Dockside, and as soon as we got close, Murphy pulled his head in from the window, scrambling up to try and sit on the console between us, straining forward, looking at the house, tail wagging wildly. And as I pulled into the driveway and he got more and more excited, I knew this was the proof, even more so than the computer's confirmation. Murphy knew where he was, and was desperate to get back. When I killed the engine and opened the back door, he bounded out of the car and ran straight for the house, clearly delighted to have found his way home at last.

Truth and Daring

chapter eighteen

I WAS ALREADY AWAKE AT TWO A.M. WHEN MY PHONE RANG. I HAD no I idea why I hadn't been able to sleep, and it was enough to make me wonder if my dad had been onto something with his talk about the diner's coffee. I'd been lying awake for the last few hours, because having no social life meant that you went to bed early, even on nights where there was more excitement than usual.

My mother had been equally upset at Warren, for bringing the dog home fully accessorized without checking with her first, and at the renters, for abandoning him in the first place. She hadn't been able to reach them at the number she had, but she'd called Henry's dad and found out that they had had a dog all last summer, a puppy they'd gotten right when the they'd moved in. Henry's dad remembered because it had gotten into their trash a few times, and the Murphys hadn't seemed to care very much about it.

Gelsey had gone into paroxysms of delight over the fact that Murphy had come home with us—even though, as my mother kept stressing, this was just a temporary situation. My father hadn't come down one way or another, but I noticed him slipping the dog bits of his dinner throughout the meal, and when Murphy clambered onto his lap after the plates were cleared, my dad didn't push him away, instead rubbing his ears until the dog made a sound that I'm pretty sure was the canine equivalent of purring.

Luckily, Murphy seemed to be housebroken—and even better, housebroken for our house. He knew our house with a familiarity that was a little unnerving, as we watched him settle in by the front windows that faced the street, pressing his nose against the glass, head resting on his paws. Even though Gelsey had begged to have him sleep in her room, my mother had refused, and had set up the dog bed just outside the kitchen. When we'd all gone to sleep, I'd been listening for any sounds of whining or whimpering—but the dog was quiet, and presumably sleeping better than I had been able to.

I'd rolled on my side and looked out my window, out into the sky dotted with stars. I was debating simply trying to go back to sleep or turning on my light and trying to read, when my phone rang.

This was surprising enough that I didn't move for it right away, just stared at it on my dresser, lighting up the corner of the room with an unexpected brightness, beginning to launch into the chorus of my ringtone. By the second ring, though, I had pulled it together and had rolled out of bed and grabbed it before it woke the whole house—or at least my mother, who was a notoriously light sleeper. I didn't recognize the number—or the area code—but answered it quickly anyway, wondering if it was a wrong number. I couldn't think who else would be calling me at two a.m.

"Hello," I said quietly into the phone, taking it back with me to bed and moving to the far corner of it, as if this would reduce noise traveling through the house. There was a long pause on the other end.

"Who is this?" a girl's voice asked, slurring slightly.

"Taylor," I said slowly. "Who is this?"

"Oh, shit," the girl on the other end muttered, and just like that, I knew who it was.

"Lucy?" I asked, and I heard her sigh deeply.

"Yeah?" she asked. "What?"

"I don't know," I said, baffled as to why we were even having this conversation. "You called me."

She sighed again, and there was a rustling sound for a moment before she was back on the line. "Dropped the phone," she said. "So I need you to come to the beach."

I sat up straighter. "Why?" I asked, suddenly panicking that I hadn't closed the concession stand properly or something. Though I had no idea why Lucy would be calling me, apparently tipsy, to tell me about it. "Is everything okay?"

"Would I be calling you if everything was okay?" she asked. "Just come here, and—" I heard the rustling sound again, and then the line went dead.

I held the phone for a moment, thinking. I was going down there—the option of not going there only crossed my mind for a second. Because I knew that if I didn't, I really wouldn't be able to get any sleep, as I'd just be lying awake, wondering what was going on down at the beach. But mostly, I was trying to figure out how to get there. I knew that if I took one of the cars, my mother—not to mention my dad or siblings—would wake up. And though we hadn't discussed curfew hours for this summer, I had a feeling that leaving at two in the morning wouldn't exactly be cool with her. I let my eyes drift outside, where I could see, at the end of the driveway, the garage. This gave me an idea, and I climbed out of bed quickly, pulling on jean shorts and changing from my giant, much-washed sleeping shirt to a tank top. I tiptoed out into the hallway, listening for any sounds of movement. But the house was peaceful, no light spilling out from under my siblings' doors, and no sound from my parents' bedroom upstairs. Even the dog was sacked out, lying on his back in his dog bed, his back leg twitching occasionally, as though in his dream, he was chasing something down or running away from something.

I crossed the open-plan downstairs, not needing to turn on any lights as the moon was streaming in through the front windows, letting in giant rectangles of light across the floor. I passed through one

morgan matson

as I walked to the front door, half-expecting it to feel warm, like I was walking though sunlight. I let myself quietly out the front door and locked it behind me, grabbing my flip-flops from the jumble of shoes. Then I walked down the front steps to the garage—where my bike, newly restored for me by my dad, was waiting.

chapter nineteen
five summers earlier

"SO I HAVE NEWS," LUCY TOLD ME OVER THE PHONE. IT WAS ALWAYS her favorite way to introduce a subject, even if it turned out that her news was something trivial, like the new ice-cream flavor of the week at Jane's, or the fact that she'd mixed two nail polish colors together to create a custom blend.

"Me too," I said, not able to contain a smile from breaking out across my face. I tucked the cordless phone under my ear as I stepped out onto the screened-in porch. I knew exactly how far I could go and still get reception. It was after dinner, and my mother was setting up the Risk board, but I knew that I'd be able to talk to Lucy for a few minutes undisturbed, particularly if Warren insisted on supervising Mom while she did it.

I hadn't told Lucy about the movie date with Henry the week before—because until the moment that he'd taken my hand, there had been nothing to tell. But he had held my hand through the rest of the movie, and we stayed sitting that way, palm to palm, our fingers laced, until the credits rolled and the lights came up and the employees came in with their brooms to sweep up the fallen popcorn. And of course, I'd tried to call Lucy immediately after, but she never seemed to be at the house of the parent I tried to call, and her cell had been suspended while her parents argued over who was going to pay for it. So these days, it seemed like I was waiting for Lucy to call me so that I could talk to her.

"Me first," she said, and I laughed, feeling in that moment just how much I missed her.

"Taylor!" Warren opened the door and frowned at me, pushing up his glasses, which were constantly slipping down his nose. "We're getting ready to play."

I covered up the earpiece. "I'm on the phone," I hissed at him. "Long-distance." On the other end, I could hear Lucy giggle.

"New Jersey is not long-distance," Warren scoffed. "In fact, it's short-distance. Only one state away."

"Leave me *alone*," I said, trying to push him out of the door.

My brother just shook his head and looked at me with his I'm-so-mature expression. "We're starting in five minutes, so if you're not there, you forfeit your armies." But he finally stepped out of the doorway, and I lifted up the phone again.

"Sorry about that," I said. "Warren's being Warren."

"It's okay," Lucy said. "You guys are playing Risk? Like, all of you?"

"Yeah," I said, trying not to notice the note of wistfulness in Lucy's voice. "But anyway. I have news, you have news. . . ."

"Right!" Lucy said, immediately excited again. "So I like a boy."

"Me too!" I said, beyond thrilled that we had reached this at the same time. That was the only thing that had given me pause when I considered telling Lucy about Henry. I hadn't wanted to move on to something this big without her. But if she liked a boy at the same time I did, everything would work out. Whenever we talked about the future, it was one of the assumptions we always made—that we would experience things at the same time. This included boyfriends, prom dates, and eventually, a double wedding.

"No way," she said, laughing again. "Okay, I'll go first. I totally like Henry Crosby."

I opened my mouth to say something, and finding no words, closed it again. But Lucy didn't seem to notice, and kept on going.

"Ever since I first saw him this summer—he got so cute last year—I had a crush on him. I wasn't going to say anything, but since I got home I can't stop thinking about him. And because you two are friends, I thought maybe you could see if he likes me. But, you know, in a subtle way."

I opened my mouth again, even though I wasn't sure what I was going to say. But I had to tell her—about the date, and the Outpost, and the hand-holding. "Listen, Luce . . ."

"Taylor?" I turned around, and my dad was standing in the doorway, Gelsey flung over his shoulder in what he always called "the sack of potatoes," her head hanging down by his side, my dad holding on to her feet. I could hear Gelsey giggling hysterically, upside-down. "We're about ready to get started, kid. Prepare yourself for swift and bloody devastation."

"I'll be right there," I said. A minute earlier, I would have complained, cajoled, done anything to stay on the phone with Lucy. Now, I was thrilled to have an excuse to end the conversation.

"And one more thing," my dad said, looking around exaggeratedly. He turned in a half circle from side to side, Gelsey swinging around as he did so. "Have you seen your sister? I can't seem to find her *anywhere*." This caused Gelsey to go into shrieks of laughter, and he flipped her around, tossed her up in the air, and caught her before putting her back on the ground, now laughing along with her as he headed inside.

"I should go," I said to Lucy, grateful for a reason to get off the phone.

"So you'll talk to him?" Lucy persisted. "You'll see if he likes me?" I swallowed hard and tried to see if I was brave enough to just tell her now that *I* liked Henry. But I was afraid she would accuse me of something she'd been saying since we were little—that I was copying her. That I just liked whatever and whoever she liked, did whatever she did. And as I thought about my wispy bangs, I realized that she wasn't entirely wrong.

"Right," I said, regretting the word even as I was saying it but somehow not able to take it back. "I'll talk to you soon."

"Definitely. Miss you!"

Lucy hung up, and I walked slowly inside to join my family around the coffee table. Warren was quoting from something called *The Art of War*, and my dad was going over strategy with Gelsey (they were on a team) while I just stared into space. My mind was spinning with justifications for what I'd done—or, more accurately, hadn't done. She'd caught me off guard. I didn't even know what might happen with me and Henry. Lucy might not even be back until the summer was over. There was no point in causing trouble or making anyone feel bad.

"Ha!" Warren said triumphantly, and I looked down at the board to see that, right under my nose, he had just swept away most of the armies that I thought were safe.

chapter twenty

As I wobbled down our street on my mom's old bike, trying to do everything I could not to topple over, I realized that riding a bike was, in fact, something you could forget how to do. In my defense, it was a bike I wasn't used to, and nothing like my old mountain bike that was now Gelsey's. It was a beach cruiser, and heavy, with a sloping crossbar and no handbrakes. Though I'd stuck a flashlight into the bike's white metal basket as kind of a DIY bike light, once I made it to the street, it became obvious it wasn't going to be necessary. It was an incredibly clear night, and the moon that had been shining through our downstairs windows was lighting up the road.

I made slow, wavering process down the street, the bike threatening to fall over every few seconds until I got the pedals going and straightened out a little. But by the time I turned off Dockside, I was feeling better about my progress. The streets were empty, and I had them to myself as I swerved across both lanes and made figure eights. The wind was lifting my hair, and I could feel it stream behind me as I coasted down the small hills. I pedaled faster, picking up speed, until I realized where I was—at the top of Devil's Dip.

I began to brake, even though I knew from long-ago experience that this was the moment to pedal fastest, gain the momentum I would need to get myself up the other side. But up at the top of it, looking down into the dip without the benefit of being in a car, I could understand why this had seemed so insurmountable when I was eight. Had I really once done it as a matter of course? And even more than that, had this really been a hill I had raced Henry up, both of us red-faced and puffing with exhaustion as we tried to beat each other to the opposite side? I braked a little harder, but the incline had already started pulling me down the hill. I could have just let myself enjoy the ride down, but instead, as the bike slipped out of my control, I felt myself braking, hard. My front wheel hit a patch of gravel, and before I knew what was happening—it only seemed to take a fraction of a second—the wheel was turning, and I was losing control. I felt the whole bike waver, off its axis, and then my foot was getting tangled in the wheel, and then I was on the ground, the bike resting on top of me, front wheel still uselessly spinning.

As I shoved the bike off me and pushed myself to my feet, I was especially grateful that it was very late—or early—and there had been nobody around to see me wipe out like that. I was more humiliated than hurt, but the palms of my hands and both of my knees

morgan matson

had gotten scraped. I brushed off the dirt and gravel and pulled the bike up. I walked it the rest of the way down the Dip, then back up the other side. I was embarrassed, but mostly I was mad at myself, that I had chickened out on doing something that I'd conquered when I was still in elementary school. When I made it up to the other side, I got back on the bike, looking forward at the road, riding extra quickly toward the beach, as though this would make up for bailing out on the Dip. It wasn't until I was nearly at the beach that I realized that I could have given it a second try, rather than walking my bike. I could have picked myself up and tried again. But I hadn't. I had just left. I tried to push this thought away as I steered my bike toward the beach. But unlike so many other times, it didn't go easily.

Since Lucy had just told me to come to "the beach," I had no idea what to expect, or if I'd have trouble finding her. But this didn't turn out to be a problem, because when I got close to the beach, I saw her standing on the side of the road yelling into a cell phone.

"It is so over," she said. "And you should know, Stephen, that you just lost the best thing you're ever going to—" She stopped, and her expression changed from fury to disbelief as she listened. "Oh? Is that so? Then why don't you have the guts to come out here and explain yourself?"

I slowed the bike, feeling very much like I was intruding, even though this confrontation was going down in the middle of the street. I noticed that the driveway of a nearby house was filled with cars, and I could hear, faintly, the thumping bass of music playing and random party sounds—yells and laughter.

"And I will have you know—" Lucy finally saw me, and she frowned as she lowered her phone and stared at the bike. "What is that?"

"What's what?" I asked.

"Where's your car?" she asked. She looked around, swaying slightly, as though it might be hiding behind me.

"I didn't bring it," I said.

Lucy stared at me. "Then how are you going to drive me?" Stephen must have weighed in then—I could hear his voice, loud and a little whiny, through her phone. "I'm done here, you asshole," Lucy snapped, though I noticed she didn't hang up, but appeared to be listening.

I felt incredibly stupid as I stood in the middle of the road, with my bike, at two thirty in the morning. And I could feel myself getting mad at Lucy for the first time in a long time. Ever since we'd met again, I'd been constantly aware of what I'd done, and why she was mad at me. But she had dragged me out of bed to give her a ride home when she would barely talk to me at work? And hadn't even been able to specify that I should bring a car?

Even though Lucy was still on the phone, I felt the need to defend myself. "For the record," I said, raising my voice to be heard over Lucy's phone call, "you didn't tell me you needed a ride—or ask me to give you one, by the way," I said. "All you said was 'come to the beach.' So I biked here."

"Well, I would have been more specific," Lucy said, "but I'm in the middle of breaking up with this *complete moron*—" She yelled these last two words into the phone, and Stephen might have finally had enough, because a moment later, she lowered the phone. "He hung up on me," she said, incredulous. "Can you believe it?"

Actually, I could, but thought this might not be the moment to tell her this. "Was he in there?" I asked, pointing at the party house.

"Yes," Lucy said, huffy, as she picked up her purse from the ground, dropped her phone into it, and rummaged through it. She came up with a bag of Skittles, and ripped open the top, tossing a handful back like they were pills and not candy. She kept the bag in her hand as she closed her purse and slung it a little too vigorously over her shoulder. "I storm out of the house and he doesn't even have the decency to follow me. Just stays where he is and *calls*. What a loser." But as she said this last word, her bravado seemed to crumble a little, and she glanced down the driveway, biting her lip. "God," she muttered, her voice shaky. "And I really liked him too. I thought we'd at least be together through June." She looked at me, and my bike, and sighed. "I guess I'm walking. Thanks for coming, though, Taylor." She gave me what I'm pretty sure was supposed to be a smile, then turned and headed up the road, weaving slightly.

I wheeled the bike around and caught up with her. As safe as Lake Phoenix was, I wasn't about to let a tipsy Lucy wander home on her own. Not to mention the fact that she looked about ready to give up halfway there and take a nap next to a tree. "I'll walk you home," I said, as I got off the bike and walked alongside it.

"You don't have to do that," she said, just as she stumbled over a rock on the side of the road, which sent her veering into my bike. She didn't protest after that, and we fell into a rhythm, walking next to each other, the bike in between us. We continued on in silence, the only sounds coming from the cicadas around us and the gravel crunching under my tires.

"So," I said after a second, glancing over at her, "do you want to talk about it?"

Lucy stopped at that and turned to me, and I stopped as well. "Talk," she repeated. "To you."

I could feel my face heating up, and shook my head and started wheeling my bike again to cover it. "Never mind," I said. "Forget it."

Lucy fell back into step with me, and as we walked on and the silence grew more uncomfortable. I found myself wishing that I had, in fact, brought my car. There were so many more things to distract you in cars. I wouldn't have been feeling this awkward if I could have turned up the volume on the radio and pretended it wasn't happening.

"Thanks for offering," Lucy said finally, sounding half-genuine

morgan matson

and half-sarcastic. "But it's not like we're friends anymore, Taylor."

"I know," I said. I looked down at the bike, concentrating on wheeling it in a perfectly straight line, trying to ignore the lump that was threatening to rise in my throat.

"And whose fault is that?" Lucy asked. Since I knew the answer to this, and suspected she did too, I didn't say anything, just tightened my grip on the handlebars for a second before letting them go again. "You shouldn't have just left like you did," Lucy continued. "Without any explanations or anything. It was a really shitty thing to do."

"Do you think I don't know that?" I asked a little sharply, surprising myself. I glanced over at her and saw that she looked taken aback by this as well. "Do you think I don't feel bad about it?"

"Well, I don't know," Lucy said, sounding annoyed. "It's not like you've, you know, *apologized* or anything."

She was right. I had tried, but halfheartedly. Just like I'd done with Henry, and then blamed my lack of courage on circumstances that had swept those potential moments away. I took a breath and stopped walking my bike. I'd been given, and ignored, too many opportunities to change. So I decided to take one, there in the middle of the road, with the moonlight streaming down over us and casting our shadows on the ground. "Lucy," I said, looking her right in the eye, "I'm really, really sorry."

She looked at me for a long moment, then nodded. "Okay," she said, starting to walk again, weaving a little in the road as she concentrated on shaking another handful of Skittles into her palm.

"Okay?" I asked, half-running alongside the bike to catch up with her. "That's it?"

"What did you want me to say?" she asked, yawning and covering her mouth with her hand. "I accept your apology."

"Thank you," I said, a little stunned it had been that easy. But I realized, as we walked on, that we weren't going to revert to being friends again. She may have accepted my much-too-late apology, but it wasn't like she'd forgiven me.

"I'm sorry too," she added after a moment. I turned to her, confused, and she shrugged. "I've been a total bitch to you at work."

"Not totally," I said, but I could hear that I didn't exactly sound convincing. Lucy looked over at me, we both burst out laughing, and for just a moment, it was like we were twelve again. I nodded at the bag of Skittles. "You don't eat them by color anymore?"

She blinked at me, then, remembering, smiled. "Nope," she said. "Not for years now." She peered at me in the darkness. "Why, do you?"

"No," I lied, trying to sound nonchalant. "I was just . . . asking." Lucy arched an eyebrow at me but didn't say anything. I looked away, as though concentrating on the road, and realized we'd reached the top of the Dip. You either lived on one side of the lake or the other, and the Dip was pretty much the dividing line. This

morgan matson

had been the spot we'd always parted ways when we had ridden somewhere together, usually with our extra-long, very complicated hand-claps. But Lucy continued on, heading down the hill, away from her house. "Where are you going?" I called.

Lucy stopped and looked up at me. "Your house," she said, as though we'd decided this in advance. "I can't go home like this. My mother would kill me."

I wasn't sure my mother's reaction would be any less extreme if she discovered me sneaking in at three a.m. with an intoxicated Lucy, but at least I would be clearly sober. I began to walk my bike down the hill after her, then stopped, feeling my heart start to beat a little bit faster, my adrenaline pumping in anticipation of what I was about to do. "Meet you on the other side," I called down to her as I slung one leg over the crossbar.

"What?" Lucy asked, turning to look at me. I pushed off, pedaling full-speed down the hill. I passed her quickly, and made myself pedal even as I could feel gravity pulling me down faster and faster, forcing myself ignore the instincts that told me this was dangerous, that I was going too fast, that I was going to get hurt. I just kept pedaling, and before I knew it, I had reached the bottom of the hill, and my momentum was beginning to carry me up the other side. But I knew it wouldn't last, and I started pumping my legs harder than ever. Sure enough, the climb began to get very hard very quickly, and I could feel my calves burning with the effort to bring me—and my mother's ridiculously heavy bike—up the hill. But I didn't think about giving up this time. Not only did I have Lucy watching me, but I'd already given up on myself once tonight. I could feel my breath coming shallowly, but I forced myself, gasping, to the top of the other side. Once I'd made it, I stepped down off the pedals and let myself collapse over the handlebars, breathing hard.

I looked down and saw Lucy making her way up the hill. But even from far above her, I could see that she was clapping.

"Shh," I reminded Lucy as I kicked off my flip-flops on the porch and crossed to the door, taking my key out of my pocket.

"I know," she said, stifling another yawn. "Don't worry."

I turned the knob slowly, and pushed open the door an inch at a time, hoping it wouldn't squeak. I glanced at the clock on the microwave as we stepped inside and saw that it was 3:05 a.m.—not a time I wanted to be waking up either of my parents.

"Wow," Lucy said, not as quietly as I would have liked, looking around, "it looks just the same."

I eased the door shut behind us. "I know," I whispered as I crept past her, motioning her down the hall to my room. "Come on."

"No, I mean it looks *exactly* the same," she repeated, even a little louder. In his basket by the window, one of Murphy's ears twitched, and I realized the last thing I needed was the dog waking up and starting to bark. "It's weird." Her eyes fell to the

morgan matson

ground, and the sleeping dog. "When did you guys get a dog?" she asked, now not even whispering at all, but just talking in a normal volume.

"Today," I murmured. "It's a long story." I took another step toward my bedroom, hoping that she would follow me. But Lucy was still looking around, her mouth hanging slightly open. I realized as I watched her that she must have been feeling the same thing I had when I'd come back—like entering an odd sort of time machine, where nothing had changed in the last five years. If we'd been coming up here all this time, undoubtedly the house would have changed with us. But instead, it was perfectly preserved from the last time she'd been in it—when we'd been very young, and best friends. "Lucy," I said again, a little louder, and this seemed to snap her out of whatever reverie she'd been in.

She nodded and followed me down the hall, but stopped short halfway to my room. "You're kidding me," she murmured. She pointed at one of the framed pictures hung along the hall, where Lucy and I, at ten, smiled out at the camera, our mouths stained red and purple, respectively, from the popsicles we'd no doubt just consumed.

"I know," I said quietly, standing next to her. "It was a long time ago."

"It was," she replied. "God. Wow."

I looked at the two of us in the picture, standing so close, our arms so casually thrown over each other's shoulders. And in the glass of the frame, I could see us reflected as we were now, seven years older, standing several feet apart. After looking at it for another minute, Lucy continued walking down the hall again. And not until she opened my door did I realize that of course she didn't need me to show her the way—that at one point, she'd known my house as well as her own.

Lucy changed into the T-shirt and shorts I found for her, and I made the trundle bed with the extra sheets from our linen closet. When she came back from the bathroom, I had changed for bed as well and was experiencing a very strong sense of déjà vu. I had spent years in this same spot, with Lucy in the trundle bed looking up at me, as we talked for hours, long after we were supposed to have gone to sleep. And now here she was again, exactly the same, except for the fact that everything had changed. "This is weird," I whispered as she climbed into the trundle bed, pulling the covers up around her.

She rolled on her side to face me, hugging her pillow the same way she'd done when she was twelve. "I know," she said.

I stared up at the ceiling, feeling strangely uncomfortable in my own room, all too aware of every movement I made.

"Thanks for tonight, Taylor," Lucy said around a huge yawn. I peered over the edge of my bed to see that her eyes were drifting closed, her dark hair fanned out across the white pillowcase. "You saved my butt."

"Sure," I said. I waited a second longer, to see if she wanted to talk—about the disappointing Stephen, or the circumstances of the night. But then I heard her breathing grow slow and even, and I remembered that Lucy had usually fallen asleep before me. I'd always envied the way she could fall asleep at the drop of a hat, while it sometimes took me what felt like hours to drift off. I lay back down on my pillow and closed my eyes, even though I had a suspicion that I wouldn't be falling asleep anytime soon.

But the next thing I knew, light was streaming in through my windows, and when I sat up, I saw that the clothes I'd lent Lucy were neatly folded on the trundle bed. On top of them was the bag of Skittles, the top rolled over. And when I opened it, I saw that it contained only the flavors that had always been mine.

chapter twenty-one
Five summers earlier

I WOKE UP WITH MY ARMS AROUND THE STUFFED PENGUIN, WHO still smelled slightly of funnel cakes and cotton candy. I smoothed his scarf down, running the soft felt across my fingers, feeling myself smile as I opened my eyes, replaying the scenes from last night in my head. It had been a perfect night, and I didn't want to forget a single moment of it.

I'd been going to the Lake Phoenix carnival since I could remember. It lasted the entire weekend, and Henry and I had gone to the first night of it. That was the night I'd always liked best. Before the grass became muddy and trampled, before you got queasy at the sight of the Slurpee booths, before you saw how few people actually won at the carnival games. When everything was still shiny and magical, the way it had been last night.

Since our movie date, Henry and I had continued to spend our days together, but things had definitely changed from the easy, race-you-to-the-snack-bar friendship we'd had before. Things were more complicated now, but also infinitely more exciting, and I'd return home every night, barely even paying attention to my dinner, instead turning over in my mind a thousand little moments with Henry—the dimple in his cheek when he smiled, the way he'd brushed my hand when he handed me my ice-cream sandwich. He hadn't made any move to kiss me yet, but the possibility seemed to infuse every day, and I found myself wondering when it would be—when he took my hand to pull me up to the raft, and I yanked him into the water instead, and we surfaced at the same time, so close that I could see the water droplets on his eyelashes? When he biked me home, and then paused, clearing his throat and looking at the ground, like he was trying to gather the courage? Neither of these had been the moment, but that didn't stop them from being that much more exciting, and making me feel like after spending my whole life reading about things happening to people in *Seventeen*, things were finally happening to *me*.

The only thing that dimmed the perfection of it was Lucy, who was insistent on knowing if I'd asked Henry about her. I was vague whenever she asked me about this, and found myself trying to get off the phone with her as soon as possible, once she brought it up.

But I tried to push Lucy out of my thoughts as I sat up in bed and propped the penguin on my knees. Henry and I had spent the carnival together, just the two of us. This hadn't been easy to arrange, especially with Gelsey trying to follow me wherever I went, but I was able to bribe Warren into looking after her for the night with five dollars of the ride money my dad had given me, as well as promising to buy him ice cream the next time we went to Jane's.

After finishing the protracted negotiations with Warren, I'd headed across the carnival in search of Henry, feeling my heart pound hard with excitement. It was early yet—the sun hadn't totally set, and the neon on the rides and along the sides of the booths was just starting to glow. The *clank* of the machinery mixed with the shrieks from the people on the rides, and the yells of the workers in the booths, calling for people to step right up, test their luck, take a chance.

The funnel cake stand was almost at the opposite end from the entrance, and as soon as you got close, you could smell the scent of fried dough and powdered sugar, a combination that always made my mouth water. The sign that advertised FUNNEL CAKES/ SOFT DRINKS/ LEMONADE was in spelled out in pink and yellow neon, and standing under it, the glow from the sign reflecting on his dark hair, was Henry.

"You look really nice," he said when I finally reached him.

"Thanks," I said, smiling wide at him. Even without Lucy's help in the getting-ready department, I felt like I had been able to do an okay job with my hair and was wearing my new T-shirt. "You too." I noticed that his normally shaggy hair had somehow gotten much neater, and I could see the comb tracks through it.

The air all around us smelled sweet, and Henry reached over

and took my hand, threading his fingers through mine, and smiled at me. "Where do you want to start?" he asked.

We started with the Scrambler, then went to the Round-Up, then the Ferris wheel (we rocked the car as much as we could before the attendant yelled at us to settle down up there). Then, after we'd gotten most of the stomach-churning out of the way, we split funnel cakes and popcorn, and then shared a bright-blue cotton candy that stained our teeth and made our fingers sticky.

I'd gotten the penguin when we passed one of the game booths, and the attendant of the watergun-horse-race game had yelled out, "Hey, kid! Win a prize for your girlfriend!"

He'd said this last word with a smirk, and had probably intended to embarrass us, but Henry had just walked over to the booth, plunked down a dollar, and won (not the top prize level, but the one just underneath it) on his first try.

By the end of the evening, the neon was glowing brightly against the dark. My mom had arranged to meet me and my siblings at the entrance at nine thirty—my dad, who usually never missed coming to the carnival with us, had been working the whole weekend on some case. Henry was meeting his mom around the same time, and so we walked over together to the entrance. Just before we left, however, he took my hand and pulled me a few steps away, separate from the crowds, into the shadow of the ticket booth. And as I realized what was happening, Henry tilted his head and closed his eyes, and I closed mine just in time, and then he kissed me.

After all the articles I'd read that detailed how to kiss, I'd been worried that I wouldn't know what to do. But the second his lips touched mine, I realized I hadn't needed those articles. It had been easy.

I hugged the penguin tight, remembering. I'd been kissed. I was now a person who had been *kissed*. I rolled out of bed and practically danced out to the kitchen, though I quieted down when I saw my dad at the dining room table, on the phone, frowning at his laptop, piles of paper in front of him.

Feeling like I was full of more joy than the house could contain, I slipped out through the screened-in porch and ran down to the dock. I just wanted to lie in the sun and turn it all over in my mind, every moment of the night before. When I reached the end of the dock, though, I stopped short.

Across the water, I could see a pink bandanna tied to the leg of the dock opposite ours. Lucy was back.

chapter twenty-two

"AND DID YOU KNOW THAT THEY THINK THE FIRST VETERINARY records they can find date back to 9000 B.C.? And that the first veterinary school was founded in France in 1761?" I looked over at my brother and wished that I'd had the foresight to bring my iPod out to the dock with me. "Did you?" Warren persisted.

I just shook my head. I'd given up asking him not to tell me facts about vets twenty minutes before. "I know!" Warren enthused, looking down at the book on his lap. "It's fascinating!"

It was my day off again, and I'd finally made it down to the dock, where I'd had plans to sunbathe the afternoon away. I hadn't planned on the company of my brother, who had shown up not long after I'd arrived with my towel and cracked open my magazine. Now he was sitting on the edge of the dock with his feet dangling in the water, while I stretched out on my towel in my bikini, hoping I could pull a Lucy and just drop off to sleep. Ever since we'd gone into Doggone It!—four days ago—my brother hadn't been able to stop talking about veterinarians, and what a fascinating field veterinary medicine was.

It became clear after only a day or two—despite my mother's attempts to track down last year's feckless, dog-abandoning renters—that we now had a dog. Murphy had settled in, to the delight of my sister. Surprisingly, though, it was my father that the dog really seemed to connect with. When I left for work—always biking now, unless it looked like rain—he was usually on my dad's lap, looking at his computer screen as though he understood what was happening, and he usually reclaimed his spot after dinner as well. I'd even caught my mother patting Murphy's head the other day when she thought that nobody was watching. And to an outside observer, Warren would appear to be the dog's biggest fan—nearly every day he bought Murphy more treats, another squeaky toy, extra rawhide bones. But I knew that this, like his sudden love for the veterinary sciences, had nothing to do with affection for the dog and everything to do with Wendy, the girl who worked at Doggone It!.

"And—" Warren started, as I pushed myself up on my elbows and shook my head at him.

"No," I said firmly, pushing my sunglasses up on top of my head. "No more vet facts. I've reached my limit. Go torment Gelsey."

Warren looked offended for a second, but then just sighed and shook his head. "I can't," he said, kicking at the water's surface. "She's off with her other half."

I smiled as I lay back down on my towel. Gelsey and Nora had become a unit quickly, which seemed to make her parents very happy. They'd explained, one night as they came over to say hello and collect her, that they'd been working toward a script deadline and hadn't been able to spend much time entertaining her. But this was no longer an issue. Gelsey and Nora had become pretty much inseparable after that first day. They'd arranged to be in the same tennis group, and when they weren't tormenting their tennis instructors, they were riding their bikes in tandem, heading out in the morning, to the pool or the beach. Every night, Gelsey was burbling over with things that Nora had said, facts about Nora's life in Los Angeles, reports of their adventures. As I listened at dinner, I realized that Gelsey finally had her first best friend. "Then go tell Mom or Dad," I said to Warren, as I turned my head to the side and closed my eyes. "Because I'm done."

The *beep-beep-beep* of a truck backing up sounded, and I sat up straight and looked back toward the driveway, even though not much of it could be seen through the screened-in porch. "FedEx?" I asked, as Warren turned and squinted.

"UPS," he said, shaking his head. "FedEx was here this morning."

In addition to his work packages, my father had started ordering things like crazy, and was getting a lot of deliveries. It seemed like every day, multiple packages arrived—books, DVDs, chocolates from Belgium, steaks from Omaha packed in dry ice. He'd continued to get up early, and we'd had two more diner breakfasts, complete with our question quiz. (I'd learned that he had dreamed of being an astronaut when he was little, that the food he hated most in the world was lima beans, and that he'd gone to a ballet every night for a month after meeting my mother, to catch up.) Every night after dinner, we all gathered in the family room and watched a movie, and he was usually still up by the time I went to bed, reading a book, surrounded by an ever-growing stack of them.

I'd been unable to fall asleep a few nights before, and had gone out to the kitchen to get a drink of water, more because I was bored than thirsty, and had found my dad stretched out on one of the couches, the embers of a dying fire still crackling a little in the fireplace. The dog was sleeping on his feet, and he had his reading glasses on and a thick book propped up against his chest.

"Hi," I whispered, and my dad turned his head and smiled when he saw me, pulling his glasses off.

"Hi, kid," he said quietly. "Can't sleep?"

I shook my head and crossed to sit on the couch across from his, leaning forward to try to see his book. "What are you reading?" I asked.

"T.S. Eliot," he said, holding it up for me. The cover showed a black-and-white photo of a mournful-looking man. "Ever read it?" I shook my head. He settled the book on his chest again. "*The Love*

Song of J. Alfred Prufrock," he said. "I remember it was my favorite in college." He settled his glasses on the bridge of his nose again and squinted at the text. "I can no longer remember why, exactly, it was my favorite in college."

I smiled at that and curled up on the couch, resting my head on the decorative pillow that was scratchy against my cheek. It was so peaceful out here—the intermittent crackle of the dying fire, the dog's breathing, interrupted by an occasional snort, the presence of my dad—that I had absolutely no desire to go back to my own room.

"Want to hear some of it?" my dad asked as he looked over the book at me. I nodded, trying to remember how many years it had been since someone had read to me. I'd always wanted my father to do it when I was little, even though most nights he wasn't home until long past my bedtime. But when he was there, he was the only one I wanted to hear stories from—he added in details my mother didn't, like the fact that Hansel and Gretel were guilty of trespassing and willful destruction of property, and that the Three Little Pigs could have pursued a harassment charge against the Big Bad Wolf. "Okay, here we go." He cleared his throat and started to read in a voice that seemed somehow weaker than the big, booming baritone I'd always associated with him. I told myself it was just because he was trying to be quiet, and not wake the whole house. And I closed my eyes and let the words wash over me—about women talking of Michelangelo, and yellow fog, but mostly, a refrain about how there will be time, time for you and time for me. And these last words were echoing in my head as my eyes got heavier, and the last thing I remembered before falling asleep was my dad placing a blanket over me and turning out the light.

"I'm not sure what he got this time," Warren said now as he looked back toward the driveway and the UPS truck. "Personally, I wouldn't mind more steaks."

"I hope it's something as good as those chocolates," I said, hearing my voice go up a little higher than normal, into the range of forced cheerfulness. "They were amazing."

"They really were," Warren said, and I noticed he had the same bright, high tone to his voice. He met my eye briefly before looking back at the water. We weren't talking about the reason why our dad had suddenly turned slightly manic—or about the fact that he wasn't eating many of the gourmet treats he was having flown to the Poconos from all over the world, and had started to get noticeably thinner.

I flipped a through a couple more pages of the magazine, but it no longer seemed particularly interesting, and I tossed it aside after a few minutes—but carefully, since it was one I'd borrowed from Lucy. Things had been better with us since our impromptu sleepover. We weren't good friends again by any stretch of the imagination, but the atmosphere at work had gotten a lot more cordial. Elliot, upon hearing about Lucy's breakup, had started dropping a lot more things when we were all working together, confirming what I'd begun to suspect—that he had a crush on her. But as far as I could tell, he hadn't done anything about this except exponentially increase the amount of cologne he wore to work. I was worried that if he kept it up, customers might start to complain.

"So what's going on with the Crosbys?" Warren asked, making me jump.

"What do you mean?" I asked, wondering why this simple question was making me so nervous. I hadn't seen Henry since I so thoroughly embarrassed myself at Movies Under the Stars, but I'd been thinking about him—Henry now, and the Henry I'd known before—much more than I ever would have admitted.

"I mean that tent by their house," Warren said, looking through the gap in the trees, where you could see a flash of Day-Glo orange vinyl. "It looks like they're harboring vagrants."

I shook my head and lay back down. "I seriously don't think they are."

"Well, I know that's what you think, but statistically . . ." I let Warren drone on about the legal definition of squatting, which somehow turned into him telling me that "hobo" actually stood for "homeward bound," and I was just beginning to be able to tune him out when I heard a familiar-sounding voice right above me.

"Hey there." I opened my eyes and saw Henry standing on the dock, wearing a faded Borrowed Thyme T-shirt and surfer-style swim trunks, carrying a towel.

"Hi," I stammered, sitting up and trying to fluff up my hair, which I had a feeling had gone limp with the heat.

Warren pushed himself up to standing and tilted his head to the side, then asked, "Henry?"

Henry nodded. "Hey, Warren," he said. "It's been a while."

"I'll say," Warren said. "It's nice to see you again." He crossed to the end of the dock and held out his hand. After a tiny pause, Henry shifted his towel to the other arm and they shook. "I heard that you guys were next door to us now. How've you been?"

"Pretty good," Henry said. He glanced over at me and met my eye for only a second, but it was enough to set my pulse racing. "How about you?"

"Oh, fine," Warren said. "Good, really. Heading to Penn in the fall, spending the summer doing some reading." Henry nodded politely, not seeming to realize that Warren was just getting started. "Like, right now I've been reading up on the history of veterinary sciences. And it's really fascinating stuff. For instance, did you know that—"

"Warren," I interrupted. He looked over at me and I smiled at him, all the while trying to convey with my thoughts that he should really stop talking, or better yet, leave.

"Yes?" he asked, apparently not understanding any of these mental messages.

"Didn't you, um, have to help Dad? Inside?" Warren just frowned at me for a moment, causing me to question, not for the

morgan matson

first time that summer, if my brother really was as brilliant as everyone seemed to think.

"Oh," he said, after a too-long pause. "Right. Sure." He waggled his eyebrows at me in what was a very un-Warren, but incredibly annoying, way before he turned to go. He'd only taken about two steps when he pivoted back around to face Henry. "Actually, about that tent on your lawn—" he started.

"*Warren,*" I said through clenched teeth.

"Right," he said quickly. He gave Henry a quick wave, then turned and headed up the grassy slope toward the house.

"Sorry to bother you," Henry said as he walked up to where I was sitting on the dock, dropping his towel next to mine. "I didn't realize you guys were out here."

"Oh, no," I said, and could hear how high my voice sounded. It was as if I'd suddenly become part Muppet. I was suddenly very aware that, in my bikini, I wasn't really wearing all that much. "It's fine. Totally, totally . . . fine."

Henry spread out his towel and sat on it, stretching his long legs out in front of him. I was conscious that there was not a lot of space between us, and couldn't help thinking back to that moment in the woods, his hands on my back, the only thing separating his skin from mine the thin fabric of my T-shirt.

"Your brother doesn't like the tent?" he asked, bringing me back to the present moment.

second chance summer

"It's not that," I said. "He just . . . wondered what was going on with it. He was worried that you were taking in hobos or something."

Henry smiled at that, a smile that crinkled the corners of his green eyes and made me smile back, almost like a reflex. "Not hobos," he said. "But close. Davy's living in it."

"Oh," I said, then paused, waiting for more of an explanation. When Henry just leaned back on his elbows, and looked out at the water, I asked, "And why is Davy living in it?"

"He's been on this whole wilderness kick for a few years now. He'd sleep in the woods if my dad would let him. This was their compromise. And he's only allowed to sleep in it in the summers."

Thinking of the occasional weekends we once used to spend up here in the winters, and how frigid cold they could be, I nodded. "Did he get it from you?"

"Get what from me?" Henry turned to face me, eyebrows raised.

"The whole in-the-woods thing," I said. Henry continued to look at me, and the directness of his gaze was enough to make me look away and concentrate on smoothing out the wrinkles in my towel. "You were always trying to get me to come with you and look at different bugs. You used to love that stuff."

He smiled at that. "I guess I still do. I just like that there's a system in the woods, an order to things, if you know how to see it. I always find myself in the woods when I need to think something out."

Silence fell between us, and I realized that this was the first time, since our initial meeting on this dock, that it had been just the two of us—no little brothers or customers or blond girlfriends. But it wasn't an uncomfortable silence—it was companionable, like the silences we used to have when we'd spend rainy days in the tree-house, or hours lying out on the raft. I looked over at him and saw that he was already looking at me, which surprised me, but I didn't let myself look away. I took a breath to say something—I had no idea what; in my head I hadn't gotten any further than his name—when he stood abruptly.

"I think I'm going to go for a swim," he said.

"Oh," I said. "Okay, have—" But I lost whatever I was going to say next, because that's when Henry took off his shirt. Dear God. I swallowed hard and looked away but then, remembering my sunglasses perched on top of my head, I lowered them as casually as possible so that I could look at him and not have it be totally obvious that I was staring. And I don't know if Henry had been lifting sacks of sugar or flour at the bakery, but his shoulders were broad, and his arms were muscular, and his stomach muscles were defined. . . .

It suddenly seemed much warmer on the dock than it had just a moment before, and when Henry nodded at me before diving into the water, I tried to wave back casually. I watched him swimming—the stroke I recognized, the one we'd both been taught by our long-ago swim team instructors—until I couldn't see him any longer, then pulled on my shorts and T-shirt, picked up my towel, and headed inside.

As I came close to the house, I became very aware of two things— opera and popcorn. A soprano was wailing, hitting her high note as I crossed in from the screened-in porch to the kitchen, where I discovered the source of the popcorn smell.

There was what looked like a movie theater's worth of popcorn on the dining room table—popcorn in tins, popcorn in bags, balls of popcorn wrapped with cellophane. Warren was standing nearby in the kitchen tossing a popcorn ball up in the air, while my father sat by the table, the dog sleeping in the crook of his arm, humming along to the music, reading along with the liner notes.

"Hi," I said as I dropped my sunglasses and magazine on the kitchen counter. I looked around at all of it, and since the house hadn't been a popcorn factory when I'd gone out to the dock, I figured this must have been what arrived in the UPS truck.

"Taylor, listen," my dad said, holding up a finger. Warren caught the popcorn ball, and we all listened to the woman sing something in Italian. He smiled at me when she'd finished her aria, and I noticed for the first time how white his teeth looked against his skin, which was getting a more yellowish cast. "Isn't that lovely?"

"Very nice," I said, as I headed over to the table and helped myself to a handful of what looked like kettle corn from an open bag.

"It's *The Barber of Seville*," my dad said. "Your mother and I saw a production of this when we were first married. And I always told myself I'd go see it again, someday." He looked down at the liner notes, turning the pages slowly, and I took a bite of my kettle corn, which pretty much put all the other kettle corn I'd ever had to shame.

"This is incredible," I said, and my dad gestured for me to give him some. Though he took a handful, I noticed he ate only a few kernels and winced slightly when he swallowed. But he smiled at me nevertheless.

"Supposed to be the best popcorn in the country," he said. "I thought we should try it out, especially if we're finally going to watch *The Thin Man* tonight." I exchanged a glance with Warren, who tossed the popcorn ball up in the air again. Though none of us had ever seen it, my dad had been talking about *The Thin Man* for years. He claimed it was the perfect bad-day antidote, and was always offering—or threatening, depending on how you looked at it—to play it for us when we were in bad moods. "You kids will love it," he continued. "And I think Murphy will get a kick out of Asta." He jostled the dog, who opened his eyes and yawned, resting his head against my dad's arm.

At least, that had been the plan. But then Gelsey came home, thrilled with the news that Nora had been given permission to sleep over. And it seemed my mom had volunteered Warren and myself as babysitters, because she'd made reservations to go out to dinner with my dad at what had been their favorite restaurant in Mountainview. Since the opera was blaring again downstairs, Gelsey was bouncing-off-the-walls excited about her sleepover, and Warren was back to the subject of How Interesting Vets Are, I retreated to the front porch with my magazine and a Diet Coke. The shadows of the trees were just starting to stretch across the gravel when my mom stepped out onto the porch, calling, "Taylor?"

"Yeah?" I turned around and saw that mother was dressed up in a way I hadn't seen her in a while—white summer dress, her hair up in a chignon, her eyes done. I could smell her light, floral perfume, the kind she only ever wore when going out, the one that conjured all the nights I'd spent when I was younger, sitting on the bathroom counter and watching her get ready to go out with my dad, convinced that she was the most beautiful woman in the world. "You look great," I said, and meant it.

My mom smiled and smoothed down her hair. "Well, I don't know about that," she said. "But thank you. You're okay watching the girls tonight?"

I nodded. "Sure. It's fine." Even though Warren would be home as well, I had the feeling he would disappear with his book at the first available opportunity. She lingered on the porch for a moment, twisting her hands together. In the silence that followed, I was aware of just how much I wished things were different. I wanted to be able to talk to her, and tell her how afraid I was of what was going to happen, and have her tell me everything was going to be all right. But the way we'd always behaved stopped me, and all I could see were the barriers and walls I'd put up between me and my mother—casually, unthinkingly, not realizing that at some point I might want to take them down.

"Ready to hit the road?" My dad joined my mother on the porch, looking more like the version of himself that I had grown up with. He was wearing a blazer and a tie, and I tried not to see how big his clothes were on him, how he seemed to be disappearing in them. As they waved good-bye to me, my mother calling out last-minute instructions while I nodded, I realized that as they walked to the car in the slowly falling darkness, they could have been just any couple heading for a dinner out. They could have been just my parents, both of them healthy and whole, the way I'd always known them, and the way I had stupidly always assumed they'd stay.

Two hours later, I stuck my head into Gelsey's room. "You guys okay?" I asked. I expected to see a typical slumber party unfolding—snacks (God knows we had enough popcorn), magazines, makeup, maybe a stolen trashy novel. But instead, Nora was sitting on the carpet, playing a game on her phone while Gelsey, on her bed, paged through a ballerina biography.

"We're fine," Gelsey said. Nora just gave me a nod without looking up from her phone.

"Okay," I said. I looked at the scene for a moment longer before backing out into the hallway. "So . . . just call if you need something."

"Sure," Gelsey said. I closed the door and stood outside it for a moment, wondering if they'd just been quiet because I was there, waiting for the laughter and shrieking of a normal sleepover. But there was nothing but silence.

Without even thinking through what I was doing, I retrieved my cell from my bedroom and scrolled through my contacts until I found Lucy's number, and pressed it before I could change my mind. She answered on the second ring.

"Hi, Taylor," she said, her voice slightly wary. "What's up?"

"Sorry to bother you," I said as I walked down the hallway toward the kitchen. I pulled open the fridge door and saw that we had—in addition to a truly absurd number of bottles of chilled ketchup—cookie dough and Sprite. Perfect. "It's just that my sister and a friend are having a sleepover."

"Okay," Lucy said, stretching out the word. "And?"

I thought back to what I had seen in Gelsey's room, how sedate and utterly free from makeovers it had been. "And they're doing it wrong."

There was a pause. "How wrong?"

"They're not talking. My sister's reading and her friend is playing a video game."

There was another pause. "That's not good."

"I know," I said. "Clearly they don't know what they're doing. And I was just thinking back to our sleepovers. . . ." I didn't have to finish the sentence; I had a feeling Lucy would understand. Our slumber parties had been epic, and whenever I'd had sleepovers with friends back in Connecticut, I always found them wanting in comparison. I shifted the phone to my other ear and waited.

When Lucy came back on the line, her voice was brisk and businesslike, as though we'd had a previous arrangement all along. "What do you need me to bring? I'm not sure what kind of snacks we have here."

I felt myself smile as I pulled open the kitchen cabinets. "We have more popcorn and chocolate than anyone could possibly want," I said. "But maybe if you have any candy or chips?"

"Done and done," she said. "Cookie dough?"

"Covered," I assured her.

"Good," she said. "All right. I'll see you in ten."

After we hung up, I excavated my makeup case from where it had been gathering dust on my dresser, since I hadn't felt much need to wear any so far this summer. I had been expecting Lucy to drive or bike over, so it came as a shock when, not even ten minutes later, I got a text from her that read *Am here on dock need hlp w stuff.*

I hurried out through the screened-in porch and down the steps to the hill that led to the dock. Even though it was past eight, there was still some light left—it was one of those long summer twilights

second chance summer

that seem to go on forever, the light somehow tinged with blue. I could see Lucy climbing up on the dock and hauling a one-person kayak up with her.

"Hey," I called as I stepped barefoot onto the dock. "I thought you'd be biking."

"This is way faster," she said. She dropped two overstuffed canvas tote bags on the dock and dragged the kayak over to the grass, the paddle resting inside it. "Plus, no traffic this way."

"Were you able to see?" I asked, as I hoisted one of the bags over my shoulder. Lucy lifted up a flashlight from the kayak and turned the beam on and off once. "Gotcha," I said.

She joined me on the dock and picked up the other bag, and we walked together toward the house. "Did you get in trouble the other night?" she asked, lowering her voice even though it was clearly just us in the backyard. "I didn't think I woke anybody up when I left, but you never know."

"You were fine," I assured her. I had spent a somewhat anxious morning, worrying that someone had heard us, and that I would have some tricky explaining to do, but it appeared that we'd gotten away with it.

"Good," she said, with a relieved smile. We reached the front door, and Lucy followed me inside. Warren was in the kitchen, attempting to juggle three of the popcorn balls. When he saw Lucy,

morgan matson

his jaw dropped open, and all three of the balls fell to the ground, one right after the other.

"No way," he said, shaking his head. "Lucinda?"

Lucy shook her head. Warren had always insisted that her name just couldn't be "Lucy," but had to be short for something, and as a result, had called her as many permutations of this as he could find. "Hey there, rabbit Warren," she said, and Warren turned red before bending down and picking up the popcorn balls. I had found the expression when I'd read *Watership Down* in sixth grade, and told Lucy about it, so that she could have some of her own ammo against him calling her Lucifer. "Long time no see."

"Likewise," he said. "Taylor mentioned that you were working together, but I didn't know you were coming over tonight." Warren shot me a questioning look, mostly, I suspected, because he didn't want to have sole responsibility for the preteens.

"Lucy's here for the slumber party," I told him as I headed down the hallway, Lucy following behind. "You better not eat all the cookie dough!"

Two hours later, the slumber party had been salvaged. Gelsey's hair had been teased out until it was twice its normal size and accessorized with glittery clips, and Nora's was in two elaborate French braids. My hair had been worked on by both girls simultaneously, and so I had a row of three ponytails on Nora's side and a head full of mini-braids on Gelsey's. And we were all sporting dramatic new makeup, thanks to Lucy. When she'd arrived, she'd pulled out a professional-grade tackle box that Fred would have most likely envied. But instead of lures and fishing line, it contained the largest assortment of makeup I had ever seen. Gelsey was now wearing so much makeup that I was already planning the explanation to my mother if she came home before I could get it off her. Nora's eyes had been done in a cat-eye style. She'd shrugged it off as "okay," but I couldn't help notice that she was peeking into Lucy's hand mirror every chance she got, looking at her reflection with a tiny smile on her face.

We'd turned Gelsey's bedroom into a proper slumber party room—blankets on the floor, pillows arranged in a circle, the food, magazines, and makeup in the center. We'd eaten our way through an entire tin of the kettlecorn, had made Sprite floats with vanilla ice cream I'd uncovered in the freezer, and had devoured the entire bag of tortilla chips Lucy had brought. We'd read through the advice section of *Seventeen* (I'd hidden Lucy's *Cosmo* when I saw Nora looking at it a bit too interestedly) and had taken all the quizzes. We'd had a very unsuccessful round of Light as a Feather, Stiff as a Board—Lucy conceded that you really needed six people to do it properly—and now, we were playing Truth or Dare.

"Okay," Nora said, crossing her legs, leaning forward, and

looking among the three of us. "Lucy," she said, after a dramatic pause. "Truth or dare?"

Most of the dares so far that night had been pretty tame, and the majority of them had involved tormenting Warren. And so—maybe figuring that there was safety in numbers—Warren had taken the dog with him to the family room where, last I checked, he'd been sitting on the couch, back to the wall, book in his lap, protected against any further sneak attacks.

"Truth," Lucy said. I shot her a slightly admonishing look, and she gave me one back that said, *Don't worry about it.* It was surprising that after all the time apart, I could still read her. Almost as surprising as finding out that she could still read me. And she had picked up that I was nervous about just how truthful she was planning to be. Gelsey had always liked her—Lucy, an only child, had been willing to spend hours playing with my sister, and what's more, seemed to enjoy it. But after seeing her makeup collection, and finding out she was captain of her gymnastics team back in New Jersey—something that had been news to me as well—I could see the girls moving into full-on idolization mode, and I didn't want them hearing the full truth about Lucy's exploits. After seeing her flirt with practically every guy who came to the snack bar, I had a feeling that she'd had a number of them.

"Okay," Nora said. Gelsey motioned her over, and they had a whispered conference before Nora returned to her seat and fixed

Lucy with her direct gaze. "When did you have your first kiss? And who was it with?"

My mind immediately switched to my own answer, the one I'd given at so many other sleepovers. *When I was twelve. Henry Crosby.*

"When I was thirteen," Lucy said now, "with Henry Crosby."

I stared at her, wondering if this was some kind of a joke, as Lucy helped herself to some of the jalapeño-flavored popcorn. "What do you mean?" I asked, feeling a jealous burn in my chest.

"Sorry, Taylor, but it's Gelsey's turn next," said Nora, who had taken it upon herself to administer the rules of truth or dare.

Lucy looked at me and raised her eyebrow. "What?" she asked. "Did you never expect him to go out with anyone else, ever again?"

"No," I spluttered, wishing I didn't sound so defensive. "I just . . . didn't know." Lucy tossed back another handful of popcorn. "Did you two date or something?"

Nora and Gelsey were looking between the two of us, riveted, and I had a feeling this drama might turn out to be the highlight of the party.

Lucy shrugged. "For about a month. And we were *thirteen*. It wasn't serious."

I recognized the tone—it was the same one I had used when I'd laughed off my relationship with Henry. It was only in hearing it from someone else that I realized how untrue it was when I said it. Because even if I tried to make light of it, Henry hadn't just been

morgan matson

some guy who didn't matter, nothing but a story to tell about a random boy I dated when I was younger. He had mattered, and he still mattered—which explained why all of our interactions had been so charged. It was why I was suddenly feeling possessive and incredibly jealous of Lucy, who had already moved past this story and was continuing on with the game.

I was caught up in these thoughts until I heard Gelsey say something about getting to first base, and my attention snapped right back.

"What?" I asked, staring at my sister. She just stared back at me, her freckles showing though Lucy's application of concealer and foundation. It wasn't like we'd been close, or that she'd ever told me her secrets, but I still would have thought I would have known if something like this had happened. "When was this?"

"At the dance last year," Gelsey said with a shrug. "With a couple of different guys."

"What?" I could hear my voice rising to the level of shrill, and Lucy shot me an alarmed look. I was suddenly regretting ever letting Gelsey put on makeup, and I was already planning in my head the conversation I was going to have with my mom when she got home.

"Just to clarify," Lucy said, her voice serious. "Remind me. What's first base again?"

"Holding hands," said Nora and Gelsey in unison, and I could feel myself relax, hugely relieved that my sister hadn't turned into some kind of sixth-grade hussy. Lucy bit her lip, and I could see that she was trying not to laugh.

Nora may have picked up on this, because she shot Lucy a withering look. "You know, holding hands is a *really* big deal," she said, and Gelsey nodded. "It *means* something. And you don't hold hands with just anybody. You only do it with someone you really care about."

Nora and Gelsey continued on about the importance of hand holding, but I tuned them out when I thought I heard the sound of tires crunching on gravel. Sure enough, a moment later, I heard the sound of the door opening and closing and my dad calling out, "Kids? We're home!"

My mother did her patented two quick knocks before opening the door, and not actually giving you enough time to say "Come in" or "Stay out"—which, actually, may have been her intention. "Hi," she said. Her gaze traveled around the room, her eyes widening when she saw the amount of makeup my sister was wearing, and then stopped on Lucy. "Oh, my goodness," she said. "Lucy, is that you?"

"Hi, Mrs. Edwards," Lucy said, scrambling to her feet. While my mom and Lucy made small talk, catching up over the last five years, Gelsey tossed Nora the now dog-eared *Seventeen*, and they bent their heads over it together, Gelsey bursting out laughing at something Nora pointed to. As I watched, I felt myself smile, and realized our work here was done.

morgan matson

After we left the girls with the rest of the snacks, and instructions to make cookies at midnight, Lucy packed up her things and we headed down the corridor, my mother and Lucy still talking.

"So great to see you again," my mom said as we reached the from door. "And be sure to tell your mom hi for me."

"I will," Lucy assured her as my dad came in from the family room, the dog, as usual, under his arm.

"Can this be Miss Marino?" my dad asked, smiling wide, pretending to be shocked. "All grown up?"

"Hey, Mr. Edwards," Lucy said, but I could see her smile falter a little bit as she looked at him. Even though he was laughing and rubbing the dog's ears, I could see what he looked like through Lucy's eyes—much too thin for his frame, the kind of thin that always seemed to convey sick, not just dieting. The yellow cast to his skin. How much older he looked than he should have.

We walked out to the screened-in porch in silence, each of us carrying one of Lucy's bags. I led the way down the three steps, and felt the grass, cool on my bare feet. The night was clear, the moon huge over the lake, and the stars were as numerous as I'd ever seen them. But I barely noticed this as we started walking down toward the dock. I had a feeling Lucy was going to say something, so I turned to her first, asking the question that had refused to leave my mind. "What happened with you and Henry?"

Lucy stopped and adjusted the bag on her shoulder. "What do

you want me to say?" she asked. "We dated, and it didn't work out, and so we split up, and now we're friends. Kind of."

"Whose idea was it to go out?" I asked. "Yours or his?"

"Mine," Lucy said evenly, looking right at me. "I liked him, as I think you were aware."

I felt my face get hot, but at the same time, it was freeing to talk directly about the things we'd been mad about, but not ever naming, all summer. "I know," I said. "But just for the record, Henry and I had started dating before you told me you liked him. I just didn't tell you because I didn't want ..."

"What?" Lucy asked.

I shrugged. It seemed so stupid now, and so long ago, and yet, the ramifications of it all were still playing out, even now. "I didn't want it to get in the way of our friendship," I finally muttered.

"Ah," Lucy said, nodding. Deadpan, she added, "Well, that sure worked out." I met her eye and we both burst out laughing. "Have you told Henry this?" she asked.

"No," I said, looking over at her. Lucy shrugged.

"It might help," she said lightly. She gave me a look that let me know she could tell what I was thinking, even after five years, even in the semidarkness. "Just so you know, most people don't get this upset when they find out their childhood boyfriend dated someone else," she said. She arched an eyebrow at me. "I'm just putting that out there."

Not really wanting to respond to this, I started walking down toward the dock again, Lucy falling into step next to me. "So," she said after a moment. The way she hesitated, I had a feeling that she was choosing her words carefully. "Is your dad okay?"

Even though I'd had a feeling this was coming, the question still made my chest tight, like someone was clenching my heart, making it hard to breathe. "He's sick," I said, hating how even this simple, obvious admission made my voice waver, and made me aware that there were tears lurking behind my eyes somewhere. And that maybe they'd been there, just waiting for their chance, ever since we'd found out.

Lucy looked over at me, and I found myself incredibly grateful that she didn't ask, "With what?," that she somehow knew not to ask this. "He has cancer," I said out loud for the first time. I swallowed hard and made myself go on, saying the word that I hadn't even known a few months ago but now hated above all others. "Pancreatic."

"I'm so sorry," she said, and I could hear from her voice that she meant it. "Is he . . . ," she started, then looked away from me, and I could feel her uncertainty. "I mean, will he . . ." She looked back at me and took a big breath. "Get better?"

I felt my face crumple a little, my chin start to tremble. I shook my head, feeling tears flood my eyes. "No," I whispered, my voice hoarse, and next to me, I could hear Lucy draw in a breath. I kept walking toward the dock, focusing on the water in the moonlight, and I tipped my head back slightly, trying not to blink. I knew that if I blinked, it would be all over. I'd be crying, and I had a feeling I might not stop for a long, long time.

"Oh, my God," she murmured. "Oh, my God, Taylor, I'm so sorry. That's just . . ." Her voice trailed off, as though words wouldn't be able to describe it.

We walked on, me fighting back tears, and then I felt Lucy's fingers brush mine as she took my hand and held it firmly in hers.

As she did this, I could feel the first hot tear hit my cheek, and then my chin was trembling, out of control again. As I looked out at the water, I realized there was nowhere to go, nowhere left to run. And I just had to stay here, facing this terrible truth. I felt, as more tears fell, just how tired I was, a tiredness that had nothing to do with the hour. I was tired of running from this, tired of not telling people, tired of not talking about it, tired of pretending that things were okay when they had never, ever been less okay. I attempted to pull my hand away, but Lucy just held it, squeezing mine hard, all the way to the end of the dock. And there was something about it—maybe the fact that she was letting me know, physically, that she was there, that she wasn't going anywhere—that made me feel like I could finally just let myself cry.

When I'd pulled myself together a bit, Lucy headed back to get her kayak, dragging it across the dock. She took out the paddle and flashlight and placed the kayak on the edge of the dock. "Can I do anything?" she asked.

I shook my head. "No," I said, running my hand across my face. "Thanks, though."

Lucy didn't take the easy out, though, continuing to look at me intently. "Will you let me know if there is anything I can do?" she asked. When I nodded, she pressed, "Promise?"

"Promise," I said. She dropped the kayak in the water and climbed in, and I handed her down the paddle and flashlight.

"Hey," she said, looking up at me in the moonlight as she bobbed below the dock, "do you remember any of those codes we used to have?"

I felt myself smile as I thought back to all those messages we had figured out how to send each other across the water. "I think so," I said.

"Good," Lucy said, using the paddle to push off the dock and propel herself forward with swift, practiced strokes, the beam of her flashlight bobbing on the water. "Just stay out here for a minute, okay?"

"Okay," I called back. She waved the paddle at me, and I sat down on the dock and watched her progress, my eyes straying only occasionally to the carving at the end of it, the inscription that joined my name with Henry's.

When I looked back at the lake, I couldn't see Lucy anymore, and figured she must have made it home. Just as I thought this, a beam of light flashed across the water at me. One flash, then three. Then two more, then three.

It came to me after a moment, and I felt myself smile as I translated the message she was sending me.

Good night, Taylor. I'll see you tomorrow.

chapter twenty-three
Five summers earlier

"TAYLOR?" I LOOKED UP FROM MY LOUNGE CHAIR AND LOWERED MY
dark sunglasses. Lucy was standing in front of me, wearing a bathing suit I'd never seen before, and an expression that fell somewhere
between happiness and annoyance.

"Hey, Luce," I said as I stood up and we hugged, my excitement
at seeing her tempered by all the half-truths I'd been telling her
about Henry, not to mention the secrets about him I'd been keeping
from her. Even though I'd seen the bandanna a week and a half ago,
I'd been avoiding her as much as possible. I was spending most of
my time with Henry. We had carved our initials into the dock the
day before. Part of me thought it was the most romantic thing that
had ever happened, but another part of me kept looking across the
lake, worried that Lucy would see us. She'd been calling every day,
and I'd promised Warren my dessert for a month if he would make
up excuses and not ask questions. Because I knew I wouldn't be
able to talk to her without telling her everything that had happened
with Henry—which meant explaining that I'd never actually talked

to him about her, even though almost a month had gone by since she'd asked me.

My mother, saying that my father needed peace and quiet to work, had shooed me out of the house. Not wanting to go to the lake, I'd gone to the pool with a pair of my mother's old sunglasses and took one of the least desirable lounge chairs, hoping to fly under the radar.

"I've been looking everywhere for you!" Lucy said, pulling me into another hug, and as she did, I realized with a pang just how much I'd missed her, and how she was the only person I wanted to tell about all the Henry stuff—that even my first kiss didn't seem complete, because I hadn't been able to discuss it with her. "We have so much to talk about," she said, grabbing me by the hand and pulling me in the direction of the concession stand.

"Where are we going?" I asked, letting myself be pulled.

"Snacks," Lucy said, grinning at me. She pulled a ten-dollar bill out of her pocket and waved it at me. "I think it's guilt money. Both my parents are giving it to me. My treat."

Lucy talked a mile a minute as we waited in line, and got Cherry Cokes and a frozen Snickers, to split. She only seemed to notice I hadn't been saying much once we'd paid and were heading toward one of the wooden tables. "What's been going on with you?" she asked, finally taking a breath.

I set my can down and brushed my fingers through the lines

of condensation that were already starting to form on it. "Actually," I said, a little haltingly, "there's something I have to tell you." Lucy smiled and leaned forward, but then she looked past me, and her smile froze, turning into something much less relaxed.

"Oh, my God," she breathed, sitting up a little straighter, a faint blush coming into her cheeks, "he's here. Do I look okay?"

I turned around to look behind me, and felt my stomach plunge when I saw Henry heading toward me, smiling. Before I could say or do anything—although what I would have said, I had no idea, as I felt totally frozen—he had reached us.

"Hi," Lucy said, in a giggling, high-pitched voice I wasn't sure I'd ever heard before. She smoothed down her bangs and tucked her hair behind her ears, smiling wide at him. "How's it going, Henry?"

"Fine," he said, glancing at me, and giving me a smile. "When did you get back?" I saw him start to reach for my hand, but I immediately stiffened, and moved my hands so that both were around my Cherry Coke can.

"Oh, about a week ago," Lucy said, her voice still high-pitched and giggly. "Did you miss me?"

"What?" Henry asked, looking baffled. He took a step closer to me. "Um, I guess."

"Taylor," Lucy said, turning to me, still smiling brightly but a little fixedly. She jerked her head in the direction of the concession stand. "Why don't you go get us some napkins or something?"

She was trying to get rid of me. She was trying to get rid of me so that she could talk to Henry—my Henry, who just a second before had tried to hold my hand. I closed my eyes for a moment, wishing that all of this would just stop, the whole time knowing it was my fault this was happening at all.

"Taylor?" Lucy asked again, her voice a little sharper this time.

"I'll come with you," Henry said, taking a step closer to me and, before I could stop him, taking my hand in his. "Lucy's being *weird*," he whispered in my ear.

Lucy was staring at the two of us, and she looked much paler than she had just a moment ago. "Taylor, what's going on?" she asked, her voice no longer giggly.

Henry looked between the two of us, uncomprehending. "Didn't Taylor tell you?" he asked with a wide, happy smile. He squeezed my hand and swung our linked hands a little. I just stood there, feeling like I was rooted to the spot, not able to speak, or look away from the expression on Lucy's face.

"She didn't tell me *anything*," Lucy said, her voice now laced with anger.

"Oh," Henry said, his smile dimming a little. He looked at me, frowning slightly. "Tay?"

I cleared my throat, and even when I spoke, it was like the words were sticking there. "Listen," I said haltingly. "Lucy, I didn't . . ."

Lucy narrowed her eyes at me, then turned to Henry. "The only thing Taylor told me about you was that she doesn't like you. That you just want to spend all your time in the woods. That you're a huge dork." She looked back at me, her expression hard. "Isn't that right, Taylor?"

Henry's face fell, and he also turned to me, looking more hurt—and confused—than I had ever seen him look. "Taylor?" he asked. He dropped my hand. "What's she talking about?"

I looked between the two of them, and I realized how much I'd hurt them—both of them. I didn't see any way that I could make things better, or even start to fix anything. And I was backing away from the table before I even realized I'd made a decision. But by then, it was too late—I just went with it. I turned and ran for the entrance, leaving them both—the two people who meant the most to me, who I had just managed to hurt simultaneously—behind.

I had left all my things back at the pool, but I didn't care. None of it seemed to matter anymore. I biked home on autopilot, tears blurring my vision. I had no idea what I was going to do, but I knew I needed to be home. I could figure things out once I got there.

I threw my bike onto the gravel of the driveway and ran toward the house. I had just opened the door when I almost crashed into my father, who was heading out of it, his weekend bag in his hand.

"Taylor?" he asked, looking down at me. "You okay?"

"Are you leaving?" I asked, looking at the bag. Usually my father was up only for the weekends, but he had planned on taking this whole week off, now that it was August, and things usually quieted down at his office. "Now?" I could hear the disappointment in my voice.

"I know," my dad said with a grimace. "Work has just gotten crazy, and I have to be there. Sorry, kid."

I nodded, but my mind was suddenly racing ahead with all kinds of possibilities that I knew I really shouldn't let myself consider. But once the idea was planted, it was all I could think about. I took a deep breath before asking, "What if I went back with you?"

"What do you mean?" he asked. He put down his bag and frowned at me. "You mean go back to Connecticut?"

"Yes," I said, trying to sound casual. Lucy's face flashed into my mind, but I tried to push it away, not wanting to think about Lucy. Certainly not wanting to think about Henry, and what he must be feeling right now. Instead, I made myself smile at my father, as I said in a voice so confident that I almost believed it myself, "Yeah. I'm kind of tired of it all up here, anyway. When should we leave?"

Ten minutes later, I'd thrown my clothes into a bag and we were heading down the driveway. I'd looked at the stuffed penguin for a long moment, wanting so badly to take it with me, to try to hold on to the feeling I'd had when I'd woken up the morning after the carnival. But instead, I left it on my bed, knowing that I wouldn't be able to take seeing at it every day in Connecticut.

We had reached the end of the driveway when my dad stopped the car. "Isn't that your friend Henry?" he asked.

I looked up, alarmed, and saw Henry biking up the street, his hair askew, looking out of breath, heading toward our house. "No," I said, looking away from where Henry was approaching, and at my dad. "We should just go."

"Are you sure?" he asked. "We can wait a moment if you want to talk to him."

"I don't," I said as firmly as I could. "Seriously, we should go."

"Okay," my dad said in an *if-you-say-so* kind of a voice. He turned down the street, and we passed right by Henry as we went. I met his eye for just a moment—and saw how confused and unhappy he looked—before looking away, facing forward, and pretending I hadn't seen anything at all.

The Beginning of a Beautiful Friendship

chapter twenty-four

"JERKFACE." I THREW DOWN MY CARDS ONTO THE COUNTER.

"Jerkface." Lucy followed suit immediately, causing Elliot to look at us over the top of his remaining cards and sigh.

"Seriously?" he asked, as Lucy nodded, fanning her cards for him.

"Read 'em and weep," she said in triumph.

"I think it's the name," Elliot grumbled as he scooped up the cards and started shuffling them. "I can't get used to it."

We were technically playing Asshole, but after Elliot had yelled it a little too loudly in triumph, just as a mother was approaching with her toddlers, we had figured that it might be time to institute some precautionary measures. Lucy was sitting cross-legged on the counter, I had pulled up a high stool, and Elliot was standing, so that he could pace while he considered his strategy.

"Another round?" he asked, clearly hoping that we'd forgotten the stakes of the game.

"Not a chance," Lucy said with a laugh. "Next three customers are yours." She hopped off the counter and crossed to the side door, holding it open for me.

"But what if there's a customer who needs something complicated? Or grilled?" Elliot asked. "What then?"

"Then call for us," I said, going to join Lucy by the door. "We'll just be outside."

Elliot shook his head, grumbling, as he continued to shuffle. Lucy stepped outside into the sunshine and I followed, letting the door bang shut behind me. Though he'd never said anything, I got the feeling that Elliot wasn't thrilled that Lucy and I were friends again. Not that he was happier when it had been drama-and-tension-filled—he actually told us that he was glad, since before that, working with the two of us had been like being stuck in some terrible reality show in which the main characters, who hate each other, are nonetheless forced to interact. But in the days that followed, it became clear that Lucy and I finding our way back to friendship meant that neither of us was spending as much time hanging out with him.

It wasn't like it had been a perfectly easy transition. For one thing, we were dealing with a five-year gap, and for both of us, a lot had happened in those five years. So even as we were having fun catching up, there were moments that illustrated just how vast the holes in my knowledge were—like when Lucy was talking about someone named Susannah, and I hadn't realized that this was the name of her stepmother. And she would occasionally say something, or make a reference to something that Elliot would immediately get, while I would be utterly in the dark. It was a strange combination of making a new friend while simultaneously getting to know an old one. But something had changed that night after she'd come to the slumber party. We had been able to let go of the past, the reasons why we'd stopped being friends, and I'd been reminded just how good a friend Lucy was. Not to mention how much fun we had when we were together. I'd forgotten that when you were around Lucy, there always seemed to be the possibility of something *happening*. She could somehow make going to the PocoMart to get snacks feel like an adventure. But we could also just gossip and talk for hours, the conversation rarely flagging.

We'd discovered that we both liked the grassy area with the picnic tables. It had a balance of sun and shade, and looked out at the water—but, most importantly, it provided an excellent view of the parking lot, which meant that we would be able to see Fred's truck if he happened to drop by. He did this occasionally, and it always indicated the fish had refused to bite for him that day—meaning he would already be in a disgruntled mood and would probably not be too happy to see two of his employees lying out in the sun while on the clock.

We headed straight for what had quickly become our favorite spot. Elliot handling the next three customers could mean, in the late-afternoon lull we were in, that it might be half an hour before we had to return to the snack bar. Lucy kicked off the flip-flops we weren't technically supposed to be wearing in the kitchen and sank down cross-legged onto the grass. I followed, lying back on my elbows and turning my face up to the sun.

"So," Lucy said, turning to look at me. "How's everything going?" Since we'd been working together all day, I knew this wasn't just an idle inquiry. It was her coded way of asking about my dad, which she did every few days, always careful not to press it if I didn't want to talk. I hadn't realized how much I would appreciate someone else knowing about him. It was so nice to just be able to shrug off the question, and to know that she would listen if I wanted to talk—which I hadn't, really, yet. But the opportunity was there. Mostly, it was just a relief not to have to pretend, as I was still doing with almost everyone else, that things were still just fine.

"About the same," I said, squinting out at the water. This was pretty much the truth. My father seemed to be doing basically the same. He was working on his case and on his project, which remained a secret despite Warren's many attempts to crack the mystery. My dad seemed to have calmed down a little bit in terms of the mail order—we were no longer deluged with gourmet packages from around the world—but he was still trying to read as much and see as many movies as possible. Possibly as a result of this, he had started taking a nap every afternoon. He was also thinner than ever, despite all the Belgian chocolates. We'd been to the diner for breakfast two more times but with each visit, he seemed to eat a little bit less of whatever he ordered. My mother had started trying to counterbalance this at dinner by simply serving him double the portion that the rest of us were eating, and then watching him like a hawk throughout the meal, so that she barely ate anything herself. At dinner two nights ago, my dad had only picked at his food, starting to wince whenever he took a bite, and he'd finally looked up at my mother and sighed.

"I'm sorry, Katie," he said, as he moved his plate away. "I just don't have any appetite."

My mother had sent me for a vanilla milkshake from Jane's for him, but by the time I'd come back with it, he'd already gone to bed. I'd ended up sitting on the back steps, drinking it myself as I looked out at the moonlight hitting the surface of the lake.

I kicked off my own flip-flops and stretched out my legs in front of me on the grass, hoping Lucy would understand that I wanted to change the subject. "So what's up with Kevin?"

"Kyle," Lucy corrected. "Kevin was last week." She wiggled her eyebrows at me, and I shook my head, smiling. Since her breakup with Stephen, Lucy had been dating her way through all of Lake Phoenix's eligible—and not-so-eligible—guys. She seemed to still be completely unaware that Elliot was pining openly for her and messing up most customers' orders as a result. And the one time I'd tried to hint to her that there might be dating prospects with someone she already knew, someone she was friends with, she'd thought I was trying to set her up with Warren, and things had briefly gotten very uncomfortable.

"But you could have Kevin!" Lucy said, her face lighting up. "And then we could double. Perfection."

"Luce," I said, shaking my head, and Lucy sighed. Ever since she'd reentered the dating scene with a vengeance, she was always trying to get me to go out with her. But I had resisted every invitation, knowing full well the reason why.

"Is this because of Henry?" she asked, fixing me with her direct gaze.

"No," I said, much too quickly for it to be the truth. Because it absolutely was. I hadn't talked to him since we'd been on the dock together, but whenever I'd gone into Borrowed Thyme to pick something up, I'd been disappointed when it wasn't him behind the counter. I'd seen him a few times at a distance, in his kayak on the lake, silhouetted against the sun.

"You need to do something about that," Lucy said as she lay back down on the ground and closed her eyes. "Either become friends with him again, or tell him how you feel and get it over with." Before I could respond, Lucy's phone beeped with a text, and she grinned as she sat up. "Bet you it's Kyle," she said, drawing out the syllables of his name. But her face fell as she read the text. "It's just Elliot," she said, dropping her phone back on the grass again. "He says he needs you to come back." Since I'd started to have more of a social life, I'd begun carrying my phone again, but Elliot would always call Lucy's phone, even when the message was for me.

"Fine." I sighed, but I was already standing up and sliding my feet into my flip-flops. I was actually grateful to have some time to think about what Lucy had said. I wasn't going to ask Henry out—he had a girlfriend with annoyingly perfect hair—but maybe we could be friends again. Did I really have anything to lose?

"Don't let him trick you into staying," Lucy said as I started toward the snack bar. "We still need to talk about the Kyle situation."

I nodded as I headed to the employee entrance. I had a feeling that Elliot might actually need my help, because if he just wanted one of us to keep him company, he would have asked for Lucy. "What is it?" I asked, as I came in through the side door, going temporarily blind as my eyes adjusted to the darkness after the brightness of the day outside.

Elliot tipped his head toward the front window. "You were requested specifically," he said. Gelsey and Nora stood in front of the window, my sister smiling, Nora looking impatient.

"Hey, you two," I said, stepping up to the center of the counter. "What's up?"

"Where were you?" Nora asked, folding her arms across her

chest. While she'd gotten slightly less grumpy recently, she certainly hadn't become sunshine and light, by any stretch of the imagination.

"I was just taking a break," I said, wondering why I was justifying myself to a twelve-year-old. "Do you guys want something?"

"Sprite," they said in unison. "And barbeque chips," Gelsey continued, "and frozen M&Ms."

Nora peered into the darkness of the snack bar. "Is Lucy here?"

"She's up on the grass," I said, pointing. The girls' adoration of Lucy had been cemented when, the day after the slumber party, they'd come to the beach and Lucy had taught them how to do round-offs.

Elliot filled the sodas and grabbed the snacks while I rang them up. I handed Gelsey back the change, and after a moment's consideration, she magnanimously put a single quarter in the tip jar.

"Thanks," I said. Nora took a sip of her soda and Gelsey opened the bag of chips, but neither of them made any effort to leave. "Was there something else?" I asked. We weren't exactly besieged by customers, but apparently Fred didn't like people just hanging out in front of the snack bar, as it discouraged the people who didn't want to wait on line.

"Uh-huh," Gelsey said, crunching down on a chip, then tilting the bag toward Nora, who pursed her lips and carefully selected one. "You need to pick up the dog from the groomer's when you're done with work."

"You're kidding." I sighed. "Again?"

Both Gelsey and Nora nodded. "Again," Nora confirmed. "Your brother has a problem."

Last week, my mother, shocked at just how many squeaky toys Murphy had managed to accumulate in a very short time, had forbidden all of us (but specifically Warren, since he was the only one buying them) from getting the dog any more accessories. And so, Warren had been devising increasingly desperate and obvious excuses to go to Doggone It!, see Wendy the vet-in-training, and possibly get up the nerve to say more than hello. The first time he'd spilled something on the dog, we'd thought it was an accident. Warren claimed that he'd just been drinking some tomato juice when the dog had run into the kitchen. He took the dog to get groomed, and nobody thought anything of this until, two days later, Warren managed to spill grape juice on him. Back Murphy went to the groomer, and when I caught Warren stalking the dog with a bottle of ketchup (because the dog, no fool, had started to flee whenever he saw my brother approaching), I'd finally confronted him about it.

"You need to stop tormenting the dog," I told Warren as I forcibly removed the ketchup from his hands and stuck it back in the fridge. "You're going to give him some kind of skin rash or something. I don't think dogs are supposed to be washed this often."

"Want me to tell you about the dog that crossed over three

thousand miles to get back to its family?" Warren asked, clearly choosing to change the subject, rather than own up to the fact that he'd been attempting to douse the dog with ketchup.

"No," I said, automatically. "But want me to tell you about the guy who traumatized his dog because he couldn't ask a girl for a date?" Normally, I never would have said something like this to my brother. Maybe it was because I was so much more aware of what was happening in his social life now, in a way that I hadn't ever been in Stanwich.

Warren blushed bright red. "I don't know what you mean," he said, crossing his arms and then uncrossing them again.

"Just ask her out," I said, as I knelt down to look under the table. Murphy was cowering there, shaking slightly, but when he saw that I wasn't Warren—or wielding a liquid to throw at him—he seemed to relax slightly. I gestured for him to come, but the dog stayed put, clearly not sure if I was on Warren's side or not. I straightened up to find my brother looking uncharacteristically confused.

"And, um," he said, clearing his throat and then opening and closing the fridge for no reason whatsoever, "how exactly should I do that?"

"How should you ask her out?" I echoed. "You know. Just—" I stopped short when I saw the look on my brother's face and realized that he might not, in fact, know how to do this. "Just strike up a conversation," I said. "And then steer it toward whatever you want the date to be."

"Uh-huh," my brother said, and he looked around the kitchen, his fingers resting on the legal pad we always kept by the phone. I had a feeling that he was on the verge of taking notes. "And can you give me an example of that?"

"Well," I said. I had never asked anyone out directly, but I had certainly encouraged guys in the right direction. "Like, if you want to take her out to dinner, mention that you know a great pizza restaurant, or whatever. And then hopefully she'll say she loves pizza, and then you ask if she wants to eat some with you."

"Okay," Warren said, nodding. He paused for a moment, then asked, "But what if she doesn't like pizza?"

I let out a long breath. If I hadn't known my brother had a near-genius level IQ, I certainly would never have believed it after this conversation. "That was just a hypothetical," I said. "Pick anything you want. A movie, or miniature golf, or whatever."

"Right," Warren said, looking lost in thought. "Got it." He headed out of the kitchen, then took a step back in and gave me a slightly embarrassed smile. "Thanks, Taylor."

"Sure," I'd said, and then tried to see if I could coax the dog out from under the table.

After that, the dog had gone unassaulted for a few days, so I assumed that Warren had taken my advice, or at least abandoned this particular strategy. But it seemed that Murphy had to once again suffer the ineptitude of my brother's flirting techniques.

I looked over the counter at Gelsey and Nora, who were now passing the bag of frozen M&Ms between them. "What was it this time?" I asked.

"Syrup," Gelsey said. "Mom was really pissed."

"I bet," I said, thinking what a sticky mess that must have created.

"So she isn't letting Warren pick him up. She wants you to do it. And then pick up some corn for dinner."

"Got it," I said, glancing back at the clock. I stretched my arms over my head, glad that I had only half an hour left on my shift.

"What's wrong with your dog?" Elliot asked, apparently deciding to join this conversation.

Nora frowned at him. "Who are you?"

"Elliot," he said, pointing to his name tag. "Taylor's boss."

I rolled my eyes at this. "No, you're not."

"Her superior, at any rate," he amended, unfazed.

"Anything else?" I said, turning to the girls.

"Nope," Gelsey said. She held out the bag of frozen M&Ms to me, and I shook three into my palm. Unlike Skittles, I didn't care what color my M&Ms were. "See you later!"

"Bye," I called as she and Nora walked away, heads bent toward each other, already deep in conversation.

"Your sister?" Elliot asked, pushing himself up to sit on the counter.

I nodded. "And next-door neighbor. They're kind of a package deal these days." I heard my phone beep with a text, and pulled it out of my back pocket. It was from Lucy, but instead of the message I'd been expecting, asking me to come back to our spot so we could keep talking, there was just one word: *FRED!!!*

"Fred's here," I hissed to Elliot, as though Fred would somehow be able to hear me. Elliot hopped off the counter and I looked around for something that I could pretend to clean, when the side door opened and Fred, looking sunburned and grumpy, stepped in, with his tackle box and a large cardboard box that he dropped on the ground with a thump.

"Hello, Fred," Elliot said, in a much-more-cheerful-than-usual voice. "How were the fish?"

Fred shook his head. "Not good. Haven't gotten a bite in days. I swear, it's like they all got a memo or something," he said, taking off his hat. I blinked, then made myself look away. The top of his head—which was covered by his fishing hat—was a totally different color than the red below it, with almost a straight line dividing the two. I wondered if I should be the one to tell Fred about the magical invention of sunblock. He looked around and frowned. "Where's Lucy?"

"Right here!" she said as she pushed the door open. "I was just doing some inventory," she said, not meeting my eye as she crossed the snack bar, wearing her best "responsible employee" expression.

"Uh-huh," Fred said, clearly not buying it. He gestured down at the box at his feet. "I just picked up the posters for the movie night. I'll expect you three to do your part and ask the local businesses to hang them up. Okay?"

"Sure," I said, and Elliot gave Fred a thumbs-up.

"Are we all set for Friday?" he asked, speaking directly to me this time.

"Absolutely!" I said, trying to sound much more confident about the movie night than I actually was. This time around, I'd had more to organize. It was up to me to pick the movie, rent the screen and projector, and order the posters. I was pretty sure everything was taken care of—except my introduction. I was trying not to think about it too much, and hoping that if I felt as nervous as I had about the last one, Elliot or Lucy would step in and do it for me.

Fred left after that, and I tore open the cardboard box, holding up one of the posters and admiring it. When I'd looked at the beach's collection of movies, and had seen the title printed on the side of the box, I'd known there was only one choice.

"What's the movie?" Lucy asked, peering over my shoulder.

"*Casablanca*," I said, scanning the poster quickly for spelling mistakes, feeling like I probably should have done this before I'd given the text to Jillian in the office.

"Never seen it," Lucy said with a shrug as Elliot made scoffing noises.

"Me neither," I said. I felt myself smile as I remembered what my father had said. "But I have a feeling it's going to be great on the big screen."

chapter twenty-five

I LEFT WORK A LITTLE BIT EARLY, SO THAT I COULD COLLECT THE dog, who was most likely thinking that he'd had it better when he'd been wandering free around the neighborhood. Life had probably been more restful, at any rate. I also had some posters with me, figuring that I could ask Wendy if Doggone It! could put one up, and maybe Henson's Produce as well. I had just pedaled up Main Street and secured my bike, and was all set to head into the pet store when I looked across to the bakery. Without really thinking it through, I was walking across the street, posters in hand, my heart pounding hard.

I pushed open the door and stepped inside, glad that I was the only customer. Henry was leaning over the counter, reading a book, and he looked up. "Hey," he said, looking surprised but not upset or angry, which I took as the evidence I needed to press forward.

"I think we should be friends," I blurted, without thinking about it first.

"Oh," Henry said, his eyebrows raising. "Um . . ." He clearly didn't know what to say after that, as nothing followed.

"I just," I started, as I took another step into the store, "I think that it would be good. Bury the hatchet, and all that."

"I didn't know there was a hatchet," he said, smiling faintly.

"You know what I mean," I said. Even though every instinct I had was telling me to turn and go, just leave the store and keep on walking, I made myself cross the floor until I was standing in front of him at the counter. Which might not have been the best idea, because now I was close to him—close enough to see the freckles across his nose, and the smudge of flour on his cheek, and the confusion in his green eyes. I looked away, then took a breath and continued. "What I did was horrible," I said. "Just leaving like that, with no explanation."

"Taylor," Henry said slowly, his brow furrowed. "Where is this coming from?"

I didn't want to tell him about my conversation with Lucy or what I'd realized the night of the slumber party. But I couldn't stop thinking about him. And if I was totally honest with myself, I hadn't ever really stopped. That in a lot of ways, he'd been the only boy that had mattered in my romantic life so far. My first love, even if I hadn't been able to admit it, before I even really knew what those words meant. "I just . . . miss you," I said, wincing at the words even as I said them, hearing how lame they sounded. "And I'd really like to be friends. Just friends," I amended, remembering the girl at the ice-cream parlor, not wanting him to think I was hitting on him.

"Well," Henry said, looking a little shell-shocked. "Anything else?"

"And I was wondering if you could put this up in your window," I said, as I placed the stack of posters on the counter and slid one over to him. I kept my eyes on his face, trying to see what he thought about what I'd just said, incoherent as it had been.

"That I can do," he said, taking the poster and looking at it. "*Casablanca*," he said thoughtfully. "Nice pick."

"My pick," I interjected quickly.

He looked up from the poster and gave me a surprised smile. "You like it?" he asked.

I could feel my face start to get hot, though by now I was finally tan enough to hide it. I found myself wishing I hadn't said anything, feeling like this was joining the long list of things that had gone wrong during the conversation. "No," I said. "I've never seen it. I've just . . . heard good things."

Henry looked down at the poster, like it might have the answer he was looking for. "I don't know, Taylor," he finally said. "A lot's happened in the last five years."

"I know," I said, feeling all at once just how embarrassed I was, like there had been a time delay on it until that moment. "Sorry," I said. "I shouldn't have . . . I mean . . ." Whole sentences did not appear to be forthcoming, and I had an almost palpable sense of relief that I would finally be able to give in to what my instincts had been screaming at me to do since I first stepped inside the store— that is, leave immediately. "Sorry," I muttered again, turning away and heading quickly for the door. I had just reached for the handle when Henry spoke.

"Taylor," he called. I turned, feeling a tiny flutter of hope in my chest. But he was just holding up my stack of posters. "You forgot these."

I hadn't known it would be possible to be more embarrassed than I had been, but apparently new and unseen depths were still being uncovered. "Ah," I murmured. "Right." I crossed toward him quickly, and grabbed the stack, trying to avoid eye contact as much as possible. But to my surprise, Henry didn't let go of the posters right away, making me look up at him, into those eyes that still startled me every time with their greenness. He took a breath, as though he was going to say something, looking back into my eyes. But after a moment, he broke our eye contact and looked away, releasing his hold on the posters.

"I'll see you around," he said, and somewhere in my mind, I registered that this was what I'd said to him the first time we'd met again, on the dock.

"I think that's inevitable," I said, echoing his words back to him.

I made myself smile as I said it, to take some of the sting out. I turned and walked, fast, to the door, and this time he didn't say anything to call me back.

My pulse was racing as I crossed the street and walked toward the pet store. I yanked open the door with probably more force than I needed to. I had a feeling that it would probably be best for everyone if I could just be by myself until I shook off this jumpy, reckless feeling. But because of my brother's social awkwardness, I had to collect the dog, and there was no way around it.

"Hey there!" Wendy said, smiling at me, even though I hadn't seen her since I'd brought Murphy for microchip identification. But she saw my dog enough that she probably felt like she knew me really well too. "I've got your little guy here for you." She reached under the counter, and I heard the faint click of metal. A moment later, she emerged with Murphy, whose tail started wagging when he saw me.

"Great," I said, dropping the fliers on the counter and taking the dog. I placed him on the ground, looping his leash over my wrist, which turned out to be a good thing, since he immediately lunged in the direction of the kittens. I glanced down at the posters on the counter, and suddenly felt a surge of sympathy for my brother, having just experienced how humiliating it was to walk up to someone and get shot down. "So. Wendy," I said, and she looked up from the computer, where she had been no doubt adding this latest service to our bill, "are you dating anyone?"

She blinked at me. "No," she said, looking maybe a little concerned. "Um, why?"

"Just wondering," I said. I pushed one of the posters across the counter at her. "Want to go on a date with my brother?"

The whole interaction had gone much more smoothly than I'd been expecting it to. Wendy had agreed almost immediately, and she knew exactly who Warren was—she hadn't even needed a photo reminder, which was a good thing, since the only picture of him that I had on my phone was a terrible one I'd taken while he was in the midst of telling me how potato chips were invented. I'd taken the picture to try and get him to stop talking and the result was Warren looking both annoyed and out of focus.

As I walked Murphy over to my bike after picking up the corn and some licorice for my father, I was feeling a tiny bit better. Even if I hadn't been able to make things right with Henry, I had gotten my brother a date and, hopefully, saved the dog from any more excessive grooming.

It wasn't until I faced the reality of getting home, with the dog, that I realized I'd hit a snag. Presumably, Warren had dropped him off in the car. It turned out that Murphy did not like the concept of my bike basket, and kept trying to get out of it, his nails scraping for purchase. When one of his paws got stuck between the metal slats, he started whimpering in a way that hurt my heart, so I dropped the kickstand and lifted the dog out immediately. "It's okay," I said, pulling him close to me for a minute. I could feel that he was trembling. "We don't have to go in the basket. It's okay." I ran my hand over his wiry head for a moment, and felt him settle down a bit.

But even though I'd made this blithe promise, I wasn't sure exactly how we were going to get home. I tried riding the bike, holding the dog's leash to the side, but it kept getting tangled in the wheel and Murphy proved himself to not be the world's fastest learner in avoiding this. And the same thing happened when I tried to walk the bike and the dog at the same time. So finally, I decided we were just going to have to go on foot. I locked my bike up by the diner, tucked the posters under my arm, and started walking Murphy home, probably undoing all the grooming work that had just been done. I was pulling out my phone to call home and let my mother know that the corn—not to mention me and the dog—were going to be a little late, when a car slowed to a stop next to me.

It was a slightly battered SUV, with Henry in the driver's seat. He lowered the passenger side window and leaned across the seat. "Hi," he said.

"Hi," I replied. Maybe he just wanted to continue our conversation from earlier, but this seemed like an odd place to do it.

"Do you need a ride?" he asked. The minivan behind him slammed on its brakes, and then honked loudly. Henry waved him around, and I realized that this was not a moment to really consider the question, or wonder why he was asking after he'd so effectively shot me down less than an hour before.

"Sure," I replied, picking up the dog and opening the passenger door. I got into the car and slammed the door, looking over at him as he shifted the car into gear. "Thanks. The dog hasn't mastered the concept of riding in the bike basket."

"No problem," he said, pulling back onto the road. "We're going to the same place, after all. It seemed rude not to offer."

I nodded and I stroked the top of the dog's head and looked out at the trees on the side of the road. So it wasn't anything except politeness. I really shouldn't have been surprised. I focused on making sure Murphy's bow—pink polka dot, again—was straight and concentrated on not speaking. I'd made such a fool of myself earlier that I didn't see the sense in making it worse. But the silence between us felt oppressive, like it was a physical force closing in on me from all sides.

Henry might have been feeling this as well, because he turned on the radio, then turned it off when a twangy, country-sounding voice started singing about lost love. We drove without speaking for a few moments, and then he glanced over at me. "I didn't know you had a dog," he said.

"Yeah," I said, scratching the spot between the dog's ears that always made his back leg thump. "It's kind of new." Henry just nodded, and silence fell between us again. I was about to leave it at that, but then, figuring that this was a safe and non-humiliating topic, took a breath and continued. "He belonged to the renters who had our house last summer."

Henry glanced over at the dog, comprehension dawning on his face. "Yes," he said, "that's where I know him from. It's been bothering me ever since I first saw him." He paused at a stop sign, looking from the dog to me. "So why do you have him?"

"They left him behind," I said. "We haven't been able to track them down, so we've kind of just taken him in."

"They left him," Henry repeated, his voice strangely flat.

I nodded. "At the end of the summer," I said. I looked over at Henry, expecting some kind of reaction. Everyone else's responses— even my grandfather's, over the phone—had been angry, distressed, concerned. But Henry's hands just tightened on the wheel, something closing off in his face.

We drove the rest of the way home without speaking, and Henry passed my driveway and pulled into his, confusing the dog, who had sat up straight when we neared our house, his nails scrabbling against the glass of the window, eager to get home. He clearly hadn't put it together that this was also the place where people dumped syrup on him. "Thanks for the ride," I said, when Henry had turned off the engine, even though he made no move to leave his car.

"Right," he said, his voice sounding far away. "Sure." I looked over at him, wondering what I'd said, or if this was just the residual tension from earlier. It seemed that in my efforts to put the past behind us, I'd unwittingly made things even more uncomfortable. I started to say something—anything—to try to get us back to a more amicable place, when the dog started full-on whining, standing up on my lap, straining to get back home again, which must have seemed extra frustrating now that it was so close.

I pushed open the door and slid out of the car, dropping the dog down to the ground, where he immediately started pulling against his leash. I was about to say something else to Henry, but he was still sitting in the driver's seat, looking lost in thought. So I just closed the door gently, and then headed up his driveway, being tugged by much more force than I would have thought a small dog was capable of, wondering what had just happened.

An hour later, I was sitting on the front porch with a glass of Diet Coke, extra ice, shucking the corn for dinner. My siblings were with me, and they were, technically, supposed to be helping. But instead, Gelsey was doing her ballet exercises using the porch railing as a barre and Warren was pacing back and forth, barely avoiding getting whacked in the face by Gelsey's *grands battements*, peppering me with questions about his upcoming date.

"And she said yes?" Warren asked, as I peeled back the green husk from an ear of corn, exposing the yellow and white kernels underneath. I felt my stomach growl just looking at it. Fresh corn was one of the best things about the summer, and Henson's corn was always spectacular. I dropped the husk into the paper grocery bag resting at my feet, then looked up and gave my brother a look.

"Yes," I said, for what had to be the eighth time. "I asked her if she wanted to go to the movie on Friday, she said yes, and I took the dog and left."

"And you're sure she knew it was with me?" Warren asked. I met Gelsey's eye just before she sank down into a *grand plié*. She gave me a tiny smile before looking away, stretching her arm over her head.

"I'm sure," I said firmly. "You have a date. You're welcome." I shook my head, wondering if I'd done the right thing. After all, Warren and Wendy sounded like some kind of terrible folk duo. Not to mention the fact that she was now going to be subject to my brother's endless wellspring of trivia.

"Right," Warren said, as though just now realizing I had something to do with this. "Thank you so much, Taylor. If there's something I can do to repay you—"

"There is," I said, handing him the half-shucked ear of corn, and picking up my Diet Coke glass—I was due for a refill. "Finish these." I headed in, through the screened-in porch to the kitchen. My mother was slicing up tomatoes, and I recognized the fixings for hamburgers on the grill.

"Corn done?" she asked as I opened the fridge to retrieve my Diet Coke.

"More or less," I said, glancing out to the porch, where it looked like Warren was talking to Gelsey, wearing a dreamy expression, but not actually accomplishing anything.

"More or less what?" my father asked, walking into the kitchen. He was holding the dog tucked in the crook of his arm and he looked a little rumpled, the way he always did when he woke up from his nap. He had also stopped dressing as though he was going to be called into the office at any moment, and today was wearing an American Bar Association T-shirt with his khakis. Without meaning to, I looked behind him to the calendar on the fridge, and saw that we had some-how ended up in the middle of June. Like every year, the summer was moving much too quickly—but I now had more of a reason to need it to slow down than just not wanting to go back to school.

"The corn," my mother said, bringing me back to the present moment as she turned down the heat on one of the burners.

"Oh, *shucks*," my father said, his pun expression spreading over his thin face. I smiled, and it looked like my mother was trying not to. "Oh, I'm sorry," he said, with mock contrition, "was that too *corny*? Personally, I thought it was a-*maize*-ing."

"Enough," my mother said, shaking her head, even though she was laughing. "We need to get these burgers on the grill." She left the kitchen, brushing my father's arm lightly with her fingers as she passed, and walked onto the porch, where I could hear her telling Warren to get a move on.

"And how was your day?" my dad asked, turning to me. "Did you do great things?"

I smiled at that, pretty sure that serving people sodas and fries didn't count. "I don't know about that," I said. "But I did get these." I crossed to the table and handed him one of the movie night posters. "What do you think?" I asked, uncharacteristically nervous as I watched him reading it.

"Did you pick the movie?" my dad asked, his voice sounding a little hoarse.

"I did," I said, and my father nodded, his eyes not meeting mine, but still on the poster. "You said it was your favorite," I said after a minute, when he still hadn't spoken. "And that you'd never seen it on the big screen . . ."

My dad cleared his throat and looked up at me. "Thanks, kid," he said. He looked back at the poster. "This is great. I can't believe you did this for me."

I nodded, then stared down at the kitchen floor tiles. What I couldn't somehow bring myself to say was all I could think about—that I had done it because I loved him and wanted to make him happy, and I had wanted him to see his favorite movie again. But implicit in that was what was staring me in the face every time I looked at the calendar—that this would probably be the last time he would see it. That it would, most likely, be one of the last movies he ever saw. I swallowed hard before I felt like I could speak again.

"And," I said, trying to keep my voice upbeat, "Warren has a date to the movie."

"Does he now?" my dad asked. He jostled the dog in his arm. "Does that mean he'll stop tormenting this poor thing?"

"Let's ask him," I said, heading out of the kitchen. My father followed behind me out to the porch where Gelsey was now stretching, her foot up on the porch railing, and her head bent toward her knee at an angle that, no matter how many times I'd seen it, always made me wince.

"Shoulders back," my mother said, and I saw Gelsey make the correction. My dad crossed over to sit next to Warren, who appeared to still be holding the same ear of corn that I'd left him with. I couldn't help but notice that my dad looked a little winded by the trip from the kitchen to the porch, that he already needed to rest from it. He settled the dog, who seemed more than happy to just be toted around in the crook of his arm, and smiled at my brother.

"So I understand you have a date," he said, startling Warren, who turned red and finally started shucking the corn.

"Really?" my mother asked, smiling at Warren, as she joined my dad, sitting on the arm of his chair. "Since when?"

"Since Taylor asked her out for him," Gelsey piped up as she straightened up from her stretch.

"What?" my mother asked, frowning, and I laughed and crossed over to help my brother with the corn while he began to recount the story. And as I sat there and listened, chiming in when necessary, it occurred to me that we had somehow never done this back home—just hung out, talking over details of our lives. If we'd been at home, my father would have been at work, and the three of us would have no doubt been doing various activities. And despite the circumstances that had brought us here, I couldn't help being glad for just a moment that we were sharing this together, as a family, at last.

chapter twenty-six

I COULDN'T SLEEP. THIS SEEMED TO BE THE THEME OF THE summer, as I found myself lying awake for hours every night, even when I'd worked all day and was exhausted and should, by all rights, have fallen fast asleep as soon as my head hit the pillow. But whenever I lay down, I would find myself tossing and turning for hours, my thoughts keeping me awake. It just seemed like ever since we'd arrived in Lake Phoenix, I was constantly being confronted with all the things that I'd done wrong and had been trying to avoid thinking about for the last five years. And it was always at night, when I couldn't escape them, that they took up residence in my head, refusing to go away.

What was keeping me up tonight, oddly enough, was the dog. There was something in Henry's reaction to hearing he'd just been left behind that had stuck with me. Because as much as I'd wanted to demonize the renters for leaving their dog behind, it was basically what I'd been doing for years now—running away or quitting whenever things got hard. I'd just never had to deal with the reality that this came with a cost. In fact, most of the time, I'd done my very best to avoid ever having to confront the consequences of my actions. But Murphy was the living proof that leaving something or someone was never just free and easy.

When I couldn't take it any longer, I rolled out of bed and pulled on a sweater, figuring that some fresh air might help, or at least clear my head a little. I tiptoed down the hall and let myself out through the screened-in porch. I didn't bother with shoes, and just stepped barefoot out into the grass.

It was a gorgeous night, the moon huge in the sky, and just as huge reflected on the surface of the lake. There was a little bit of a chill in the air, a light breeze that ruffled the leaves, and I pulled my sweater a little tighter around me as I headed down to the dock. It wasn't until I'd walked down the steps that I noticed the dock wasn't empty. This wasn't that unusual—I'd noticed Kim and Jeff out there one night, each holding pieces of paper, pacing around the dock, apparently trying to brainstorm. I slowed down as I squinted, trying to make out who was sitting on the edge of the dock. Then the figure turned slightly to the left and I saw that it was Henry.

I froze, wondering if I could walk away now without him noticing me. He hadn't turned his head far enough to see me, but I was worried that sudden movement would attract his attention. Though a second later, I thought back to all those moments that had just been keeping me awake, reminding me that I'd run away when I should

morgan matson

have stayed. But with Lucy, and now maybe with Henry, it seemed like I was getting an opportunity to at least try and make things right. So I took a deep breath and kept on going, putting one foot in front of the other until I had reached the dock. Henry turned toward me, and it was only then that I considered that he might not care about my need to confront my faults—that he'd probably come out to the dock to be by himself, and had most likely already had far too much of me that day. Also, that I was wearing what I had slept in—very short terry cloth shorts and a tank top with no bra. I was suddenly very grateful for the sweater, and hugged it even closer around me. I nodded rather than lifting one of my arms to wave at him. "Hi," I said.

"Hey," he said, sounding surprised. I made myself keep walking toward him, sensing that if I stopped or hesitated, the part of me that I usually listened to would take over and I'd turn and go hustling back inside rather than risk humiliating myself in front of him for the umpteenth time that day.

I sat down next to him at the end of the dock, careful to leave at least a person-space between us. I extended my legs until they reached the water. The lake was cold but felt good against my feet as I moved them in small circles under the surface. "I couldn't sleep," I offered after we'd been sitting in silence for a moment.

"Me neither," he said. He looked over at me and smiled faintly. "Cold?"

"A little," I said, as I hugged the sweater around me. He seemed comfortable in the cool night air, wearing a gray T-shirt that looked much-washed and soft, and a pair of drawstring shorts. I suddenly wondered if this was what he'd been sleeping in as well, and the thought was enough to make me avert my eyes, quickly, back to the lake and the moonlight.

"I'm sorry about before," he said, looking out at the lake as well. "In the car. I didn't mean to shut down like that."

"Oh," I murmured. I hadn't known that's what had happened. "Was it . . ." I started, then paused when I realized I wasn't sure how to say this. "Did I say something wrong?" I finally ventured.

Henry shook his head and looked over to me. "Not really," he said. "It just . . ." He let out a breath, then continued. "My mom left," he said. He kept his eyes on mine as he said this, and trying not to betray my shock, I made myself keep looking into his eyes, not letting myself look away. "Five years ago," he said. "At the end of the summer." He broke our eye contact and looked back out to the lake. I looked down and saw that his fingers were curled around the edge of the dock, and his knuckles were white.

"What happened?" I asked softly, trying not to let the shock I was feeling seep through my voice. But inside, I was reeling. Mrs. Crosby had just *left*?

Henry shrugged, and kicked one foot in the water, sending out a series of ripples that grew and grew, until finally the water stilled again. "I knew she was having some trouble that summer," he said, and I tried to remember back. Truthfully, in a summer that had mostly been defined by first dates and carnival kisses and drama with Lucy, I hadn't been paying a lot of attention to Henry's mother. She had seemed like she always had—a little distant and not particularly friendly. "I hadn't thought it was anything. But the week before we were supposed to go back to Maryland, she went into Stroudsburg to do some shopping. And she didn't come back."

"Oh, my God," I murmured, trying—and utterly failing—to imagine my mother doing something like that. For all the times we'd argued or disagreed, for as hard as I'd sometimes tried to push her away, it had never once entered my mind that she would go.

"Yeah," Henry said with a short, humorless laugh. "She called later that night, I guess so my dad didn't wouldn't call the police. But then we didn't hear anything from her until she contacted us two years ago, when she wanted a divorce."

This was somehow continuing to get worse. "You haven't seen your mother in five years?" I asked, a little faintly.

"Nope," he said, a hard edge coming into his voice. "And I don't know if I ever will again." He looked over at me. "You know what the worst part was? My dad and I were at a baseball game. She just left Davy alone in the house."

I did the math and realized that Davy would have been seven then. "Was he . . ." I swallowed hard. "I mean, did anything . . ."

Henry shook his head, thankfully stopping me from having to

finish the sentence. "He was fine," he said. "But I think it's the reason he got so into wilderness survival after that. Even though he tells us it's because of a show he saw on Discovery."

Slowly, things were beginning to come together. "Is this why you moved up here full-time?" I asked. It was also, of course, the reason that none of us had seen Mrs. Crosby the whole time we'd been here.

"Yeah," he said. "My dad needed to do something else, find a job where he could be around more. He'd always liked it up here. We had to move houses, because in the old place Davy and I were sharing a room. Not that he ended up needing a room of his own," he added, his lips curling in a small smile as he looked toward his yard, where Davy's tent sat. Henry shrugged, and kicked at the water again. "My dad was kind of a mess for a while after she left," he said, his voice quieter. I waited for him to say more, give me details about it, but he was already continuing. "So moving here . . . it just seemed like the right thing to do."

I nodded, but was still trying to wrap my head around everything. It suddenly struck with a force that sent a chill through me, that only a week or two after I had suddenly left with no explanation, his mother had done the same. "Henry," I said quietly, and he looked back at me. "I'm really, really sorry." I hoped he knew that I meant it, and wasn't just tuning out these words as I had been doing with everyone who had tried to offer them to me.

"Thanks," he said quietly, but not meeting my eye, and I couldn't tell if he believed me or not. "I just wanted to let you know why I flipped out like that."

"It didn't look like flipping out," I said.

"I tend to flip out very quietly," Henry said, deadpan, and I smiled. "Sorry to tell you all this," he said with a shrug.

"I'm glad you did," I said. He met my eye and gave me a small smile.

I realized there was something I had to tell him in return. I took a breath, but somehow, telling him out here in the darkness didn't seem quite as impossible. "My dad's sick," I said. Immediately after I said it, I could feel my eyes prick with tears, and my bottom lip start to shake. "He's not going to get better," I said, making myself go on, and sparing Henry having to ask. "That's the real reason—" My voice caught in my throat and I looked down at my feet in the water, forcing myself to get through it. "The real reason we're up here. To have a last summer." As I finished speaking, I felt a tear spill over, and I wiped it away, fast, hoping Henry hadn't seen, willing myself to keep it together just a little bit longer.

"I'm so sorry, Taylor," Henry said after a moment. I looked over at him, and saw in his face something I hadn't seen from any of the people who knew—a recognition, maybe, of what I was going through. Or someone else who, at least, had gone though something that most other people were unable to really understand.

"I probably should have told you that first day," I said. I ran my hand over the smooth planks of the dock and thought that it was fitting, maybe, that we were here, at the place where we'd first met again—that we had come full circle like this. "But I think I wanted to pretend it wasn't happening."

"I can understand that," he said. We sat in silence for a moment, and the breeze kicked up again, blowing Henry's hair over his forehead. "What you said earlier," he said. "About being friends. I think we should do it."

"Really?" I asked. Henry, his face serious, nodded. "But what about what you said—about all the stuff that's happened in the last five years?"

Henry shrugged and gave me a smile. "So we'll catch up," he said. He pulled his feet out of the water and turned to face me. "Should we start now?"

I just stared at him in the moonlight for a second, not quite able to believe that this was being offered to me so readily. It made me ashamed for thinking so little of Henry—feeling like he wouldn't be willing to forgive me, just because that's how I would have acted. But in that moment, it was like I'd suddenly been given a second chance. It was one I knew I didn't deserve, but it was one I was getting anyway. I pulled my feet out of the water as well, and turned toward him. "Yes," I said, feeling myself begin to smile, just a little. "Now sounds perfect."

morgan matson

chapter twenty-seven

THE DAY AFTER HENRY AND I MADE OUR PEACE ON THE DOCK, HIS brother showed up on our porch with a proposition.

Henry and I had stayed up talking until almost five a.m. We sat on the dock, occasionally dipping our feet in the lake, and swapped stories—but not in a rushed way, trying to cram everything in. Instead, we traded them back and forth easily, the way we'd once traded comic books (I'd been partial to Betty & Veronica, he'd had what even he now admitted was an unhealthy obsession with Batman). Henry didn't really say any more about his mother leaving, and I didn't want to talk about what was happening with my dad. And neither of us discussed any other romantic history we might have had in the intervening years. But every other subject, it seemed, was open.

Henry had told me about how he almost got a tattoo—and showed me the one mark from this experience, a dot on his tricep that looked like a freckle, and was going to be a tribal design until he'd felt the first needle go in and had realized he was making a mistake. "And they still charged me for a whole tattoo, can you believe it?" he'd asked me, as I peered at the tiny almost-tattoo in the moonlight.

I told him about my brief desire to be a marine biologist, until I realized that fish really grossed me out and that I tended to get seasick on the open ocean—things that it would have been helpful to know before starting a summer-long oceanography camp.

He told me about how he'd failed the driver's test twice before barely passing the third time, and I told him about the speeding tickets I'd been able to talk myself out of. He told me about the first vacation he and Davy and his dad took after Mrs. Crosby left, and how he'd wanted it to be perfect. And they'd ended up camping in a snowstorm, everyone freezing and unhappy, until they all called it quits and spent the rest of the vacation watching TV and eating takeout in a motel room. I told him about last Christmas, when we'd gone to St. Maarten and it had rained every single day, and Warren had been so desperate to find out about his admissions letters that he tried to call our mail carrier, and my mother finally confiscated his phone. We talked about music (he got offended when I labeled his penchant for barefoot singer-songwriters "crunchy"; he mocked me for knowing the names of all three Bentley Boys, despite my protests that I only knew about them through Gelsey) and snack bar gossip—it seemed he'd been in on Elliot's Lucy crush weeks ago, and had given up trying to get him to do something about it when

Elliot assured him that he was actually *was* doing something about it, that he had a plan, complete with flowchart.

And as we talked, I remembered just why we'd been such good friends when we were kids. It was in the way he listened when you were talking, the way he wasn't just waiting to jump in with his own story. It was the way he always weighed his words, meaning I always knew that when he responded, it had been carefully considered. It was in the way that every time he laughed—which wasn't often—it seemed earned, and made me want to do everything I could to get him to laugh more. It was his enthusiasm for things, and how when he discussed what he was passionate about—like how much he loved being in the woods, how he felt things made sense there—I found myself getting swept up in it along with him.

As the hours passed, our pauses between stories grew longer, until we were just sitting in comfortable silence together and looking out at the water, and the first ribbon of daylight showed up on the horizon.

That's when we parted and headed to our separate houses. As I'd crept into the kitchen, I'd been stunned to see that it was five a.m., and was sure, as I headed to my own room, that I'd have no problem getting to sleep now. But once I'd settled myself in, I realized that there was something missing. And I'd gone to my closet, and returned with the stuffed penguin, settling him next to me on the pillow.

I didn't even mind it all that much (maybe because I hadn't had

second chance summer

a chance to really fall asleep) when my father tickled my feet at eight a.m., waking me up for our breakfast. Though it seemed to me that he was eating even less than usual—even Angela the waitress commented on it—we worked our way through the new placemat quiz. (It turned out that he was scared of roller coasters and was allergic to ginger.) After breakfast we'd collected my bike from where I'd left it outside the diner the night before, and I'd driven us home. Nobody in my family had said anything, but in the last few days, my father had stopped driving. He had walked around to the passenger side of the Land Cruiser without comment, leaving me to fumble with the keys and head over to the driver's seat, trying to pretend that this was just totally normal.

When I pulled into the driveway, I saw, as expected, Murphy behind the door of the screened-in porch, jumping around excitedly at the sight of my father returning. But I was surprised to see Davy Crosby sitting on our front steps. He was wearing a variation on what he'd been wearing every time I'd seen him—a T-shirt, cargo shorts, and moccasins.

"Hello there," my father said, as he got out of the car a little unsteadily. I noticed that he reached for the porch railing right away, and leaned on it heavily even as he smiled down at Davy.

"Hi," Davy said, standing up and offering my father his hand, which my father shook. "I'm Davy Crosby. I live next door to you. I was wondering if we might speak."

"By all means," my father said. He looked down at Davy's feet and smiled. "Nice moccasins, son." He glanced back at the house. "Was there nobody here to let you in?" Davy shook his head and my father looked at me, a question on his face.

"Probably at the Rec Center," I said, realizing that this was Gelsey's ballet day, and she and my mother were probably occupied. And since when I left that morning, I'd noticed Warren laying out every article of clothing he owned, and muttering over them, I had a feeling that he might have gone along to try and convince them to take him on a last-minute, pre-date shopping trip.

"Ah," my father said. "Well, shall we discuss this inside?"

"Sounds fine," Davy said, and my dad pushed open the screen door, sending the dog into paroxysms of joy. He scooped up the dog and met my eye for just a second, and I could see that he was trying to conceal a smile, which he had successfully done when he sat in his normal seat and Davy settled in opposite him.

"So," my father said, his voice serious as he scratched the dog's ears. "Your proposition?"

"Yes," said Davy, sitting up straight. "I couldn't help but notice that you have a dog." My father nodded gravely, and I bit my lip to stop myself from laughing. "I would like to propose that I walk him for you." Davy looked between my father and me. "I don't expect payment," he clarified. "It's just that I like dogs. And Dad says we can't have one," he added, sounding like a kid for the first time that conversation.

"Well," my father said after a pause, in which I noticed that the corners of his mouth were twitching violently. "I think that sounds fine. Come by anytime, and I'm sure that the dog will be happy to be walked."

Davy's face broke into a smile. "Really?" he asked. "Thank you so much!"

My father smiled back. "Want to start now?" he asked, since that was what Davy very clearly wanted. He started to push himself up from the chair, but immediately winced, and I sprang up from mine, heading toward the kitchen, pretending I hadn't noticed this.

"I'll get the leash!" I called. I grabbed it from the hook by the door, and when I came back out onto the porch, my father had put Murphy on the floor, and Davy was patting the dog's head tentatively. "Here," I said, handing the leash to Davy. He clipped it on carefully, and Murphy started straining toward the door, clearly eager to get on with it.

"Have fun," my father said, settling back in his chair with a smile as Davy and the dog started out the door.

"Thanks," Davy said. He paused in the doorway and turned back to my dad. "I heard you were sick," he said. "I'm sorry about that." I looked at my father and saw, with a sinking feeling in my stomach, some of the happiness drain right out of his face, like someone had hit a dimmer switch.

"Thank you," I jumped in, when it didn't look like my dad was going to be able to respond to this. Davy nodded and headed down the driveway, the dog running as far in front of him as the leash would allow. After a moment, I looked over at my dad. I knew it was my fault—the only reason that Davy knew was that I had told his brother—but I wasn't sure if this was something I should apologize for, or something we were just going to pretend hadn't happened.

"That's Henry's brother?" my dad asked, looking out to the driveway, where Davy and Murphy were just passing out of view, then back to me.

"Yes," I said. "He's Gelsey's age."

My father nodded, then looked over at me with a smile that I knew from experience meant trouble. "Henry's a nice boy, isn't he?"

"I don't know," I said, feeling my cheeks get hot, even though there was no reason for them to. "I mean, I guess so."

"I've seen him at the bakery," my father continued, opening his *Pocono Record* slowly, as if he actually had no idea that he was torturing me. "And he's always been very polite."

"Yeah," I said, crossing and uncrossing my legs, wondering why it felt like my face was on fire. Henry and I were barely friends again, let alone . . . anything else my father, in his oh-so-knowledgeable voice, might have been implying. "Dad, want me to bring you your laptop?"

"Sure," he said, turning to the crossword, and I let out a silent breath of relief that he was going to drop the subject. I stood to head into the house so my father could work on his mystery project. "You know," he said, when I had my hand on the doorknob. I turned back to him, and saw that my father was still smiling. "The window in the hallway upstairs faces out toward the dock."

I gripped the handle harder. "Does it?" I asked. I was trying to keep my voice light, even though, technically, I hadn't done anything wrong. I didn't think that it was that bad, after all, that I'd snuck out of the house at three a.m. if the only place I'd gone was the backyard.

"Mmm," my father said, apparently still engrossed in the paper. After a moment, though, he looked up and smiled at me. "Like I said," he said, "he seems like a nice boy."

I felt my cheeks flame again. "Laptop," I said, in my briskest voice, as I headed inside to the sound of my dad chuckling. But even after I'd retrieved his laptop from where it had been charging on the couch, I found that I couldn't quite stop smiling.

chapter twenty-eight

"YOU'LL BE FINE," LUCY SAID, REASSURINGLY. SHE TURNED TO Elliot, who was shuffling his ever-present deck of cards and, when he didn't agree, whacked him hard on the arm. "Won't she?"

"Ow!" Elliot yelped. "I mean . . . um, yeah. Totally. You'll do great. Way better than last time. Which I'm not . . . supposed to mention," he said, noticing that Lucy was giving him a death glare. He gave me a big smile and a thumbs-up, and I felt my stomach clench. Movies Under the Stars had arrived again, and neither of my coworkers were letting me out of doing the introduction. Lucy had just read the self-help book of a former reality TV star, and this woman was apparently big on "confronting your demons." I'd seen some of this woman's show, and it appeared that she was big on confronting everything, but this argument made no headway with Lucy. And once Lucy took a stand with something, I knew Elliot would never disagree with her. I had, however, gotten him to promise to rescue me if I crashed and burned again.

The days leading up to the movie had passed in a blur of what had become the normal routine—breakfast and questions with my father, work with Lucy and Elliot, nights eating dinner with my family on the screened-in porch. But now thrown into the mix was Henry. It turned out that we reported to our respective jobs at the same time, and the day after our dock talk, he'd caught up with me as I was attempting to simultaneously bike and drink coffee from my to-go mug. Though we hadn't talked much on the ride (I was still getting into biking shape, and found that I needed my breath for other things, like getting to the top of Devil's Dip) it had been nicely companionable. The next morning, I'd caught up with him, and we'd been biking into work together ever since. We hadn't had any more long talks on the dock, though I found myself checking it several times before I went to bed every night—just to make sure nobody was out there. And even though I knew she'd be interested, I hadn't told Lucy about it. For one thing, he had a girlfriend. And I didn't want it getting back to him that I had any interest in him again. Which I wasn't even positive that I did, so there was no point in pursuing it.

There was also the fact that every time I found myself staring into space at work, and starting to think about Henry, something inside my head would snap to attention and remind me of what really mattered. What was happening with my dad was what was really important, and I shouldn't let myself forget that, even if my father had developed the annoying habit of asking me far too many

morgan matson

pointed questions about Henry, always with a knowing smile. But none of that seemed as pressing at the moment as the fact that I was possibly about to humiliate myself in front of fifty people for the second time.

"You know," Elliot said with fake nonchalance, "if we had gone with one of my movies, I'd have no trouble talking about it. We should think about that for the next one."

"No," Lucy and I said in unison. She turned to me as Elliot started his shuffle again, muttering about people with no cinematic taste. "You'll be fine," she said, giving me an encouraging smile. "And if you're not, I'll start doing cartwheels in front of you, okay?"

I couldn't help laughing at that. "Luce, you're wearing a skirt."

She smiled wider. "All the more effective, then, right?"

The cards flew everywhere as Elliot lost control of the deck. Red-faced, he bent to pick them up as Lucy rolled her eyes. I took the opportunity to check out the crowd and possibly throw up or faint, if need be. The sun was huge and low in the sky, having begun the process of setting, reflecting its oranges and reds onto the lake. I looked at the clock and saw that it was getting close to eight thirty, the start time that Fred had scheduled for tonight's show.

"Taylor!" I turned at the sound of this distraught voice to see my brother, wearing his usual uniform of khakis and a polo shirt, holding a bouquet of flowers with a death grip, and looking like he might be close to fainting himself.

"Hey," I said. I scanned the towels and blankets—I hadn't seen my family arrive. "Where are Mom and Dad?"

"There," Warren pointed, and sure enough, I saw our blanket spread out on the sand. My father had his arm around my mother's shoulders, and she was laughing. For some reason, there was a beach chair just to the side of our blanket, but it was sitting empty. Next to our blanket, I saw that the Gardner family had set up theirs, with Nora and Gelsey leaning over the space between them, talking. "But listen," he said, and I turned back to my brother, who looked even more anxious than he had before taking the SATs for the third time, in pursuit of the elusive perfect score (he'd achieved it). "Do I look okay? Or do I look stupid? Gelsey said I looked *fine*. What is that supposed to mean?"

Somehow, in my own panic about public speaking, my brother and his romantic travails had slipped my mind. Which wasn't good, because this was pretty much my doing, and if things went horribly wrong, I had a feeling I would be blamed in perpetuity. "You look great," I assured him. "Just . . . um . . . breathe. And if you can help it, maybe don't tell her how anything was invented. Just on the first date."

"Right," Warren said, nodding for much longer than people usually nodded. "Okay." I looked up toward the entrance, where I saw Wendy, her hair out of her normal braids and hanging long over the white sundress she was wearing.

"Your date's here," I said, pointing. Wendy saw me and waved, and I waved back. Warren, on the other hand, just stared, his mouth opening and closing a few times.

"Go," I said, poking him in the back. "Breathe."

"Right," Warren said in a voice that indicated he wasn't doing much of that, but he did start walking toward the entrance. Wanting to give him a little bit of privacy, I scanned the beach again.

It wasn't like I was looking for Henry specifically. However, he'd come to the last one, and I'd given him the poster, so I knew he knew about this one, so it wouldn't have been unexpected to see him there or anything. But my eyes moved from blanket to blanket with no sign of him.

I looked back to the snack bar to see Elliot tapping his watch and Lucy giving me a thumbs-up. I knew that the moment had arrived. I signaled to Leland, who gave me a nod, and then walked in front of the screen and took a deep breath. "Good evening," I started, and must have been loud enough, because most people looked up at me. I could feel how damp my palms were, and I twisted my hands together behind my back, hoping nobody else would pick up on this. "Welcome to Movies Under the Stars, and tonight's screening of *Casablanca*." For some reason, this caused some people to burst into applause, which gave me a second to collect myself. What did I normally do with my hands? I had no idea, and I was going to keep them behind my back until I remembered.

"The, um, concession stand will be open for the first twenty minutes. So . . . that's how long." I could feel that I was babbling, but at least it was better than the never-ending silences of the last time. I looked up, and my eyes traveled right across to my family's blanket. My mother was wearing a rather fixed smile, and Gelsey was frowning as if she wasn't sure what I was doing. But when I met my father's eye, and saw his steady, encouraging expression, I felt myself let out a long breath. Suddenly, I knew exactly what to say. "*Casablanca* has been called, by some film scholars, a perfect movie, from first frame to last," I said, seeing an expression of happy surprise come over my dad's face as I said this. "I hope you agree. Enjoy the show!" There was another smattering of applause as I scurried away from the projector and toward the safety of the snack bar just as the movie started, the old-fashioned Warner Brothers logo, in black and white, taking over the screen.

Twenty minutes later, we closed down the snack bar as quietly as possible. I'd been watching what I could of the movie in between serving up sodas, ice cream, and popcorn, and I thought I'd gotten the general gist of it.

"You staying?" Lucy asked me after we'd locked up the snack bar.

I nodded, looking back to my family's blanket. "I am. You?"

She shook her head and yawned. "I don't think so," she said. "I'll give it a miss this time."

"Me too," Elliot interjected, stepping in between us. "So are you heading home, Luce? Want a ride?"

"No, thanks," Lucy said. "I biked here."

"Great," Elliot enthused. "Want some company biking home?"

"But didn't you drive?" I asked, feeling that Elliot's crush was wreaking havoc on his logic.

Elliot's face fell as he seemed to realize this as well. "Technically, yes," he murmured. "But . . . um . . ."

"You're a nut," Lucy said, shoving his arm good-naturedly. "See you tomorrow!" she called as she headed to the parking lot. I watched Elliot literally slump when she passed out of view.

"I think you're going to have to tell her how you feel," I told him. "I don't think she's getting your signs."

Elliot blushed. "I don't know what you're talking about," he said. He also turned to leave, which seemed like a good idea. From what I'd been able to grasp about the movie so far, it seemed to be about a guy pining for a girl, so it was maybe not the best thing for him to see in his current state.

I picked up the Diet Coke I'd poured for myself before we turned off the soda machine and tiptoed across the sand, ducking until I reached our blanket.

"Nicely done," my father stage-whispered to me. I looked across the blanket and saw that he was giving me small, silent claps.

"Thanks," I whispered back. "I was just quoting the experts." I looked for my brother and saw that, a few rows back, he'd set up his own blanket and was sitting next to Wendy. I noticed that every few seconds he would look away from the screen and glance at her, and I couldn't help but be glad that I'd chosen a first date for them that would make it impossible for Warren to inundate her with facts if he got really nervous.

I settled in and tried to pay attention to what was happening. I was shocked by how many lines I recognized even though I'd never seen the movie before. They were either things I'd heard my father quote, or lines that seemed to be part of the zeitgeist, references I'd known without even realizing it. I was getting caught up in the movie, the thwarted love story, when I became aware of something to my right. I turned away from Rick and Ilsa and saw Henry sitting next to me.

"Hi," he whispered.

"Hi," I whispered back, surprised, and feeling myself start to smile. "What are you doing here?"

He raised an eyebrow at me, a smile playing around the corners of his mouth, which I made myself look away from. "Seeing a movie," he said, as though this should have been obvious.

I could feel my cheeks get hot, and was glad for the cover of relative darkness. "I got that," I whispered back to him. "I just thought, when I didn't see you earlier . . ."

"Oh, so you were looking for me?" Henry asked, settling himself in next to me and leaning back on his hands. I shook my head, looking back at the screen for a second, where Humphrey Bogart was lighting what had to be his fortieth cigarette of the movie so far. "I had to help my dad with some of the prep for tomorrow," he explained after a minute.

I turned my head slightly to look at him, the shadows from the screen flickering across his face. I realized, now that he'd said it, that he smelled sweet—a mixture of cake flour and something like cinnamon. When I realized that I was staring, I looked away fast, back to the screen and the world of Rick's Café that I had, until just a few moments ago, been utterly absorbed in. I could feel my heart beat fast and was thinking that it would just take a few inches for me to extend my hand and have it touch his. Which was why I made myself keep looking at the screen as I asked, trying to keep my voice light, "So where's your girlfriend?"

"Girlfriend?" Henry sounded so genuinely confused that I turned to look at him again.

"Yeah," I said. "The girl who was with you at Jane's? And I've seen her at your house. . . ." My voice trailed off, as Henry shook his head.

"That's Davy's babysitter," he said. "He really doesn't need one, but my dad gets worried."

"So you're not . . . dating her?" I asked, thinking of the way she'd looked at him at the ice-cream parlor, at how their fingers had brushed.

"No," Henry said quietly. "There was a moment when maybe that was going to happen, but . . ." He trailed off, running his hand across the sand for a second, as though smoothing it out, and I held my breath, waiting for whatever would come next. "But I changed my mind," he finally said, looking back at me.

"Oh," I murmured. *Oh.* I wasn't sure what that meant, but I was pretty sure about what I wanted it to mean. It suddenly hit me that Henry, single Henry, was sitting next to me in the darkness, as we watched a movie. And just like that, those butterflies I'd first felt at twelve made a reappearance.

"So what'd I miss?" Henry whispered after a few moments. I glanced over at him, fully aware of how close together we were, how close he'd sat next to me, even though there was ample room on the blanket.

"I thought you'd seen this," I whispered, looking back fixedly at the screen.

"I have," he said, and I could hear that there was smile in his voice. "I just wanted a refresher."

"Well," I said, turning my head to face him a little. "Rick's really mad because Ilsa just left, without a real explanation." As soon as I'd said this, I realized that the statement might apply to more than just the movie. I think Henry realized this as well; when he spoke again his voice was a little more serious.

"She probably had a good reason for that, though, right?" He wasn't looking at the screen anymore, but right at me.

"I don't know," I said, looking down at the blanket and both our legs extended, just a hand's width between them. "I think she was just really scared, and ran away when things got hard." This was no longer about the movie at all, because we'd just learned that Ilsa did have an actual reason for leaving Rick behind in the rain, whereas I had only my own cowardice to blame.

"And then what happens?" he asked. I looked at him and saw that he was still looking at me.

"I don't know," I said, feeling my heart start to pound again, certain that we had stopped talking about the movie entirely now. "You tell me."

He smiled and then glanced back at the screen. "I guess we'll have to wait and see," he said.

I looked back at the screen as well. "I guess we will," I said. I watched the movie, trying my best to pay attention to what was happening—Nazis, French resistance, everyone trying to find some letters of transit—but after a few minutes, I gave up even trying to follow the plot. The movie was unfolding before me, but all I was really aware of was Henry's presence next to me, how close to me he was sitting, how I noticed every time he moved or turned his head slightly. I was so aware of his presence that by the time the famous last line was uttered—the one about the beginning of a beautiful friendship—our breath was rising and falling in the same rhythm.

chapter twenty-nine

"AND THEN WHAT?" LUCY DEMANDED, EYES WIDE.

I took a sip of my soda, and shook my head, smiling at her. "And then nothing," I said. "Seriously." Lucy groaned and I looked out to the nearly deserted beach, wondering if at some point we could just admit that nobody was coming to the snack bar and go home early.

I was telling her the truth—nothing had happened at the movie. That is, nothing had happened between me and Henry. We had simply watched the rest of the movie in silence, and when it ended, I'd hustled to the front of the now-blank screen, thanked everyone for coming, and told them that the next movie night would be in a month, and I'd managed to do it without babbling or taking too-long pauses, which seemed to me like some kind of progress. When I'd returned to the blanket, Gelsey and Nora were engaged in some kind of complicated hand-clap game, and my mother was folding up our blanket and talking to the Gardners, who were going on about how the movie had one of cinema's most perfectly structured screenplays. In the midst of this, my father was struggling up out of the beach chair. He had moved to sit in it during the movie's second half, the sight of which had made me lose track of the plot altogether for a while, as I kept glancing back at my dad, looking somehow diminished in the beach chair that he had always sworn he'd never use.

Henry was already walking toward the parking lot, but he met my eye and raised his hand in a wave. I waved back, and felt myself watching, out of the corner of my eye, until he passed out of sight. Because I was facing the parking lot, I saw Warren and Wendy heading out, not holding hands, but walking awfully close together. I caught Warren's eye for a moment, and he gave me a wide, happy smile, the kind that I'd never seen on my brother, who before this had seemed to specialize in the sardonic smirk.

I'd locked up the projector and screen and thanked Leland, who was yawning so enormously that I was just grateful he hadn't fallen asleep during the movie. Gelsey ended up riding home with the Gardners, as my father's back was hurting again, and he needed to stretch out across the backseat. I'd buckled myself into the passenger seat and turned around to look at him. In the fading light—my mother's car lights would flare when a door was opened but then slowly dim, as though transitioning you to darkness—I saw how thin my father was, how his skin was stretched over his cheekbones.

"Did you like the movie, kid?" he asked, startling me. His eyes were closed, and I'd assumed he'd fallen asleep.

"I did," I said as I turned to face him fully. He opened his eyes and smiled at me.

"I'm glad I got to see it on the big screen," he said. "That's how Ingrid Bergman was meant to be seen." I laughed as my mother opened her door and my father gave me a wink. "Don't tell your mother," he added.

"Don't tell me what?" my mom asked, smiling, as she started the car and pulled us out of the now mostly deserted parking lot.

"Just something about Ingrid Bergman," my dad said, his voice sleepy, his eyes drifting closed again. I saw my mother glance back at him in the rearview mirror, her smile fading.

"Let's go home," she said in a voice that sounded like it was straining to be upbeat. "I think we're all tired." She'd pulled back out onto the road, and by the time we made it home, five minutes later, my father was totally asleep.

My parents had gone to bed as soon as we'd gotten back and my mother had collected Gelsey from next door. I'd noticed that, as they made their way up to their bedroom, my mother was now walking slightly behind my father, watching him carefully, like she was worried that he might fall backward. And as I noticed for the first time how slowly my dad was taking every step, how heavily he was leaning on the railing, it seemed like this might have actually been necessary.

I'd gotten ready for bed, but felt far too keyed-up to even try to go to sleep. When I'd heard a car pull into our driveway, I'd walked out to the porch, where I saw Warren just sitting in the Land Cruiser, the engine off, looking straight ahead. When he saw me, he got out of the car and walked up to meet me on the porch steps. Technically, he walked. But there was something about him that made it seem more like floating.

"Taylor," Warren said, smiling at me pleasantly, like I was some-one he'd known, vaguely, many years before. "How are you?"

"I'm fine," I said, crossing my arms over my chest and trying not to grin. "How are *you?*"

"I'm good," Warren said. He smiled again—that big, genuine smile that I was still getting used to. "Thanks so much for arranging it."

"Sure," I said, looking at him closely. I really wanted details, but this was so outside the realm of what my brother and I normally talked about that I had no idea how to even broach this subject. "Will you need me to arrange another one?"

My brother's expression became slightly disdainful, and there-fore much more familiar. "I don't think so," he said. "We're going out tomorrow night. Miniature golfing."

"Sounds fun," I said, smiling, suddenly very impressed with Wendy and her ability to get my brother to do something that I knew, only a few days before, he would have scoffed at.

Warren started to head toward the door, then stopped and looked back at me. "Did you ever have a night that just . . . seemed to change everything?" he asked, sounding happy but a bit bewildered.

"And everything is different afterward?" I didn't, and Warren must have seen this on my expression, because he shook his head as he opened the door. "Never mind," he said. "Forget it. 'Night, Taylor."

"'Night," I called to him. And even after he'd gone inside, I stayed out on the porch for a few minutes, looking up at the stars above me and turning over Warren's words in my mind.

But for now, I was at work. It was a cloudy, overcast, humid day—the kind that threatened rain, but never quite delivered it. It was chilly to boot, which meant that we'd had approximately three customers that morning, all of whom had either wanted coffee or hot chocolate, and all of whom had wanted to complain about the fact that this wasn't summer weather.

Lucy looked at me closely, clearly not ready to let me off the hook that easily. "Just because something didn't happen with Henry," she said, "doesn't mean that you don't *want* it to."

I felt myself flush as I looked around for something to do and started straightening a stack of cups. "I don't know," I said. And I didn't, even though thoughts of Henry had kept me awake most of the night before. I had no idea what he wanted, and was just getting used to the idea that we could be friends. The possibility of more made my stomach clench, in a good way, but also in a real and scary way.

"Don't know what?" Lucy asked, pushing herself up to sit on the counter, looking at me, waiting for my answer.

The cups were as straight as they were ever going to be, and I shoved the stack away. "There's a lot going on right now," I said. I met her eyes and saw that she knew what I was talking about. "So I'm just not sure it's the right time. . . ."

Lucy shook her head. "There's no such thing as a perfect moment," she said with great authority. "Look at me and Brett."

Brett was a new guy she had just started going out with, despite the fact that he was only in the Poconos for a week. I pushed myself up to sit on the counter and sat cross-legged facing her, increasing the number of health-code violations we were currently in violation of, glad that the topic had shifted away from me. "Maybe," I said, in what I hoped was an offhand manner, "there's someone here who already likes you and is going to be around for the whole summer. Possibly someone who likes card tricks?"

I watched her closely for her reaction, but Lucy just shook her head. "I get enough of that with Elliot," she said. "No, thanks."

"I don't know," I said as casually as I was able. "I don't think Elliot's so bad."

Lucy shook her head. "He's great," she said, offhandedly. "But not exactly someone I want to date."

"Why not?" I asked, and Lucy frowned for a second, as though considering this. But before she could answer, her phone beeped and she pulled it out of her pocket.

"Gotta go," she said, smiling at the screen. "Are you okay here? Brett wants to hang out."

I nodded as I slid off the counter, and Lucy followed suit. She slung her bag over her shoulder and was reaching for the door, when she stopped and looked back at me. "I'll call you later," she said. She looked around the deserted snack bar and added, "Think you can handle the crowd without me?"

I smiled at that. "I think I'll be fine," I said. "Have fun." She waved and left, and I tried to fill the rest of the work shift by cleaning the ice machine and attempting to sort through what, exactly, I was feeling about Henry. I didn't think I'd been imagining that something was going on last night, but in the cold light of day, I couldn't be sure.

As soon as five rolled around, I locked up the snack bar and zipped a hooded sweatshirt over my cutoffs (I'd leaned my lesson as far as sweatshirts and overcast days went), feeling myself shiver. The wind had just started to pick up, tossing the tree branches violently. It was a truly miserable day, and I just hoped that there would be a fire going when I got home.

I biked to Henson's to pick up some corn and tomatoes for dinner, per my mother's request. At the register, I found myself hesitating over the bags of licorice. I'd been getting them for my dad whenever I'd gone in, even though he'd stopped asking for them. And when I'd gone in search of some chips the night before, I'd seen three of the licorice bags in the cabinet, shoved behind a box of saltines. But somehow not bringing a bag for my father seemed like an admission of defeat.

"That too?" Dave Henson asked cheerfully, pointing to the licorice bag I'd picked up, and helping me make my decision.

"Sure," I said, paying for my items and shoving them into my bag. "Thanks."

"Get home safe, now," Dave said, looking outside. "I think we're about to get some weather."

I waved good-bye to Dave and headed out as a rumble of thunder sounded in the distance. I groaned and flipped the hood of my sweatshirt up just as the first drops of rain splattered on the road. Main Street wasn't crowded—it seemed like the weather had kept people in, but those that were on the street either ducked under awnings or hustled to their cars. I knew the signs, and I hurried to my bike and dropped my bag in the basket. I was trying to decide if it made more sense to call home for a ride and duck under an awning, or just see how far I could get before the storm really hit. I had a feeling that if I called home for a ride because it was raining, I might never hear the end of it. But on the other hand . . .

The thunder sounded again, closer this time, and that decided it for me. So I'd get a little wet. I would certainly survive. And it would be better than Warren—not to mention my dad—mocking me for the rest of the summer. I climbed on my bike and headed down

Main Street, noticing that puddles were already starting to form on the pavement. As I pedaled through them, water splashed against my feet and bare legs, and I realized that this really had not been the day to wear shorts.

I biked on, getting soaked as I rode. The thunder was getting ever closer, so loud that I found myself jumping slightly whenever it sounded, my hands tightening on the handlebars. As I stopped for a moment to brush some of the rain off my face and fix the bag in the basket, I saw a flash of lightning in the distance.

"Crap," I muttered, pulling my hood up higher and looking down at my bike for a second, taking in the fact that it was pretty much made of metal. I was fairly sure the rubber of the tires would keep me from getting electrocuted, but it wasn't something that I was dying to field-test. I was soaked through to the skin, and I could see the droplets rolling off my bare legs. The rain was coming down in sheets now, so hard that I could barely see the road in front of me. But it somehow seemed that I was getting wetter standing still than I had when I was in motion. Wiping my wet hands on my even wetter sweatshirt, I swung my leg back over the bike when someone skidded up next to me.

"Taylor?" I turned and saw Henry on his own bike, looking almost as drenched as I was, though not quite—he was wearing a baseball cap that seemed to be keeping some of the rain off his face.

"Hey," I said, momentarily grateful that I had my hood up, since

I could only imagine how bad my hair looked. But a second later, the reality hit. *I had my hood up.* I probably looked like a half-drowned elf.

"This is intense," he said. He was practically yelling to be heard above the sound of the rain and wind.

"I know," I called back. I felt myself smile, realizing how ridiculous we probably looked—two people, standing still in a rainstorm, having a conversation on the side of the road.

"Ready?" he asked, and I nodded, standing up on my pedals and starting to bike against the wind. The rain was starting to come down sideways, and the wind was blowing so hard that I was having trouble keeping my bike upright. It kept wobbling, and I kept having to put a foot down to steady myself. Because of this, Henry had ridden on ahead of me, though he would always stop and wait for me to catch up. I thought this was what was happening when I reached him and he was stopped, a foot resting on the ground. I biked on ahead, figuring that he would be right beside me, but after a few seconds, I turned and saw that he was still stopped.

"You okay?" I yelled over the rain, thinking that this was really not the day to have mechanical problems.

"Yeah," he called back. "But this is insane. I think we should just wait out the storm. It's not going to continue like this."

"No, but . . ." I shivered. I didn't even need a fire any longer; all I wanted was a shower so hot that it would steam up the bathroom mirror in seconds, and I planned to stand under it until our tiny hot-water heater ran out. I looked back to the direction of Main Street, which was the only place any shelter could really be found. But the thought of biking all the way back there, and then having to go home, was not exactly appealing.

"Come on," Henry called. He looked both ways, then biked across the street. Confused, I watched as he got off his bike and started wheeling it up a driveway.

"Henry!" I called across the street, "what are you doing?" I couldn't tell if he heard me, but at any rate, he just kept wheeling his bike. I didn't understand what was going on, but it appeared like he, at least, had some sort of plan, so I checked for oncoming traffic before riding across as well.

As soon as I made it onto the driveway, the tree cover cut down on a little bit of the rain. I looked around for Henry and saw that he was rolling his bike toward a house, I now realized, that was very familiar. I squinted through the rain to see the sign, and sure enough, we were at Maryanne's Happy Hours—also known as Henry's old house. The driveway was empty and the house was dark, so at least it seemed like Maryanne wouldn't be chasing us off her property. I walked my bike past the house, following Henry around to the back. By the time I reached it, Henry had stopped where the woods began, and leaned his bike against a tree. I did as well, noticing that when I stepped into the woods, the denseness of the trees really did

morgan matson

begin to provide some shelter from the rain. I just wasn't sure that it had been worth stopping for. I was about to say this to Henry when I saw that he was walking into the woods. And that's when I saw what he was heading toward—the treehouse.

"You okay?" he asked, as I concentrated on getting a grip on the wooden planks, nailed into the tree trunk, that served as the ladder.

"Fine," I said, reaching up for the next rung. Henry was already in the treehouse, looking down at me—he'd climbed up with no problem whatsoever. It wasn't the kind of treehouse that you some-times saw in catalogs, the ones that came with a kit and instructions and were meant to look like log cabins, or pirate ships, all right angles and smooth wood. It had been built by Henry's dad, without any fancy blueprints, just to fit in the space between three support-ing trees, which made it triangle-shaped. There was a roof, two walls and a floor, but nothing so fancy as a door. Instead, the front was just open, slightly overhanging the trunk that served as the ladder. It seemed fitting that we were there now, as the only times I could really remember being in the treehouse was when it had been rain-ing. I wasn't sure I'd actually ever seen it from the inside when it was sunny out.

"Need a hand?" Henry asked, and I nodded. I extended one upward, and he grasped it—his hands cool against mine—and gave me a pull, allowing me to throw a leg over onto the wooden planks of the floor. I let go of Henry's hand and pushed myself to my feet, starting to stand. "Careful," he said. He pointed upward. "It's a little low in here."

I saw that I had been just about to whack my head on the roof. "Wow," I murmured as I crouched down. When I'd been here last, I'd been able to stand up to my full height with no problem. The treehouse didn't appear to have changed much. There was nothing inside it except a plastic pail in the corner that I saw was positioned under a leak; every few seconds there would be a muted *ping* sound as another drop fell in.

Henry was sitting at the front of the treehouse, his legs dangling in the air. He took off his baseball cap and ran his hands through his hair, brushing back that one lock that sometimes fell over his forehead. I crouch-walked over and sat down next to him, hugging my knees to my chest and rubbing my legs with my hands to try and warm them up a bit. If my sweatshirt had been bigger, I would have tucked them inside without a thought to how ridiculous I looked.

Now that we were under a little bit of shelter, I could see how gorgeous the woods were in the storm. Everything seemed greener than normal, and the sound of the rain was muted, making it seem much more peaceful than the deluge we'd been exposed to out on the road. It was still very windy, and I watched the trees around us as they bent and swayed in the wind. Mr. Crosby's carpentry skills

morgan matson

seemed to be holding up, though, and the treehouse wasn't moving or even feeling unsteady.

"Better?" Henry asked.

"Much," I said. I leaned forward and glanced at Maryanne's house. I could see it through the trees—though it was still dark, it was worryingly close. "Won't Maryanne mind?"

Henry shook his head. "Nah," he said. "I come here sometimes to think, and she doesn't mind it."

"Got it," I said. We sat there in silence for a moment. The only sound was the rain falling all around us and the wind whipping through the trees. I glanced behind me to the treehouse again, still marveling at the fact that it looked the same—just a little shrunken. "I can't remember the last time I was up here," I said. "But it hasn't changed much."

"It would have been that last summer, right?" Henry asked, turning to me. "When we were twelve."

I nodded, looking straight ahead at the branches that were swaying and dipping. "Probably." And maybe it was the disorienting effect of being caught in a rainstorm, or the conversation I'd just had with Lucy, but before I could consider what I was saying, I asked, "Do you ever think about that summer? I mean, when we were . . ." I paused, hesitating over the right word.

"When we were going out," Henry finished for me. I looked at him and saw that he was still looking at me. "Of course."

"Me too," I said. I wasn't quite brave enough to tell him what I'd realized at Gelsey's slumber party—how much it had impacted me, our first attempt at something like love. It was the only time, I supposed, when you could go into something totally fresh, with no baggage, no idea of how you could get hurt and hurt others in return.

"I mean," Henry said, "you were my first girlfriend, after all."

I felt myself smiling at that. "And there have been lots of others, I take it, in the interim?"

"Scads," Henry said, straight-faced, making me laugh. "Just dozens and dozens."

"Same here," I said, deadpan, hoping he knew that I was joking. Because other than my cheating ex, Evan, and two very short-lived relationships sophomore year, there was nobody of significance to tell him about.

"You know," Henry added after a moment, "I really liked you back then."

I took a deep breath. "I shouldn't have done that to you," I said. "I shouldn't have left like that. And I'm really, really sorry."

He nodded. "I just didn't know what was happening. I didn't know if I'd done something. . . ."

I shook my head. "No," I said. "It was all me. I just . . . tend to run away when things get to be too much." I shrugged. "I'm working on it."

"I couldn't believe it when you showed up on the dock," he said with a laugh. "I thought I was hallucinating for a minute."

"Me too," I confessed. "I thought you'd never speak to me again."

"I tried," he reminded me, and I smiled at that. "But seriously," he said, looking right at me, his tone a little more measured, "you're a hard habit to break."

I looked into his eyes and could feel my heart begin to pound a bit faster. The air around us suddenly seemed charged, and it felt like we were standing at a crossroads—that things could go either way from here, but there was a decision that had to be made.

Slowly, inch by inch, Henry moved closer to me. He reached down and touched my hand with his, making me shiver, even though I was no longer cold. He picked up my hand and looked into my eyes, as if making sure this was okay. It more than was, and I hoped he could see that in my expression. He leaned a little closer to me and tipped back my hood and I didn't even care what my hair looked like. He placed one hand on my cheek, stroking it with his thumb as I shivered again. And then he leaned toward me and I could feel my heart beat hard, and we were so close, just a breath apart. I closed my eyes and, as the rain and wind whipped all around us, he kissed me.

It was soft at first; his lips touching mine lightly. Then he pulled back and cupped my cheek under his hand and kissed me again.

This time it wasn't so tentative, and I kissed him back, and it was a kiss that was both familiar and brand-new, making me remember a kiss from five years ago, and making me feel like I'd never been kissed before in my life. And I realized that maybe Lucy was wrong—maybe sometimes there was such a thing as a perfect moment. His arms were around my back, pulling me closer, and I looped my arms around his neck and ran my hands over his jawline, suddenly not able to stop touching him. And while we kissed, up there among the trees, the rain tapered off until, at long last, the sun came out.

The Best of Times, the Worst of Times

chapter thirty

"TAYLOR!" I OPENED MY EYES AND SAW LUCY, LYING ON MY DOCK IN her bikini, waving at me. "Hello?"

"Sorry," I said, sitting up and trying to remember what Lucy had been talking about. I had not been paying attention in the least. "What was that?"

"Let me guess," Lucy said, shaking her head. "You didn't hear what I was saying."

I smiled involuntarily, causing Lucy to groan. "Oh, my God," she said. "It's so hard to have a conversation with you when you keep slipping into makeout flashbacks."

I thought about denying it, but I had a feeling it would be pretty useless. I pulled my sunglasses down to cover my eyes and lay back down on my striped towel, stretching out in the late-afternoon sun.

It was almost July, a little over a week after Henry and I had kissed in the treehouse. And Lucy wasn't entirely wrong to complain. In fact, she'd been right on the money—while she'd been talking, my mind had been drifting to the night before, when Henry and I, once we had been sure our respective families were asleep, had made out on this very dock, stretching out on a blanket under the stars. At one point, we'd paused to catch our breath, and I'd looked up at the sky as I rested my head on his chest, feeling his breath rise and fall. "Do you know any constellations?" I asked, and I'd felt his laugh rumbling in his chest before I heard it.

"No," he'd said, and even without looking, I could hear the smile in his voice. "Want me to learn some?"

"No," I said, my eyes still on the stars above us. "I was just wondering." He'd smoothed his hand over my hair, and I'd closed my eyes for just a moment, still a little amazed that this had happened, that we'd somehow ended up here.

In the short time we'd been together, I knew that this was like none of my other relationships. And it was also not like we'd been before, when we were so young and inexperienced. It was like all the obstacles that had made my other relationships so complicated— gossip, drama at school—were just removed. He lived next door, my parents liked him, and we had no schedules or responsibilities beyond our not-very-taxing jobs. And unlike Warren's fledgling relationship with Wendy, being with Henry wasn't causing me a lot of stress.

Not that Warren wasn't happy—in fact, he had developed an annoying humming habit, and he did it constantly, even in the shower—but he was still spending far too much time before every date picking out which shirt to wear, and then afterward, wanting to go over everything she'd said, as though looking for hidden clues or meanings. Warren and I would often end up returning home around the same time, and so we would sit outside, usually on the porch steps, and I listened as he dissected and analyzed his evening for me. But unlike Warren's relationship, I was finding that being with Henry again was surprisingly relaxing. It was like I could just be myself when I was with him. After all, he already knew my flaws, especially the biggest one of all. And this meant that in quiet moments, lying with my head on his chest, I could close my eyes and just breathe, reveling in the peace.

But it wasn't *all* quiet and peaceful. There was a spark between us that I'd never felt with any of the other (four) guys that I'd kissed. When we were making out, it was almost impossible for me to keep my hands off of him, and kissing him could stop time and cause me to forget where I was. Just thinking about kissing him made my stomach flip over, and I had burned several batches of fries at work as I stared into space, going over in my head the events of the night before—his fingers, tracing a line down my neck, the spot he'd found just underneath my earlobe that I hadn't ever considered before, but that now could make my knees weak. The way I would run my hands through his hair, always pushing back that one errant lock as we kissed, the softness of his cheek against mine, the warmth of the back of his neck where he was always faintly sunburned.

But now, I attempted to pull myself away from all such thoughts and focus on Lucy. "Sorry," I said sheepishly. "Really. What's up?"

She frowned at me for a moment before pulling out her phone. "Okay," she said. "For the second time." She raised an eyebrow at me and I tried to look properly contrite. "It's Brett. He keeps texting me, saying he wants to keep in touch, maybe do the long-distance thing, which is crazy, because we went on, like, three dates."

"Well," I said slowly. "Maybe you should just keep your options open for now. It's not like Brett's even here. And maybe there's someone around here you haven't even thought of."

"If there was someone around here, I'd have noticed," Lucy grumbled. I opened my mouth to say something—maybe plead Elliot's case once again—when she glanced back to the house and smiled, shaking her head. "Look who's here."

I turned and saw Henry walking down from his house, wearing his Borrowed Thyme T-shirt, raising a hand in a wave. I felt myself smile, wide, just at seeing him.

"Oh, my God," Lucy said, rolling her eyes at my expression. "I'm going to take that as my cue to go."

"No, stay," I said, but even I could hear how halfhearted this sounded, and she laughed.

"Nice try," she said. "You're a terrible liar."

"See you tomorrow?" I asked.

"Definitely," she said. She stood and pulled a pair of shorts and a tank top over her bikini, stuffing her towel and the magazines we'd been paging through into her canvas bag just as Henry arrived on the dock. "Hey," she said, walking past him and giving him a good-natured shove. I had been worried, probably more than I would have admitted, about seeing them together after learning that they'd dated. But watching them interact for a few minutes had been enough to make me see that there was nothing between them. More than anything else, they seemed to behave like brother and sister now.

"Oh, are you leaving?" Henry asked her, and even though he was clearly trying to sound disappointed, I could tell what Lucy meant—Henry was also a terrible liar. Lucy just shook her head and waved good-bye.

"Hey," I called to him, shading my eyes with my hand against the sun.

"Hi, yourself," he said, reaching me and sitting down on the dock next to me. I saw his eyes widen at the sight of my bikini, and I laughed as I leaned over and kissed him. He tasted sweet, like buttercream frosting, and I had a feeling he'd been on icing duty that day at work.

When we broke apart, he reached for his backpack and unzipped it. He pulled out a square green bakery box, the smallest one that Borrowed Thyme used, and held it out to me. I had a feeling that I should protest, just out of politeness or out of respect for his dad's profits, but I knew I wouldn't be able to do it convincingly. As I took the small box, I found myself smiling. There were very definite benefits to dating someone who worked in a bakery, I had found out. "What is it today?" I asked as I opened the lid and peered inside. A cupcake sat inside, yellow cake with white icing. A *T* had been placed on top of the icing with mini chocolate chips. "This looks great," I said, feeling my stomach growl just looking at it.

"Lemon cupcake," he said. "And my dad's new lemon-vanilla frosting. He wants your input."

"Happily," I said, closing the box carefully. I had learned the hard way that if I didn't wait until after dinner—and then share with my siblings—it was Henry who bore the brunt of it the next time he came by the house. "Thank you."

"And, um," Henry said as he pulled out a small plastic bag filled with cookies, "these are for your dad. Double chocolate chip, fresh-baked."

"Thanks," I said, as I placed the bag next to my cupcake box, feeling a now-familiar lump start to rise in my throat. When I'd told Henry about the fact that my dad wasn't eating much, he'd taken to counteracting this (along with his father, I'd later learned) by trying to find the one dessert or bread that might bring my father's appetite back again. Despite their best efforts, this didn't seem to be working. My dad always made a big show over the treats, oohing and ahhing, but he only had a bite or two before claiming that they were just too good to keep all to himself.

My father was doing about the same—that is, doing a little bit worse every day, even though it wasn't possible to see until I looked back and realized that, this time last week, he hadn't slept from afternoon until dinnertime and had been able to walk up the stairs without Warren's help, my mother walking behind, ready to catch him if he tumbled backward. He'd stopped reading late into the night, and his voice, the one I used to be able to hear across the house, had continued to diminish, and now I could sometimes barely hear him across the dining room table.

We were still doing our diner breakfasts twice a week, even though he'd taken to just ordering toast, and even then, only eating a few bites of it, no matter how Angela scolded him. But even though he didn't eat much, we continued to do our questions. I couldn't remember how it had happened, but we had moved past the questions on the placemat quiz, and had just started talking. I had always loved my father, of course—even though I hadn't yet found the right moment to tell him this. But it wasn't until we started having our breakfasts together that I really got to know him.

I learned about how my dad had almost gotten fired from his first law job, and about the trip around Europe he took after college, and how the first time he'd seen my mother, he'd fallen in love. The one thing that I had been most surprised by, though, he'd told me two days before. We'd been talking about our shared past, all those childhood moments that I, at one point, had been sick of hearing about. It wasn't until now, when every day I had with my father was suddenly numbered, that I realized just how precious they had been. A thousand moments that I had just taken for granted—mostly because I had assumed that there would be a thousand more. My father had just finished telling the story (even though I'd heard it at least twenty times) about how I'd come to his office for Take Your Daughter to Work Day when I was six and had drawn all over a very important piece of evidence, when he stopped laughing and just looked at me over his coffee cup.

"Here's one I bet you don't know," he said, giving me a smile. He was thinner than ever, and his skin continued to darken from yellow to a darker tan, like he had had a very unfortunate experience at a tanning bed. It made his teeth look startlingly white in contrast.

I still couldn't get used to the physical changes that were happening so quickly in my father, proof that there was something very, very bad going on inside of him. Something that wouldn't stop until it killed him.

But these changes didn't hit home until I saw the proof, like in a picture, or saw the way that other people looked at him. My father was attracting attention now, in a way that made me feel simultaneously embarrassed, angry, and protective. Other people in the diner would stare just a moment too long, looking back to their eggs quickly when I met their eyes.

morgan matson

"What's that?" I asked, moving my cup to the edge of the table so that Angela would give me a refill the next time she came by. I didn't really even want more coffee, but the more filled my cup was, the longer our time here would be. These mornings were the only time I had alone with my father, and I had started trying to extend them as long as possible.

My dad smiled and leaned back in his seat, wincing slightly as he did so. "When you were first born," he said. "I used to go into your room and watch you sleep. I was terrified that you weren't breathing."

"Really?" I asked. I'd never heard this one, and as the middle child, I had very few stories that were mine alone, so I was fairly sure I'd heard them all.

"Oh, yes," my dad said. "With your brother, we never had to worry. He was wailing every few seconds. I don't think your poor mother got more than five hours' sleep that first year. But you slept through the night right away. And it used to terrify me."

Angela arrived with her pitcher, filling up my coffee and nudging my father's toast closer to him, as though the reason he hadn't eaten it was that he hadn't noticed its presence on the table.

"So," he continued, taking a sip of his coffee, "I used to just stand in your doorway, listening to you breathe. Making sure that you were still with us. Just counting your breaths until I was convinced that you were sticking with us for a bit."

And then Angela had dropped off the check and we'd moved on to other things—how he'd driven across the country after high school and got lost in Missouri, and how I had actually figured out the truth about Santa Claus when I'd noticed he had the same wrapping technique—sloppy, with masking tape—as my father. But the image of him standing in my doorway, watching over my breaths in the first few weeks of my life, had stayed with me.

Now though, I was on the dock with Henry in the sunshine, and that seemed very far away. "We'll see if these do the trick," I said, setting the cookies aside. When they were out of the way, I leaned over to kiss him again. One of the best things about kissing Henry was that it could make the rest of the world—like my dad, and what was happening to him—go away for a little while. It never totally disappeared, but like a TV you could hear in the next room, I was able to think about it less when Henry's lips were on mine and his arms were around me.

"So," Henry said. It was a while later, and we were taking a break. We were stretched out together, and I was lying in what I had already come to think of as my spot—there was just a place where I seemed to fit perfectly. His arm was around my shoulders, and my head resting on his chest, one of my legs thrown over his, our feet tangled together. "Do you have any plans for the Fourth?"

I hadn't been expecting this question, and I propped myself up to look at him. "I think we're watching the fireworks," I said. "Out here, probably." There was always a fireworks display over the lake, and we'd usually gathered on the dock, as a family, to watch it.

"Great," he said. "Well, don't make any plans for afterward, okay? I've got a surprise."

I propped myself up even farther, looking into his eyes. "A surprise?" I asked, not quite able to keep the excitement out of my voice. "What is it?"

"You should get Warren to tell you the definition of the word *surprise*," he said as I felt myself smile. "It involves not revealing what something is."

We lay there together for a little longer, watching the sun over the lake as it finally started to go down, and twilight started to fall all around us, the fireflies starting to wink in the grass. When I felt the first mosquito bite me, I slapped it away and sat up, checking the time, and realizing that I should probably head in for dinner.

"Time to go?" Henry asked, and I nodded, standing up and extending a hand to help him up. He took it, but didn't really exert much pull on it as he stood and I zipped up a sweatshirt over my bikini. I gathered up my towel, sunglasses, and desserts, and we walked across the dock together, holding hands.

When we reached the back of my house, he squeezed my hand. "I'll see you tomorrow," he said.

"See you then," I said, feeling how wide I was smiling, but

knowing I wouldn't be able to stop myself. He leaned down and kissed me, and I stood on my tiptoes to kiss him back.

"Ugh." We broke apart, and I turned to see Davy standing a few feet in front of us, Murphy at his feet. Davy made a face. "That's disgusting."

"You won't always think so," Henry assured him. "Were you walking the dog again?"

Davy nodded and held out the leash to me reluctantly. Ever since my father had given him the go-ahead to walk the dog, Davy had taken his responsibilities very seriously, coming over to walk the dog several times a day. It had gotten so that Murphy was exhausted by early evening, falling asleep on my dad's lap immediately after dinner.

"Thanks," I said, taking the leash from him. Davy nodded and I smiled at Henry. "See you," I said.

"Bye," he said, smiling back, causing Davy to groan. Henry walked toward his house, with Davy running to catch up with him, already talking about something.

"And how was your day?" I asked as I picked up the dog, who looked utterly wiped out. I held Murphy, who seemed thrilled to get a little bit of a break, under my arm and scratched his ears as I headed up toward the house. "Did you do great things?"

The first thing I noticed as I headed up the porch steps was that there was music playing. And not one of my mother's ballets or her classical music—old-school rock. I dropped the dog on the porch, unhooked his leash, and opened the screen door. Murphy trotted inside, making a beeline for his water dish; a second later I could hear the sound of him slurping.

I stepped inside the house, and the music got even louder. It sounded vaguely familiar, like maybe I'd heard it on an oldies station or in a movie soundtrack. I dropped the cookies and cupcake on the kitchen counter and continued on inside, noticing that the house seemed to be fairly empty, and turning some lights on as I went. I found the source of the music and my dad at the same time. He was sitting on the ground in the TV room, an old turntable in front of him and stacks of records surrounding him.

"Hi," I said, turning on the light, and making us both wince slightly as the room lit up. He was wearing sweatpants and a T-shirt, but I noticed that his hair was parted as sharply as ever.

"Hi, kid," he said, starting to cough. After it had passed, he cleared his throat and continued. "What's the news?"

"No news," I said, smiling at him. I looked around at the records, and at the one spinning on the turntable. I had to say, I liked this better than the opera. I knelt down and picked up one of the sleeves—it was for someone named Charlie Rich. The album art—and his beard—both looked very seventies. "What is all this?"

He smiled at me and turned down the volume of a song about California. "I was just puttering around the workshop," he said, "and

I found my old record player and albums. And I was just going to go through them, but then I started listening to them. . . ." His voice trailed off as he picked up one of the albums and turned it over.

"So who is this?" I asked, as the song ended and the next one began, slower and softer this time.

"This," my dad said, reaching behind him and wincing, picking up the album cover and handing it to me, "is Jackson Browne."

"Did you used to listen to him?" I asked as I looked down at the album cover art, a car sitting under a single streetlight.

"All the time," my dad said, smiling faintly, as though remembering it. "It drove my father crazy."

"So turn it up," I said, sitting next to him and leaning back against the couch leg.

My dad cleared his throat, then pulled a handkerchief out of his pocket and coughed into it. He folded it carefully and replaced it. "You don't have to listen to this," he said, giving me a smile. "I know it's not exactly your style."

"I like it," I protested. And I did—the lyrics seemed almost like real poetry, layered with meaning in a way that the Bentley Boys' songs certainly weren't. "Tell me about this song."

My father leaned back against the couch leg as well and just listened for a moment. "This is a song that I always liked, but started to like a lot more after I met your mother," he said, and I could hear the smile in his voice. "It's called 'For A Dancer.'"

I smiled at that, and we sat there as it got darker and darker outside, me and my father, listening to the music he'd loved when he was my age. I knew that soon, the moment would be over—my mother and Warren and Gelsey would return home, bringing with them noise and news and bustle. But for now, there was my father and me, and a moment that I didn't try to preserve, but just let happen, as I sat next to him, listening to the song, as the record spun and the music played on.

chapter thirty-one

THE FOURTH OF JULY WAS SUNNY AND CLEAR, AND IT FELL ON A Saturday, which meant that the beach was packed. Lucy, Elliot, and I had run around all day and had sold out by noon of the tricolored Firecracker ice pops. Even Fred was there, hovering around, mostly getting in the way as he clearly just wanted to get back to his fish. But when the ice machine broke down in the middle of a rush, I was very glad that he was there, since he was the only one who knew how to fix it.

My mother had decided at the last moment to invite the neighbors to a barbecue before we would all head out to the dock to watch the fireworks, and had enlisted me with bringing home supplies. Five p.m. couldn't come soon enough, though it was more like five twenty by the time we got through the line of people who wanted fries and sodas and water and—shockingly for the beach—burgers. As we locked up, I reminded Lucy about the barbecue, and when Elliot heard that Lucy might be coming, he invited himself along too. By that point, I figured that more was definitely merrier, so

I invited Fred, who only thanked me without committing, and Leland, who told me regretfully that he'd have to miss my rager, as he was one of the people on the water with the company that was setting off the fireworks from the middle of the lake.

"They needed a lifeguard," he explained as I unlocked my bike from the beach entrance. "You know, in case someone gets hit by a firework or drowns setting one off or something."

I didn't exactly find this reassuring, but I told him to be careful, then biked to Henson's and grabbed all the rest of their corn on the cob, hoping it would be enough for however many people ended up coming. I walked my bike past the bakery, peering inside, wanting to see Henry, if only for a few minutes. But Borrowed Thyme was packed, and though he caught my eye through the window and waved, I could tell that he looked stressed-out, and I had a feeling this wouldn't be the best time to bother him.

So I biked home alone, feeling the wind through my hair and smelling the scent of backyard grills as I went. The Dip didn't faze me anymore—it wasn't until I'd coasted down it and crested up the other side that I looked back and realized how far I'd come.

I leaned my bike against the porch and headed up the stairs, feeling desperately in need of a hot shower, so that I wouldn't smell like fryer grease and the batch of lemonade that I'd spilled on myself. I had no idea what the surprise Henry had promised me might be, but just thinking about it was enough to make me smile.

But I snapped out of it as soon as I stepped into the kitchen. My mother was stalking between the counters, her hair frizzy and coming out of its normal neat bun. She was banging pans much harder than was necessary, and I felt myself instinctively shrinking back, remembering in a rush why I'd never liked it when we entertained up here—the smallness of the kitchen always seemed to exponentially increase my mother's stress. Murphy had apparently picked up on this as well, and he slunk past me, his ears pressed down against his head, and huddled behind my ankles. I bent down to pet him, and as I did, it was then that my mother turned around and saw me.

"Finally!" she snapped, brushing back a lock of hair. I could see that her face was flushed and her eyes looked red-rimmed. "Did you get the corn?"

"All they had left," I said, holding up the Henson's bag but making no move to come any farther into the kitchen. "So I'll just shuck it outside, okay?"

"I need you to set out condiments and plates," my mother said, either not hearing or just choosing to talk over me. "And then if you could get the junk off this table, I'd appreciate it. I don't even know how many hamburgers to make; I guess Warren's girlfriend is coming, but he's not sure. . . ."

"Oh," I said quietly, suddenly regretting the invitations I'd extended at work. But this was supposed to be a barbecue; I wasn't sure why my mother was getting so stressed-out about it. "Well, I

morgan matson

actually invited some people from work. So we might have three extras as well."

My mother slammed down the pot she'd been lifting up and turned to face me. I suddenly wished that Warren or Gelsey were here, so maybe we could spread around some of my mother's anger a bit. She didn't get mad often, so when she did, it was like all her pent-up frustration got unleashed at once. And now, it seemed, it was being unleashed on me. "God, Taylor," she snapped. "Did you ask me? Did you realize that this might be a huge inconvenience? Did you consider checking with me first?"

"I'm sorry," I said, taking a tiny step out of the kitchen. I could feel what always happened when someone confronted me—my flight instinct, kicking in, telling me to be anywhere but there. "I didn't think—"

"No," she interrupted me, moving another pot off a burner and slamming it down. "You didn't think. Because that would have involved thinking about someone else, wouldn't it? Someone other than yourself?"

I felt tears prick my eyes, and suddenly wanted nothing more than to go back to five minutes before, when I'd been riding my bike and everything had still been fine. "Sorry," I muttered, feeling how hot and tight my throat was, and not wanting to cry in front of my mother. "I'll go shuck." And I took the bag of corn and walked out to the front porch as fast as I could. Once there, I looked for a long moment at my bike, but I knew that if I left, I'd just be making things worse. And besides, where would I go?

I sat down on the nearest chair and picked up the first ear of corn with hands that were trembling. As I pulled back the husk, I felt a tear hit my cheek. My heart was still beating hard and I was, for whatever reason, more upset now than I had been when my mother was yelling at me. I wiped my hand across my eyes, took a shaky breath, and started to shuck the corn.

"Hi." I looked over and saw a pair of feet standing in first position, then up to see my mother, biting her lip. She sat down on the small table that stood between the two porch chairs and leaned forward. "I'm sorry, sweetheart. You didn't deserve that."

"I just," I started, having to take a breath before I could continue, feeling like I was on the verge of starting to cry again. I gave the husk a hard yank and dropped it into the bag at my feet. "I'm sorry for inviting people. I didn't think it would be a big deal. I can call them and tell them not to come."

My mom shook her head. "It's fine. I promise. The thing is . . ." She sighed and looked out to the road for a moment. Two people walking a golden retriever passed by, waving to us. My mother waved back, then looked back at me. "I just kept thinking, all day, about how this is your father's last Fourth," she said quietly. This didn't do much to keep my tears at bay and I pressed my lips together hard. "I just wanted everything to be perfect," she said. I looked over at her, and saw to my alarm that there were tears in her eyes, threatening to fall.

This, frankly, was a lot more frightening than the yelling. Seeing my mother sad, vulnerable, *scared*—it was too much for me, and I grabbed another ear, careful not to look at her again.

"There's just nothing worse than a ruined holiday," she continued, but she sounded less like she was about to cry, and I could feel myself relax just a tiny bit.

"I know," I said, without even thinking about it. When my mother didn't say anything, I looked up at her. "My birthday?" I prompted, then immediately wished I hadn't said anything, as her face crumpled a little bit and she looked like she was about to cry again. "Sorry," I said quickly. "I didn't mean that, Mom. Don't . . ."

My mother shook her head and looked away from me. Murphy padded tentatively out to the porch, maybe figuring that as long as we were no longer yelling, it was safe to emerge. To my surprise, my mother scooped the dog up, resting her cheek against his wiry fur for just a moment. "I thought you didn't like him," I said.

My mom smiled, and settled the dog on her lap. "I guess he's growing on me," she said, running her hand over the top of his head. We sat in silence, and as I dropped one ear of corn in the bag and extracted a new one, my mom shook her head. "Leave the rest," she said. "Warren and Gelsey can do them when they get home." I dropped the ear back, surprised, and my mom leaned forward. "And I am sorry about your birthday, sweetie. I promise I'll make it up to you."

"You don't have to," I said. I meant it too. I'd been upset about the birthday thing, at first, but so many other things had happened since that it had lost a lot of its importance. "And I promise it'll be fine tonight. We'll make it a good night for Dad." She looked at me, and I gave her a slightly trembly smile, realizing how strange it was to be the one consoling her, trying to cheer her up, when I'd known a lifetime of it being the other way around.

"I hope so," she said quietly. And then, she leaned a little closer to me and smoothed my hair down, then rubbed my back in small circles the way she'd done when I was young. The things we'd been fighting about no longer seemed to matter. After a moment, I surprised myself by leaning into her and resting my head on her shoulder, in a way I hadn't done since I'd been very little, and her shoulder had seemed a lot bigger, big enough to hold up not only me, but the whole world. And for just a second, as I closed my eyes and she ran her hand over my hair, it felt like it might still be true.

Despite all the stress, the barbecue turned out fine. Gelsey and I had set up citronella candles all around the backyard (she insisted on doing *grands jetés* to go between them) and my father had taken over grill duties, piling the platter high with cheeseburgers and hot dogs, wearing pressed khakis and a polo shirt that now looked much too big on him.

Henry and his dad had to do some prep work for the bakery that night, so my mother had invited Davy over and Mr. Crosby had given his babysitter the night off. All in all, it was a bit of a mixed group, but everyone seemed to be getting along. Fred showed up, bringing Jillian as his date and bearing two sea bass that my father grilled, and that everyone had effusively praised, making Fred turn even redder than normal. As soon as she had arrived, Lucy had been seized by Nora and Gelsey, and was now running an impromptu backbend lesson on the side of the lawn. Elliott had freaked out when he learned Jeff was a professional screenwriter. They had discovered a mutual love of science fiction movies, and had spent most of the barbecue talking only to each other. My mom had dragged some chairs out to the back lawn, and she hovered near my dad while he sat next to Fred, the two of them laughing about something. Davy was trying to teach the dog—unsuccessfully—to fetch, but he nonetheless seemed committed to his task.

I saw Warren and Wendy holding hands and talking to Kim, and I headed over to join them. "It's just such a fascinating area!" Kim was saying as I joined their circle. I noticed that Wendy looked particularly patriotic—she was wearing a red-and-white-striped shirt with blue shorts, and had pulled back her hair with a red headband. "We're definitely looking at getting an animal tech—or maybe a vet—into this pilot we're developing," Kim said.

"Wendy's going to be a vet," Warren said, and I just stared at him for a moment, beaming at the girl next to him. It was like I barely recognized him anymore.

"Well, we'll see," Wendy said with a laugh, her cheeks turning slightly pink. "I'm just starting college in the fall."

"But you should see her in the store," Warren gushed, as though Kim was actually interviewing Wendy for a job and needed to hear all about how fabulous she was. "She has an incredible way with animals."

"Can you help out over there?" I asked Wendy, pointing in the direction of Davy. Murphy was now circling him while he threw the stick. The dog watched the stick arc across the lawn, and then went back to jumping up at Davy, missing the point of the exercise entirely.

Wendy shook her head. "I'm not sure how effective I'd be," she said, giving me a smile. I noticed she rarely stopped smiling, and Warren hadn't seemed to stop all night. Before she had shown up, I truly hadn't been aware my brother had this many teeth.

"It's still very impressive," Kim said, taking a sip of her wine. "If we get this show going, we'll have to hire you on as a consultant."

Wendy blushed, turning the same color as her headband. "Oh, I don't know how much help I'd be," she murmured.

"She's just being modest," Warren said. He put his arm around her shoulders a little carefully, like he was still getting used to doing this. "She knows everything there is to know about animals. Tell them what you told me yesterday. The thing about the elephants?"

"Oh," Wendy said. "Well, Warren and I were talking about . . ." She paused and threaded her hand through my brother's, up by her shoulder, and I saw her give his hand a quick squeeze before continuing. "Death," she said, glancing at him once before looking back to Kim. "And I was telling him about how animals actually have grieving rituals, funeral procedures. . . . It's not just limited to humans."

"Really?" Kim asked, raising her eyebrows. "See, that's just the kind of stuff that would be great to have on our show. What kind of rituals?"

"So," Wendy said. She started to talk about llamas dying of broken hearts, of elephants trying to lift their dead babies, of gorillas sleeping in the nests of their dead parents and refusing to eat. And while a part of me was listening, I was really just trying to process a few things. One was that my brother had somehow found someone who liked facts—and sharing them—as much as he did. And the other was that he was talking to Wendy about death—which meant that he was talking to her about Dad, and what he was feeling. I thought about all the times Lucy had asked me if I wanted to talk, all the times that Henry had asked me leading questions about how things were at home, and how I had put them both off—with Lucy, by changing the subject, usually to one involving her love life, and with Henry, by kissing him. I had just assumed that Warren would have been the same way, and the fact that he wasn't was, weirdly, making me feel a little betrayed—like he'd broken an unspoken agreement that we'd had.

Kim was now asking Wendy if vets ever lived above their offices—this was apparently one of the premises of the show, along with a wacky receptionist—when the first *hiss* of a firework sounded, and I looked over toward the lake. Sure enough, there was the first firework, streaking across the darkening sky like a comet, exploding with a loud *bang* and turning into a red, white, and blue light. Everyone on the lawn clapped, and then began moving as a group down toward the dock, the better to watch the show.

Fourteen people—and a dog—were probably a few too many for our dock, but we all crowded on and had more or less settled by the time the next firework shot up into the sky, almost directly above us.

I ended up toward the back of the dock, sitting near the chair my mother had carried down for my dad. I glanced behind me, to see if Henry was coming over from his house, but so far, no sign of him. I had no idea how long the work at the bakery would take, and all he'd told me about my surprise was that it would happen after the fireworks. But after checking for him a few times, I let myself just relax and enjoy the show. And maybe it was that I hadn't seen a fireworks display on the Fourth in a few years (I'd been out of the country or trying to learn to speak another language), but it seemed pretty impressive. Certainly more so than I remembered from the last time we were up here to watch them.

I tipped my head back and just watched the bursts of color and light that were taking over the sky, reflecting on the water below. After a series of particularly spectacular ones, the group on the dock clapped, and the dog raced toward me at full speed.

"Sorry," Davy, who'd been holding him, said as he turned back to me. I grabbed the dog before he fell into the water—we weren't sure of Murphy's swimming abilities—and picked him up. As I did, I noticed that he was trembling violently. "I don't think he likes the noise."

"I'll bring him inside," I said, pushing myself up to standing.

"Thanks, kid," my dad said, giving the dog's dangling paw a squeeze as we passed. "He probably doesn't understand what's happening. Poor thing must think he stumbled into a war zone."

"Actually," I heard Wendy say from farther up the dock, "dogs' ears are amazingly sensitive. So what we're hearing is being amplified ten or twenty times for him."

I walked up to the house, feeling the dog flinch in my arms whenever a firework exploded. And I realized my father was probably right—if you had nobody to tell you we were only celebrating, you could easily think that the world was coming to an end. I dropped him inside the house, where he immediately fled down the hall to my room. Maybe it was because I had a bedskirt, but I'd noticed that the dog tended to hide under there whenever it was thunderstorming. It was, apparently, his safe place.

As I started to head down the hill again, I realized that the sound of fireworks had stopped—I'd missed the finale. And sure enough, I saw the group on the dock begin to stand and make their way up the hill. I continued down, figuring that I would probably be needed to help and not wanting to risk my mother's wrath a second time.

Fifteen minutes later, I had helped my mom clean up, said my good-byes to everyone, thanked people for coming, and promised to call Lucy later and tell her what Henry's surprise had been about. My father, exhausted, had gone right to bed, with Warren helping him up the stairs.

"I guess that's it," my mom said, as she picked the last abandoned plate up off the lawn and looked around, as though making sure that everything was in order. Gelsey was still on the lawn, darting from one citronella candle to the other, blowing them out. "Gels," she yelled to my sister, "bedtime!"

In the light left by the last candle, I watched as my sister dropped into a low arabesque, her leg almost parallel above her. "Five minutes!" she called back, her voice slightly muffled.

My mother nodded and turned back to me. "And not too late for you," she said. I nodded as well, feeling myself smile. I'd received a text mid-cleanup from Henry, asking me to meet him on the dock in twenty minutes for my surprise. Even though I had no idea what we'd be doing or how long we'd be out, my curfew, such as it was, had gotten very relaxed over the summer. All my mother had asked was that I come in at a reasonable hour, and quietly.

I set out for the dock a little early, which was when I noticed that Henry was also walking toward the dock, the white of his shirt bright against the darkness of the night. "Hey," I called, and Henry stopped and turned around, smiling when he saw me.

"Hi there," he said. Taking advantage of the darkness, and the fact that his brother wasn't around to make gagging sounds at us, I slid my arms around his neck and kissed him. He kissed me back, hugging me hard and lifting me off my feet for just a second, which he seemed to like to do occasionally, if just to remind me that he was now taller than I was.

"You missed the show," I said, when we broke apart after a moment.

"Did I?" he asked, his tone strangely neutral. "Too bad."

"So?" I asked, looking around. "My surprise?"

Henry smiled and took my hand. "At the dock," he said. We were walking down together when I heard a noise behind me and turned to see my sister was still on the lawn. I was about to say something, remind her to go inside, when I saw her shaking a sparkler out of the box. As I watched, it suddenly burst into flame, and Gelsey held it up as she danced her way back toward the house, big traveling leaps and a series of small *chine* turns, the sparker leaving streaks of light behind her until she rounded the corner of the house, her light still burning brightly behind her.

It turned out there was a good reason that Henry had told me my surprise was down at the dock. It was a boat.

"More than a boat," he said. He'd assembled everything down at the dock, and had turned on the Coleman lantern that he was now holding up to give us some light. Tied up to the dock, bobbing in the water, was a rowboat. It was lined with sleeping bags and it looked surprisingly cozy—something I'd never thought a boat could really be.

"Where did you get this?" I asked, as I climbed down the dock ladder and stepped carefully into the boat, which immediately pitched from side to side, and for one heart-stopping moment, seemed like it was going to turn over. I knew that the Crosbys had a few kayaks, but I was pretty sure I would have noticed the rowboat at our dock.

"Borrowed it from one of Dad's best customers," he said. "I'm giving him a coffee cake tomorrow to thank him. But we have to get going."

"Okay," I said, completely confused about what the rush was, but settling myself onto the front bench. Henry took the back, and started to row us across the lake with surprising skill. I turned to face him, and pulled my knees up to my chest as I just enjoyed the ride, the way we skimmed fast over the lake until we were far enough from the dock that it appeared tiny.

Henry stopped rowing and hooked the oars over the sides. Then he pulled out his phone to check the time, the light of his screen unexpectedly bright. "Okay," he said. "Almost time."

I looked around. We were in the middle of the lake; I couldn't see what we were almost on time for. "Henry?" I asked.

He smiled, and turned off the lantern. He lowered himself onto the floor of the rowboat, on the sleeping bags, and gestured for me to do the same. I did, crawling up to meet him. When I was next to him, he lay back down and I followed, ducking under his arm and finding my spot. We rocked in the boat for a moment, the only sound that of the water lapping against the sides and the cicadas humming all around us. He leaned down and kissed me quickly, then traced his finger down my cheek and smiled at me. "Ready for your surprise?" he asked.

"I am," I said, looking around, wondering if I was missing something. "But—" Just as I started to say this, I heard the *hiss* of another firework being let off. And then, right above us, a firework exploded, huge and golden, seeming to take up the whole sky. "What is this?" I asked, looking up at him, but only briefly, as more fireworks were coming, one right after another.

"I go to school with one of the guys who works for this company," he said. "And he agreed to delay a couple, so that we could get a really good spot to see them."

"This is amazing," I murmured, looking straight up above me into the night sky, watching it get overtaken by bursts of color and light. I had never before seen fireworks lying in a boat and looking up at them, but I knew as I watched them above me, that it would be now the only way I would ever want to see them. "Thank you," I said, still not quite able to believe that Henry had arranged this—a private fireworks show, just for us. I stretched up and kissed him, and behind my closed lids, I could still see the flashes of light as the display continued in the sky above us.

After a few more fireworks, the show ended, and Henry and I clapped from the boat, even though we knew that nobody would be able to hear us. And even though watching the fireworks had been the whole reason for taking the boat out, it was so nice, just drifting there, that neither of us seemed to feel any need to go back right away. We unzipped one of the sleeping bags and slipped into it, as it was starting to get a little chilly, not to mention damp, out on the lake.

We kissed until my lips were numb and my heart was racing, and we were both out of breath, and then our kisses changed to ones that were more lingering and softer, and then, when we were taking a small break to get our breath back, we just started talking, as we drifted across the lake, the sky huge and star-filled above us.

Maybe it was because it was dark, or because we weren't looking

morgan matson

right at each other, or because it was just what happens when you're lying in a rowboat with someone. But we started talking about much more serious things than we had yet talked about. I told him what had happened with my mother, and how seeing her about to cry had scared me so much. He told me about how he worried about Davy, especially since he would be leaving for college in a year and wouldn't be there to take care of him. And I told him what I hadn't said out loud yet, but had been thinking for the last few weeks—that I knew my father was getting worse, and I was terrified about what was going to come.

The gaps in our conversation got longer and longer, and I finally closed my eyes and rested my head against Henry's chest, feeling warm and secure in his arms, surrounded by the soft flannel of the sleeping bag, with the boat rocking me gently back and forth. I felt myself yawn, and a moment later, I heard Henry echo me, and even though I'd had trouble sleeping all summer, I could feel myself falling into sleep, right there in Henry's arms, under the stars.

It was starting to get light out by the time we woke up and rowed back to the dock. I'd woken up to find that I had a series of mosquito bites on my neck—pretty much the only piece of me that had been out of the sleeping bag—while Henry had gotten about five on his hand. At first, I'd been incredibly embarrassed that I'd fallen asleep, wiping my mouth quickly, just hoping that I hadn't drooled on him by accident, hoping that my breath wasn't terrible. I'd never slept next to anyone (unless Lucy on my trundle bed counted, and I had a feeling that it didn't) and was worried that I'd accidentally kicked him, or muttered in my sleep, or something.

But if I had, Henry didn't mention it and didn't seem bothered. I pulled the sleeping bag around my shoulders as I sat next to him on the back beam while he rowed us home. Henry had a faint crease mark along the side of his face, from where he'd slept on the sleeping bag's seam, and his hair was sticking up in little tufts all over. And for some reason, this made him look even cuter than he normally did.

We tied up the boat and took the equipment out of it, moving quickly. Mr. Crosby normally left for the bakery a little before six, and Henry wanted to get inside so that he could pretend he'd been sleeping there the whole time.

"Thank you for my surprise," I said, trying with all my might to resist the urge to scratch at the mosquito bites on my neck.

"Of course," he said, leaning down and kissing me quickly. "I'll call you later?"

I felt myself smile, and as I stretched up to kiss him again, I found I no longer cared if my breath was terrible.

I walked up the yard and around the side of the house, humming the tune that Warren had gotten stuck in my head. I was about to head inside when I stopped short—my dad was sitting at the table on the screened-in porch, a mug of coffee in front of him.

I swallowed hard and climbed the porch steps, feeling my face get hot. "Hi," I murmured, trying to smooth my hair down, knowing exactly what this looked like.

My father was wearing his familiar blue pinstripe pajamas, with a plaid robe over them. He shook his head at me as he took a sip of his coffee, but there was something in his expression that let me know just how much he was enjoying this. "Late night?" he asked.

"Kind of," I said, feeling myself blushing harder than ever. "Um, Henry took me out in a rowboat to see some fireworks, and then we kind of fell asleep." Just hearing it, I realized how ridiculous it sounded.

My dad shook his head. "If I had a dime for every time I'd heard that excuse," he said gravely, making me laugh. He arched an eyebrow at me, and I recognized the pun expression, even on my father's much thinner face. "I'm afraid that excuse isn't going to *float*," he said, as I groaned, and took the seat next to him. "It's kind of an either-*oar* situation. And if it doesn't *hold water* . . ."

"Enough," I said, laughing. I looked at him as he lifted the mug with both hands and took another sip. "Why are you up so early?"

He faced the back of the screened porch, the side that looked out to the water. "Wanted to watch the sunrise," he said. I looked in that direction as well, and we sat in silence for a moment. "I should probably be lecturing you," he said, glancing over at me. "But . . ." He trailed off and smiled at me, shrugging. He pointed outside, where the whole sky was turning the palest shade of pink, the color of Gelsey's pointe shoes. "Isn't that beautiful?" he asked, his voice not more than a whisper.

I had to clear my throat before I could speak again. "It is," I murmured.

"I don't know how many of these I've missed, or just taken for granted," he said, his eyes on the lake. "And I told myself I was going to get up for one every morning. But I have to tell you, kid," he said, looking over at me, "I'm just so tired."

And as he said it, I realized that he did look exhausted, and in a way that I'd never seen before. There were deep lines in his face I didn't recognize, and bags underneath his eyes. It looked like the kind of tired that a good night's sleep wouldn't come close to making up for, the kind of tired that went down to your bones.

There was nothing I could do to fix this, or make it better. So I just nodded and pulled my chair a little closer to my dad's. And together, we watched the sky lighten and transform, as another day began.

chapter thirty-two

I FINALLY GOT WHAT DICKENS WAS TALKING ABOUT. IT WAS THE best of times and the worst of times, all mixed into one. Because things were great with Henry, with Lucy, at work, even with my siblings. But every day, my father got worse. The FedEx truck bearing my dad's work documents stopped coming, and I'd thought it was just an anomaly until three days went by. Mom told me when my dad was napping one afternoon that his firm had pulled him off the case. This sent my father into a funk like I'd never before seen from him. He didn't get dressed, barely combed his hair, and snapped at us when we tried to talk to him—making me realize how much I had relied on him being who he was, the cheerful and punning father I'd taken for granted.

But it did give me an idea. Leland and Fred both agreed, and it was arranged while my dad took his late-afternoon nap. When he woke up, Warren helped him outside, where the Movies Under the Stars—Edwards Family edition—had been set up. Leland had agreed to run the projector, and we'd spread out blankets on the back lawn, down by the water, to watch what my father had always promised was the perfect bad-day antidote.

It was a much smaller crowd than normally assembled at the beach—just us, Wendy, Leland, the Gardners, and the Crosbys. I turned the introduction duties over to my dad, and we all got very quiet while he did his best to raise his voice so he could tell us, in no uncertain terms, how much we were all about to enjoy *The Thin Man*. And as we watched, I was able to pick out my father's laugh above everyone else's.

The movie helped shake him out of his funk, but just seeing him like that had been enough to scare me. The next couple of weeks fell into a pattern almost like a pendulum, with the good and the bad in constant flux, and I could never fully enjoy the upswing because I knew that there would be a downswing coming shortly thereafter.

We all started staying in at night, and spending the time after dinner sitting around the table, not rushing off to meet our dates (me and Warren) or catch fireflies with Nora (Gelsey). After much protesting from my mother, we excavated the old battered Risk board and set it up in the living room, where it became a shrine to strategy. And later on, when it got too dark or cold to stay on the porch, we all came inside to play the game, until my dad started yawning, his head drooping, and my mother would declare détente for the night and she and Warren would help my dad upstairs.

• • •

"Because," I said as angrily as I could, to my mother, "I haven't trusted you since you left me for dead in Paraguay. That's why."

"You tell her, Charlie," my brother said in a monotone, as my mother flipped pages, frowning.

"Sorry," she said, after a minute, as Kim and Jeff both groaned. "I don't—"

"Page sixty-one," Nora hissed. "At the bottom."

"Oh, right," my mother said. She cleared her throat. "I'll ruin you, Hernandez," she said to me. "I'll wreck you and your whole family until you beg for mercy. But mercy won't come." She looked over at Kim and Jeff and smiled. "That's very good," she said, causing Nora to throw up her hands and my dad to applaud her performance.

Because we weren't going out, people started to come to us. The Gardners occasionally stopped by, mostly to use us as impromptu actors to hear the current draft of their screenplay read aloud. Nora would take notes for her parents, and they kept casting my mother, despite the fact that she was constantly pausing mid-scene to offer her opinions.

When we weren't butchering the Gardners' script with our terrible line readings or playing Risk, we'd watch movies on the old corduroy couch, all my father's favorites. And while he'd start off telling us more trivia than we ever wanted to know about *The Americanization of Emily* or *Mr. Smith Goes to Washington*, he would usually fall asleep halfway through.

Sometimes Wendy or Henry came over for the movie or to take sides in the battle for global domination—it was only with Henry's help that I'd finally conquered Russia—but usually it was just the family, just us five. And I found I liked it. I kept thinking back to all those nights in Connecticut, when I was out the door as soon as dinner was over, yelling my plans behind me as I headed to my car, ready for my real night to begin—my time with my family just something to get through as quickly as possible. And now that I knew that the time we had together was limited, I was holding on to it, trying to stretch it out, all the while wishing I'd appreciated what I'd had earlier.

But it wasn't like I was spending the whole night inside. I would usually sneak out later, once everyone had gone to bed. Sometimes I'd paddle the kayak across to Lucy's dock and we'd sit for hours with our feet dangling in the water, talking. She remained oblivious to Elliot's crush but had also given up on Brett after he'd sent her a booty-call text by accident—it had been intended for someone named Lisa. One Saturday night, we'd all met up at the beach at midnight—me, Henry, Elliot, Leland, and Lucy. Rachel and Ivy, the other lifeguards, had bought us a few six-packs in exchange for Leland taking over some of their shifts, and we'd had a party on the dark, empty beach. We'd gone nightswimming and played I Never—it turned out that Lucy pretty much Always Had—and I'd ridden back on Henry's handlebars as it was starting to get light out, my damp hair twisted up, closing my eyes and feeling the wind against my face as he brought me home once again.

But parties on the beach or nights with Lucy were the exception. If I was sneaking out, it was usually to go next door. I knew by now which one was Henry's bedroom, and he knew mine. Luckily, we were both on the ground floor, and I became practiced at creeping across to his house, and drumming my fingers lightly on the glass of his window. Henry would meet me, and we would either go out to the dock, or his old treehouse, if he knew Maryanne was out of town. If it had been a particularly bad day with my dad, I'd always find myself going over to Henry's. There was something so terrible in what was happening to my father, made all the more awful because I was powerless to stop it. And as he deteriorated, each new version of him replaced the other, and I had trouble remembering when he hadn't just worn pajamas and a robe all day, when he hadn't struggled to eat all his meals, his hands shaking as they tried to bring food to his mouth, coughing as he tried to make himself swallow. When he hadn't needed help to stand or sit or walk upstairs, when he'd been the one to lift our heavy boxes, and throw Gelsey over his shoulder like a sack of potatoes, and when I was very little, carry me in from the car after long drives when I'd pretend to fall asleep. It was getting hard to remember who he'd been last week, let alone who he'd been four months ago, when everything had seemed fine.

He had started sleeping late in the mornings, though I still found myself jerking awake at eight, expecting him to be there, tickling my feet, telling me to get a move on, that we had pancakes to eat. I continued to go to the diner on my days off, getting our food to go, and bringing it home to him. But after three trips with his toast in its Styrofoam container sitting on the counter, uneaten, I'd stopped.

After the particularly bad nights—like when he'd snap at my mother, then look immediately regretful, and like he was on the verge of tears—I'd head to Henry's as soon as the house was quiet and sleeping. Despite our talk in the rowboat, I usually didn't want to go into what was happening, even though he always gave me the opportunity to. Mostly, I just wanted to feel his arms around me, solid and true, while I tried to shut out the feelings that were hurting my heart with a thousand tiny pinpricks, which was somehow worse than having it broken all at once.

Whenever it got really bad at home, I would know that there was happiness waiting for me just around the corner, right next door. But whenever I found myself in a moment of happiness— laughing with Lucy, kissing Henry, conquering Asia with a shoestring army—I'd suddenly get shaken out of it, since I knew that much worse was coming down the pike, and really, I had no right to be enjoying myself when my father was going through this. And there was always the uneasy knowledge that, soon, there would be a breaking point.

• • •

morgan matson

"And this," Henry said, wrapping his arms around my waist, "is where the magic happens."

"Is it?" I asked, stretching up to kiss him. We were behind the counter at Borrowed Thyme, through the stainless steel swinging doors, back where the ovens and prep stations were. I'd had the day off, so I had come downtown to pick up some things for my mother and to visit Henry. Finding the store in a between-customers lull, he'd taken me behind the counter to show me how things worked.

"I was just about to ice some cupcakes," he said, pointing to a mixer bowl full of white buttercream icing that, even from here, smelled delicious. "Want to help?"

"Maybe," I said, sliding my hands around his waist and kissing him again. I was in a great mood—my dad had had a good morning, been up and alert and making terrible puns at breakfast, I didn't have to work, I was with Henry, and there was a lot of frosting just there for the taking. Lucy was caught up in her latest boy—I had a feeling he wasn't going to be around long, so I'd just taken to calling him Pittsburgh—so I knew she wouldn't give me a hard time for not hanging out with her, which meant I had all afternoon to spend kissing Henry. Breaking the moment, my phone trilled in my bag across the counter. I listened for a second—it was the ringtone for the house's landline. I started to go to answer it when I realized that it was probably Gelsey.

"Do you need to answer that?" Henry asked.

"Nope," I said. I crossed to my phone and turned the ringer off so that it wouldn't interrupt us again when she inevitably called back. "It's just my sister wanting me to help her get ready." When Henry still looked perplexed, I added, "It's the first night of the carnival." Gelsey had been freaking out about it all week, and she'd finally told me that she had a crush on a boy in her tennis group—which actually explained why she'd stopped complaining about her lessons recently. She, tennis boy, Nora, and the boy Nora had a crush on, were all meeting up for what Gelsey kept insisting was *not* a double date. Nevertheless, when she'd found out that I didn't have work today, she'd assumed that I would be spending the afternoon helping her primp—by which she meant I would give her a make-over, using my makeup. And while I was willing to help Gelsey get ready, I was not about to spend four hours doing it.

"Ah, the carnival," Henry said with a smile. He brushed some hair back from my forehead and smiled at me. "I remember the carnival." I smiled back, pretty sure that we were both remembering the same thing. He kissed me again before we headed over to where the frosting was. "Cupcakes."

Henry showed me the proper icing technique, and even though I insisted on tasting the frosting every few minutes, just to make sure it wasn't going bad, we were soon making progress. "Not too hard, right?" he asked.

I nodded, admiring my handiwork. The bell dinged out front

just as we were finishing the batch, and I realized that I should probably be getting home—I'd let Gelsey dangle long enough. I took a cupcake for the road and kissed Henry good-bye. I biked home, humming Warren's tune under my breath, waving at the people I knew as I passed. Halfway home, though, I pulled out my phone to turn the ringer back on and realized that something was wrong. I had seven missed calls and two voice mails.

I started biking faster, hoping that it was just Gelsey wanting me to help and being a pain. But as soon as I stepped onto the porch, I could feel it in the air, a kind of crackling tension that made the hairs on the back of my neck stand on end. My mother was on the phone in the kitchen, but she slammed it down when she saw me.

"Where have you been?" she demanded. Her face was red, and her expression was scared and angry in equal measure.

I swallowed hard, thinking of all the calls I'd ignored, just assuming they were Gelsey. A terrible dread was creeping over me. "Um," I said, feeling my heart begin to pound. What was happening? "I was downtown. My ringer was off. What's going on?"

"Your dad—" my mom started, but her voice broke and she turned away from me slightly, wiping her hand across her face. "He's not doing well. I'm going to take him to the hospital in Stroudsburg and see what they say."

"What's wrong?" I made myself ask, even though my voice was no more than a whisper.

"I don't know!" my mother snapped, turning back to me. "Sorry," she said after a moment, a little more quietly. "I'm just . . ." Her voice trailed off and she gestured helplessly around her.

"Where's Gelsey?" I asked, looking around the house, as though I was going to spot my siblings, like maybe they were just hanging out on one of the sofas while all this was happening. "And Warren?"

"Your sister's next door at Nora's," my mom said. "And Warren went somewhere with Wendy; I haven't been able to reach him."

"Okay," I said, making myself take deep breaths. "What can I do?"

"Help your sister," my mom said, and I felt immediately ashamed of myself that I'd spent the afternoon trying to avoid doing exactly that. "And don't tell her we went to the hospital. She's looking forward to tonight. I'll tell her when I get back."

I felt my breath catch in my throat, noticing the singular pronoun. "But Dad will be coming back too, right?" I asked slowly.

My mother shrugged, her chin trembling, and I felt my stomach plunge. She pressed a hand to her eyes for a moment and took a deep breath. When she spoke again, she was more composed, back in her efficiency mode. "I'm going to need your help getting your dad into the car," she said. "And then please be either here or by your phone tonight, in case I have updates." I nodded, feeling a second wave of shame crest over me that I had been actively ignoring my phone all afternoon. "And," my mother said, biting her lip. She

morgan matson

seemed to be weighing something in her mind. "I'm going to need you to call your grandfather."

"Oh." This was not what I'd been expecting to hear. "Sure. But why am I doing that?" My father's father was a former naval officer who now taught at West Point and had always reminded me of Captain Von Trapp from *The Sound of Music*—just without the easygoing personality or penchant for songs about flowers. He'd always terrified me, and the few times a year I saw him, we never seemed to have all that much to talk about.

"He wanted to know . . . when we got to this point," my mother said. "He wanted to come and say good-bye."

I nodded, but it felt like the breath had just been knocked out of me. "What point?" I asked, even though I didn't really want to hear the answer, because I was afraid that I already knew it.

"He wanted to come," my mother said, slowly, like she was having to think about each word before she spoke it, "when your father would still understand what was happening. When he would still . . . be here."

I nodded again, mostly just so that I would have something to do. I couldn't believe that only twenty minutes ago, I'd been eating icing and making out with Henry. "I'll call him," I said, trying to sound competent and together, and not like I was feeling, which was the exact opposite.

"Good," my mother said. She rested her hand on my shoulder for just a moment, and then she was gone, heading upstairs, calling to my father.

Fifteen minutes later, each of us taking one arm, my mother and I got my father down the stairs and into the backseat of the car. The change in my dad from just that morning was startling—his skin had taken on a grayish tone, and there were beads of perspiration on his forehead, and his eyes were, for the most part, closed tightly against the pain that he was so obviously feeling. In the past, I could not remember my father ever complaining about his own discomfort, and I'd never seen him cry. But now his forehead was furrowed, and he was making a low moaning sound in the back of his throat that scared me in a way that nothing else yet had.

When Murphy saw us loading my dad into the car, he rushed full-out down the driveway, and scrambled up into the backseat. I reached for him, but he darted past me and settled behind the driver's seat.

"Taylor, would you get the dog?" my mother asked, as she put a large duffel bag on the passenger seat. I was about to ask what it was, when I realized that it was probably clothes in case she—or my dad—had to stay over.

I reached for Murphy, who tried to get away, clearly only wanting to be where my dad was. "Stop it," I said, more sharply than I needed to, as I snatched him up and shut the car door.

"I'll call with updates," my mother said, climbing behind the wheel.

"Okay," I said, holding tight to the dog, who seemed to be ready to make a break for it again. "I'll be here." I made myself smile and wave as the car backed down the gravel driveway, even though my mother was concentrating on reversing, and my father's eyes were closed.

When it disappeared from view, the dog seemed to droop a little in my arms. I stroked his wiry head, and felt myself let out a shaky breath. I knew exactly how he felt.

Fortunately, Gelsey was too excited about the carnival to ask many questions. When she got home from Nora's, I told her that Dad had a doctor's appointment, which I figured sounded much less scary than going to the hospital, and she simply accepted it without question.

I flat-ironed Gelsey's hair while she took calls from Nora on her cell, getting an update every time there was an outfit change. As I stood behind my sister and looked at her excited expression in the mirror, as she giggled with her best friend, I felt both envious that she could still be this lighthearted, and anxious knowing that soon, she wouldn't be laughing like that. That none of us would.

Once her hair was straight—and with hair as curly as Gelsey's, it took a while—I had her sit on the bathroom counter while I did her makeup, less than she wanted, but probably more than my mother would have approved of. When I was finished, I twisted the cap back on my mascara and stepped back so that she could take in her reflection.

She leaned closer, examining her new self closely. "What do you think?" she asked. "Do I look like you?"

I stared at her. She had wanted to look like *me*? I blinked, then smoothed down the back of her hair. It actually explained why she'd wanted it straightened. "You look better," I said, smiling at her through the mirror. Gelsey smiled back at me for a moment before her phone rang, and she hopped off the counter, already chattering to Nora as she headed down the hall to her bedroom.

Kim and Jeff were driving the girls to the carnival, so they came over with Nora. "Where are Katie and Rob?" Kim asked me as Gelsey and Nora got their purses and checked the mirror one last time. "Is everything okay?"

"They had to go to Stroudsburg," I said, trying to keep my voice level. I looked over at Kim and saw that she was still waiting for more, worried. "To the hospital," I said, and I lost control of my voice on the last word. I took a deep breath, knowing that I had to keep it together for just a few more minutes, so I wouldn't ruin my sister's night.

Kim nodded, and even though I could see she wanted to, she didn't ask any more questions, for which I was grateful, since I didn't have the information to answer them. "Well," she said after a moment, "just please let us know if there's anything we can do. Your dad's in our thoughts."

"Actually," I said, "would it be okay if Gelsey slept over?" I wasn't sure when—or if—my mother was getting back tonight, and this just seemed like a way to buy some time.

"Of course," Kim said. She smiled. "Nora asked me the same

thing, so I was going to ask your mom. Gelsey!" she called, heading over to join Jeff, who was fruitlessly trying to get Murphy to fetch. "Want to stay over after the carnival?"

The prospect of a sleepover *and* the not-date raised the decibel level in the living room significantly, and Murphy finally escaped and fled to my room, no doubt seeking solace under my bed. When Gelsey and Nora were finally ready, they all piled into the Gardners' Prius, waving at me through the back window as the car headed down the street.

I watched them go, then closed the door, walked inside, and sat down on the nearest couch to think. I couldn't get my mother's words out of my head when she asked me where I had been. And I knew why I hadn't told her—because of how silly and frivolous it would make me look. I wasn't around to help out with my father because I'd been giggling like I was Gelsey's age and kissing Henry. I hadn't been where I was needed. What was happening with my father was more important than my summer romance, and I shouldn't have let myself forget it.

But it was more than that, I realized as I got up and paced to the kitchen, getting a Diet Coke I didn't really want out of the fridge. It was how I'd come to depend on Henry, how I'd been running over there every night when I needed to be consoled. What would happen when he wasn't there? What would happen when the summer ended and I went back to Stanwich and had to learn how to be without him? From what my dad's doctors had said, we had all been expecting that we would make it through the summer. But nobody was really hoping for beyond that. And if I was dealing with a terrible breakup on top of just losing my dad—I couldn't really let myself even finish that thought. Feeling the need to stay in motion, as though I could somehow escape this, I walked outside, closing the screen door behind me, heading down the driveway to the dock.

There was also the fact that I could glimpse, still half-hidden in shadow but there, what a mess I'd be once the terrible inevitable happened. And did I really think it was right to put Henry through that? Especially knowing how he tried to take care of Davy—of everyone, really, even my dad, attempting to cure him through cookies. He was always trying to help people. I had known this from the moment we'd met, seven years earlier, the first time he'd come to my rescue. I knew that he would stick with me afterward. Because it would be the Right Thing to Do. And I didn't want to force that responsibility on him. Henry had been through enough already.

I walked to the end of the dock and sat down, hooking my legs over the edge. It was twilight, the sky slowly darkening and the first stars just beginning to appear, but I barely noticed it. The facts were hard to argue with. I needed to end it with Henry before he was pulled along with what was inevitable. I needed to end it before things got more serious, before he felt like he had any obligation to me. Suddenly, the very fact that I'd started anything at all with

morgan matson

him seemed monstrously selfish. There were so many reasons why it wasn't a good idea to stay together. It was impossible to ignore. I saw the light in Henry's bedroom come on, and I pulled my phone out of my pocket. I would do it fast, before I could reconsider, or let myself remember how we'd laughed together, or how his kisses had melted me. It would be like pulling off a Band-Aid—painful at first, but in the end, better for everyone.

I took a deep breath and sent him a text, asking him to meet me on the dock.

Henry was smiling as he walked toward me, and even though I wanted to look away, I made myself look back at him, memorizing what he looked like when he was happy to see me. I had a feeling that it would be the last time I would be seeing it.

"Hi," he said, reaching the dock and coming close, his hand stretching out for mine, clearly expecting me to meet him halfway. But I locked my hands together behind my back and took a tiny step away, going over in my mind the list of reasons why I had to do this. Henry's smile dimmed a little, and one of his eyebrows went up. "Is everything okay?"

"I think we have to stop this," I blurted out. It hit me that this was how I'd first proposed becoming friends, as well. For whatever reason, there was something about him that made it impossible for me to ease into a subject. Henry looked confused, and I clarified, "You and me. What we've been doing. We should stop."

Henry looked at me for a long moment, then out across the lake before turning back to me. When he did, I couldn't help but see the pain in his expression—pain that hadn't been there only a few seconds ago. "Why?" he asked me. It was a gentle question, not demanding an explanation, even though he was entitled to one. "What's going on, Tay?"

I knew that if I lied to him, he'd be able to tell. And plus, he deserved better than that. "I just," I started, taking a deep breath, "need to spend my time with my family right now. And it's not fair to ask you to just hang around while I go through this."

"So I'm supposed to just go away?" Henry asked, sounding equally baffled and hurt. "Is that the plan?"

"I just don't want you to—" I started.

"Taylor," Henry said, taking a step toward me. Suddenly he was right there, so close, close enough that I could have leaned forward and kissed him, reached out for him, done all the things that I wanted to do. "Don't think about me. Really."

It was hard to do, nearly impossible, but I made myself take a step away from him. "I just can't be with you right now," I said. "With anyone," I clarified quickly, lest he think I'd suddenly developed some bizarre crush on Leland. "I just think it's for the best."

"Okay," Henry said. He looked at me steadily. "But we can still be friends, right?"

I swallowed hard and made myself shake my head. I knew that

if he was in my life, I wouldn't be able to stop myself from wanting to kiss him, needing to find solace in my spot. "No," I whispered.

Henry's face changed, and he looked angry for the first time in this conversation. "Are you cutting out Lucy, too?" he asked. I just looked down at the planks of the dock, giving him my answer. "I just don't see," he said, more quietly now, "why I have to be the only one shut out."

I had no idea how to respond, how to tell him the truth that was behind this—that I could feel myself falling for him, and I was already on the cusp of losing someone I loved. And the closer we got, the harder it would be when I lost him, too. "I'm sorry," I whispered. "But you don't understand what this is like, and—"

"I do," he said, causing me to look up at him. "My mother's gone, and—"

"But she's not dead," I said, my voice coming out sharp. "You can talk to her if you want. You could find her. She doesn't have to be gone. That's your choice." Henry took a step back; it was like I'd slapped him. "I'm sorry," I said after a moment, knowing I'd gone too far.

Henry let out a breath and looked back at me. "I just want to be here for you," he said, his voice quiet and pained. "I don't understand what's changed."

Suddenly, all I wanted was to tell him, about the hospital, about my grandfather, about all of it. I wanted to feel his arms around me, the one thing that made sense while everything around me was falling apart. But I had a feeling that if I did, I'd be hurting him—and myself—much more after the summer than either of us was hurting now. "I can't explain it," I said, making my voice as cold as I could, trying to push him away hard enough so that he'd go, and stay gone. "Sorry."

Henry looked up at me, and for a second, I saw all the pain—all the pain that I was causing—cross his face. Then he nodded, and just like that, he was back to being what he'd been to me at the beginning of the summer—a little distant, a little cool. "If that's what you want," he said. I nodded, and pressed my nails hard into my palms to stop myself from telling him otherwise. He looked at me for one moment longer, then turned and walked off the dock, shoving his hands in his pockets as he went.

As I watched him go, I felt a tear hit my cheek, then another, but I didn't even bother to wipe them away. When I was sure he'd gone inside, I walked slowly up the dock myself, making sure not to look back at what we'd carved so long ago—the plus sign, and the heart, that was a lie once again.

chapter thirty-three
seven summers earlier

I WAS OFFICIALLY LOST.

I turned in a complete circle, but all I saw around me were trees, and trees that all looked exactly the same. Any sign of the path I had taken when I'd stomped into the woods was totally gone. The trees were blocking out the light above me, and this deep in the woods, it was darker than I had realized it would be. I could feel my heart start to beat faster, and made myself close my eyes for a moment and take a deep breath, like I'd seen my father do before he had court, and once when he saw what his car looked like when my mom rammed it into the tree that came out of nowhere.

But when I opened my eyes again, nothing had changed. I was still lost, and it was now a little darker out. I hadn't intended to go into the woods. But I'd been so mad at Warren, for cutting me out of his stupid game. And when I'd told my mother about it, she was helping Gelsey with her new ballet slippers and told me she didn't have time to deal with me right then. So I'd headed out the door, planning on just taking my bike and going down to the lake, or maybe seeing if Lucy was around and wanted to hang out. But the more I thought about it, the unfairness of it all, the madder I got, until I'd convinced myself that all I wanted was to be alone. And at first, I'd been so busy noticing things—a huge anthill that I would have told Warren about if I'd been speaking to him, the springy moss that grew at the roots of trees, the thousands and thousands of ferns—that when I stopped and looked around, I realized I had no idea where I was. Figuring I couldn't have gone that far, I headed toward where I was sure the road back to my house was, only to find woods, and more woods. So I'd changed direction, but that hadn't helped, and had only served to make me more turned around. And now it was getting dark, and I was starting to feel myself panic, despite all the deep breaths I was taking. I had a ton of freedom up in Lake Phoenix, and could pretty much do what I wanted with my day, so long as I was back for dinner. And even though my mom always complained when I did this, I sometimes went for dinner at Lucy's and forgot to call. So it could be hours before anyone realized that I was gone, that something was wrong. And it would be dark by then. And there were bears in the woods. I could feel the first hot tears start to build up behind my eyes, and blinked them away hard. I could find my way out. I just had to think rationally, and not panic.

A twig snapped behind me, and I jumped, my heart hammering harder than ever. I turned around, hoping with everything

morgan matson

I had that it would just be a squirrel, or better yet, a butterfly, basically anything but a bear. But standing in front of me was a kid who looked around my own age. He was skinny, with scraped-up knees and shaggy brown hair. "Hey," he said, lifting one hand in a wave.

"Hi," I said, looking at him more closely. I didn't recognize him, and I knew all the kids' whose families had homes in Lake Phoenix—most of us had been coming up here since we were babies.

"Are you lost?" he asked. And though he didn't say it mockingly, and I was, I still felt my cheeks get hot.

"No," I said, folding my arms across my chest. "I'm just taking a walk."

"You looked lost," he pointed out, in the same reasonable voice. "You kept turning around."

"Well, I'm not," I snapped. I felt the urge to toss my hair at him. The heroine in the book I was reading tossed her hair a lot, and I'd been looking for an opportunity, even though I wasn't quite exactly sure how to pull this off.

He shrugged. "Okay," he said. He turned and started to walk in the other direction, and after he'd gone a few steps, I yelped, "Wait!"

I hurried to catch up with him, and he waited for me until I got there. "I'm maybe a little lost," I confessed as I reached him. "I'm just trying to get back to Dockside. Or really, any road. I'll be able to find my way back."

He shrugged. "I don't know where that is," he said. "But I can take you back to the street my house is on, if you want. I think it's called Hollyhock."

I knew exactly where that was—but it was a ten-minute bike ride away from my house, and I realized just how turned around I had actually gotten. "Did you just move in?" I asked as I fell into step next to him. He was a little shorter than me, and as I looked down at him, I could see an explosion of freckles across his nose and cheeks.

"This afternoon," he said, nodding.

"Then how do you know where you're going?" I asked, and I could hear my voice rise a little, as I started to panic again. Were there now two of us lost in the woods? Were we going to provide the bears with multiple entrée options?

"I know the woods," he said, in the same calm voice. "We have some behind our house in Maryland. You just have to look for markers. You can always find your way out again, no matter how lost you think you are."

That seemed highly unlikely to me. "Really."

He smiled at that, and I could see his front teeth were slightly crooked, the way Warren's had been before he got his retainer. "Really," he said. "See?" He pointed through a gap in the trees and I saw, to my amazement, the road, with cars going by.

"Oh, wow," I said as I felt relief flood through me. "I thought I was never going to get out of here. I thought I was bear food. Thank you so much!"

"Sure," he said, with a shrug. "It was no big deal."

As he said this, I realized he wasn't bragging, or telling me that he'd told me so, or being a jerk about the fact that I'd lied and then needed his help anyway. And as I looked at him, and his steady green-brown eyes, I was suddenly glad I hadn't tried to toss my hair. "I'm Taylor, by the way."

"Nice to meet you," he said, smiling at me. "I'm Henry."

chapter thirty-four

My dad returned from the hospital the next day, but it was clear that things weren't going to go back to whatever normal we'd established. His doctors no longer wanted him to go unmonitored, and apparently, he was going to need help soon that we wouldn't be able to provide. So, as a condition of being able to come home, we would now have round-the-clock home health care workers. He also wasn't supposed to climb stairs any longer, so a bed—the kind with a remote that could raise and lower it, the kind in hospitals—had been installed in our living room, the table we never used pushed aside to make space. A wheelchair sat in the corner of the screened-in porch, like a terrible sign of things to come.

And adding to the feeling that the summer as we'd known it had ended was the presence of my grandfather. After I'd had my conversation on the dock with Henry, I'd gone inside and cried for an hour. This seriously frightened Warren, who'd come home with Wendy and a pizza in tow for dinner, and hadn't expected either the news about Dad or to find his sister in an emotional meltdown.

When I'd composed myself, with Warren standing by for emotional support, I'd called my grandfather in New York and told him the situation. I'd barely gotten the words out before he was telling me what bus he would be on, and when I should pick him up. So as my mother was dealing with the medical-supply people and setting up the bed, and Warren was taking Gelsey out for ice cream to tell her what was happening (never mind that it was ten in the morning), I was driving to Mountainview to meet my grandfather's bus.

I arrived early and parked near the bus station, but it wasn't until I got out of the car to wait that I realized I probably should have pulled myself together a little more. I wasn't even wearing shoes, which was never really a problem in Lake Phoenix. My feet, by now, had toughed up so that I could easily run up the driveway barefoot, and I preferred to drive barefoot, always with a few lone grains of sand clinging to my feet and the pedals. Nevertheless, I almost always remembered to throw some flip-flops into the car so that I wouldn't look like a total hick when I got out of it. But between lying awake the night before, wondering if I'd done the right thing with Henry, and this morning, with the new equipment and people traipsing through the house, I wasn't really in the best frame of mind.

The bus arrived right on time, and I walked up the hot sidewalk to meet it, as the doors swung open and the passengers disembarked. My grandfather was the third passenger off, and I waved as he got closer, getting a curt nod in response.

Even though it was a Saturday morning, and the temperature was in the high eighties, he was wearing a collared shirt and a blue blazer, khakis with pleats, and boat shoes. His white hair was sharply parted and he carried a small leather duffel bag and a larger suitcase easily, as though they weighed nothing. As he got closer, I realized with a sudden pang that my grandfather, who had always been *old*, was now in much better shape than my dad was.

"Taylor," he said as he reached me, pulling me into a quick hug. He didn't look much like my father—my dad seemed to take after my grandmother, at least in the pictures of her I'd seen—but I noticed now, for the first time, that he had the same blue eyes as my dad. And me.

"Hi," I said, already feeling awkward around him, and wondering how long he was going to end up staying. "The car's this way." As I headed over, I saw him look down at my feet and raise his eyebrows, but he didn't say anything, which I was grateful for. I wasn't sure what explanation I could give for having forgotten to wear shoes that morning.

"So," he said, after I'd started driving toward Lake Phoenix. I noticed that his posture was, as always, ramrod-straight, and I found myself sitting up a little straighter in response. "How is Robin?"

It took me a moment to translate this to my dad. I knew his name was Robin, of course, but he went exclusively by Rob, and my grandfather was practically the only one I had ever heard call him this. "He's back from the hospital," I said, not really trusting myself to say more. My dad had been asleep most of the morning, even through the setup of the hospital bed, which had been loud enough to send Murphy running for cover. My grandfather nodded and looked out the window, and I tried to remember the last time he'd seen my dad—it would have been months ago, when he still seemed healthy, and strong, and normal. I had no idea how to prepare my grandfather for the changes in him—I could barely process them myself. "He's not doing so well," I said, looking straight ahead, concentrating on the brightness of the red light in front of me. "You might be a little surprised by how he looks."

My grandfather nodded again, squaring his shoulders a little as though steeling himself to face this. After a few minutes of driving in silence, my grandfather pulled something out of his bag. "I made this for your sister," he said. "I finished it on the bus." He extended it to me just as I reached another stoplight and slowed for the yellow. "Do you think she'll like it?"

I looked at the item on his outstretched palm. It was a tiny carved wooden dog, remarkably detailed. "You made this?" I asked, stunned. The car behind me honked, and I realized the light had changed. I drove on, and my grandfather turned the dog over in his hands.

"Whittling," he said. "I learned to do it on the first ship I served on, when I had kitchen duty. I could make a potato look like *anybody*." I felt myself smile, a little shocked. It seemed my grandfather could be funny. "Your mother told me you got a dog, but she didn't tell me what kind. So it's kind of a mix."

"So's the dog," I assured him, sneaking another glimpse at the tiny figure. "I think Gelsey will love it." As I thought about him carving it for her, I was suddenly ashamed that my first thought upon seeing him was how long he would be staying. And as I thought about him carving it on the bus, I was just glad he hadn't flown. Somehow, I had a feeling the TSA wouldn't have approved.

"Good," my grandfather said, tucking it back in his suitcase. "I know this is probably so hard on her. On all of you." I nodded, tightening my fingers on the steering wheel, telling myself to hold it together a little longer. I didn't want to cry in front of my grandfather, of all people.

When I pulled into the driveway, the medical supply van was gone, but there was still an unfamiliar car parked next to my mom's, which I figured belonged to the nurse who was taking this shift. "Here we are," I said, even though that was probably pretty obvious by the fact that the car was in park and I had just killed the engine. My grandfather collected his things, waving me off when I tried to help, and I led him into the house.

My father was lying on the couch, listening with a faint smile on his face as Gelsey perched nearby, apparently telling him all about the carnival. She stopped talking as she looked up at us, standing in the doorway. My father's head slowly turned as well, but I was watching my grandfather's face when he got his first glimpse of my father.

I had never seen my grandfather cry. He was not one for any kind of displays of affection, and he and my father had always seemed to greet each other with a handshake and a pat on the back. I'd never even seen him get even slightly emotional. But when he saw my father, his face seemed to crumple, and it looked like he aged about five years, right in front of my eyes. Then he squared his shoulders again and walked to the couch, nodding at Gelsey as he went.

But as I watched, surprised, my grandfather went right up to my father and hugged him gently, starting to rock him back and forth, as my dad gripped his hands. I signaled to Gelsey, and she got up and headed over to me. "Is Grandpa okay?" she whispered to me as I stepped out of the front door and she followed.

"I think so," I said. I looked back for a second into the living room and was struck by how small my dad looked in my grandfather's arms. Probably almost like he had a long time ago, when he'd been Gelsey's age, and younger, just a little boy himself. I eased the door closed behind me, giving my grandfather a moment alone with his son.

I couldn't sleep that night. This in itself was not so unusual. What was unusual was that I wasn't the only one.

Normally, I would have gone next door, to find Henry, to try to forget a little bit. And somehow the fact that I couldn't do this—and that this had been my own choice—was making lying there unbearable.

Things were made more complicated by the new sleeping arrangements—my grandfather had been installed in Gelsey's room, and Gelsey was currently snoring away on my trundle bed. We'd agreed to switch off taking the trundle bed, but as I listened to her breathing in and out, I found myself wishing that I'd offered to take the first night. It would have been much easier to leave the room without having to climb over her. But when I couldn't take it any longer, I slipped out of bed and held my breath as I stepped over her. She didn't wake, just sighed a little in her sleep and rolled over again. I let out a breath and turned the doorknob, stepping out into the hallway.

"Hiya." I made a kind of squeaking noise and literally jumped, even though it had been a very quiet greeting. But I'd totally forgotten about Paul, who had the night shift with my dad.

"Hi," I whispered back, trying to get my racing heart to slow a little bit. Paul was sitting in a chair near the hospital bed, where my dad was sleeping, his mouth open, his breath labored. I'd met Paul that afternoon when he'd replaced Melody, the nurse who had smiled but hadn't said anything to anyone all day. Paul at least had seemed a little friendlier. "I was just, um, getting some air," I said. Paul nodded and went back to reading what looked like a graphic novel. I noticed that Murphy had abandoned his dog bed and was curled up under my father's bed. I motioned to the dog as I opened the door, but he didn't move, just stayed put and rested his head on his paws.

I stepped outside and stopped short, getting my second surprise of the last few minutes—my grandfather was standing on the porch, in pajamas, robe, and leather slippers, peering through an impressive-looking telescope. "Hi," I said, too shocked to really say anything else.

"Good evening," my grandfather said, straightening up. "Couldn't sleep?"

I shook my head. "Not really."

My grandfather sighed. "Me neither."

I couldn't stop looking at the telescope. It was huge, and beautiful, and I was, frankly, a little amazed that my grandfather had brought it with him. "What are you looking at?" I asked.

He gave me a small smile. "Do you know your stars?" he asked. "I think I did give you a book on it, years ago, actually."

"Right," I said, feeling my cheeks heat up, not sure how to tell him that I hadn't read it beyond the most superficial flip-through. "I don't, really," I confessed, taking a step closer. "But I'd been hoping to learn."

My grandfather nodded. "You can't be a sailor without knowing your stars," he said. "They've tried to get me to give it up at the Academy. These newer officers telling me that with GPS, it's not necessary.

But as long as you know your constellations, you're never lost."

I took a step closer, peering up at the sky. There were so many more stars here than there ever seemed to be back home; maybe that's why I'd suddenly gotten fascinated by them this summer. "Really?" I asked.

"Oh, yes," my grandfather said, clearly warming to his theme. "No matter what else happens, your constellations don't change. And if you're ever lost, and your precious GPS is on the fritz, they'll tell you where you are. And then they'll get you home."

I looked back up at the stars above me, then again at the telescope for a moment. "Can you show me?" I asked, suddenly wanting to name what I'd been looking at for the last few months.

"Of course," my grandfather said, sounding a little surprised. "Step right up."

I lowered my eye to the eyepiece and suddenly, right there and brilliantly clear, was what had been right there above me, shining down on me, all summer long.

It was August. The days turned hot and muggy, and my father started to get worse, much faster than I'd somehow been expecting. I found myself grateful for the four nurses who passed through, changing shifts every eight hours, simply because we were now out of our depth in terms of helping my dad. He needed help getting out of the bed, help walking, help going to the bathroom. We started using the wheelchair to get him around the house, but didn't use it much, as he was spending most of the time sleeping. He was getting medications and pain management administered by syringes, and we now had a bright-red medical waste container in the kitchen that the nurses took away, that didn't go into the bearbox with the rest of the trash.

I'd stopped going into work. I'd talked to Fred, and he told me he understood—he'd apparently learned about the situation when he came to the Fourth of July barbecue. Elliot would send me goofy, joking text messages, and Lucy stopped by every day after work, with a fountain Diet Coke for me, ready to listen if I wanted to talk and happy to chatter on and gossip if I wanted to be distracted.

Our kitchen—and fridge—was soon filled up with casseroles and baked goods. Fred kept bringing over coolerfuls of whatever fish he'd caught that day, and whenever Davy came to walk the dog, he always had something with him in a green Borrowed Thyme bakery box—muffins, cookies, pies. The nurses had come to really love it whenever Davy appeared. Even the Gardners, who didn't cook at all, brought by a pizza every few days.

I was still thinking about Henry much more than I wanted to, and I still wasn't sleeping. But my grandfather also wasn't sleeping, and so at night, we continued our star lessons. He'd whittle and tell me where to point the telescope, asking me to describe what I saw and then, later, to identify them myself. I learned how to find the constellations, so that I could see them even without the telescope. I was amazed to learn that there were things that could be seen with the naked eye, like other planets. And they'd been there all along, I just hadn't known what was I was seeing.

All of us were staying pretty close to home, running errands or going into town only if we absolutely needed to. My dad still had a few good hours every day when he wasn't sleeping, and none of us wanted to miss them. Which was why when Lucy came over as usual one Tuesday, I was surprised when she suggested taking a walk and my mother agreed, practically insisting that I go with her.

"It's okay," I said, frowning at my mother, who'd suddenly joined us on the porch. My dad had gone to sleep about four hours ago; I knew he'd be up soon and I wanted to be around for it.

"No, you should come," Lucy said. "I need to talk to you about something private."

I was on the verge of telling Lucy that we could just talk on the dock, or in my room, but she looked so anxious that I shrugged. "Fine," I said. "Just a short walk."

"Good," my mother said quickly and I just looked at her for a moment, wondering why she was so eager to get me out of the house. But maybe she was just worried that I'd been here too much. Warren still saw Wendy, and they'd go out sometimes, and Gelsey still went next door to see Nora. Maybe since Lucy always came to me, my mom was just worried I wasn't leaving the house enough.

morgan matson

"Let's go," I said, standing up. Lucy scrambled to her feet as well, then glanced back at my mother for a second before hurrying on ahead so that I had to rush to catch up with her.

When we reached the road, Lucy paused, shaking her head for a moment. "I can't believe you guys still don't have a sign," she said, as she turned left, and I followed, shrugging.

"We've never found anything that fits," I said. "I think if we were going to have found the right thing, it would have happened already." I turned to face her. Lucy still seemed intent on walking briskly up my street, even though we were heading away from downtown, just toward other houses. "What did you want to talk to me about? Trouble with Pittsburgh?"

"What?" Lucy asked, looking startled. "Oh. Him. Um . . . no. It's . . ."

She looked so uncomfortable for a moment, that I suddenly realized what this might be about. "Is it Elliot?" I asked. If he'd finally declared his crush, and now it was just the two of them at work, I could see how that might get awkward.

"Elliot?" Lucy repeated, sounding surprised. "No. What about him?"

I knew it was none of my business, but I decided to jump in anyway. "He has a crush on you," I said. "He has all summer."

Lucy stopped walking and looked at me. "Did he tell you that?"

"No," I said, "but it's totally obvious. I'm sure even Fred knows." Lucy looked thoughtful for a moment, then shook her head and continued to walk. "Luce?" I asked, catching up with her.

"It wouldn't work," she said definitively.

"Why not?" I asked. He wasn't my type, but Elliot was cute, and they got along well—and he was much more of a prospect now that he'd learned to tone down the cologne.

"Because," Lucy said. "He's Elliot. He's . . ." She paused, apparently having trouble coming up with an adjective. She took a glance down at her phone. "Let's turn back!" she said cheerfully, turning in the other direction.

But I wasn't going to let myself be distracted that easily. "Seriously," I said. "He's a nice guy. You guys get along great. He makes you laugh. Why not?"

"Because," Lucy repeated. But she didn't seem as dismissive as she had earlier, and I could tell that she was thinking about it.

"I'm just saying," I said, as we rounded the corner before my house, "the nice guys are the ones worth dating." I thought back to Henry, and all his small kindnesses, and felt a tiny pain in my heart.

"I know I haven't really yelled at you about this like I wanted to," Lucy said, looking at me closely, "but I still don't understand why you dumped Henry."

I winced at this even though it was technically accurate. "It was just going to be too hard," I finally said. "I could tell. And I knew we were both going to get hurt." I realized that we were now in front of the Crosby house, and I made myself look away as Lucy and I headed into my driveway.

"You want to know something about gymnastics?" Lucy asked, falling into step next to me.

"Always," I said, deadpan, and she smiled at me.

"The thing is that people only get hurt—really hurt—when they're trying to play it safe. That's when people get injured, when they pull back at the last second because they're scared. They hurt themselves and other people."

This was all hitting home until the last part, and I frowned. "How do they hurt other people?"

"You know," Lucy said, clearly stalling. "If they land on a spotter or something. The point is—"

"I get the point," I assured her. We had reached the house, and I started to head to the porch when Lucy grabbed my hand and pulled me around to the back. "Lucy, what are you—"

"SURPRISE!" I blinked at what was in front of me. There was a table set up with a cake, and balloons tied to the chairs. Gelsey was there, and my mom, and Warren and Wendy. Kim, Jeff, and Nora were there, along with Davy and Elliot and Fred. Even Leland was there, and I suddenly worried about who was working at the beach. Finally, I saw my dad, sitting in his wheel-chair, my grandfather behind him, both of them smiling at me.

"Happy birthday, sweetie," my mother said, giving me a hug. "I thought we should give you a second chance at a party," she whispered to me, and I felt myself smile, even though I was also pretty sure I was about to cry.

"Thanks," I whispered back. My mother ran her hand over my hair for a second, then turned to the table.

"Cake!" she called. "Come and get it!"

I looked around at the crowd, my eyes searching, even though I knew Henry wouldn't be there. But it wasn't until I knew he was absent that I realized how much I wanted him to be there. I took a step closer to the table and saw that the *Happy Birthday, Taylor* was written in his handwriting. My mother started serving up the cake, and I realized that just to the side of it were two small containers of ice cream from Jane's. I could tell without tasting them that they were raspberry and coconut. "Mom," I said, trying to keep my voice casual, "where did the ice cream come from?"

"It came with the cake," she said. "Henry insisted. He said it would bring out the flavor. Wasn't that nice of him?"

"Yes," I said, as I took the piece she gave me, which happened to have the *T* of my name, feeling the lump in my throat. "It really was."

chapter thirty-five

TIME WAS RUNNING OUT. THIS WAS CLEAR NOT ONLY IN HOW EACH day got a just a little shorter but also in what was happening to my dad. He was a little more confused every day, and his stretches of wakefulness and awareness of what was going on were getting shorter and shorter. It became difficult for him to talk, and somehow this was the hardest for me to see—my dad, who I'd watched command courtrooms with his deep, booming voice. Now, he struggled to speak, and to find the words he wanted to use.

We'd started taking turns spending time with him while he had his lucid periods. My sister talked a mile a minute, like she was trying to tell him everything she was ever going to want to, all at once. My brother would sit by his bedside and they would talk about, from what I could overhear, famous law cases, swapping their favorite facts, my brother usually talking more than my dad. My grandfather would sit next to him and read the paper out loud, usually the human interest section. His voice, so like my dad's had been, could be heard across the house, as he'd say, "Now, you'll like this, Robin. Listen to what happened yesterday in Harrisburg."

My mother didn't say much when they were together. Sometimes I'd hear them talking about financial things, making arrangements, plans. But mostly, she held his hand and just looked at his face, studying it, like she knew that she wasn't going to be able to see it soon.

When it was my turn with my dad, we played our question game that had taken us through so many breakfasts. But now he didn't seem to want to talk about himself. Now he seemed to want to know everything about me, while he still could. "Tell me," he'd say, his voice as scratched as one of his old records, "my Taylor. When have you been the happiest?" And I'd try my best to answer, attempting to deflect the question, but he'd always have another one lined up. What was I thinking about in terms of college majors? Where were places I wanted to visit? What did I want to do with my life? What was the best meal I'd ever had?

Sometimes I wouldn't be able to answer; I'd break down crying, and that's when we'd listen to his records. I knew them all by now—Jackson Browne, Charlie Rich, Led Zeppelin, the Eagles— a lot of shaggy-haired guys that my grandfather still didn't like, if his reaction when he came into the room and heard them was any indication. And the music, and the questions, would continue on, as I'd try to tell my father who I was and who I hoped to be, while we still had time.

Throughout all of this, the dog refused to leave his spot under my dad's bed. We finally had to move his food and water bowl under there, even though Roberto, who was the most by-the-rules of the nurses, worried about germs. Davy still came by twice a day, and the dog let himself be pulled out from under the bed and taken for a very quick walk. But aside from that, he didn't move from his spot.

I had finally given up and claimed the trundle bed as mine, since I was barely sleeping anyway. The night nurses were used to it by now, just giving me a nod as I crept out to the porch. Sometimes my grandfather was awake, and would sit with me while I looked up at the stars, needing to see something fixed and permanent while everything else in my life seemed to be breaking apart. When he was in bed, he left the telescope out and in position for me. There was a meteor shower that was expected at the end of the month, and according to my grandfather, things tended to get very interesting, stargazing-wise, before a meteor shower, so I was keeping an eye out.

The nights when my grandfather wasn't there were the nights I cried. I was no longer even trying to stop myself. We were all more or less trying to keep it together for my dad and one another. But at night, alone, with all the moments of the day finally hitting me, I would let myself just sob, out on the porch. And though I knew it was a stupid, pointless reaction to what was happening, I also realized it was all I could do. I cried, I tried to think of puns that might make my father laugh one more time, and I looked at the stars.

• • •

I had just come in from a night without my grandfather, a night I'd finally found Sirius on my own, when I saw Paul standing over my dad. It felt like my heart stopped for a moment before it started beating much faster, in a panic. "Is he okay?" I whispered, looking down at my dad, suddenly more scared than I'd ever been in my entire life.

"He's okay," Paul said quietly back to me, and I could feel my panic start to recede. "He's just having a hard night. Poor guy."

I looked down at the hospital bed that now seemed like it had always been part of our living room. My dad, thin to the point of being emaciated, his skin yellowed and leathery-looking, was sleeping, his mouth open, looking so small in the big expanse of white bed. His breaths were labored and rasping, and I found myself listening for each one, then waiting for the next one.

It seemed wrong, somehow, to just go back to my own room and sleep my easy sleep. So I curled on the couch that was nearest to the hospital bed, and looked at my dad sleeping in the shaft of moonlight that was coming through the windows, falling across his face. As I listened to his breathing, my heart starting to pound whenever there was a pause, a break in the rhythm, I realized that this was what he had done for me, years ago, when I was a baby.

I wished that there was something I could do to make it better. But all I could do was to lie there and listen for each labored, rasping breath, counting them. I was aware that he didn't have that

morgan matson

many left, and somehow, to not pay attention to each one seemed like the worst kind of indifference. And so I lay there, just listening, knowing that each breath was another moment he was still here and, simultaneously, that meant that he had just moved a little closer to being gone.

I heard a door hinge squeak, and looked up to see Gelsey standing in the hallway. She was wearing an ancient, much-washed nightshirt that had once been mine. "You weren't in bed," she whispered. "Is everything okay?" I nodded, and then, without knowing I was going to, motioned her closer.

I expected her to go to one of the other couches, but she came right to mine, curling up against me. And I put my arms around my sister, smoothing back her soft, curly hair, and we lay there together in the dark, not speaking, just listening to our father breathe.

I thought about Henry, of course. During one of our talks, my father had even brought him up. I had evaded the question, but I still found myself turning over our time together in my head. Usually I was pretty sure I'd made the right decision. But sometimes—like when Wendy stopped by and was sitting with Warren on the porch, and I'd watch her lean her head against his shoulder, comforting him, and my brother let himself be comforted—I wondered if I actually had done the right thing by ending it with Henry. There was a part of me that was afraid that I'd dressed it up and called it a new name, but that it was my same flaw, rearing its ugly head once again. I was still running when things got too real—I'd just learned how to do it, at last, by staying in the same place.

Even though I knew when the meteor shower was coming—that morning's *Pocono Record* had even done a special feature on the best time to try and catch it—it still took me by surprise. Since it was predicted to arrive an hour before dawn—when even I had usually gone to sleep for the night—I'd set my alarm. When the alarm beeped four thirty, waking me but not Gelsey, I'd switched it off and contemplated just going back to sleep. But my grandfather had promised it would be something extraordinary, and I felt like I'd put in enough time that summer looking up at the stars—I might as well see them deliver.

I pulled on my sweatshirt and tiptoed out of the room, even though I'd learned by now that my sister was one of the world's deepest sleepers. I headed into the hallway and nodded at Paul, who was on duty, who gave me a small wave back. My dad was sleeping, his breath rattling in his throat. I looked at him for a long moment, and Paul met my eyes and gave me a sympathetic smile before turning back to his book. Things had gotten much worse in the last two days. We'd stopped talking about my father's condition, how he was doing. We were mostly just trying to get through each day. And though my father was still with us, the last coherent conversation he'd been able to have was several days ago—and that had been just a moment with my mother before he got confused again.

I headed outside to the porch, looked up at the sky, and gasped.

The whole night sky above me was filled with streaks of light. I had never seen a single falling star before, and they were whizzing across the vast expanse of sky—one, then another, then two at once. The stars had never seemed quite so bright, and it was like they were surrounding me, much closer than I'd ever seen them, and a few of them were just on a joyride across the sky. And as I watched it unfolding, I knew that I didn't want to be watching it alone.

I hurried back inside, not sure how long meteor showers lasted and not wanting him to miss any of it. "Paul," I said quietly, and he looked up from his book and raised his eyebrows at me.

"You okay?" he asked.

"There's a meteor shower outside," I said. "It's going on right now."

"Oh, yeah," Paul said, yawning and picking up his book again. "I think I read something about that in the paper."

"The thing is . . . ," I said, shifting my weight from foot to foot. I could practically feel my anxiety building. I felt like time was running out, right in front of me, and that I needed to get my father outside as fast as possible. "I want my dad to see it." Paul looked up at me again, frowning. "Would that be possible?"

"Taylor," he said, shaking his head. "I just don't think it makes much sense."

"I know," I said, surprising myself—and Paul, by the look on his face. "But that doesn't mean we shouldn't do it. Just for a moment or two. You can carry him outside, or I can wake Warren up. I just . . ." My voice trailed off. I had no idea why I thought this was so crucial. It's not like I believed that meteor showers had some magic healing properties. I just wanted my dad to see something so extraordinary. I hated that all he saw, every day, was our living room. I wanted him to breathe in, labored or not, some of that pine-scented night air. I was searching for the words to express this, when Paul stood up.

"For five minutes," he said. "And there's no guarantee that he'll even wake up."

"I know," I said. "Thank you." Paul got up and unfolded the wheelchair, while I crossed over to my father's bedside, standing right by his head. His breathing was still labored, with a rattling to it that had shown up in the last two days, and which terrified me. It made every breath he was taking seem painful, and I hated to hear it. "Daddy," I whispered, touching his shoulder through the blanket, shocked by how bony it felt, how fragile he seemed. "Rise and shine. Up and Adam."

There was a hitch in his breathing, and for a moment I panicked, but then my dad's eyes opened, those blue eyes he'd given to only me. He looked at me, but he'd been looking at us, unseeing, lately, so I didn't know if this meant anything. But then his eyes focused on my face and one corner of his mouth pulled up in a tiny smile.

"Tayl," he said, his voice thick and slurred. He opened and closed his mouth a few times, then said, his eyes starting to drift closed again. "Hi, kid. Whas news?"

I smiled even as I could feel tears prickling my eyes. "Want to see some stars?" I asked him. I looked over and saw that Paul was standing by with the wheelchair. I nodded at him and stepped away. With practiced skill, Paul lifted my father from the bed as though he weighed nothing and settled him into the chair. I grabbed the blanket from the bed and tucked it around him, and then Paul pushed him out to the front porch. I followed, and was thrilled to see that the falling stars were still falling. That this event, which happened for a brief window just a few times a year, hadn't passed us by.

Paul stopped my dad's chair in the center of the porch and put the brake on, then looked up himself. "Wow," he murmured. "I see what you mean."

I sat down next to my dad's chair and touched his shoulder. "Look," I said, pointing up. His head was resting on the back of the chair, but his eyes opened and looked up.

I watched him watching the stars above, as streaks of light flew past. His eyes were focused, following one as it cut its path across the huge, dark canvas of the sky. "Stars," he said in a voice that was clearer than he'd yet used that night, a voice that was laced with wonder.

I nodded, and moved closer to him. His breath was rattling

again, and I could feel Paul standing nearby, waiting to bring my dad inside. But I picked up my dad's hand where it was hanging over the wheel and took it in mine. It was too bony, but it was still huge, engulfing my own. The hand that had taught me to tie my shoes and hold a pencil correctly and had held mine carefully when we were crossing the street, making sure to keep me safe.

His head was lolling back against the chair again, and his eyes were closing. And I didn't know if he'd know what I was saying—or remember, if he was going to a place where there was remembering—but I leaned close to him and kissed his much-too-thin cheek. "Daddy," I whispered, feeling my own breath hitch in my throat. "I love you."

Just when I was sure that he was asleep, the one corner of his mouth lifted in a smile. "I knew that," he murmured. "Always knew that."

I didn't care if Paul saw me crying. It didn't matter in the least. I had told my father what I needed to. I squeezed his hand, gently, and I felt him squeeze it back, so faintly, before he drifted off to sleep once again, as, above us, the stars continued to fall.

morgan matson

chapter thirty-six

I KNEW THAT SOMETHING WAS DIFFERENT WHEN I WOKE UP THE next morning. I could hear voices outside, the phone ringing, my mother's voice, low and choked. I could hear the crunch of tires on gravel, and voices from the living room, voices at a normal volume when normally we spoke softly, to let my father get his sleep.

Nobody was letting him get his sleep now. Which meant—

No.

I thought this as hard as I could. I hadn't opened my eyes yet, and I squeezed them shut, tightly. If I didn't open them, I could be anywhere. I could be in my bed, back home in Stanwich. And maybe it was five months ago, and all that had happened was just some terrible dream. And I'd go downstairs and my dad would be eating a bagel while my mother chided him about having to lose weight. And I'd tell him all about my dream, even as the details were fading and getting further away, just a crazy dream, thank God. . . .

"Taylor." It was Warren, his voice sounding cracked and broken. I felt my face crumple, my chin tremble, and even though I hadn't yet opened my eyes, two tears slipped out from the right one.

"No," I said, rolling away from him, toward the window, hugging my knees to my chest. If I opened my eyes, this became real. If I opened my eyes, there was no going back to a moment when this wasn't true. If I opened my eyes, my father was no longer alive.

"You have to get up," Warren said, his voice sounding tired.

"Tell me about Coca-Cola," I said. "What were they trying to make?"

"Aspirin," Warren said after a moment. "It was just a big mistake."

I opened my eyes. Sunlight was streaming in through my windows and I felt a sudden rage at it. It shouldn't have been sunny. It should have been dark, stormy, nighttime. I looked over at Warren, whose face was blotchy and whose hands were clutching a tissue. "It's Dad," I said, not asking a question.

Warren nodded, and I could see him swallow hard. "Paul said about dawn this morning. He was sleeping. It was peaceful."

I was crying now; I wasn't even trying to stop. I had a feeling I might never stop, ever. As long as this stayed true, I couldn't imagine that I'd ever want to stop.

"You should come out," he said, resting his hand on my doorknob. "So you can get a chance to say good-bye."

I nodded and, after a moment, followed behind my brother. The clothes I'd dropped on the floor the night before were still there. My makeup was still on the counter. How could those things, those stupid insignificant things, still be there when the world had ended, sometime about dawn? How could they still be there when my father wasn't?

I stepped out into the hallway and saw my family. My grandfather was standing in the kitchen. My mother was standing near the hospital bed, her arm around my sister. Warren leaned against the back of the couch. And in his hospital bed was my father, his mouth open, his eyes closed.

He wasn't breathing.

He wasn't *there*.

It was such a basic thing—I'd seen it on a thousand cop shows and movies. But I just stared at my father, on the bed, still. I couldn't make myself understand it. I'd never not known him alive, breathing, laughing, making terrible jokes, filling up a room with his voice, teaching us how to throw a football. That he was suddenly not alive—that he was so still, there but not there in any of the ways that mattered—was a truth I could not wrap my head around. And as I looked at his closed eyes, I realized that I would never see his eyes again. That he would never look at me again. That he was dead.

I was crying full-out now, and even though I hadn't noticed my mother move, she was suddenly right there, pulling me into a hug.

She didn't tell me it was going to be okay. I knew in that moment that things would be forever different—that today was going to be a day that split my life into before and after.

But in that moment, I just let myself cry onto her shoulder, as she hugged me tight, as though letting me know that, at least, I was not alone.

chapter thirty-seven

THE FUNERAL TOOK PLACE FOUR DAYS LATER. IT WAS A BRIGHT, sunny day, which again seemed wrong. I'd been hoping that it would rain—the night before had been cold and overcast, but I'd nonetheless sat out on the front porch steps with the dog until my feet got numb.

I couldn't get over how empty the house seemed now, and how without my dad there, none of us knew what to do with ourselves. Warren, for the first time since I could remember, hadn't been able to read. Instead, he'd been spending days down at the tennis center, hitting a ball against the wall as hard as he could, returning home tired and drained-looking. My grandfather had been whittling and taking the dog for long walks. When he came back, his nose was always red, his voice hoarse, and the dog exhausted. Gelsey hadn't wanted to be alone since that morning, and so we'd been spending a lot of time together. We weren't talking about what had happened yet, but it somehow helped just to be able to look across the room and see my sister there—proof that I wasn't the only one who was going through this. My mother had been spending her days organizing everything—the service, the casket, the flowers—and seemed as though she was handling things better than any of us. But earlier that day, I'd come outside to see her sitting on the porch, her hair damp from the shower, crying. There was still a piece of me that wanted to turn around and not have to face this, but I made myself keep going and sit next to her on the porch step. We didn't speak, but I took the comb from her hand and combed through her hair in the sunlight. When I'd finished, and released the stray hairs into the wind for the birds, my mother had stopped crying. And we just sat there together for a moment in silence, our shoulders touching as we leaned against each other.

The tiny Lake Phoenix chapel was filled with people. We were going to be doing a larger memorial service back in Connecticut, so I hadn't expected this one to be so packed. But standing by the front pew in a black dress my mother had lent me, I watched them streaming in, all these people who had shown up for my dad. Wendy was there, and Fred and Jillian, and Dave Henson, who'd sold him so much licorice. Lucy was there with her mother, Angela from the diner was there, and the Gardners, everyone from the beach—and Leland had even combed his hair.

The minister hadn't been too happy when I'd given him the mix CD of the music we had chosen. It probably was a little unorthodox—opera mixed with Jackson Browne. But I had a feeling it's what my dad would have wanted. He also wasn't happy about the dog, but my grandfather had told him that Murphy was his service animal, and so, he was sitting under the front pew, at my grandfather's feet, perfectly still.

It was just the family in the front row, Gelsey in an old black dress of mine, Warren wearing a suit that somehow made him look younger. My grandfather was wearing his Navy dress uniform, which might have been one of the reasons the minister hadn't argued with him. My mother was sitting next to me, clutching one of my dad's handkerchiefs tightly. I noticed we'd left an extra, open spot in our row, as though he might be joining us, but was just running a little late, parking the car. I couldn't somehow get my mind to accept that the still figure in the casket at the front, surrounded by flowers, was him.

The minister gestured to my mother, and the service began. I let the words wash over me, not really hearing them, not wanting to hear about ashes and dust when it came to my father. After he was done, my grandfather spoke, about what my dad had been like when he was young, and how proud my grandfather had always been of him. My mother spoke, and I gave up on trying not to cry. Warren spoke briefly, reading a section from the T.S. Eliot poem Dad had loved.

And even though I hadn't planned to say anything—or prepared any remarks—I found myself standing as Warren returned to his seat, and walked straight up to the lectern.

I looked out at the crowd and saw, standing in the back, Henry. He was with Davy, wearing a suit I'd never seen before, and his eyes were fixed on mine—supporting, encouraging, somehow giving me the confidence I needed to start.

And as I looked out at the crowd, I realized I wasn't panicking. My palms weren't sweating. And I wasn't worried about what I was going to say—it was simple. It was just the truth.

"I'd always loved my dad," I said in a voice that was stronger than I'd expected it to be. "But I actually got to know him this summer. And I realized that he'd been teaching me so much, all along." I took a big breath—not because I was nervous, but because I could feel tears building up, and I wanted to try and get through this first. "Like the importance of really bad puns." The crowd laughed at that, and I felt myself relax a little bit. "And that you should always get ice cream when the opportunity presents itself, even if it is close to dinnertime." I swallowed hard. "But mostly, he taught me this summer about courage. He was so brave, considering what he was facing. He didn't run away from it. And he was brave enough to admit that he was afraid." I wiped my hand across my face, and took another shaky breath, to try to finish.

"I'm just glad that I got the time I did with him, even—" my breath caught in my throat, and the view of the crowd got blurry. "Even if it wasn't enough time," I finished. "Even if it wasn't nearly enough."

I stumbled, half-blind with tears, down to my seat. The minister was speaking again, and now Jackson Browne was singing. And it was Warren, unexpectedly, who pulled me into a tight hug and let me cry against his shoulder.

Things wrapped up after that, with the announcement of the reception back at our house, and then the processional past the casket. I sat it out, holding Murphy on my lap, feeling like I'd already said good-bye to my father under the stars. But I noticed that as my grandfather went up, his posture so straight in his uniform, he put into the casket the figure he'd been whittling all week—a tiny carved robin, taking flight.

chapter thirty-eight

I TURNED THE CAR DOWN THE DRIVEWAY, SHUT OFF THE ENGINE, and let out a breath. I had just dropped my grandfather and his telescope off at the bus station, and it had been much harder to say good-bye than I'd been expecting. And there had been far too much of that already lately.

In the days after the funeral, we slowly fell back into the pattern of a few weeks before. But instead of playing Risk, or watching movies, we began to talk about my dad. And with every story, some of the memories of him sick faded away a little, and I started to remember him as he'd been my whole life, and not just this summer.

I was still feeling shaky, and the smallest things could cause me to burst into tears unexpectedly—like finding one of his clean handkerchiefs in the laundry and suddenly panicking about what to do with it.

But today, coming back from the bus station, I was feeling slightly closer to okay as I crossed the driveway barefoot to find my mother was sitting at the table of the screened-in porch, a manila envelope next to her.

"Hi," I said, as I sat down and looked at the envelope next to her. "What's that?" The sight of it somehow made me nervous. My mother turned it over and I saw that *Taylor* was written in my father's handwriting. My breath caught in my throat, just seeing it, and I looked up at my mother, confused.

She slid it across the table to me. "It turns out this was your father's mystery project. I found them upstairs in the closet. He wrote them to all of us."

I picked up the envelope, tracing my fingers over where he'd written my name. I didn't want to be rude to my mother, but I suddenly wanted to read my father's last words to me in private. "Sorry," I said, pushing back my chair a little from the table. "But . . ."

"Go," my mother said gently. "And then I'll be here if you want to talk about anything, okay?"

I nodded as I stood up. "Thanks, Mom," I said. I gripped the envelope carefully as I left the porch. It wouldn't have been valuable to anyone else, but at the moment, there was nothing in the world that I valued more. Before I even knew I was heading there, I found myself walking to the dock, which was deserted, the late-afternoon sunlight glinting off the water.

I kicked my flip-flops off and walked across the wooden planks barefoot, feeling them warm under my toes, all too aware that it was now mid-August and summer was starting to come to an end, that barefoot weather would be drawing to a close all too soon.

I walked to the edge of the dock and sat cross-legged, dropping my purse next to me. Then I took a deep breath and opened the envelope.

I'd been expecting a few sheets of paper. I had not been expecting, to find inside the envelope, like Russian nesting dolls, a flurry of more envelopes. I shook them out. They were all sealed, all labeled in my father's neat, slanting writing: *High School Graduation. College Graduation. When You Get Your Law Degree/PhD/Masters in Interpretive Dance. On Your Wedding Day. Today.*

I fanned through them, still a little amazed that this was happening, and pulled out the *Today* envelope, putting the others carefully back into the larger envelope, closing it with the little metal clasp, and making sure to anchor it in my bag, even weighting it down with my wallet and cell phone.

Then I opened the envelope, took a deep breath, and started to read.

chapter thirty-nine

Hi, kid! What's the news?

So if you're reading this, I've done the very terrible thing of shuffling off this mortal coil a couple of decades too early. I am truly sorry, Taylor, that I've done this to you. I hope you know that if it had been up to me—if I'd had any choice in it—I wouldn't have let anyone take me from you all. I would have fought anyone who tried, tooth and nail.

I hope you've seen now that I'm going to do my best to stick around, offering you advice, throughout the next couple of years. I hope some of it's helpful. I regret a lot about having to leave you so early. But mostly, it's that I'll never get the chance to see what you become. Because I have a feeling that you, my daughter, are going to do great things. You may be rolling your eyes at me now, but I know it. You are the child of my heart, and I know you'll make me proud. You already have, every day, just by being yourself.

I'm not worried about your making friends, having fun, learning, or making your mark on the world. The only thing that I'm a little worried about is your heart.

I have noticed in you, my dear daughter, a tendency to run away from the things that are most frightening in the world—love and trust. And I would truly hate it if my leaving before I wanted to caused, in any way, for your heart to close, or for you to shut yourself off to the possibilities of love. (And believe me, you don't want me to be unhappy. I may be looking into the haunting thing right now.)

But you have a heart that is big and beautiful and strong, and deserves to be shared with someone worthy. You get some perspective when you know you're not going to get to flip a new month on the calendar. And I've realized that the Beatles got it wrong. Love isn't all we need—love is all there is.

It will be scary. But I know you can do it. Know that I'll be with you, if there's any way that I can manage it. And know that I have always—and will, for always—love you.

Dad

I set the letter down on my lap and looked out at the lake. There were tears on my cheeks, but I didn't bother to wipe them away just

morgan matson

yet. I had a feeling I'd start crying again when I reread it anyway. I placed it carefully under my wallet with the other letters, still a little amazed that my father had done this for me. And the fact that he had made arrangements to keep talking to me—to keep our conversation going, through the major milestones of my life—made the thought of having to go through life without him just a little easier to bear.

I ran my hands over the planks as I thought about the section that had stuck in my mind the most—where my dad had called me out on my behavior. I wasn't sure when he'd written this letter, but it was exactly what I'd done to Henry. I'd pushed him away because he got too close, rather than letting him help me, as Warren had let Wendy help him. It didn't make me stronger, or a bigger person, I realized now. It just made me weak, and afraid.

I truly didn't know if I would be able to do what my father wanted me to do, and open my heart up to someone. It was a huge, unanswered question. But I knew that at some point, I would owe it to my father to give it a try.

That night I slept better, more soundly, than I had all summer. I woke up to the sunlight streaming in through my window and the birds already chiping at each other. It was another beautiful day. But I knew just how quickly time could pass. And it struck me now that beautiful days were not unlimited things. And just like that, knew what I had to do.

I didn't try to make myself look better, as I rolled out of bed and headed for the door. Henry had already seen me in every possible state this summer. But even more importantly, he had seen me—seen who I was, even when I'd been trying my best to hide it from him.

It was strange to have to search for Henry, after a summer of bumping into him when I'd been least expecting it. But there was also a piece of me that felt that this was the way it had to be— that after too many years of running away from things, I was finally going to run toward them.

Or at least walk. The woods—the place I'd had a feeling he would be—weren't exactly great for running in. I'd been walking for about twenty minutes, doing my best to avoid stepping in rotted-out tree trunks, when I rounded a curve and there he was.

Henry was sitting on the ground, his back against a tree, the sunlight dappling through the leaves and falling onto his face. He glanced up at me, even though I hadn't spoken, and pushed himself to his feet.

"Hi," I said. I let myself really look at him, in a way I hadn't since we split up. It wasn't like when I'd first seen him this summer and noticed only how cute he was. This time, I saw the kindness in his eyes. I saw how lonely his hand looked without mine to hold it.

"Hi," he replied. There was a question in his voice, and I knew he was probably wondering what I was doing there.

"Thank you for coming," I said, and I saw that he understood I meant the funeral. "I really appreciated it."

"Of course," he said. He gave me a sad smile. "I really, really liked your dad." I heard the past tense and nodded, not really trusting myself to reply. "And I thought you gave a great speech. I was really proud of you, Taylor."

I looked at him, with that lock of hair falling over his forehead, and I wanted to reach up and push it back. I wanted to kiss him. I wanted to tell him all the things I'd been feeling, all along, even if I hadn't really let myself feel them until now.

"So," he said, sliding his hands into his pockets. "What are you doing in the woods? Are you lost?"

"No," I said, and as I did, I realized just how true this was. "I'm not lost." I took a breath. I realized that what I was about to do went against everything I'd ever done. It was confronting everything I was the most scared of. But my father had wanted me to move past this. And I knew, somewhere inside, that it was time. And that this was the place, and Henry was the person. "I got scared," I said. "And I should never have pushed you away like that."

Henry nodded and looked down at the ground. There was a long silence, punctuated only by the rustling of leaves and the occasional bird call, and I knew I had to keep going.

"I was just wondering," I said, "how you felt about second chances." As I waited, I could feel my heart pound hard, wondering what he was thinking. As excruciating as this was, I had a feeling it was better to be facing it full-on—not running away and hiding and ducking. But out in the sunlight, putting my heart out and watching to see how it was received.

He looked up at me, then started to smile. "I guess it would depend on the context," he said slowly. "But generally, I'm in favor of them." I smiled back, for what felt like the first time in days. I knew we still had things to talk about, and so much to figure out. But I had a feeling that we could manage it together.

As I took a step toward Henry, closing the distance between us, I thought about those words we'd carved, years ago, on the dock— our names. And *Forever*. In the instant before I stretched up to kiss him, I hoped that they just might turn out to be true.

chapter forty

I PULLED MY SWEATER A LITTLE MORE TIGHTLY AROUND MY shoulders and sat back on the damp grass. It was almost September, and already starting to get chilly. The leaves that had been so brilliantly green all summer were starting to change just slightly, edging toward oranges and reds and gold. Even though I'd been coming here often since they put the marker in, it managed to still make me smile, groan, and miss my father, all at the same time.

We'd found his instructions for it with his will. Though he would be buried in Stanwich, he'd wanted a marker here, in Lake Phoenix, where he'd spent some of his best days. Warren hadn't believed that he was serious about what he wanted on it, but as I'd told him, there was nothing my father took more seriously than puns. So here, in the small Lake Phoenix cemetery, was the single punny epitaph: ROBIN EDWARDS. BELOVED HUSBAND AND FATHER . . . THE DEFENSE RESTS.

I looked down at it, and could still practically hear his words, see his smile. *Hey, kid! What's the news?* So I'd done my best to try to tell him, keeping him informed about our lives—how Warren and Wendy were still going strong and had worked out a detailed visiting schedule, on a spreadsheet, for when they both started college. How my mother was going to start teaching dance again. How Gelsey was already planning on spending her spring break in Los Angeles with Nora, meeting movie stars. That Murphy had, against everyone's expectations, learned to fetch. And that I was doing okay too.

I looked back and saw Henry's car pull into the small parking lot just down the hill from the cemetery. I knew he'd give me all the time I needed—and sometimes it was a lot of time, as I found this spot to be a place where it was easy to cry—not to mention totally expected. It wasn't like everything was fine, not by a long shot. There were still moments I missed my dad so much that it hurt, physically, like someone had punched me. There were moments that I got so angry, I was liable to snap at the wrong person, just to release some of the rage at the unfairness of it all. And there were days when I woke up with my eyes puffy and swollen from crying. But we—the four remaining members of the Edwards family—had somehow, against all odds, become okay with talking about our feelings. And on days when it was particularly bad, I knew that there were people I could turn to.

I pushed myself up to standing and looked down at the grave for a long time. "Bye, Daddy," I whispered. "I'll see you soon."

I turned and headed down the hill, where Henry was leaning against the car. "Hey," he said, as I got close enough to hear him.

"Hi," I said, giving him an only slightly trembling smile. It hadn't been simple, finding our way back to being together, especially with my loss so raw. But one thing that I was learning about what happened when you stuck around—it usually seemed that other people were willing to stick by you as well. Even though we were heading back to Connecticut soon, and he was staying here, the distance wasn't worrying me. We'd been through too much together to let a few hours' separation split us up now. He leaned down to kiss me, and I kissed him back, making it count. I had a feeling my dad would understand.

"Are you ready to go?" he asked when we stepped apart.

I nodded. We were having a dinner at our house, a good-bye event before everyone started leaving. Lucy and Elliot, who hadn't stopped holding hands—and making out—once he finally got up enough courage to tell her how he felt, were bringing the cups and plates (stolen, I was sure, from the snack bar). Fred and Jillian were bringing fish. Warren and Wendy were in charge of the seating plan, and I'd no doubt my brother would tell us all how the first one was invented. Kim and Jeff were bringing their finalized screenplay for some after-dinner entertainment, as well as a sneak peek at their pilot, *Psychic Vet Tech*. Henry was bringing the dessert, and I had picked up the final element that afternoon at Give Me A Sign.

I pulled it out of my purse now and held it out to Henry, who smiled when he saw it. SOARING ROBIN, it read, with a bird in flight etched beneath it.

"Very nice," he said. He glanced back up to the hill for a moment, then back at me. "I think he'd like it."

"I think so too." I glanced up and saw that it was getting dark quickly; I could see the very first stars starting to appear. "Come on," I said. I smiled at him as I threaded my hand through his. "Let's go home."

morgan matson

Take a sneak peek at
Morgan Matson's next book:

The list arrived after Sloane had been gone two weeks.

I wasn't at home to get it because I was at Sloane's, where I had gone yet again, hoping against hope to find her there. I had decided, as I'd driven over to her house, my iPod off and my hands gripping the steering wheel, that if she was there, I wouldn't even need an explanation. It wouldn't be necessary for her to tell me why she'd suddenly stopped answering her phone, texts, and e-mails, or why she'd vanished, along with her parents and their car. I knew it was ridiculous to think this way, like I was negotiating with some cosmic dealer who could guarantee this for me, but that didn't stop me as I got closer and closer to Randolph Farms Lane. I didn't care what

I had to promise if it meant Sloane would be there. Because if Sloane was there, everything could start making sense again.

It was not an exaggeration to say that the last two weeks had been the worst of my life. The first weekend after school had ended, I'd been dragged upstate by my parents against my wishes and despite my protests. When I'd come back to Stanwich, after far too many antique shops and art galleries, I'd called her immediately, car keys in my hand, waiting impatiently for her to answer so that she could tell me where she was, or, if she was home, that I could pick her up. But Sloane didn't answer her phone, and she didn't answer when I called back an hour later, or later that night, or before I went to bed.

The next day, I drove by her house, only to see her parents' car gone and the windows dark. She wasn't responding to texts and still wasn't answering her phone. It was going right to voice mail, but I wasn't worried, not then. Sloane would sometimes let her battery run down until the phone shut off, and she never seemed to know where her charger was. And her parents, Milly and Anderson, had a habit of forgetting to tell her their travel plans. They would whisk her off to places like Palm Beach or Nantucket, and Sloane would return a few days later, tan, with a present for me and stories to tell. I was sure that's what had happened this time.

But after three days, and still no word, I worried. After five days, I panicked. When I couldn't stand being in my house any longer, staring down at my phone, willing it to ring, I'd started driving around town, going to all of our places, always able to imagine her there until the moment I arrived to find it Sloane-free. She wasn't stretched out in the sun on a picnic table at the Orchard, or flipping through the sale rack at Twice Upon a Time, or finishing up her pineapple slice at Captain Pizza. She was just gone.

I had no idea what to do with myself. It was rare for us not to see each other on a daily basis, and we talked or texted constantly, with nothing off-limits or too trivial, even exchanges like *I think my new skirt make me look like I'm Amish, promise to tell me if it does?* (me) and *Have you noticed it's been a while since anyone's seen the Loch Ness monster?* (her). In the two years we'd been best friends, I had shared almost all of my thoughts and experiences with her, and the sudden silence felt deafening. I didn't know what to do except to continue texting and trying to find her. I kept reaching for my phone to tell Sloane that I was having trouble handling the fact she wasn't answering her phone.

I drew in a breath and I held it as I pulled down her driveway, the way I used to when I was little and opening up my last birthday present, willing it to be the one thing I still didn't have, the only thing I wanted.

But the driveway was empty, and all the windows were dark. I pulled up in front of the house anyway, then put my car in park and killed the engine. I slumped back against the seat, fighting to keep down the lump that was rising in my throat. I no longer knew what else to do, where else to look. But Sloane couldn't be gone. She wouldn't have left without telling me.

But then where was she?

When I felt myself on the verge of tears, I got out of the car and squinted at the house in the morning sun. The fact that it was empty, this early, was really all the evidence I needed, since I had never known Milly or Anderson to be awake before ten. Even though I knew there was probably no point to it, I crossed to the house and walked up the wide stone steps that were covered with bright green summer leaves. The leaves were thick enough that I had to kick them aside, and I knew, deep down, that it was more proof that nobody was there, and hadn't been there for a while now. But I walked toward the front door, with its brass lion's-head knocker, and knocked anyway, just like I'd done five other times that week. I waited, trying to peer in the glass on the side of the door, still with a tiny flicker of hope that in a second, any minute now, I'd hear Sloane's steps as she ran down the hall and threw open the door, yanking me into a hug, already talking a mile a minute. But the house was silent, and all I could see through the glass was the historical-status plaque just inside the door, the one that proclaimed the house "one of Stanwich's architectural treasures," the one that always seemed covered with ghosts of fingerprints.

I waited another few minutes, just in case, then turned around and lowered myself to sit on the top step, trying very hard not to have a breakdown among the leaves.

There was a piece of me that was still hoping to find this had been a very realistic nightmare, and that any minute now, I'd wake up, and Sloane would be there, on the other end of her phone like she was supposed to be, already planning out the day for us.

Sloane's house was in what was always called "backcountry," where the houses got larger and farther apart from each other, on ever-bigger pieces of land. She was ten miles away from my place, which, back when I'd been in peak running shape, had been easy for me to cross. But even though they were close, our neighborhoods couldn't have been more different. Here, there was only the occasional car driving past, and the silence seemed to underscore the fact that I was totally alone, that there was nobody home and, most likely, nobody coming back. I leaned forward, letting my hair fall around me like a curtain. If nobody was there, it at least meant I could stay awhile, and I wouldn't be asked to leave. I could probably stay there all day. I honestly didn't know what else to do with myself.

I heard the low rumble of an engine and looked up, fast, pushing my hair out of my face, feeling hope flare once more in my chest. But the car rolling slowly down the driveway wasn't Anderson's slightly dented BMW. It was a yellow pickup truck, the back piled with lawnmowers and rakes. When it pulled in front of the steps, I could see the writing, in stylized cursive, on the side. *Stanwich Landscaping*, it read. *Planting . . . gardening . . . maintenance . . . and mulch, mulch more!* Sloane loved when stores had cheesy names or slogans. Not that she was a huge fan of puns, but she'd always said she liked to picture the owners thinking them up, and how pleased with themselves they must have been when they landed on whatever they'd chosen. I immediately made a mental note to tell Sloane about the motto, and then, a moment later, realized how stupid this was.

Three guys got out of the truck and headed for the back of it, two of them starting to lift down the equipment. They looked older, like maybe they were in college, and I stayed frozen on the steps, watching them. I knew that this was an opportunity to try and get some information, but that would involve talking to these guys. I'd been shy from birth, but the last two years had been different. With Sloane by my side, it was like I suddenly had a safety net. She was always able to take the lead if I wanted her to, and if I didn't, I knew she would be there, jumping in if I lost my nerve or got flustered. And when I was on my own, awkward or failed interactions just didn't seem to matter as much, since I knew I'd be able to spin it into a story, and we could laugh about it afterward. Without her here, though, it was becoming clear to me how terrible I now was at navigating things like this on my own.

"Hey." I jumped, realizing I was being addressed by one of the landscapers. He was looking up at me, shielding his eyes against the sun as the other two hefted down a riding mower. "You live here?"

The other two guys set the mower down, and I realized

I knew one of them; he'd been in my English class last year, making this suddenly even worse. "No," I said, and heard how scratchy my voice sounded. I had been saying only the most perfunctory things to my parents and younger brother over the last two weeks, and the only talking I'd really been doing had been into Sloane's voice mail. I cleared my throat and tried again. "I don't."

The guy who'd spoken to me raised his eyebrows, and I knew this was my cue to go. I was, at least in their minds, trespassing, and would probably get in the way of their work. All three guys were now staring at me, clearly just waiting for me to leave. But if I left Sloane's house—if I ceded it to these strangers in yellow T-shirts—where was I going to get more information? Did that mean I was just accepting the fact that she was gone?

The guy who'd spoken to me folded his arms across his chest, looking impatient, and I knew I couldn't keep sitting there. If Sloane had been with me, I would have been able to ask them. If she were here, she probably would have gotten two of their numbers already and would be angling for a turn on the riding mower, asking if she could mow her name into the grass. But if Sloane were here, none of this would be happening in the first place. My cheeks burned as I pushed myself to my feet and walked quickly down the stone steps, my flip-flops sliding once on the leaves, but I steadied myself before I wiped out and made this more humiliating than it already was. I nodded at the guys, then looked down at the driveway as I walked over to my car.

Now that I was leaving, they all moved into action, distributing equipment and arguing about who was doing what. I gripped my door handle, but didn't open it yet. Was I really just going to go? Without even trying?

"So," I said, but not loudly enough, as the guys continued to talk to each other, none of them looking over at me, two of them having an argument about whose turn it was to fertilize, while the guy from last year's English class held his baseball cap in his hands, bending the bill into a curve. "*So*," I said, but much too loudly this time, and the guys stopped talking and looked over at me again. I could feel my palms sweating, but I knew I had to keep going, that I wouldn't be able forgive myself if I just turned around and left. "I was just . . . um . . ." I let out a shaky breath. "My friend lives here, and I was trying to find her. Do you—" I suddenly saw, like I was observing the scene on TV, how ridiculous this probably was, asking the landscaping guys for information on my best friend's whereabouts. "I mean, did they hire you for this job? Her parents, I mean? Milly or Anderson Williams?" Even though I was trying not to, I could feel myself grabbing on to this possibility, turning it into something I could understand. If the Williamses had hired Stanwich Landscaping, maybe they were just on a trip somewhere, getting the yard stuff taken care of while they were gone so they wouldn't be bothered. It was just a long trip, and they had gone somewhere with no cell reception or e-mail service. That was all.

The guys looked at each other, and it didn't seem like any of these names had rung a bell. "Sorry," said the guy who'd first spoken to me. "We just get the address. We don't know about that stuff."

I nodded, feeling like I'd just depleted my last reserve of hope. Thinking about it, the fact that landscapers were here was actually a bit ominous, as I had never once seen Anderson show the slightest interest in the lawn, despite the fact that the Stanwich Historical Society was apparently always bothering him to hire someone to keep up the property.

Two of the guys had headed off around the side of the house, and the guy from my English class looked at me as he put on his baseball cap. "Hey, you're friends with Sloane Williams, right?"

"Yes," I said immediately. This was my identity at school, but I'd never minded it—and now, I'd never been so happy to be recognized that way. Maybe he knew something, or had heard something. "Sloane's actually who I'm looking for. This is her house, so . . ."

The guy nodded, then gave me an apologetic shrug. "Sorry I don't know anything," he said. "Hope you find her." He didn't ask me what my name was, and I didn't volunteer it. What would be the point?

"Thanks," I managed to say, but a moment too late, as he'd already joined the other two. I looked at the house once more, the house that somehow no longer even felt like Sloane's, and realized that there was nothing left to do except leave.

I didn't head right home; instead I stopped in to Stanwich Coffee, on the very off chance that there would be a girl in the corner chair, her hair in a messy bun held up with a pencil, reading a British novel that used dashes instead of quotation marks. But Sloane wasn't there. And as I headed back to my car I realized that if she had been in town, it would have been unthinkable that she wouldn't have called me back. It had been two weeks; something was wrong.

Strangely, this thought buoyed me as I headed for home. When I left the house every morning, I just let my parents assume that I was meeting up with Sloane, and if they asked what my plans were, I said vague things about applying for jobs. But I knew now was the moment to tell them that I was worried; that I needed to know what had happened. After all, maybe they knew something, even though my parents weren't close with hers. The first time they'd met, Milly and Anderson had come to collect Sloane from a sleepover at my house, two hours later than they'd been supposed to show up. And after pleasantries had been exchanged and Sloane and I had said good-bye, my dad had shut the door, turned to my mother, and groaned, "That was like being stuck in a Gurney play." I hadn't known what he'd meant by this, but I could tell by his tone of voice that it hadn't been a compliment. But even though they hadn't been friends, they still might know something. Or they might be able to find something out.

I held on to this thought tighter and tighter as I got closer to my house. We lived close to one of the four commercial districts scattered throughout Stanwich. My neighborhood was pedestrian-friendly and walkable, and there was always lots of traffic, both cars and people, usually heading in the direction of the beach, a ten-minute drive from our house. Stanwich, Connecticut, was on Long Island Sound, and though there were no waves, there was still sand and beautiful views and stunning houses that had the water as their backyards.

Our house, in contrast, was an old Victorian that my parents had been fixing up ever since we'd moved in six years earlier. The floors were uneven and the ceilings were low, and the whole downstairs was divided into lots of tiny rooms—originally all specific parlors of some kind. But my parents—who had been living, with me, and later my younger brother, in tiny apartments, usually above a deli or a Thai place—couldn't believe their good fortune. They didn't think about the fact that it was pretty much falling down, that it was three stories and drafty, shockingly expensive to heat in the winter and, with central air not yet invented when the house was built, almost impossible to cool in the summer. They were ensorcelled with the place.

The house had originally been painted a bright purple, but had faded over the years to a pale lavender. It had a wide front porch, a widow's walk at the very top of the house, too many windows to make any logical sense, and a turret room that was my parents' study.

I pulled up in front of the house and saw that my brother was sitting on the porch steps, perfectly still. This was surprising in itself. Beckett was ten, and constantly in motion, climbing up vertiginous things, practicing his ninja moves, and biking through our neighborhood's streets with abandon, usually with his best friend Annabel Montpelier, the scourge of stroller-pushing mothers within a five-mile radius. "Hey," I said as I got out of the car and walked toward the steps, suddenly worried that I had missed something big in the last two weeks while I'd sleep-walked through family meals, barely paying attention to what was happening around me. But maybe Beckett had just pushed my parents a little too far, and was having a time-out. I'd find out soon enough anyway, since I needed to talk to them about Sloane. "You okay?" I asked, climbing up the three porch steps.

He looked up at me, then back down at his sneakers. "It's happening again."

The moving, relatable story of a girl who takes a road trip to find herself— and the guy who goes with her

"This is an incredible book— heartbreakingly funny and utterly un-put-down-able."
—Lauren Myracle, *New York Times* bestselling author of *Thirteen* and *ttyl*

★ "A near perfect summer read."
—*Publishers Weekly*, starred review

"One of the most touching, irresistible, and feel-good road trips I've been on in a long, long while. *Amy & Roger's Epic Detour* is a book to love."
—Deb Caletti, National Book Award finalist

WHAT IF

ALL YOUR CRUSHES
FOUND OUT HOW YOU FELT?

From bestselling author

JENNY HAN

Jonathan Aubrey is about to discover that one kiss is all it takes for two worlds to collide.

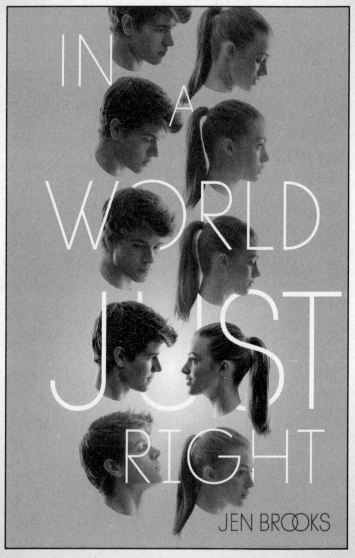